THE
FALL
OF
INNOCENCE

THE
FALL
OF
INNOCENCE

JENNY TORRES SANCHEZ

PHILOMEL BOOKS

PHILOMEL BOOKS
an imprint of Penguin Random House LLC
375 Hudson Street
New York, NY 10014

Copyright © 2018 by Jenny Torres Sanchez.
Penguin supports copyright. Copyright fuels creativity, encourages diverse
voices, promotes free speech, and creates a vibrant culture. Thank you for buying
an authorized edition of this book and for complying with copyright laws by
not reproducing, scanning, or distributing any part of it in any form without
permission. You are supporting writers and allowing Penguin to continue to
publish books for every reader.

Philomel Books is a registered trademark of Penguin Random House LLC.

Library of Congress Cataloging-in-Publication Data
Names: Torres Sanchez, Jenny, author.
Title: The fall of innocence / Jenny Torres Sanchez.
Description: New York, NY : Philomel Books, [2018].
Summary: Sixteen-year-old Emilia DeJesus struggles to overcome the aftermath of
assault when new information about what happened to her eight years before awakens
her memories.
Identifiers: LCCN 2017040890 | ISBN 9781524737757 (hardback) | ISBN
9781524737764 (e-book)
Subjects: | CYAC: Child abuse—Fiction. | Memory—Fiction. | Dating (Social
customs)—Fiction. | Family life—Fiction.
Classification: LCC PZ7.T6457245 Fal 2018 | DDC [Fic]—dc23
LC record available at https://lccn.loc.gov/2017040890

Printed in the United States of America.
ISBN 9781524737757
1 3 5 7 9 10 8 6 4 2

Edited by Liza Kaplan.
Design by Ellice M. Lee.
Text set in Bembo.
Image of crows © 2018 by Shutterstock/Novikov Alex.
This is a work of fiction. Names, characters, places, and incidents either
are the product of the author's imagination or are used fictitiously, and any
resemblance to actual persons, living or dead, businesses, companies, events, or
locales is entirely coincidental.

For Nando

THE
FALL
OF
INNOCENCE

I measure every Grief I meet
With narrow, probing, eyes—
I wonder if It weighs like Mine—
Or has an Easier size.

I wonder if They bore it long—
Or did it just begin—
I could not tell the Date of Mine—
It feels so old a pain—

I wonder if it hurts to live—
And if They have to try—
And whether—could They choose between—
It would not be—to die—

—Emily Dickinson

PART ONE

Early December 1994

Strange Puffs of White

Strange puffs of white trailed like smoke in the curiously blue sky. Emilia stared at them from the passenger-side window of her boyfriend's car. They made her think of a rocket shooting into outer space. She reached for the radio knob to turn down the music.

"Hey, you remember when the shuttle exploded?" she asked Ian as they drove to school. She unwrapped a piece of Bazooka Joe bubble gum and offered him the ridged pink square. When he opened his mouth, she popped it in and watched him chew, resisting the urge to lean over and kiss his jaw.

"The *Challenger*?" His words were garbled as he struggled with the hard piece of gum. "Jesus, that was forever ago."

They came to a stop sign and he looked at her as she tucked her long black hair behind her ears, a habit. She looked over at him, her eyes dark and serious. Then he turned onto the main road and the high-pitched screech of metal against metal that his car made filled the air.

"Remember how Mrs. McNary made us write letters to the families of the astronauts?" he said.

Emilia unwrapped another piece of gum for herself, studying the package and focusing on Bazooka Joe's eye patch. She'd seen the image a thousand times, but it was the first time she'd really noticed or thought about it. "Nope, wasn't in school for that," she said.

"That's right." He shifted in his seat. "Sorry."

"Don't apologize," she told him. She put the piece of gum in her mouth and chewed until it was soft and flexible, and then she started blowing a huge bubble slowly, so as to not break it. Her eyes widened as it got bigger, and she smacked Ian on the shoulder. He laughed and then a small tear in the stretched-out gum caused it to deflate.

"That was good," Ian said.

Emilia smiled, chewed some more while she looked at the pack of gum. A kid with an eye patch as a mascot. So weird. "What do you think happened to Bazooka Joe's eye?" She held up the packaging so he could see.

"Who knows," Ian said.

"A nasty encounter with a bazooka, perhaps?" Emilia squinted one eye. He glanced over again and laughed. She loved it when she made him laugh.

Just when she'd forgotten about the space shuttle, Ian said, "Man . . . those astronauts, though. Can you imagine being in that shuttle? Knowing you're going to . . . *explode*?"

"No . . . ," she said, her voice trailing off as she looked out the window. The puffs were faint and disappearing, but her mind filled with an imaginary shuttle. With panicked astronauts. With calls for help.

"What made you think of that, anyway?" Ian asked.

When Emilia was eight, she'd watched the shuttle explode over and over again on the television from her mother's bed. The image was seared into her memory because she'd watched it happen at least a hundred times. Smoking bits and pieces of shuttle going in different directions, white puffs trailing behind each of them. These puffs made her feel like she was back on her mother's bed again, like she'd stepped back in time. She didn't want to go back to that time in her life. Not now. Or ever. Better to stay in the present.

"Oh, I don't know." Emilia threw the pack of gum into the glove compartment. "Same thing that made me wonder about one-eyed Joe, I guess." She smiled, trying to forget it all.

They neared the street that led to their old elementary school, the one they passed every day and Emilia was always curious to go down. It was next to Hofstra University, and Emilia remembered walking over to the campus for symphony and theater field trips. Today, before she could stop herself, Emilia yelled, "Hey, turn here for a minute."

She thought this almost every time they passed the school, but she'd never said the words aloud. Today, those puffs and Ma's bed and that day and this school and even the chill in the air were suddenly so present in her mind that the words just slipped out. She felt like she had when she was little and turned at that corner every morning.

Like no time has passed, she thought.

"Here? Why?"

"Just . . . come on."

Ian flicked on the turn signal and the screeching sliced the air again. He shook his head, cursing and complaining about "this piece-of-shit car" as the school came into full view. He stopped at the corner and they stared at it.

She didn't tell Ian she hadn't been there in years. It felt surreal to be there now.

"Looks kind of small, doesn't it?" she said. Her own voice sounded foreign to her. "I used to think it was so big."

"Yeah, me too. It's kind of weird seeing it like this. So empty."

Emilia nodded and glanced at a boarded-up window. The school had closed last fall when the district decided there weren't enough students in town to keep it running, and since it was the oldest, it was the first to go. When Emilia heard about the closing, she'd been happy no more kids would come to this school.

Let's go inside.

The words crossed her mind quickly, out of nowhere. For a moment she almost said them out loud. She imagined herself and Ian in those empty hallways, sneaking into abandoned classrooms. They could skip school and spend the whole day together like they had last week when they'd kept driving and ended up in the nearly empty parking lot of a museum.

Emilia's stomach fluttered at the memory of kissing Ian in the car so much that day her lips had felt raw long afterward. Of Ian saying if they kept doing this he was going to explode. So they'd gone inside and walked through the galleries. She'd never been to that museum before, and Emilia remembered how Ian kept coming up behind her, kissing her neck, every time she wandered to something that caught her eye. She made fun of him each time because he was "going to explode" and turned her attention back to the pictures, statues, and paintings, all of them arranged so beautifully.

She looked at the school now and her stomach fluttered again. Somehow it looked strangely alive, even though it was shut down and abandoned. Those windows looked like eyes. The double front doors were a red gaping mouth, now closed and locked and silent. It looked like . . . it was waiting for something.

Or someone.

Emilia didn't want to go inside. She didn't want to walk those hallways again, even with Ian by her side.

"What do you think they'll do with it?" Emilia asked. There was still a flag on the flagpole.

But Ian had turned his attention to the house nestled at the dead end next to the school, and then he quickly said, "We should get going. We're gonna be late."

Emilia looked past him toward the group home for mentally and developmentally delayed kids. It had been there for as long as she could remember. There were a few kids and adults on the lawn, speckled by the sunlight shining through the leaves and branches of the trees that towered over the home.

They're waiting for the bus, Emilia thought. *It will come and pick them up and carry them to another school, on the other side of town, away from this one. Just like it always has.*

Emilia remembered how the bus seemed to arrive at the same time she did when she was younger, back when she walked to school with her older brother. And she would see kids walk, run, or stumble to catch it.

Flashes of those kids from the past came back to her, and she vividly remembered the one who drooled. His spit clung from the edge of his chin to his shirt, and swung in the breeze like the silk of a spiderweb as he half ran, half walked.

Some wouldn't look up, just walked with their heads down.

Like Jeremy Lance.

Jeremy Lance walked like that, his shoulders hunched, the tallest and seemingly the oldest of all the kids. A teenager, but to Emilia he looked like some kind of monster.

Emilia shuddered, remembering that morning. She'd stopped to pick up a dirty brown bracelet she found just lying there on the ground outside the school. As her brother hurried ahead with some friends, Emilia studied the entwined leather for a moment. When she looked up, a face suddenly appeared in one of the bus's windows.

He started knocking on it and smiled and mouthed something to her. But his smile scared Emilia. She dropped the bracelet and wouldn't wave or smile back. She'd looked away, but out of the corner of her eye, she could see him still knocking on the window.

And she could hear the thump of his fist as he knocked harder, trying to get her attention.

She shivered with thoughts of the past.

"Hey," Ian said. "You okay?"

She looked at him, here, now, and smiled. "Yeah, let's go," she told him. "You're right. We're gonna be late."

Ian made a U-turn, shook his head at each piercing screech his car made, and Emilia couldn't help but glance at the house again as it came into clear view on her side.

She was ashamed to admit even now that she was afraid of the kids on the lawn, just as she'd been afraid of the kids back then. Just as she'd been terrified of Jeremy Lance. Even before he attacked her on the school playground one day.

It's over now, in the past. Leave it all in the past.

Emilia leaned back, closed her eyes, and tried to clear her head of the memories.

Ian drove onto the main road.

"You sure you're okay?" he asked once they were away from the school. His voice revealed concern and love for her, but somewhere in there, Emilia thought maybe pity, too. She didn't want to be pitied. And especially not by Ian.

"Yeah, why?" But before he could answer, she went on. "Hey, you know what we should do?" She rushed, trying to get the words out so they would stop any conversation about the school, or the group home, or if she really was okay. "We should go to the museum again!" She gave him a sly look and he laughed nervously.

She loved this, the effect she had on him. She loved him. "It'll be fun. It will be the best day, I promise." She touched his neck gently, outlining the faint traces of a small fading hickey she'd put there last week. She thought of the one on her own neck, of how she liked to see it in the mirror and think of Ian, kissing her.

But he shook his head and instantly she felt foolish. Maybe the museum was a stupid suggestion.

"Or we could get ice cream at that place we went to over the summer. Remember? I *loved* that place. Do you think it closed already?" Of course it had. She knew it must have. Summer had ended and even though she'd give anything to be riding home with Ian on the last day of school, the windows down, the warmth and promise of sweltering summer days ahead, it was so far away.

Emilia was surprised at the fresh pang of sadness that hit her as she thought of another summer over. And she hated the crispness in the air that reminded her of the bone-chilling cold soon to follow, that was already finding its way to her.

"I wish I could. But I have these two tests today and I can't miss them."

"Oh," Emilia said. She sat back in her seat and put her feet against the glove compartment, sighing and resigning herself to a crappy day full of assignments and jarring bells and teachers complaining about students' lack of enthusiasm.

"At least it's Friday," he said. "And hey, Anthony's coming into town tonight."

"Anthony! Oh, that's great!" she said, immediately cheered up and excited. Emilia liked Ian's cousin. The three of them had often hung out together before Anthony graduated from high school and joined the army. She knew he was stationed a few hours away, but it was difficult to get time off, so she hadn't seen him since he'd left for boot camp a few months earlier.

"Didn't I tell you? He'll be here this afternoon, actually. And he mentioned all of us doing something tomorrow."

"Of course! Aw, Anthony's back. It'll be just like before."

"Well," Ian said. "The only thing is . . ." He looked at Emilia. "He, uh, kind of mentioned bringing this girl he met right before he left."

Emilia shrugged. "So? A double date. Sounds like fun."

"Yeah, I was thinking we could all see that movie you and I were talking about, but . . . ," he said, taking a deep breath and looking over at her. "The thing is . . ." A funny look crossed his face. "She's . . . actually, sort of, a stripper . . ."

Emilia was taken off guard for a minute but quickly recovered. "Ahh, well, like I said, sounds like fun," she told him. She blew another bubble and sucked it in, making several popping sounds.

Ian laughed. "Yeah, right. Come on! It doesn't bother you? Not even a little bit?"

"What? It's not a big deal! So she's a stripper. It's not like *I* have to be a stripper to be her friend."

"Now, there's an idea."

Emilia looked over at Ian; his face flushed as he laughed, and she smacked his shoulder. "Shut up," she said, laughing with him.

He grabbed her hand and squeezed it. She held on to him a little tighter as they pulled into the school parking lot. Ian nodded at some of his friends as he and Emilia got out of the car and made their way toward the entrance of the school. And then, without really meaning to, Emilia glanced up at the sky before they entered the crowded hallway.

Some part of her half expected to see the shuttle blowing up, but instead she noticed black birds circling above. Her crows.

She slowed and stopped for a moment, watching them glide. Their distant caws reached her ears and she wanted to call out to them, but Ian tugged at her hand and she followed him inside.

As they stood outside her first class, Ian played with the green four-leaf-clover ring on Emilia's finger. He clasped her hand, his pale against hers. "See you after school?" he said.

She thought it was funny, the way he asked this every day. This year they *did* have completely different schedules and lunch times, which meant Emilia saw him only in the morning and not again until after their last class. But still, she thought it was a funny habit.

"Duh," she said, laughing and leaning against the wall. He leaned in and kissed her as the bell rang.

When he pulled away, his eyes were still closed and he whispered, "I love you, Emilia."

She smiled, tucked her long hair back behind her ear, felt light and beautiful, and wished again they'd been able to skip school.

They could have spent the day anywhere, doing anything. They could have had whole hours of nothing but each other.

Maybe then some part of her mind wouldn't still be thinking about the past, about the school. About Jeremy Lance. Maybe she would have forgotten about all of it.

She focused on Ian's dark eyes as the hallway emptied. "I love you, too."

Emilia Woke to an Empty House

Emilia woke to an empty house the following morning. Like most Saturdays, her mother and brother had already left for work. She didn't really mind this Saturday routine, even though she did get a little creeped out being by herself. But she'd never tell her mom that. It's just that the house was so quiet, so still, that any little noise made her jump. But so did the lack of noise. No clatter of dishes, no hum of television in the background, nothing.

She should have been used to it, but she wasn't.

"Okay, Emilia, get up," she said to herself. She always did this when she was home alone—talked to herself loudly, made lots of noise, because she didn't want to hear a rustle, or a creak, or anything that might put her on edge. And even though Ma hated wasting electricity, Emilia always turned on the television when she went downstairs. She always double-checked the doors, too, sometimes without even realizing she was doing it, just to make sure they were locked. Which was stupid, because her mother *always* locked the doors.

And you think Ma is paranoid, she told herself when she realized what she was doing.

Emilia watched TV while she ate her cereal. When she finally looked at the clock, she realized it was past noon and wondered why her mother hadn't called to check up on her yet. She must have gotten busy between appointments. A fussy bride who didn't like the way her makeup turned out the first time and made Ma do it all over again.

Just as she tipped the bowl to drink the sugary leftover cereal milk, the phone rang, making Emilia jump and hit the bowl against her teeth.

Jesus Christ, she thought as she wiped away the milk that had fallen on the T-shirt she slept in. *Thanks a lot, Ma.*

"I'm fine, Ma," she said, answering the phone on the third ring.

There was a slight pause and Emilia caught herself. "I mean, hello?"

"Uh, yes, Nina DeJesus, please."

"She can't come to the phone right now. Can I take a message?"

The silence on the other end gave Emilia enough time to realize her mistake. Her mother had trained her well. *Never tell anyone I'm not home, Emilia,* her mother always told her. *Tell them I can't come to the phone.* But it was too late now. Whoever it was had heard Emilia, and it was obvious Ma wasn't actually home if Emilia had thought it was her calling.

"Hello?" Emilia said again, flustered. "Can I take a message?"

"No message," the man on the other end said. "I'll call back another time." The abrupt click left Emilia unsettled and jittery.

For a moment, she stood there with the phone in her hand before finally placing it back on the receiver. She wondered who it was, but then, noticing it was almost one o'clock, she realized she better get ready to meet up with Ian and Anthony and his stripper girlfriend.

Emilia went upstairs and looked in her closet.

What does one wear when hanging out with a stripper? she wondered. *I bet she's sexy. Strippers are sexy, aren't they?*

She pulled out a purple sweater and held it up to herself. This purple sweater was not sexy. It was horrible. Emilia threw it to the side.

I bet she's older, more interesting. Glamorous? Trashy?

Emilia put on her best pair of jeans and tried on a dozen shirts, but she looked so plain in each one. And she wanted to look *different*. She wanted to look glamorous, trashy, sexy, and like herself all at once. She didn't want Ian looking at Anthony's girlfriend, comparing her to another girl. Emilia looked back in her closet and pulled down the pile of old clothes she kept on her top shelf, the one she always meant to take to Goodwill and never did. She rifled through it, not sure what she was looking for. Finally she came across a black skirt she'd outgrown years ago. She held it up, then changed into it. It was incredibly short now and tight. For a moment, Emilia thought it was perfect.

What would Ian think? she wondered.

Emilia stared at herself for a moment, at the curves of her hips. She didn't normally wear any clothes that revealed her body like this, outlined it this way. She studied her legs, which looked longer in a skirt so short. She posed and stared at herself.

Ian would explode if he saw her like this.

She looked older. *Sexy even.*

But then, the longer she studied herself, the more ridiculous the skirt began to look. The less sexy she felt. The more she looked like a little girl playing dress-up.

She felt stupid.

Emilia slipped off the skirt and caught a glimpse of herself in the mirror, and she wondered what it would be like to be a stripper. She stared at herself in her bra and underwear, reached around to undo her bra clasp.

She imagined a room of men looking at her. Their eyes gazing at all parts of her body, going wherever they wanted, imagining whatever they wanted.

Emilia quickly clasped the hooks of her bra back together and pulled on a pair of jeans; the nakedness of her own body felt too intimate, even to herself. She picked up and put on one of the many T-shirts that now lay on the floor, and on top of that, she threw on the horrible purple sweater.

She looked at herself in the mirror again, at the judgmental image staring back at her.

Fuck it. Who cares? She's not going to show up in a bikini, for crying out loud! Be yourself!

Emilia slipped on her boots and tried to ignore the little voice that told her she was going to regret looking so boring. Because maybe Ian might be tempted to look at someone more . . . interesting.

Don't be stupid. He's not like that.

Emilia went downstairs, shaking her head at the thought of that skirt. But she stopped by her mother's bedroom to borrow some perfume and expensive lipstick. She studied her beautifully painted lips.

This was perfect.

"You look gorgeous!" she told herself as she put the lipstick back on Ma's dresser.

Yes, this was her.

But an hour later, in the car with Ian and Anthony, she felt anything but gorgeous. She stared at Ian as they pulled up behind a strip club. She knew he was trying his best to ignore her gaze.

"I didn't know strip bars were open during the day," Emilia said.

"Oh, she's practicing a new routine or something," Anthony said, looking out the window. "Has to get the boss's approval. I mean, nobody wants to see a stripper flubbing up a routine, right?" Anthony laughed, but Ian shifted uncomfortably in his seat. He hadn't told her they'd have to pick up Anthony's girlfriend, much less that it would be at the strip club where she worked.

Maybe he didn't know, Emilia reasoned. But still.

"There she is, that's Jane," Anthony said from the back seat.

I never would've guessed, Emilia thought as she took in the girl wearing tiny, shiny shorts and high-heeled shoes Emilia would kill herself in if she even tried them on. The girl was a blur of white; her hair was shockingly blond, almost as white as the short, white-feathered coat she wore and her pale, pale skin.

"She said she'd be waiting outside."

Jane's hands were tucked in her pockets and she was intermittently stomping her feet on the concrete and rubbing her legs together in an effort to keep warm. When the car pulled up next to her, she leaned down and peered through Emilia's window.

"Hey, babe!" Anthony called from the back seat as Emilia rolled her window all the way down.

"Hi!" Jane said. She was only inches away from Emilia's face and Emilia could smell her gum. "I'm sorry! I didn't want to miss you guys and I got held up, so I haven't had time to change yet. Just give me a minute to slip on some jeans. Okay?"

She was gone before any of them could say anything—in through a dark back door. Emilia looked in after her, curious, but saw only a dimly lit hallway.

"She's real nice, you guys. You're totally gonna love her," Anthony said from the back seat. "I mean, I haven't hung out with her *that* much because I met her right before I left, but we talk on the phone every night. Even the nights she works and gets out super late, we talk, because I wanna make sure she gets home all right, know what I mean? I mean, there are crazies out there, do all kinds of shit. Especially to girls like her."

17

"What do you mean?" Emilia asked Anthony. She saw Ian glance back at him.

"Well, like she told me about this one time, right, when this guy was waiting for her in the parking lot. Actually fucking waiting for her. He kept calling her sweetie or something. Man, I got so fucking mad when she told me that! Can you believe that shit?"

Emilia stared at the door Jane just went through. "I believe it," she said quietly.

"Total prick."

"So what happened?" Emilia asked.

"With what?"

"The guy?"

"Oh, I guess he was some little shit or something." Anthony laughed. "Jane said she could've beaten him up herself, but the bouncer came out just then and scared him off or whatever."

Emilia's mind flickered with the scene, with the different ways it could have turned out.

He could've hidden in some bushes. He could've been waiting for just the right moment when Jane was alone again.

"I just can't stop thinking about her, though, you know?"

The words snapped Emilia back to reality.

"And it's not like we're totally committed or anything, but"—Anthony shrugged—"I don't know. The guys rib me about the long-distance shit, but they all have their little girlies back home, too, so screw 'em."

Emilia wondered if Anthony had met Jane here, while she was

dancing. Did he hang out at strip clubs? She looked over at Ian. Had he ever come here with Anthony?

"Sounds stupid, huh?" Anthony said.

Emilia turned back to look at him. Anthony had sleepy eyes and he was crude. He'd had a wealthy upbringing but liked to appear rough around the edges. It was his way of rebelling against his parents' expectations and wealth. Emilia thought it was juvenile, but he was a good guy.

He smiled, and Emilia shook her head. "No, I think it's great. You're in love," she teased.

"Oh, for fuck's sake, don't start with that shit," he said. But he laughed and looked away, and Emilia thought maybe she was right.

Moments later, Jane came back out the door.

"Hey!" she said as she got in the back seat with Anthony, breathless and minty and smelling of some other sweetness Emilia couldn't identify. "Sorry about that. I'm Jane, by the way."

She brought the cold into the car with her, and Emilia felt it sweep across the back of her neck and creep under her hair.

"Hi," Emilia said, and smiled. She looked at Jane and tried not to immediately picture her naked, or notice the tight shirt she wore, or the size of her breasts. She tried not to look over at Ian in the driver's seat and quietly accuse him of noticing the same things.

"Babe," Anthony said to Jane. "This is my cousin, Ian, and his girl, Emilia."

Emilia gave Jane a small wave and stared at her purple-lipstick smile. Anthony put his hand on Jane's knee.

"Emilia . . . ," Jane said, and nodded. "Now, that's a real sweet name. I love it. Not like mine. Plain Jane." She gave Emilia a *what can you do?* kind of look and smiled. Her teeth gleamed against her bright lips.

Emilia knew she should face forward again because she could *feel* herself staring at Jane and wondered if Jane realized it, too. Maybe she didn't. Maybe Jane was used to this. Emilia's eyes searched Jane for a single plain feature, but she could find none.

"Thanks," Emilia said. She was suddenly self-conscious of the lipstick she'd borrowed from her mother. She felt like she was playing dress-up again. Jane looked mature, probably twenty, maybe even a little older. Jane looked like Barbie, and Emilia felt like a dark-haired, dark-skinned version of that stupid little-sister doll Skipper.

She turned back around, but not before she noticed Jane wink at her playfully. Did she think Emilia was little and adorable? She stole a glance over at Ian, but he kept his eyes on the road.

Emilia listened to Anthony and Jane talk in the back seat. Out of the corner of her eye, she could see how they pressed into each other and touched each other's arm, or leg, or shoulder. Every so often, Emilia would turn around and ask Anthony a question about where he lived, or training, and she noticed how Jane stared at him when he answered, listening to his every word, ready to either throw her head back laughing or nuzzle into him. Emilia thought she looked exuberant.

An exuberant stripper.

"I'm starving!" Jane said suddenly, finally looking over at Ian and Emilia.

"We could get something to eat before the movie," Anthony offered.

"Could we? Oh, that would be fantastic!" Jane said.

"Uh, sure," Ian said.

"The movie starts at three, though," Emilia said. "And there's not another one until tonight."

"Oh," Jane said, but she didn't urge them to forget about getting something to eat.

"So we miss the movie. I mean, we can just hang out instead, right?" Anthony said, looking between Emilia and Ian. "You guys aren't *that* into seeing it, are you?"

"I'm good with whatever," Ian said.

Emilia looked over at Ian, but he kept his eyes on the road, avoiding her stare. Maybe he was just being nice, making things easy for Anthony, but she felt sort of betrayed. She and Ian had just talked about how they wished they'd seen this movie when it first came out and promised to go together when they saw it advertised at the dollar theater. But now he was so willing to ditch it, just to accommodate Jane.

Emilia looked back at Jane and Anthony. "Yeah, sure. No big deal," she said finally.

They decided on a diner nearby and soon they were sitting in a torn-up booth, sipping cold, murky glasses of water. Jane took off her coat and Emilia looked at Ian, who somehow managed to not look at Jane's chest.

"So, are you glad you enlisted?" Emilia asked Anthony.

"Oh, I like it okay. You know, there are some assholes, but yeah, I like it."

"Your parents cool with it now, or what?" she continued.

"Nah." Anthony shook his head and sat back in his seat. "I mean, they're accepting because they have no choice, right? If there's anybody more powerful than my dad, it's the freaking United States Army. But I still hear it from them. It makes me not even want to come home, but, you know." He shrugged.

Emilia vaguely remembered Anthony's father was some sort of hotshot stockbroker. Anthony's parents had been majorly upset when they found out their only son was going into the service. *What about college? What about really making something of yourself?* Anthony had mocked when he told Emilia and Ian about the whole thing.

"They're still snobs. What can I say?" Anthony said, reaching for a glass of water.

"My parents are the same way," Jane offered.

"Are they out in Manhasset, too?" Emilia asked.

Jane nodded. "They think their money means they get their way, which is only compounded by the fact that everything always works out the way they want it to. It also means they think they're better than everyone else somehow."

"Exactly," Anthony said, lighting a cigarette. "But the service is cool. I feel like I'm finally doing my own shit. Not depending on my parents for everything."

"Maybe I should look into it," Ian said. Ian worked for everything he had. His parents were far from rich. But why did he suddenly want to join the army?

Emilia gave him a funny look.

"What?" Ian said. "It pays for school."

"Yeah, you should definitely consider it, man," Anthony said. "It's good money."

Jane nodded. "Would your parents get all pissed?"

"Nah, I mean, my mom would probably get sad, but they wouldn't get angry. Might even be proud," Ian said.

Emilia suddenly felt left behind in the conversation. Was Ian being serious?

"That's cool. I guess your parents let you live your own life," Jane said. She turned to Emilia then, as if trying to include her. "Wouldn't you love to see this guy in uniform?" She tossed a sly glance Ian's way that made him laugh and look down at the table. "And knowing he's serving his country. I mean, that's honorable, you know? That's sacrifice. And means a whole lot more than a fucking college degree in my book."

Jane looked over at Anthony and he pulled her into him again.

When the food arrived, Emilia watched Jane eat. She wondered what made her so hungry.

All the dancing? All the stripping? Was it tiresome?

Why are you being so bitchy, Emilia? she asked herself.

23

She tried to clear her mind of the sarcastic commentary running through her brain, but she couldn't help it.

Ketchup squirted and settled in the corner of Jane's lips, and Emilia watched Jane's tongue come and whisk it away. Emilia imagined Jane in that club—a dark, smoky place—onstage in those shiny shorts and probably some sort of bejeweled bra.

Before it comes off?

"So . . . sweet Emilia," Jane said suddenly, interrupting Emilia's thoughts. "Do *you* think you could, you know, do what I do?"

Emilia choked on a fry and Jane burst out laughing.

"Careful!" she told Emilia. "Put your arms up, like this, up in the air, just like that."

Emilia recovered and Ian stroked her back.

"What?" Emilia croaked, suddenly certain Jane had been able to read her thoughts, had taken in the way Emilia observed her and knew what she'd been picturing in her head. Then a stranger thought—that Jane somehow knew Emilia had been thinking of this when she was getting ready—entered Emilia's mind.

"Could you do what *I* do?" Jane said matter-of-factly. "Strip? Dance? Whatever you want to call it. You must have already asked yourself the same question, right?" She turned to Ian and Anthony. "All girls do."

Emilia was speechless for a moment as she took in Jane's words. *All girls do.* What did Jane know? It bothered her that Jane spoke with that kind of authority. And that she was right.

Ian coughed and Anthony looked amused and said, "Aw, come

on, Jane, give the girl a break!" He looked over at Emilia. "She's a real ballbuster, this one. Don't take it personally. It just means she likes you." He laughed in a way meant to assure Emilia that Jane was harmless.

"Oh, I know, I know. I'm just being a brat! And Anthony's right," Jane said, smiling. "You kind of remind me of me a few years ago." Jane reached out and placed her hand softly on Emilia's.

Emilia could not imagine any reality where she and Jane might seem anything remotely alike.

Jane looked back and forth between Ian and Emilia. "You know something else? You two are real cute. High school sweethearts. That's really, really sweet." She removed her hand from Emilia's and took a sip of her drink.

Ian and Anthony and Jane moved on to some other conversation, while Emilia sat there feeling stupid. She watched Jane tease and joke with Anthony and Ian and wondered, *Does she have the world figured out somehow? Maybe doing what she does gives her some kind of insight into the way the world works, or the human existence? Does she sit on laps and listen to the whispered confessions of tortured individuals?*

The more Emilia sat there, listening to Jane, the more she was bothered by her. Who did Jane think she was? And why did she speak like she knew who Emilia was?

Jane laughed loudly and Emilia stared at her.

"No way could I do what you do," Emilia said suddenly, the words surprising her and causing her heart to beat a little faster.

"What?" Jane's laughter trailed off.

Emilia looked at Jane and shrugged. "You asked. I don't think I could do what you do."

Jane smiled and nodded. "Right. Okay. That's cool."

Jane turned a little, as if she was going to move on, but Emilia felt brave. "Why would you ask, anyway?" Was it to make her feel uncomfortable? So Jane could have some kind of upper hand?

Jane stared at Emilia as if she was deciding something, then she just shrugged and said, "Just wondering, I guess. I know it's what girls must ask themselves when they meet me. It's what I thought when I met the girl you could call *my mentor*."

Emilia looked at Jane. She was smiling at her again and Emilia found it unsettling, but it also made her wonder if Jane was covering up something.

Did something happen to you, too?

The thought almost took Emilia's breath away. It was there so suddenly, made total sense, that Emilia immediately wondered if she had gotten Jane all wrong. Maybe she wasn't that bad. Maybe Emilia was being too judgmental. She knew she could be like that sometimes.

She changed her tone. "So," Emilia said, looking at Jane with curiosity. "What's it like?" Ian and Anthony shifted in their seats, and Emilia suddenly wished it were just she and Jane in this diner.

Jane leaned in to her. "Do you really want to know?" Her eyes were so blue, and seemed to hide something just beneath the surface. Or maybe, more likely, somewhere deep inside. "It feels sort of like nothing," Jane said. "It doesn't even feel like me on that stage." Her face took on a strange look as she explained to Emilia. "Sometimes it feels like I'm . . . onstage, but also floating somewhere in the audience, looking at myself. And I can't quite believe that it's me up there, even as I look out into that dark room. At first, it was scary. Then it felt powerful. But now it feels like I'm not even there. Like I'm just wondering who that girl onstage is . . . the one who thought she could never do that, either."

Jane sat back, looking at Emilia for some sort of reaction.

Emilia thought the blue in Jane's eyes would crack like ice and she would see the truth seep up from where Jane carried it. But Emilia saw nothing, and a slight coldness ran through her body.

Anthony nudged Jane and the spell was broken.

"Jesus, enough of this, okay? I'm right here, you know. These girls, right?" he said to Ian. Ian shook his head and forced a laugh.

"Oh, whatever, it's no big deal," Jane said. She leaned over and kissed Anthony on the cheek. "Don't be jealous," she said. He rolled his eyes and she smiled before looking over at Emilia. "And you, don't look so scared, sweet Emilia!"

It bothered Emilia that Jane thought she was scared; she tried to shake it off. She wasn't scared. Of what? Jane? Jane was no one to be scared of.

"I'm not scared," Emilia said, just as Ian cleared his throat and said over her, "Let's get out of here, already. Find something else to do."

But Emilia didn't feel like doing anything else. She was sure Jane was harmless and probably just liked attention, and Emilia wanted to give her a chance. But there was something about her that bothered Emilia, and she couldn't quite figure it out.

Jane's forwardness? The way she placed her hand on Emilia's? Something.

"We can go to a different movie. Something has to be playing," Anthony said.

Ian looked over at Emilia in a way that asked if she wanted to. Emilia shrugged. "Sure."

When they made it to the mostly empty theater, Jane and Anthony sat in the back row while Emilia and Ian chose seats in the middle. She was glad they wouldn't have to pretend not to notice Jane and Anthony making out while she and Ian shared popcorn and whispered about how bad the movie was.

They laughed at the awful comedy, and Emilia stole looks at Ian, noticing the way the light of the screen flickered on his face and made it glow. He looked handsome and she cheered up, not that she was sad. But it made her feel better about the night. And she was glad she was there with Ian.

When the credits rolled and they left, Emilia didn't even mind that Jane hooked her arm through hers and led her to the car, saying, "Come on, sweet Emilia!" She even laughed as Jane made her skip along ahead of the guys, and sang some old TV show theme song.

It felt good to Emilia. To just be a girl, laughing with another girl, as their boyfriends trailed behind them.

She didn't even mind when they had to drive Jane forty minutes away to drop her off at home. They laughed in the car and talked about the movie, and the conversation in the diner felt like forever ago. Maybe it hadn't even happened at all, or maybe it hadn't happened the way Emilia thought it had.

By the time they got to Jane's neighborhood, where they had to stop at a gate while Jane showed the guard her driver's license to be allowed in, Emilia felt bad that she'd even thought Jane was strange and too forward. Sometimes she saw things in people that weren't there. Thanks to Ma, Emilia was always suspicious of others. She looked at Jane now and the way she was with Anthony, and she thought, *She's just different, that's all. What's wrong with that?*

"This place is beautiful," she told Jane as they drove through the neighborhood of sprawling yards and brick-paved driveways, each one leading to a large house that looked like it belonged in the movies.

"I guess it's all right. Here, this one," Jane said when they came up on one of the largest houses. Rows and rows of windows stared at them, reflecting the moonlight of a darkening sky.

Ian came to a stop and Jane and Anthony got out. Emilia watched how they walked together, how Jane threw her arms around him and kissed him goodbye over and over again, even kicking her legs up behind her as she hung from his neck. Some part of Emilia wished she could be like that. Not care if everyone watched her kissing Ian. Kick her legs up, feeling free. Jane knew Ian and Emilia were watching, but she didn't care. Emilia felt a pang of jealousy.

She could never be like that.

When Jane went inside her house, Anthony turned and ran back to the car. The cold brushed past Emilia's neck and shoulders again.

"Told you guys she was something!" he said as they pulled out of the driveway. Emilia stared at the house.

"Yeah," she said to him, "she's definitely something."

Emilia Washed

Emilia washed the few dinner dishes there were in the sink. She dried and put them away, too.

When she opened one of the cabinets to stack the plates, she saw a new set of colorful striped salt and pepper shakers tucked away in the back. Her heart beat faster as she stared at the glossy ceramic and reached in for one. She held it up to Ma, who was putting some leftovers in the fridge.

"Cute," Emilia said, studying her mom.

"Hmmm?" Ma looked over at her. "Oh, yeah, I got those at the consignment store, you know, down the block from the pharmacy?"

Emilia nodded. "Festive."

"Really? I think they're a little summery," her mom said, shrugging. "More for a cookout or something. Not for winter or the holidays. Guess that's why nobody wanted them."

Emilia put the shaker back, wondering when her mother started caring about seasonal kitchenware.

For a cookout?

They hadn't had a cookout in years. Besides, these looked brand-new. She stacked the plates and closed the cabinet.

"Well, I'm going to do some homework and go to bed."

"Okay, good night, sweetheart," Ma said, barely looking up at Emilia.

Emilia lingered for a moment, watching Ma go about her usual routine of checking the doors and locks before heading to her own room.

Upstairs, Emilia stopped in the doorway of her brother's room directly across from hers. Tomás was reading on his bed and barely glanced up as Emilia came in and threw herself near him, shoving his feet away.

"So I hung out with a stripper earlier today," she said to get his attention. Tomás looked up from his book and gave her an amused look.

"Oh yeah?"

"Ian's cousin's girlfriend."

"Anthony? I thought he was off in the army."

"He is. He's just visiting."

"Oh. So, well, this date with the stripper? Was it everything you dreamed it would be?" Tomás closed his book.

Emilia laughed and shoved his feet again. "Shut up."

He chuckled and Emilia noticed his hair was already getting darker, having lost most of the golden brown the summer sun always turned it. Emilia looked up at the ceiling. "It was weird, I guess. She's nice, but . . . I don't know. Something about her bothered me."

She propped herself up on one elbow and looked at her brother.

"It's not like it's a big deal, that she's a stripper or whatever. I don't care about that, but it was weird. She asked me if I thought I could do what she does."

Her brother raised an eyebrow and Emilia continued.

"I think it's her go-to line when she meets people. Like, 'Hey, nice to meet you. Think you could be a stripper, too?'"

"Yeah, that is kind of weird. But she's probably just insecure."

"That's what I thought, too. But like the whole night, I kept picturing her stripping. Is that weird?"

Tomás shrugged. "Not really. I mean, you can't help it once you know stuff about people. And the harder you try to fight an idea or thought, the more it keeps running through your mind."

Emilia looked at her brother again. "Yeah, I guess you're right. When did you get so smart?"

He laughed. "I'm not smart." But he was. Like their father. For a moment Emilia blurred her eyesight and she could see a younger version of their father in front of her. She thought of telling Tomás this, but decided to keep it to herself.

"I guess this would be a bad time to tell you," he said, "with you thinking I'm so smart and insightful, that Ian's mother bought hemorrhoid ointment today."

"Oh god, gross!" Emilia yelled.

"Extra strength," Tomás said.

"Ewww, extra strength?" They laughed so hard, Emilia could hardly speak.

Tomás nodded. "Yep. And she kept talking to me, like I

wouldn't notice if she just talked enough. Oh, I noticed, lady! And I took *extra* long to check out her items."

Emilia couldn't stop laughing. "Good! Good for her!" She thought of Ian's mom in her discomfort and felt only a little guilty because she disliked Emilia. "Oh man, what else?" Emilia asked finally, after wiping a few tears away.

Tomás always gave her a rundown of all the private things people in their town bought at the pharmacy. Condoms, tampons, hemorrhoid ointment, pregnancy tests. Emilia liked knowing these things about people. It seemed so many people knew about her—why shouldn't she know about others? About their private matters.

Tomás shook his head. "That's it, that's all I got."

Emilia lay back and stared at the ceiling again, smiling as her laughter faded away. She took a deep breath and then asked Tomás about what she'd been wondering since she got home.

"Hey, does Ma seem okay to you?"

"Sure, why?"

"I don't know. I just thought she seemed tired today."

"She's always tired," Tomás said. "Wakes up early to get into the city, then books all those appointments, then the commute home."

"I know, I know." Emilia thought of how her mom had to drive from Uniondale to the Hempstead train station to get into the city each morning. Tomás was probably right. Besides, she didn't want Tomás to worry. Emilia knew he worried just as much as Ma did in his own quiet way. She could see it in his face sometimes, how he worried about her and the house and the bills. It was why he quietly went out and got a job as soon as he could, picked up every extra shift, and started paying some of the household bills without even telling Ma. It's why he hadn't started his classes at the community college, even now, a year after he'd graduated from high school, though he always talked about it.

She looked at her brother, someone who seemed simultaneously wise beyond his years and also the purest person she knew. She didn't want to add to the stress he already carried by worrying him about Ma, too. So she just said, "All right, see you in the morning." Then she rolled off his bed and headed to her room.

Later that night, the salt and pepper shakers flashed in Emilia's mind as she tried to fall asleep. The colorful stripes reminded her exactly of a pair of galoshes she got when she was younger.

It was after the attack, when she'd recovered physically but still wasn't talking. And one morning, instead of Ma getting frustrated as she tried to guide Emilia through yet another home-school lesson, Ma stared at her from across the table and said, *Let's go somewhere. Wherever you want. Maybe we just need to get the hell out of the house.*

Emilia didn't want to go anywhere. And she didn't want to do the stupid lesson, either. She did, and didn't, want to crawl into the bed she'd been in for what seemed like forever, that smelled like her own sweat, and watch cartoons she didn't even care about anymore. But Ma got up, and Emilia followed right behind her like she'd become accustomed to doing.

Do you want to get sandwiches? Have a picnic in the park? Ma asked.

Emilia quickly shook her head and Ma understood. No park. No playground. No place like it. So they ended up at Kmart, where they went up and down aisles, Ma picking out notebooks, stickers, markers, anything, and holding them up for Emilia, who just wasn't interested.

Please, Ma said. *You can have anything you want.*

Emilia wouldn't respond, and Ma grew tired of asking, so they went through the rest of the store.

And then Emilia suddenly found herself in front of a shelf lined with boots; she ran her fingers over the smooth rubber and bright stripes. *Emilia,* her mother called, even though Emilia was standing right next to her. Ma always did that now, called out her name—*Emilia, Emilia*—if her eyes were turned away even just for a second.

Emilia reached out and touched her mother, reassuring them both as Ma spoke to her. Ma was always talking to her, ever since the appointment with Dr. Lisa, where Emilia had overheard the doctor telling Ma to keep talking to Emilia: *Keep having conversations with her, even if she doesn't respond. Don't forget she's there.*

Emilia felt a pull to go to one of those memories in Dr. Lisa's office, but forced herself to stay in the store with her mother.

We'll get your brother some underwear, Ma said as Emilia eyed the boots. *He really needs new ones. But don't tell him I told you that. You'll embarrass poor Tomás. You know how he is. So shy. Emilia? Emilia?*

Emilia squeezed her mother's hand.

Her mother looked down at her. *Those are pretty,* Ma said.

They were beautiful.

Ma looked at them. *You want to try them on?* she asked quietly.

Emilia nodded.

Go on.

Emilia sat on the ground, took off her sneakers, and slipped her feet into the cool rubber boots. They looked perfect. She stood up, stomped in place a few times. They felt magical. And so, Emilia closed her eyes and pretended they had some sort of special power. She felt a fire start in her heels, sparking yellow flames. She imagined the boots transforming her, turning her plain corduroys into glittering electric-blue tights and Emilia herself into some kind of superhero. Or a rock star, like the one she and Tomás had seen on television, the man with red hair and a red-and-blue lightning bolt painted over one of his eyes.

Emilia felt herself levitating, then a burst of power as she soared and punched through the ceiling of the store.

Emilia, Emilia. Her mother brought her back down to earth.

She looked at her mother. Emilia loved the boots. She wanted them. She couldn't stand the idea of leaving them behind. They would feel abandoned and forgotten. She couldn't do that. Her mother had said she could have anything she wanted. She wanted these boots.

Can I have them? she asked. Her mother stared at her. Emilia was surprised by the sound of her own voice, how the words tumbled out of her mouth. She had thought her voice was gone, all used up and carried away in the cold wind of the afternoon of her attack. But there it was, and not thin and breakable, but loud. The sound of it jarred her.

Emilia, Ma whispered under the fluorescent lights of the store and a background of camping gear.

Even now Emilia could still picture her mother's face perfectly, the look of shock when she had uttered those words after so many months of not speaking. Emilia's mother had pulled her into her arms, squeezed her so hard that Emilia squeaked like a chew toy, and her mother had laughed and said, *Yes, yes, of course you can have them. Come on!*

Emilia tumbled back, deeper into the memory.

Her mother's hand shook as she took Emilia's hand and led her past fishing poles and tents, past the registers, and out the automatic doors of the store. Emilia thought of her old sneakers left behind on the floor and tried to run back to get them, but her mother held her hand tighter and pulled her to the car.

You can have anything you want, Emilia. Anything, Ma said as they walked.

Her mother opened the door to their beat-up car and Emilia got in the back seat. She stared at her new boots as her mother slipped into the front seat. She could do anything in these boots. She could land on the moon and different planets. She smiled at them, her boots.

Do you want ice cream? Ma asked. She turned back and Emilia saw she was happy, deliriously happy, but her face was wet with tears and it scared Emilia to see her that way. Emilia nodded. But her mother abruptly faced forward again.

Do you want ice cream, Emilia? she called out.

Emilia nodded again. But her mother refused to look back.

Say yes or no, Emilia. Do you want ice cream?

The car filled with a long silence before her mother repeated the question again. *Emilia, answer my question. Just answer my question. Please.*

Emilia felt as though they sat there forever, her mother's head down as if she was looking at something in her lap. Emilia wondered if she had fallen asleep. Or was praying. Or had died.

She searched for her voice to muster her mother, to bring her back the way the crows had brought back Emilia.

Caw, Emilia cried. It came out loud and piercing, and Emilia saw her mother jump, startle. *Caw,* Emilia cried out again. But her mother would not turn back.

A coldness ran along Emilia's arms and she felt herself pulled out of the store memory and in her bed once more. She hugged the blanket around herself tighter, wondering where the gust of cold was coming from. Had she left the window open?

Emilia.

Emilia.

She heard her name and wondered if it was her mother calling her, or the wind outside, or her birds, who sometimes spoke to her and sent her messages on the wind. She used to hear them so much when she was younger. When they were always with her. When they told her to fly, to join them in the sky. Over time, they spoke to her less and less. But maybe they were calling her again now. Saying, *Join us, Emilia. Leave the world below. Come with us. Feel the wind. Fly to the sun. Forget everything down there.*

She was tired and wanted to fall into a dreamless sleep, but each way she turned, a new image was waiting.

Jeremy Lance rode into her mind on his turquoise bicycle. He turned and looked at her. Emilia wanted to run, but fear glued her to the sidewalk. He waved, started riding toward her with that ridiculously exuberant grin, and she felt the terror in her chest rising to her throat. She looked away. And when she looked back, Jane was suddenly on the bike instead of Jeremy Lance.

Emilia, now, that's a sweet name, her purple lips said. She smiled.

And Emilia suddenly realized what bothered her about Jane. Her smile, wide and somehow painful. It was like Jeremy Lance's.

You're just dreaming, Emilia told herself. *Think of something else. He can't get you anymore.* Emilia pushed Jane and Jeremy and their smiles out of her mind, but other thoughts floated in—terrible thoughts that Emilia kept away during the day but that often came to her at night when she was in that half-asleep state and couldn't tell the difference between what was a dream and what was real and what was just imagined.

In that half-asleep state, she would wonder if another kid would turn up, half dead, and then maybe another. Sometimes she saw their bodies in the woods next to hers. She would wonder if that feeling that everyone was watching her was real. And she thought of her father dying as she fell deeper into sleep. She imagined him stuck in the snow in Alaska, not a single soul hearing his cries for help.

She saw him in the snow now, his beard coated with ice. He could have been out there all night; he could have been out there for days, weeks.

Was he under some trees, looking at sky?

Were vultures circling him?

Or my crows, was that where they were headed?

Did a wolf find him?

And slash into his belly?

She could almost see his bright blood on the snow.

She needed to get to him, to save him. Emilia felt herself grow large wings and she flew upward and upward into a white sky. It was smoke and fog. It was cold. She soared higher and watched the world become smaller. She looked over snow-covered fields for signs of her father and pictured the look on his face as she landed in front of him.

Emilia? he'd say. Would he recognize her? Would he know it was her under those dark feathers? Yes, he'd know immediately.

I've come to save you, she'd tell him.

Emilia surveyed the ground beneath her, looking for him.

But the snow and trees disappeared and were replaced by only darkness. Emilia flew and flew, looking for somewhere to land, but found nothing.

Something is wrong . . . , Emilia thought as she drifted completely to sleep. But she didn't know quite what it was.

Earlier That Day

Earlier that day, while Emilia was deciding what to wear on her movie date with Ian, Anthony, and Jane, Emilia's mother had just arrived at her second appointment. She looked at her appointment book to see what the occasion was for this one, but saw no notes next to the woman's address and phone number. Regardless, it should only take about an hour, giving her plenty of time to drive to the bride across town.

Too much time, she thought. *I'll have an hour to kill.*

Still, she looked forward to having a break between appointments for once.

She arrived at the large house, drove through impressive black gates, and rang the doorbell, half expecting a butler to answer. This was the kind of house where one could expect a butler. Instead, a woman in a dark figure-hugging dress answered. Her hair was impeccably done and she smiled brightly as she opened the door. This was definitely the lady of the house.

"Mrs. DeJesus?" the woman asked.

"Yes, hi, call me Nina," Emilia's mom answered.

"Nina, all right. Come in," the lady said. "You must be cold."

She followed the woman in; their shoes clicked loudly on the white marble floor that looked too precious to walk on. Nina looked around the room, gleaming white except for a pop of red and blue here and there from sculptures and paintings of bulls and horses and Spanish matadors. It was an odd but beautiful room. Nina tried not to seem too in awe.

"Lovely home," she said quietly. Her very voice felt like it could disrupt the room's beauty, break the fragile art.

"Thank you."

The woman led Nina through an arched doorway, then through a large room with a grand piano at its center and no other furnishings. They walked through yet another room with a long table that had no doubt seen countless dinner parties. *Or not,* Nina thought as her footsteps echoed in the otherwise silent house. They finally came to a set of French doors that opened dramatically to a room constructed completely of glass panels. The walls, the ceiling let in the natural light from outside through the impossibly clear panes.

Nina stared at the scenic room. Purple and pink and white orchids in glass bowls hung by invisible strings at varying lengths from the ceiling. Lush ferns and bushes and trees lined the perimeter. Glass domes held plants too beautiful and rare to be exposed to the rest of the world while bunches of lavender and ivy and fragrant white petunias burst and trailed everywhere. In the middle of it all was a gilded birdcage—the centerpiece—atop an extravagant, tiered brick pillar.

"How sweet," Nina said of the two finches in the cage. The cage door was open and Nina whistled gently. One of the birds cooed back. "Don't they escape?"

The woman looked at Nina and smiled. "They can't really escape," she said, gesturing to the glass panels around them.

Nina nodded.

"They're a curious pair, though," she said, standing next to Nina and peering in lovingly. "The female finch—she's the brown one there—lays eggs, but destroys them. You see that little straw house, the straw inside?"

Nina nodded.

"She could lay them there, but she doesn't," the lady of the house continued. "She lets them drop onto the cage floor so they crack. Every single time."

Nina peeked in closer at the female finch, her small bird eyes that seemed to hide some kind of secret.

"I suppose she doesn't want any baby birds," the woman said.

The light brown finch flew out of the cage, sweeping past Nina's face, followed by the gray one. Nina watched them fly away, disappear into the lushness of the greenhouse. She was awed by it all, the many shades of green and life, the female finch's curious behavior. But the woman said, "This way," and gestured to a table and chair set not too far away from the cage, partially hidden by a plant with massive, drooping leaves.

Nina snapped back to reality but was sorry she had to work. What she would like to do is walk the paved paths of this secret glass garden. To go to the very back of it, where, she was certain, there was a soft, giant fern large enough for her to sit in, large enough to wrap its leaves around her and hold her gently.

"I know it's slightly warm in here," the woman explained as she gestured to the plants and flowers, "but I prefer to have my makeup done in this natural light, and this is the best room for it, as you can see. You can set up now."

"Of course," Nina said. She peeled off her coat, gathered her long dark auburn hair in a ponytail, and pushed up her sleeves.

The woman sat down and closed her eyes. Nina draped a protective smock over her, and focused on the woman's face instead of the flowers and plants around them. She studied her complexion before choosing an appropriate foundation.

"Are you headed to an event now or later in the evening?" Nina probed, wondering if she should choose lighter or darker shades. The woman sat so still and peacefully, Nina thought perhaps she didn't hear her question or was meditating.

Just as Nina was about to repeat herself, the woman spoke. "No event. Do whatever you'd like."

Nina was used to clients relying on her expertise, and so, taking inspiration from her surroundings, she continued. She didn't say anything, just allowed the woman to decide if and when she wanted to speak.

Her skin was thin. Her eyelids seemed especially fragile and Nina could see the tiny blue veins just under the translucent skin. Nina watched how they fluttered slightly, the way her eyeballs moved underneath as Nina gently applied the foundation.

Suddenly she noticed tears coming out of the sides of the woman's delicate eyes, the way she took a deep breath and let it out slowly, the furrow of her brow. For a moment, an anguished look fought its way to the surface. Nina watched as the woman tried to regain control, to suppress some pain, which came surging in those quiet moments, in the intimacy of someone delicately touching your face.

The woman let out a gentle, shaky breath and Nina grabbed a tissue and pressed it to the corners of the woman's eyes.

She wondered what had happened.

Perhaps she's headed to a funeral, Nina rationalized.

No one thinks people other than the deceased get their makeup done for funerals, but Nina knew some people did.

No, this is an old pain, Nina decided as she dusted a rose color on each eyelid. *This is the kind of pain that suddenly comes out of nowhere, for a moment fresh and raw, but is able to be constrained and pushed away. New pain takes over.*

New pain leaves you trembling.

Within a few moments, the woman had complete control of her emotions again. She relaxed and Nina continued working.

Perhaps it was a memory that suddenly flashed in her mind, or the ache for a dead husband. Or a dead child.

Could she have lost a child?

Nina thought this of almost every woman she saw or met. She

tried to read their hearts. *Did you turn your back for a moment? Was your child found? Or lost forever? Is your pain like mine? Worse?*

She sucked in her breath.

There is worse, Nina . . . Remember that.

But oh, how dreadful Nina knew it was to live your life always with that thought.

Nina let her thoughts wander, but too much, and before she could stop them, her own memories came flooding in with a rush. She suddenly saw Emilia when she was eight, stiff and unable to move, the day after coming home from the hospital. She saw the two of them in Nina's bedroom, a version of her younger self quickly putting out a cigarette in the ashtray on top of the dresser. She hadn't wanted Emilia to see she'd started smoking again. The only time her children had seen her smoke was when their grandmother died. Nina didn't want Emilia to think she, too, was gone for good.

Emilia's eyes were glassy, and they rolled around a bit while she tried to take in her surroundings.

Emilia, Nina said. She heard her own voice, how strained and close to tears it sounded as she said her daughter's name. She cleared her throat and tried again. *Emilia, how do you feel?*

It had been a simple question, but Emilia couldn't answer. She only moaned, and Nina realized how stupid she was to ask it.

No, no, I'm sorry, Nina said. *Don't, sweetheart! Don't try to talk.* Emilia's eyes widened as she suddenly seemed aware of her swollen tongue. She had bitten through it so badly it required stitches. She tried to talk again, but her eyes filled up with tears.

Don't, Nina said gently, and sat down on the edge of the bed. She looked at Emilia and saw the bewilderment, and so she explained again, *Do you remember anything? Don't try to talk. Just nod or shake your head. Stop, don't try to talk. Your tongue has to heal.*

It was Emilia's terrified look, the confusion there, that made Nina feel like cold water had been splashed against her insides, against the burning hate and rage that now kept her going. She felt brittle. She heard herself cracking.

Keep it together! she thought. *Keep it together for Emilia.*

Emilia, she said softly. Nina closed her eyes and steadied herself before she spoke again. Her daughter reached up; her fingertips grazed Nina's cheek, then her eyelids. Nina opened her eyes and started explaining.

You're home now. You were in the hospital, but you're safe now. Somebody . . . somebody very horrible attacked you . . . She didn't know what else to say. This was all she could say to her daughter. She knew it didn't make sense.

That was when Emilia's eyes went wild. She tried to stick her fingers in her own mouth. And all Nina could do was gently pull her hand down, tell her she was safe now.

Don't try to talk. Your tongue needs to heal. You need to heal.

She could hear her daughter's breathing coming faster, heavier.

Calm down. It's okay, Nina said, pulling Emilia's arm away, placing it back down on her chest, and then keeping her own hand there, feeling the violent thumping of her daughter's heart, trying to keep it from exploding. *We found you. You're okay now, Emilia.*

Nina carefully got in bed with her, tucked herself next to her daughter's small, broken body, so carefully, wondering just how broken she was inside.

You're okay now, she whispered again. *I love you.* She repeated this over and over, like a poem, until Emilia got sleepy. Until they both got sleepy and the only sound was the crackling voice of someone on the television, counting down.

Ten.

Nine.

Eight.

Nina felt her daughter's body becoming less tense next to her. The sound of the man's voice droned on. Until moments later, she opened her eyes and looked at the screen.

Fire. And smoke. And blue sky.

Nina sat up and watched the *Challenger* explode, saw the families staring up at the disaster, not knowing what had happened, the tragedy not settling into their understanding yet, not yet, even as they saw it with their own eyes.

Oh god, Nina thought. She looked down at her daughter. Then got up, turned off the television, and went to the bathroom to weep. She thought of those poor astronauts, their parents in the crowd as they watched their children explode, her own daughter, asleep in the next room. And Nina wept harder, with her whole body, but quietly. She couldn't let Emilia hear her. Or Sam. He was home, but she hoped he was downstairs in his office. Nina knew he couldn't deal with Emilia's broken body. He would not be able to deal with Nina's own brokenness on top of that. But how she wished he were right there, next to her.

Nina snapped back to the garden. Back to carefully brushing rose-colored blush onto this stranger's cheekbones. She took a tissue from the makeup table and quickly dabbed her own eyes before her client could see her tears. She reeled herself away from the past, busied herself with choosing a shade of lipstick and applying it carefully.

When she was done, she stepped back and examined her work. The woman looked beautiful. Nina held up a mirror and the woman looked at herself.

Usually she could see exactly how her clients studied the application of their eyeliner, or the placement of the blush on their cheeks. But this woman didn't. She looked at herself in the mirror head-on, as if she were looking inside herself. When she still hadn't said anything after a long while, Nina wondered if she was dissatisfied. But no, "Lovely," she said finally, and offered Nina a genuine smile before putting down the mirror and removing the smock.

The woman got up and looked pensive. Nina got an irrational urge to ask her about her life, to ask her the reason for the garden she had built here; Nina knew instinctively that it was this woman's project, her design, her conservatory. She felt that if she waited long enough, the woman would reveal some kind of secret.

But the woman didn't speak. She simply walked over to the nearest flowers and touched the petals. Nina cleaned her brushes and put them away.

"Could you . . . let yourself out? The check is right there," the woman said without turning back.

"Yes, of course. Thank you," Nina answered as she looked at the check on the makeup table. She folded it, put it in her purse, glad she would be able to cover the water bill this month.

The woman continued down the path, until she was no longer visible. Nina finished packing up, took a last look at the flowers before walking out of the magnificent garden, through the large rooms, and back out into the gray day.

She was driving past the gates when she started wondering how it was possible that she had just been in the midst of a beautiful garden. Had it been real?

How is it possible that those flowers could exist in the middle of this cold world?

For a moment, Nina imagined that nothing she thought was real actually was. Maybe even the past was just a terrible imagining.

Did it really happen?

Someone beeped. Nina proceeded past a stop sign. She glanced at her watch and knew she would be too early if she went to her next appointment now. Up ahead, a Kmart came into view and Nina made her way to it.

She walked in and went down the aisles, looking for anything they might need at home, but knowing already she'd buy nothing.

The neatly lined orange and green jugs of laundry detergent depressed her more than usual today. The stacked boxes of toothpaste brought tears to her eyes.

Keep it together, she told herself.

But the woman and the garden and now the rows of everything so neat, so orderly, and the memory of Emilia in bed, and the past, *the past*, had invaded her mind. Her whole body. She felt the urge to run her hand along the shelves, sending the soap, the bottles of shampoo and conditioner, falling to the floor.

Stop, she told herself.

But she remembered more. So much more. She remembered walking the aisles of the grocery store with Emilia. The heavy gazes of their neighbors as Nina walked dazed, hypnotized, and confused by the order of the shelves, her little bird at her side. And that day, oh that day, when Emilia spread her arms and screeched and cawed and ran throughout the store. She looked like she would bite anyone who might come near her—not that anyone did.

They just watched.

They watched as Nina ran and ran after her strange bird, swift and fast and impossible to catch.

But eventually she did catch Emilia. And she'd had to wrestle Emilia into her arms. And Emilia had scratched at Nina's face and neck as she was carried outside, screeching and kicking and *cawing*. From the grocery store windows, they watched.

All those people, who shook their heads as if I were terrible, as if we were terrible.

Emilia flapped her arms and tried to climb her mother like a tree, reaching for the sky. Only when they were in the car with the doors locked did Nina look over and see the cans of green beans she'd been holding and had absentmindedly thrown into her purse while she'd tried to get control of Emilia. She looked at Emilia in the rearview mirror, flapping around in the back seat, exhausting herself. Exhausting them both. Nina flipped down the visor and looked at herself in the driver's-side mirror there—the red welts on her face from Emilia's sharp fingernails that looked as bad as they felt, the line of little red dashes where she'd drawn blood.

As Nina waited for Emilia to calm down so she could get a seat belt on her, she worried for a moment about the green beans, until she realized the ridiculousness of worrying about the fucking green beans. About what those people—those people who had been *watching them*—thought. About worrying about anything other than Emilia. And she thought, *Fuck you! I'm taking them. I earned the damn green beans. They're mine.*

So when Emilia, finally drained of all energy, whimpered softly and looked at the sky, Nina gently buckled her in and drove away. And as she looked at the store in the rearview mirror, where those *people had the nerve to judge her and her daughter*, Nina took pleasure in knowing the green beans were there in her purse.

Nina blinked back tears and kept walking down the Kmart aisles.

What are you searching for?

The question floated into her mind and startled her.

She looked at the shelves and racks and endcaps, trying to find an answer on those neat rows. Trying to find *something* in all those things, so many things.

She moved from cleaning supplies to home decor, looking at bedsheets and throw pillows. She saw a pair of brightly colored salt and pepper shakers. She picked them up, studied the stripes, and put them in the shopping cart before slowly heading to the clothing department. There she found a soft brownish-pink shawl, the same shade as the eye shadow she had put on the woman's eyelids just a short while ago. Nina took the shawl off the hanger. There was a delicate, glimmering gold thread running through the material. She ran her finger across it and tried it on.

Somewhere, a child cried.

Nina tried to focus on the shawl. On the glimmering thread.

But the child cried louder, higher. A girl. It was a girl. Her cries filled the store, filled Nina's ears. Nina closed her eyes and tried not to wonder how Emilia must have cried. She tried not to imagine the sounds that must have erupted from her daughter that cold afternoon.

Like that? Had she cried like that? Screamed like that?

No, it must have been worse. So much worse.

Nina wrapped the shawl around herself, tighter and tighter, as if it would help restrain her from going to the small girl, grabbing her, tucking her under her arm, and running.

She opened her eyes and checked the time. She should get going.

Nina looked down at the shopping cart, empty except for the salt and pepper shakers. She searched her purse for her keys, and quickly dropped the shakers in before abandoning the cart.

Then Nina adjusted the shawl on her shoulders and walked out of the store.

He's Hiding

He's hiding something, Emilia thought. It'd been a few days since their date with Anthony and Jane. Ian and Emilia were in his car driving to school once again. But Ian seemed nervous and fidgety. When he turned the wrong direction, his car screeched and Emilia looked over at him.

"I've got a surprise," Ian said.

"Oh yeah? Another date with a stripper?" Anthony had gone back to Virginia, where he was stationed, and there was no chance of another date with him and Jane. But the snide remark came out anyway.

He gave her a funny look. "You said you weren't mad about that."

"I'm not. I'm just kidding," she said, shaking her head and smiling. "What is it? What's your surprise?"

Ian looked relieved and continued. "I found out they have a new exhibit at that museum and . . . I thought we could go . . . if you want."

"Now?"

"If you want to. I mean, I know it's kind of . . ."

"No, no!" Emilia said. "I mean, yes, let's go! It sounds perfect." She looked over at him, at her Ian, and felt so lucky. This really was perfect. And *he* was perfect. And this was exactly what she needed.

They drove on and she reached for his hand, held it, wanting to apologize for her silly remark about dates with strippers. She stared at him, willing him to look over at her, and when their eyes locked, she reached over and brushed his cheek with her fingertips before he glanced back at the road.

"You okay?" he asked.

"Yeah . . . ," she said. She wanted to talk to him, but she couldn't exactly explain that she wondered where Ma had really gotten the salt and pepper shakers. And she couldn't tell him that she felt like something was wrong, that she felt strange somehow, and that she was worried it might have to do with her father. Not because Ian wouldn't understand, but because Emilia was afraid to talk about these things. Like if she talked about them, said them aloud, they would be true.

"I'm just tired," she said, which was true. She'd had trouble sleeping lately. She would wake up in the middle of the night suddenly, cold, paralyzed, afraid to even look out her window because she felt like she might see *him* out there—Jeremy Lance, trying to get her attention, pounding on the window over and over again. Breaking it. Climbing in. Dragging her off the bed by her ankles.

"It's nothing," she reassured Ian, and smiled.

When they arrived at the museum, Ian turned off the car. He

looked at Emilia for a moment, and then he started kissing her. His kisses became more urgent, his body harder against hers, and even though she loved him, even though she wanted this to be just like last time, it wasn't.

She pulled away.

"Can we . . . Do you mind if we just go inside?" she asked.

He looked hurt but quickly said, "Yeah, of course." Emilia breathed a sigh of relief when he didn't make a big deal about it. Maybe he felt it was different this time, too.

They went inside and Ian paid their admission. Together, they walked through the open glass doors, where a man in a blue suit took their tickets and quietly told them to enjoy themselves.

They walked to the gallery directly in front of them. Walls had been erected within the large room, and there was an entryway to the smaller room those walls created. A projector hung from the ceiling, flickering scenes onto the erected walls. Emilia watched the blue-toned images of an ocean surround them. She felt like a stranger, standing inside someone else's house, looking out a window to the ocean just beyond. Blue and gray, but somehow still sparkling and gleaming.

The ocean changed to mountains. And Emilia got the sense she was flying as the mountains rushed toward her. She could practically feel the cold wind as she flew above them, dipping down here and there. It took her breath away. She wanted to stay in those mountains, but then the walls filled with clouds. Fast-moving clouds, rolling and rushing and rolling.

And then suddenly, the image of still trees and thin branches with small, fragile leaves dangling and swaying in the breeze like trinkets filled her vision.

It was as if whoever made this movie was trying to capture what it felt like to be a bird in flight.

It's a sign, she thought.

She'd felt this before, in her dreams, in her memory, a thousand times. Emilia extended her arms and she imagined the wind going through her as she soared over the trees, over the oceans. As she swooped past mountains and filled the sky with her large black wings.

She looked at her shadow projected on those walls.

"Emilia?" Ian said. The sparkling ocean cued up again. She stared at the outline of her body, her arms outstretched, and then she saw the strange look on Ian's face.

She lowered her arms and said, "This reminds me of when I used to go to Jones Beach with my parents and Tomás."

When my dad was still around, she thought.

She looked back at the water curling, coming toward them, and retreating, and she felt like she was moving with it, like she was being hypnotized.

"Let's see the rest of it," Ian said, reaching for her hand. She followed him then, because if she didn't, she felt like she might stay there forever.

"Look at this," Ian said as they entered the next gallery. There was an elaborate statue in the middle of the room resembling a human figure. It was half mannequin, half art. It had legs, but from the torso up, it was an explosion of creation.

Emilia moved closer. Thick, spongy moss covered the statue from the waist up, like it was a tree. And on the moss hung so many small, beautiful things. Tiny decorated padlocks, small gilded birdcages, various flowers and paper butterflies, and strings and strings of beads. Small, delicate, lifelike birds with beautiful feathers and tiny black eyes were perched here and there. And tiny lemons, random charms, and little porcelain statues of angels were embedded everywhere.

Emilia sucked in her breath. "This is so cool!" she told Ian. It was one of the most beautiful things she'd ever seen. She walked around it several times, took in every trinket, feeling that it was made just for her. As if someone had looked inside her, peeled back her skin, and seen this. Emilia resisted the urge to reach out and touch it.

"I wish I could take it home," she told Ian. "Put it in my room."

"Yeah? Well, I'd steal it for you but . . ." He glanced over at one of the guards and shrugged. Emilia smiled and took his hand and they walked around some more, taking in everything, even the permanent exhibits they'd seen last time. All the while, Emilia couldn't stop thinking of the statue.

"Ready?" Ian said finally.

Emilia nodded, and when they walked back outside, she looked at the sky, the same shade as the flickering images on the walls she'd just seen inside.

"What now?" she asked, because they still had so much of the day left.

Ian smiled as if he'd been waiting for her to ask. "Wait here," he said. He ran to the car and she watched him retrieve a flannel blanket and a brown paper bag from the trunk. She recognized the takeout bag from Carro's deli.

"Come on," he said, grabbing her hand and pulling her to the picnic area on the side of the museum. When they reached it, he spread out the blanket on a patch of lawn and they sat. Ian pulled items out of the bag, set them down one by one.

"When did you do all of this?" Emilia asked.

"I woke up early."

She looked at him, sitting cross-legged in front of her, at the little items displayed on the blanket. With each one, he had been thinking of her, of them, of this moment. Her heart felt full and yet there was an ache in there, too, that Emilia knew was sadness. Ian opened the sandwich for her, then his own, and she thought of how perfect today was and how much she loved him.

How can I be sad? she thought.

She wished they could hold on to this moment, this very moment here, together, but she already felt it slipping away. And the impossibility of making time stand still hit her suddenly. With every passing second, they were getting farther and farther away from this moment, this very moment here, together, and this perfect day.

Why is beauty so hard to hold on to? she wondered. And why did she feel that sadness always?

"Is it too cold?" he asked when he noticed she wasn't eating her sandwich. "I couldn't keep it hot, but I was hoping it'd still be warm."

"It's perfect," she said, taking a bite of the cold sandwich. The plastic texture of the melted and then cooled cheese tasted amazing to her.

She looked at Ian and wondered if he understood. If he knew, as she did, that someday they wouldn't be together. That the day they would break up was, at this very moment, making its way toward them, already transforming this perfect day into a bittersweet memory. A sense of dread filled Emilia suddenly, and she felt sorry for herself, for Ian, as she looked around at the bare trees and the gray sky above.

"Are you okay?" Ian asked.

"Yeah," she said, turning to him and smiling. Why couldn't she just focus on this, on Ian, who loved her and took her to see beautiful things and packed picnic lunches for them? She wanted to remember every detail of their day, so she could recall it perfectly in the future. Someday when she was sad.

"Why'd you do all this?" she asked.

A strange look crossed his face, then he smiled. "Because I love you," he said, like it was the most obvious thing in the world. "And . . . because you seem, I don't know. A little sad lately?" Emilia looked down at her sandwich and tried not to cry. But before she could stop it, her eyes filled with tears.

She'd felt strange and melancholy lately. Since their date, Ian had called and stopped by, but Emilia still felt lonely. She didn't know how to explain the kind of loneliness she felt. So she'd tried to cover it up and pretend nothing was bothering her. But Ian had noticed something was wrong anyway. And now he felt sorry for her.

"Hey," he said. "Hey, what's wrong?"

The tears rushed so fast they took her by surprise.

"Emilia?"

She shook her head. His voice, the concern in it made her eyes sting more. For a minute, she couldn't speak. Even if she knew what to say, the words would get stuck in her throat. All she could do was press on her eyes and shake her head, before taking a deep breath and letting it out.

"What's wrong?" he whispered.

"I don't know," she said finally, bringing her hands away from her face. "This is just really sweet."

Sweet Emilia.

"It wasn't supposed to make you cry," he said.

She managed to laugh. "I know, I know." She lay down and looked at the sky, which, while dreary, still hurt her eyes. She felt fresh tears form as she stared above. "I'm so stupid. *Nothing* is wrong," she said. He reached for her hand and kissed the green clover ring.

"You're *not* stupid." He kissed her hand. Then he kissed her eyes and then her cheek, and made his way to her lips. And this time she pulled him closer.

"Would you tell me?" he said. "If something *was* wrong?" He searched for some kind of answer in her face.

"Of course," she answered. "But there's nothing, I don't think. I just . . ." She shook her head. She really didn't know why she had started crying. She watched a bird fly overhead. A cold wind blew over her and she shivered.

"It's the weather," she said suddenly. *That* was all it was. The way the chilling cold came so quickly, and the world changed from the bright oranges and reds and golds of summer and fall to the sludgy gray of winter. Emilia always got this way when it got cold. Ma, too. There was something in the cold that brought back the past so quickly, and it always seemed to catch them off guard.

Emilia hated winter. It got in her bones and made her cold for months and months no matter what she did to warm up. And it marked another year without her father. Another sad Thanksgiving had already passed. Soon would come Christmas, then New Year's, when she and her mother and her brother would force more cheer and bring more attention to her father's absence by not bringing any attention to it at all.

She missed him, and most around this time.

Emilia suddenly felt relieved. "I always get this way!" she told Ian a bit too excitedly. "It's just because it's so cold. And dreary."

He lay down next to her and held her hand tight, and they stared at the sky together. She wiped her face and smiled.

Yes, it's just because of the weather.

That was why she felt this way.

"Are you sure?" Ian asked, bringing her hand up to his chest.

"Positive," she said. She rolled over and looked at him—Ian, her Ian, with the shy smile and soft brown eyes. She leaned into him. "Really, that's all," she said. She kissed him, and under that white-gray sky, she held on to that day, those passing seconds and perfect moments, for as long as she possibly could.

That night Emilia dreamed of oceans. She was at Jones Beach and she watched Ma and Dad and Tomás in the distance from where she stood just under the boardwalk. They were laughing over there, on Ian's flannel blanket. When she saw her father, in the sun, away from the cold that took him so far from them, she wanted to run to him and ask him why he'd left. But they were all laughing and she didn't want to ruin it. It was so beautiful to see them laugh. They had all been beautiful once.

Emilia started crying. Her tears flooded down her face, down her body, and into the ocean.

She looked down and had the sense of moving, of spinning and falling, as the water rushed in and out. She watched her toes sink into the warm sand, deeper and deeper, until her feet disappeared. She wiggled them, but they were cemented in the heavy sand, so she looked toward the horizon again, at the sparkling sea and faraway seagulls that looked like confetti in the sky. She heard them cry, and Emilia watched as they came closer toward her. She watched as their magnificent white glowed in the bright sun, and suddenly they changed. They turned darker, grew smaller, and Emilia realized they had transformed into her black crows.

She reached out to them, tried to walk toward them, but realized she had sunk in the sand to her knees. As she looked down, she suddenly sank to her waist.

She looked over at her family, tried to call to them, but when she opened her mouth, she tasted earth and dirt and grass. And then she felt something unwinding from her mouth, as if from a spindle, and she saw branches and moss shooting out where her tongue should be, sprouting up and around her.

They covered her so completely, she could hardly see through.

She tried to speak again, but she couldn't. None of them could hear her silent calls. She caught a glimpse of Tomás pointing to the sky, to the birds. And Emilia watched as they dove and dipped down to the water and plucked jewels from the ocean. Green and pink and white jewels that glittered and blinded her. She felt them land on her, the weight of their small bird bodies as they perched all around her branches, nestling those gifts into her mossy hair.

More and more birds came, turning the sky dark, cawing so loudly before plucking more and more jewels from the ocean. She watched her parents rush from their place on the beach. She heard them call for her.

Emilia!

I'm here! Right here!

But they didn't see her. And they couldn't hear her. They didn't see how she was sinking under the weight of all her crows, all those jewels.

She tasted the grit of sand and salt in her mouth. She felt it in her nostrils. And she looked one more time at the water, the sparkling water. Until suddenly, a phone rang in the distance. She was sure it was a phone. But on the beach? Emilia told herself it was a dream and then slowly, as she came to, felt herself back in her bedroom.

She felt her mother standing over her, too, watching her breathe. Emilia was half asleep, but she knew it was Ma. It didn't startle her; she'd grown used to Ma doing this over the years. And tonight, in that half sleep, Ma's presence comforted Emilia, made her feel like she was tucked under a warm wing, hidden, protected.

She felt her body relax; she felt the expulsion of her breath. As she fell into a deep, easy sleep, she even saw fog rising from her mouth in her dreams. And it felt so good, that release, that relief.

★　★　★

Emilia's mother watched her daughter breathing, just as she had when Emilia was a baby. But she couldn't stand there too long without being overcome with the desire to cry. Emilia was asleep, in some other world, dreaming who knew what dreams while a terrible reality was delivered the way so many terrible realities are—with the shrill ring of a phone call at night. Nothing would ever be the same.

Again.

But her mother refused to cry in that room, where Emilia might hear her, so she closed the door and, with heavy steps, went back downstairs to her own room.

The Next Morning

The next morning Emilia kissed her mother quickly before leaving for school. Ma pulled her in and gave her a long hug. Ma had been like this, melancholy and affectionate, since she woke up.

"What's that for?" Emilia said, laughing and pulling away.

"Just . . . because," Ma said. She let go and turned toward the stove.

"Okay . . ." Emilia gave Tomás a funny smile and shook her head.

Tomás shrugged and watched his sister walk down the hallway and out into the world yelling goodbye to him and Ma as she closed the door behind her.

Tomás turned his attention back to Ma. He watched as she stood by the stove and poured boiling water into her coffee cup, added instant coffee and sugar.

She was dressed for the day, but her hair and makeup weren't done yet. He hadn't thought much of Emilia's comment about Ma being tired, but now he thought, *She does look tired.* He finished half of his English muffin and wiped the crumbs from his mouth.

"You have lots of appointments today?" he asked. Ma didn't respond, so he tried again. "Ma?"

She looked over as if she just now noticed him sitting there in the kitchen.

"Tomás?" she said as if she had to place his face. Sometimes Ma forgot he was around, but it didn't really bother him much anymore. He'd grown accustomed to the way most of her attention was always on his sister. Sometimes he thought of them as one, the way she and Emilia were with each other, little separate pieces of the same whole. Tomás noticed that sometimes Emilia didn't even have to speak, because Ma had learned Emilia's silent language that year, had learned to figure out what Emilia needed or wanted even when she didn't have the words to ask for it. Even though Tomás had envied their closeness, and still did slightly, he'd taught himself to understand. Emilia had paid a terrible price for this, and he knew she and Ma would both gladly have given it up to change the past.

"You okay?" Tomás asked Ma.

She nodded. "Yes." But she stood there, still stirring.

"Do you have many appointments today?" Tomás tried again.

"Oh . . ." Ma shook her head. "I don't know."

Tomás crunched on the other half of the English muffin and observed the strangeness and silence that settled around them like a fine dust of snow.

What's wrong with her? he wondered.

The phone suddenly disrupted the silence, shrilling loudly, and Ma jumped. It rang again and again, and even though Ma was closest to it, she didn't move. Finally, Tomás walked over to answer it.

"Hello?"

"Nina DeJesus, please," the voice said on the other end of the line.

His mother stared at him, her mouth slightly open and her green eyes so wide and pale. Tomás thought she resembled a fish.

"Who's calling?" he asked. His mother rushed toward him.

"Give it to me, Tomás . . . ," she said as the voice on the other end said something about the call being "a private matter. I can only speak to Nina DeJesus."

"Tomás!" His mother's voice was piercing as she pulled the phone out of his hand and gripped it.

He stared at her and she cupped her hand over the mouthpiece. "I said I've got it."

"Okay, okay . . . ," he said. His cheeks reddened with embarrassment and a small prickle of pain stabbed at his heart. Her voice was so harsh. He felt like a small child being chastised, when he was nineteen, a man now.

Tomás stepped back and Ma said nothing more. He mumbled something about being late for work and made his way down the hall. He grabbed his jacket from the closet and stood in front of the door.

"Ma, don't worry if it's another bill collector . . . ," he yelled. She was always resentful when they called and he picked up the phone, when it was apparent that even with Tomás's paychecks, which she never wanted to accept, they were still struggling. "I get paid tomorrow," he yelled down the hall again, and waited for a moment, listened for an answer or the beginning of a conversation, but heard nothing. So he opened the door and felt the cold rush into the house as he stepped outside.

The whole way to work, he played the incident over and over in his head. Why had she let the phone ring and ring like that? He couldn't make sense of it.

Once he got there, Tomás waited for one minute before punching in at exactly 8:00 AM. He counted his drawer, then stood at the register, waiting for customers. The music coming through the store speakers was too loud and blaring for early morning.

Something's wrong, Tomás thought as he reorganized some chocolate bars. *She looked scared.*

He dropped one and picked it up, noticed it was slightly open. He threw it in the bin of damaged merchandise. It reminded him of how his mother would check their Halloween candy when they were younger.

Why is she scared?

Tomás thought back to last night. Ma had acted strange then, too, after getting a phone call. He was downstairs watching a TV movie because he'd grown bored of his book. And when he went into the kitchen to get a snack, Ma was at the sink, silent, a glass of water in her hand.

He hadn't paid too much attention to it then. Or how she'd gone upstairs to check on Emilia afterward. But she'd stayed there so long. He'd even forgotten she was up there until she came back downstairs and crossed in front of the television and went back to her bedroom without saying a word.

Has Dad been calling? Is she worried Emilia or I will pick up and it'll be him?

The thought was ridiculous. His father had been dependable in that, at least. When he left, he left for good. No forwarding address, no phone calls, no cards. Nothing. As if he fell off the surface of the earth. Tomás imagined his father floating around helplessly in space, Earth just a faraway, unreachable ball of blue-and-green swirl. That's how far away he felt.

Perhaps he would call, though, if something had happened to him?

Maybe he was sick. Maybe he was in a hospital. Tomás pushed the thought to the back of his mind, where, maybe, he might think about it later. But not now. Because he didn't know how he would feel getting that news. He'd started hating his father a long time ago.

Tomás stood there, thinking.

No, it couldn't have been that.

His mother wouldn't have reacted the way she did. She wasn't scared of their father. She was angry at him. Like Tomás. She could tear him from limb to limb. An image of his father as a tiny puppet in his mother's hand being torn apart came to Tomás's mind and made him laugh and feel sad at the same time. If Tomás answered a call and his father was on the other end, he'd just hang up.

Maybe she's worried Emilia will answer Dad's call one day, Tomás thought.

74

Maybe their father would try to come back into their lives. And disrupt the world *they*—Ma and Tomás and Emilia—had worked so hard to try to make normal again. The last thing they needed was their father.

Emilia would be so bothered if she could read Tomás's mind. She had frozen their father in Alaska to preserve him forever.

Alaska, why would you think he's in Alaska? Tomás asked Emilia once, just a few months after Dad left.

He is, she insisted.

He's gone. He left us. He's a shithead.

It was as if Tomás had slapped her. He immediately regretted it. And then he'd had to explain to Ma why Emilia wouldn't stop crying.

Just let her believe that for now, Tomás. Just give her that. Sometimes the truth is so ugly, people come up with coping methods, Ma had said. *Deep down, she knows the truth and she'll accept it when she's ready.*

And so he let Emilia have her lie, her fantasy, even though he always felt guilty about it and he worried how much of it she believed. Once or twice, he even let himself imagine it for a split second, before shutting the idea out of his mind completely.

At least his mother understood. At least, even though there wasn't the affection or attention for him that she had for Emilia, Ma knew how Tomás felt about his dad and she understood. They didn't have to pretend with each other. He could make a sarcastic remark on Father's Day around her and she wouldn't chastise him. And she was honest with Tomás. He told himself it was because

Ma must think he was stronger, could handle more. Because she didn't have to worry about him the way she always worried about Emilia.

So why wasn't she up-front about that phone call? he wondered.

She was shaking. She was scared. And this fear seemed different from the one he saw when she sat and looked at her checkbook at the beginning of each month, or when Emilia left the house for any reason. That fear was constant; it deepened the fine lines on her face and made her sigh with her whole being. But this fear was . . . raw.

This fear he'd seen only once before, all those years ago when Emilia went missing.

That day flickered into his thoughts, and he looked quickly around the drugstore for something to fixate on so he wouldn't have to remember. But his gaze fell on the women on the advertisements around him, their faces made up perfectly, their lips lined beautifully. And an image of his eleven-year-old self quickly settled inside his mind.

At the exact moment Emilia lay in the woods just beyond the playground talking to the birds, eleven-year-old Tomás was looking at himself in the mirror. He had never seen himself that way before.

The material of Emilia's dress rubbed against his skin. It was soft and made him feel alive; from the pit of his stomach a strange flutter rippled throughout the rest of his body. After years of admiring her dresses, Tomás finally had the chance to try one on because Ma had bought it too big for Emilia. It was a simple dress. Charcoal gray with a black collar.

You can grow into it, Ma had told her.

It would've made you look like Wednesday from The Addams Family *anyway,* Tomás teased.

But secretly he loved the dress. He loved it more than he thought he should. The way he had always loved Emilia's Easter dresses, and Christmas dresses, her little purple jumper that Ma matched with a purple headband, and the pastel checkered one with a thin simple bow at the waist that their grandmother had given Emilia for her birthday. He had *adored* that dress. And now this one. The warm fabric that he knew would feel just this soft when he saw it, the way the black collar looked against his neck.

Tomás stared at himself in the mirror. Then took off the dress and ran downstairs in his underwear, to his parents' room. From his mother's dresser, he took one of the many lipsticks she had and ran back upstairs.

He locked the door, pulled on it twice even though he could see it was locked, even though no one was home. He tugged at the blinds on his window even though they were already pulled down tight. And then he put on the dress again.

He uncapped Ma's lipstick and carefully applied the wine color onto his thin lips.

The color was thrilling against his skin. It transformed him even more. When Tomás looked in the mirror, he hardly recognized himself. He noticed how the dress fell on his thin body. He closed his eyes and turned, only meaning to take one small turn, but then turning and turning and turning, letting the dizziness set in until he fell to the floor, laughing.

The hem of the dress grazed his knees. He looked in the mirror and caught another unrecognizable image of himself. And oh, he was beautiful!

Hello, he said to himself.

And smiled at the person in the mirror who had been hiding inside him. *Who* is *that?*

How extraordinary to be seen.

How extraordinary to be free.

He smiled and smiled at himself.

How beautiful.

But suddenly, Tomás grew scared.

What if that person wouldn't go back from wherever she came? What if she didn't go back quietly?

He didn't know who that person was.

Stop, Tomás said.

Stop, she mocked him.

Stop! he said again.

Stop! she repeated.

He wiped his mouth roughly, staining his hands and arms with the wine tint. He tore at the buttons, let the dress fall, and looked in the mirror again, trying to find himself.

Where am I?

Tomás wiped again at his lips, trying to rub out the red that wouldn't come off. He moved closer, searching for himself in that mirror, somehow knowing he'd never find himself again. The Tomás of before fell into that glass pool and drowned.

Quickly, he got dressed, hung up Emilia's dress in her closet again. He returned his mother's lipstick, neatly lined it up with the rest of the tubes on her dresser.

And then he stood in front of the mirror again, looking like he'd always looked. But no longer himself. No, not himself. He looked like some kind of shell, some kind of clone. Where had he gone?

"Young man," someone said. Tomás turned around and saw an old woman at the register. "Are you okay?"

Tomás tried to smile. "Yes, sorry," he said as he rang up her items. He put them in the bag, handed her some change. "Have a good day," he said automatically.

"You too, dearie," she said as she collected her bag. She smiled a thick pink smile, and Tomás wished he could wipe her lips gently and apply a lighter, thinner coat. She walked out, and he leaned against the counter. He stared again at the women on the advertisements around him and thought of the women in his life.

He wondered if he should be worried about Emilia.

He wondered what the hell was wrong with Ma.

And somewhere, in the back of his mind, he wondered what he'd been wondering for as long as he could remember: *What is wrong with me?*

Emilia Was Staring at Him

Emilia was staring at him as they drove home from school. Ian felt her unwavering gaze and finally turned to her and laughed.

"What?" he said.

She gave a small smile. "Nothing, I was just thinking. And you know, thanks for the other day. For the museum." It had been a week since they'd gone. "I don't know if I actually thanked you for that."

"No problem," he said. "You don't have to thank me."

"Yes, I do," she said. "Being there was . . . so . . ." He glanced over at her, and thought she looked like she was searching for words. "I don't know, those rooms, all those . . . that one with all the trinkets." She had a faraway look in her eyes before seeming to come back. "It was amazing. And you," she said. "You're . . . you're just . . . perfect, Ian." She smiled and looked at him in a way that suddenly made him a little self-conscious.

He laughed. "No," he said, trying to shrug off the self-consciousness, trying not to read too much into the look on Emilia's face, and holding on instead to the idea that in Emilia's eyes, he was perfect. He felt a nervous warmth in his chest.

He wondered what made her think of the museum at that very moment. He was afraid to ask because he didn't want her to start crying like she had the other day. So he just said, "No," again as they turned into her driveway.

When they pulled in, Emilia got out, closed the door, and leaned down. "So," she said. "You gonna come in or not?" Her voice had a teasing tone in it that made Ian laugh and turn off the car. He got out and followed her into the house, and upstairs to her room.

He'd been in her room before, but he still always got the same flutter in his stomach when he was there and neither her mother nor her brother were home. When it was just the two of them and they would pretend to be interested in something else before they both ended up kissing on her bed. He looked around for any changes since the last time he'd been there. Sometimes she rearranged the furniture and moved posters around. But everything looked the same and he watched as she opened the window a little and put some peanuts out on the ledge. She always did this, automatically, as soon as she walked into the bedroom. It was technically the attic, which had been split up and made into two bedrooms, hers and Tomás's. Her ceiling sloped down on one side, where Ian had hit his head more times than he cared to admit. But he loved being there. Where Emilia breathed. Where she slept. Where she flickered her light on and off at night as a way to say good night to him. He could look out his own window and just make out her outline.

Emilia put on a record and sat on the bed, the record sleeve in her hand, looking at the lyrics they both knew by heart. Ian walked over and sat down next to her, reached for the record sleeve, and started reading the words to the song they were listening to. After a moment, he felt her hand on his, and he turned just as she leaned in to kiss him. He kissed her back urgently, reaching to touch her face.

"You're . . . perfect," she said to him between kisses, as she leaned back and he pressed himself against her. "Just perfect."

Ian pulled away. "Don't say that," he said to her. Not because he didn't want to believe it, but because she kept saying it over and over again. It made him feel undeserving. And worse, like she was trying to convince herself of it.

"Nobody's perfect, Emilia." He smiled at her, thought she would smile back at him, but instead Emilia's face was serious. She stared at him in a way that made him feel like she was trying to read his mind, or tell him something. It scared him, just a little. "Don't think I'm perfect," he said to her.

What was she thinking? He didn't know because she didn't say anything. She just looked at him as she reached for the bottom of her sweater and slowly pulled it over her head.

"You are," she said. Her bra was light blue with little embroidered flowers that immediately made all the blood in his body rush to his groin. She slipped off one strap, then another, and reached around to unclasp the back.

He stared at her. Beautiful Emilia.

He wondered if this was actually it, the moment he'd thought of a thousand times. He reached for her and started kissing her again, taking off his shirt, too, so he could feel her body against his. He undid his jeans and could hardly think as he reached for her pants and undid the button, pulled at them, felt her now bare legs around him. He pressed himself against her more. And kissed her a little too hard as their teeth clicked against each other. She said his name softly.

But he felt her body stiffen. She kept kissing him, but there was tension in her lips, in her whole body. Maybe it was the cold coming in through the slightly open window that made her freeze up. He should close the window. But he wanted her so badly; he'd wanted her for so long. He was afraid if he got up, for even a second, the moment would be gone.

He forced himself to slow down, trying not to be too anxious, trying not to worry about her mother coming home or what time it was. Trying not to think about anything but Emilia, here, with him, like this, whispering his name over and over. His fingers slipped below the waistband of her underwear.

"Will you take these off?" he asked. "Please."

She nodded but didn't, and his hands went farther down, to her backside, and then between her legs. She sucked in her breath, startled.

"Please," he mumbled again. But she stopped kissing him then. And pushed him off. He looked at her, but she wouldn't look back.

He rolled off her; she immediately pulled up the covers. She was shivering. Shaking. Trembling.

Ian quickly reached past her, to the window above her head, and shut it.

"Emilia?" he said. But her eyes were closed and she just shook her head.

He shouldn't have pushed it so far. He felt guilty and terrible and frustrated.

"I'm sorry," he said to her quietly. "I'm sorry. I shouldn't have . . ."

"No," she said. "Don't. I . . . I wanted you to . . ."

He reached for her hand, but it was so cold. She seemed drained of all the warmth he'd just felt in her body. He pressed her hand against his face, kissed it, tried to kiss warmth back into it.

"I'm sorry," he whispered.

She had the covers pulled up higher now, and she was tugging her hand away. Ian wanted to wrap himself around her, warm her up, but he knew he couldn't. He was afraid to touch her too much. He sat next to her in the quiet and heard her trying not to cry.

"Don't apologize, please. I don't want you to apologize." Her voice was strained, her nose stuffy.

"Should I go?" he asked. He could only see the back of her head because she was turned toward the wall, but the slight nod was unmistakable.

"Emilia," he said. He wanted to tell her he was an idiot. That he should have been more understanding. To please not cry or turn away from him. But he was afraid of what his words would do. And, like this, he was a little afraid of Emilia, too.

"Don't worry," she said, trying to hide the fact that she was crying quietly under the covers. "I'm okay. You can go, really. I'll . . . call you," she said.

Slowly, he got dressed, then stood next to the bed, wanting to kiss her softly goodbye.

"I love you," he said finally. He didn't know what else to say.

She didn't answer.

He walked to the door and opened it. And then, ever so faintly, he thought he heard her whisper, "But you're perfect."

I'm not, he thought as he looked back at Emilia hidden under the covers. Ian stood there and willed the sour taste in his mouth and the nauseating feeling in his stomach to go away. *I'm not.*

Finally, he turned and left.

Emilia Turned into a Bird

Emilia turned into a bird in third grade. She and Ian were in the same class that year, Mrs. McNary's class, and one day, when the teacher asked him to hand back a stack of graded papers, he stood at Emilia DeJesus's desk holding a spelling test with a sticker on it. She'd gotten them all right. He was impressed. And when she looked down at the grade, then up at him, and smiled, he felt like some kind of hero.

He knew Emilia, of course. They'd gone to the same school for years and she lived a few houses down. But Ian never really took much notice of her until that day, when she smiled. It was almost a prelude, something that made him feel so warm just then but haunted him later that very night, when she went missing.

All the mothers were frantic. All the fathers were quiet and angry. Ian's mother went to Emilia's house, where police cars were parked in front, their red and blue lights flashing. Kids were told to stay inside, but their faces were pressed against windows, watching. Some eventually opened their front doors, and some trickled out, down their front walkways.

What happened?

Nobody can find Emilia DeJesus.

Ian watched from his bedroom window upstairs. The one that faced the DeJesuses' house. All he could think of was Emilia's smile and the sticker on her test earlier that day. The lights flashed, people came and went, in and out of the house. The blue and red grew more alarming as night fell, and Ian wondered the number of horrible things that might be happening to Emilia. He thought of the stories he'd heard at the beginning of the school year, the one of a girl who thought she was being followed on her way to school. And the one of the group of girls who'd been flashed by some man in a coat and sunglasses. How their teachers started warning them of strangers and what they should do if *someone, anyone, approaches you*. Posters were hung in their classrooms, in the lunchroom and hallways. Families were told to have secret passwords so children wouldn't go off with a stranger claiming *I was sent by your mother to pick you up*.

What's the password? was all a child had to ask from a distance to be saved from certain harm. *Banana*. Or *apple*. Or *cuddlebug* could save their lives.

Emilia sat in class, listened to it all with Ian, never knowing, never knowing *she* had to pay extra attention. But the teachers didn't tell them what to do if a stranger was there before you realized it, if he didn't approach you kindly. If you didn't even have time to scream or make any noise. Or if your mouth was full of blood.

Now Emilia was missing.

What good had it done? Ian had wondered. He was sure Emilia was dead. He sat by his window for hours, waiting, worrying, wondering.

And then suddenly, commotion. Three figures rushed out the front door, momentarily illuminated by the porch lights. Ian watched as Emilia's mother and father were led by an officer to a police car that made a loud *beep, beep!* before it raced away. Other cop cars took off behind it, leaving only the dark figures of neighborhood women on the DeJesuses' front stoop. The eerie figures watched them go, hands over mouths, over beating hearts, arms crossed around their midsections in a way that made them look like they were holding themselves together. They stared for a long time, even after the last car was out of sight, before finally turning to one another, dazed and shaking their heads. Slowly, one by one, they made their separate ways back to their own houses, up their own stoops. They took deep breaths before opening their own doors and going inside to hold their own children.

Ian, his mother had said from the doorway as he sat on his bed. He looked up as she came over and sat next to him.

Ian, she said again.

He was scared of his mother in that moment. Her voice, her whole self seemed unnatural, like she'd been hollowed out. He couldn't ask. He was afraid.

They found her. She's alive, his mother said. Pulled him close to her, and hugged him so hard he thought he heard bones crack. And he felt how she cried as she held him there, tight.

For months after that, Ian kept watch from his window. He'd look at Emilia's heavy front door, the one she never came out of anymore. And the empty lawn where she used to play. But he never saw her. He was almost certain all the adults had lied to them about Emilia DeJesus being found. Perhaps she was still missing. Perhaps she was found dead. Emilia's existence became a mystery that Ian spent hours wondering how he would solve, and then one day, like any other, he caught sight of her.

The front door at the DeJesus house was open, finally a day hot enough so they couldn't just keep closing it and staying inside. And he saw Emilia standing behind the screen door. He pressed his face up against his own bedroom window wondering if it was really her. *Emilia DeJesus.* And then she pushed the screen door open and came out, her mother behind her.

She was careful on the stoop, looking all around, as if taking in her surroundings for the first time. She looked at the houses of their neighbors and then right at his window. Ian was sure she saw him. She walked over to her front lawn and stared at the sky above. She spread out her arms and turned in slow circles. The sun shone on her. Her mother sat on the stoop, watching. Ian ran downstairs and looked out his kitchen door, which faced Emilia's house. He went outside and watched her from his stoop until he couldn't help himself, and slowly began walking in her direction.

Closer up, she looked different. Her skin paler or grayer than he remembered, her eyes darker. He was almost afraid of her. Except, he wasn't. This was Emilia. She was alive. And beautiful. And she was looking at him and then circling around him as he stood with his hands in his pockets.

She stopped suddenly and cocked her head to the side.

Caw! she whispered.

Ian looked over at her mother, who'd stood up from where she was sitting on the stoop.

Emilia, she called. *Stop, please, Emilia . . .* But Emilia didn't stop. She cawed some more, and stared at him.

Ian couldn't move.

Will you grow a beak?

Will you sprout feathers?

Will you be a bird with me?

She didn't say those words, but that's what Ian heard. That's what he understood. So he took his hands out of his pockets and stretched out his arms.

Caw, he whispered back.

She smiled.

Caw! she yelled.

Caw! He cried louder so she would smile again. And she did. And he thought he loved Emilia DeJesus.

His mother called to him then, from the front door of their

house. He waved goodbye to Emilia and turned to run home. His heart was still racing with excitement over seeing Emilia, over her seeing him, over their small exchange.

When he went inside, his mother closed the door behind them quickly. And he'd never forget how he felt when she looked down at him and said, *Ian . . . please . . . stay away from Emilia DeJesus.*

But he couldn't.

Ian looked out his window, the terrible feeling he'd been carrying with him since he'd left Emilia's room earlier that day growing bigger. He stared at her bedroom window, the one he'd shut just a few hours ago; it remained closed. The room was dark. He wondered if she was still there under the blankets. Crying? Hating him? Thinking what a jerk he was? He wished she would come outside now, so he could go to her the way he had the day he saw her out on the lawn.

She was found.

This was something he often told himself. Sometimes he couldn't help but think of how it could've gone the other way. She could have been lost forever. He could have not ever known her—how she loved strawberry ice cream and Tomás, or how she followed the flight of birds, any kind of bird, in the sky, until it was out of eyesight. Or how her face always seemed turned up to the sky so that he knew the slant of Emilia's neck almost as well as he knew her face. He might never have known what her kiss or whisper felt like. Or her body so close to his. He could never have lain in her bed, taking in the scent of her hair, her skin, trying to match her breathing.

How had he read things so wrong this afternoon?

I'm sorry, he thought as he stared at the dark window. He was sorry he'd been such an idiot. He was sorry she thought he was perfect and he wasn't. He was sorry he hadn't been on the playground that day to follow her into the woods. That she'd gone through what she went through, what left her shivering, and shaking, and trembling. Even years later.

Suddenly the window lit up, glowing and beautiful. A second later, she was there, standing at her window. Ian felt a flutter in his heart and, cautiously, he waved.

I'm here. I'm sorry.

She waved back.

She flickered the light on and off. He rushed over to his lamp and did the same.

She forgave him.

Relief rushed through his body.

★ ★ ★

Emilia saw the light flicker in Ian's window. He forgave her.

She hadn't meant to react that way, to get so emotional.

It's in the past. You've gotten through it. Why do you keep going back to it? And why does it all get so mixed up in your head?

Any time he slipped his hand under her shirt, or just below her waistband, no matter how in the moment she was, she always felt a part of herself slip away. She'd decided today she wasn't going to stop. She just had to get past that slipping-away feeling that reminded her of the past and stay here, with Ian. But then she *had* to stop. She felt a chill graze her legs and the hard earth suddenly beneath her. And even with Ian's voice in her ear, and telling herself, *This is Ian, Ian,* she'd pictured the trees looming above and *that breathing, that panting* . . .

She cried not only because it scared her how she couldn't separate the past from the present, how her mind played tricks on her. But because she loved Ian and he loved her and she *wanted* to be with him. And she couldn't.

How long would he understand when she couldn't say aloud that those moments with him reminded her of it all in a way she couldn't explain or disentangle? She knew he would never say anything, but he had to sense it. Still, he wouldn't understand that *somehow* he became a part of that terrible day. Somehow, he got mixed up in her head with the past.

Maybe he'd think she was crazy.

Or maybe he *would* understand, but then he'd be afraid to *ever* touch her again. Instead, he'd look at her with that pitying look he thought she didn't notice deepening each day.

Emilia looked at her bed, where she and Ian had been only hours ago. She wished she could go back to that moment. She picked up the blanket that had touched his skin and wrapped it around herself.

How would he have looked at me afterward? How would I have looked at him? What would we have said?

She smiled, imagining Ian's face. She wanted that moment. She wanted that freedom. She wanted that choice.

But more than anything, she wanted the past to never have happened.

After Emilia Left

After Emilia left for school and Tomás for work, Nina stood one morning in front of the telephone. She knew she had to make the call. She'd tried several times already, but each time her mind kept going back to that incredible day when Emilia stopped being a bird. Emilia had just gotten new rubber boots and they sat together in the car in the Kmart parking lot.

Remember, she asked *for those boots,* Nina told herself. *She came out of it. We got through it.*

Nina closed her eyes, and for a moment, she felt like she was back in the car that day, willing Emilia to say *Yes,* to use her words and stop cawing.

You're not a bird anymore, Emilia. I heard you use your words. Use them again. Yes or no. Would you like some ice cream?

Emilia stayed silent in the back seat.

Caw, she crowed.

Yes or no? Nina insisted.

She waited, heard a strange moan from her daughter as Emilia struggled with the word. Nina kept her eyes closed and gave her some time.

Use your words, Emilia, she silently willed her daughter. *Please, please, please.*

It was a prayer Nina made, over and over in her head. *Use your words, Emilia. Please, please, please.*

And then she heard it, her daughter's voice. *Yes,* Emilia said.

Nina laughed and cried. She clapped her hands together and yelled *Yes!* herself as she turned to look at Emilia.

Yes, Emilia, just like that!

Her chest swelled with pride and relief as she started the car and drove out of the parking lot and asked again.

Do you want ice cream, Emilia? They turned onto the main road.

Yes! Emilia said.

Yes! Nina yelled as they went through a green light.

Yes! Emilia said again.

Yes! Nina yelled. Then together they yelled, *Yes! Yes! Yes!* over and over again as they drove all the way to Carvel, where Nina got a small sundae with pineapple topping and Emilia got one with strawberry. Between spoonfuls of melting ice cream, Nina tossed out words and Emilia repeated them like a little parrot. And Nina would say, *Yes!* and Emilia would repeat that beautiful word, too, making Nina feel as though she might burst with happiness.

How much Nina had believed everything would be all right after that day. How much it felt like the worst was behind them. It made her cry silently as she stood in front of the phone, preparing to make a call that, eight years ago, on that joyful day, she could not have imagined she'd ever have to make.

Nina ran through what she was going to say in her head, but each time she did, she got lost in the past again, in that memory. And she had to open her eyes and remind herself what she needed to do.

She'd gotten the phone call from Detective Manzetti over a week ago and she'd put this off too long already. *I'm trying to keep it under wraps as much as possible, but news stations might get ahold of it anyway,* he'd said.

She can't find out that way! Nina thought. She had to tell Emilia. But first, this. She placed her hand on the phone, willed herself to pick it up. Finally, finally, she did. And quickly Nina dialed the number that, despite never using, she had long ago memorized.

Her hands were shaking.

Why are they shaking?

She had to be steady. She could be steady. She couldn't be scared. She'd always been steady.

Emilia got through it then, Nina thought as she listened to the ringing. *She'll get through it now. She's strong.*

Yes!

PART TWO

Mid-December 1994

It Was Early Morning

It was early morning when the phone rang in Sam DeJesus's small Seattle apartment. He was sitting in the living room, looking out the window, taking note of the exact tone and slant of the sunlight as he watched a small child outside in a puffy jacket riding a small Mickey Mouse car. If he still wrote, he would be trying to describe this observation perfectly in his old leather journal. Mickey's ears were the handlebars to the car, but one of them was missing so that the car constantly steered to the left and the child had to correct it repeatedly as he continued to ride. This was the same boy who, last summer, ran out in the middle of the street, chasing a ball, and Sam had slammed on his brakes, barely missing him. Nobody ever knew. No screeching. No neighbors witnessed it. The mom came out a few minutes later, calm and unaffected. Just a secret between the boy and Sam. And a day that had haunted Sam ever since. If he'd looked away for even a moment . . . if he'd been driving even a tiny bit faster . . .

The boy's mother walked alongside her son now, a woman Sam remembered walking the neighborhood during her pregnancy. He'd watched her stomach grow larger each month and he remembered the irrational desire to warn her, to ask, *Why? Why are you bringing a child into this world?*

"Sam . . . ," came the voice over the line when he picked up the phone. He'd answered it thoughtlessly, expecting the unfamiliar voice of some telemarketer. Those were the only calls he ever got. So the blood drained from his face when he heard his wife's voice, a voice he hadn't heard in years but knew so well.

For a moment he couldn't speak. But then he asked, "What happened? What's wrong?"

Every frightful image of his family that his mind had ever conjured up suddenly flashed through his head all at once. Car accidents, fires, freak accidents, strangers . . .

"Nothing. Everyone is fine . . ."

Sam's heart pounded faster, louder, because he knew she wouldn't call if everyone and everything was fine. He knew something must be wrong. He waited for Nina to go on.

"Sam, the detective called me. Detective Manzetti . . ."

The name was both strange and familiar. Nina's words were strange and familiar, too. The dread in his gut grew, even before he was able to completely recall the man.

A vague image of a balding head and graying beard flashed in his mind. "Manzetti?"

"The detective who worked Emilia's case. He called and . . ." Sam heard her exhale, draw another breath. "He said . . . they got the wrong guy."

"What?"

"He . . . someone called, said *he* was the one who . . . attacked her." Nina was speaking like she couldn't quite get the words out. "He confessed. Because he's afraid of going to hell . . . because he wants to *go be with God*." Nina's voice rose to a strained pitch before she fell silent.

"I don't understand," Sam stuttered. "I don't . . ."

"They got the wrong guy, goddammit. And he's some sort of sociopath!" she yelled.

"Nina." Sam felt all strength leave his body.

"He said he did it, and then he said he didn't . . . My god, Sam . . ." Nina's voice cracked.

"But Emilia saw the guy." Pause. "Right?"

He heard Nina let out a sob.

"Jesus Christ," Sam said as the words registered, took on meaning, as the gaps filled in. The moment didn't feel real. He wasn't sure he was awake. He looked at the floor, at his black shoes, scuffed and old. "Are they sure?"

Sam took a deep breath and looked up and out the window just as the child outside tipped over in the car and fell. He cried and his mother picked him up, carried him inside.

"Nina, are they absolutely sure?"

"Yes, of course. I mean . . . that's what the detective said. That's what he said, so I suppose they *must* be sure." Her voice sounded thin, distant. He wondered if she was okay. If, instead of worrying about Emilia, it was Nina he should have been worrying about all this time.

"What do you mean, you 'suppose'?" Despite the cold, Sam could feel sweat breaking out across his hairline. "Did you ask them? Before you called me? Did you ask if they are *absolutely sure*?"

"Fuck you!" Nina yelled over the phone. "Did *you*? Were *you* here to ask them if they are absolutely fucking sure?" She spat out the words.

He could almost feel her breath in his ear and he was instantly ashamed. He took a deep breath, held the phone tighter.

The silence was broken by a soft, muffled crying over the line.

"I'm sorry," he whispered.

"You're sorry," she repeated.

Sam could almost picture her wiping away the tears, looking up at the ceiling in frustration. He'd seen her that way so many times. She let out a deep breath and said his name. He closed his eyes and it suddenly hit him that she had loved him once.

Before.

But then he'd left.

After the attack, Sam couldn't be fine anymore about anything.

Help me, Nina kept saying to him. *You have to help me.*

But he could hardly get out of bed. He could hardly think straight, or think about anything, except what had happened to Emilia and how he hadn't helped her. How he hadn't been there to protect her. How he couldn't protect *any* of them. And they knew it; he could see it every time he looked into one of their beautiful faces.

Thoughts he'd tried to run away from then came rushing into

his mind now—his little daughter, her bruised and broken body, her swollen face. Nina, looking at him, *help me*. And Tomás's growing disillusion with the man he once wanted to be just like.

After the attack, Sam got weaker and Nina got stronger. She figured out how to pull herself out of bed, how to do those everyday things that didn't make sense to him anymore. How to deal with the doctors, the lawyers, the trial, the psychologists. How to take care of Emilia, Tomás, Sam, herself. And he, he couldn't do anything except hide in the basement, away from it all.

"Are you there?" she asked. He could already hear the accusation in her voice, bringing him back to the moment.

"I'm here," he answered.

He watched as the mother across the street came back out of her house, without the child, retrieved his Mickey Mouse car, and took it inside. He stared at the empty street, the gray-white day.

"Sam, it's not over," Nina said through the phone, but it felt as if she were right next to him, looking out the window together. "I knew it wouldn't be. I feel like I've always been waiting."

He understood. They'd both felt that it would never really be over. Isn't that why he left? Because he couldn't handle it? And hadn't he always been waiting for this call confirming it? Hadn't he always, in that split second before he heard the benign voice of a telemarketer, been expecting Nina's voice?

Sam pulled the phone away from his ear, hung up without another word. He sat down and closed his eyes, heard Nina's voice from the past echoing in his head, about what they needed to do, what strategies she'd learned from the psychologist. And then that day when Nina told him what the psychologist had said.

There might be triggers that might make her revert to that bird behavior, but, oh, Sam, she's talking! Dr. Lisa says Emilia shows every sign of being strong and capable of overcoming the trauma of the attack. Isn't it great?

That was when Emilia finally stopped cawing, stopped flying.

A coping method, Nina told him. *It stops when she feels she doesn't need it anymore.*

But Sam always felt like Emilia was ready to take off again at any moment, to some unreachable, impossible height from which they'd never get her back. He'd felt that danger constantly, no matter how much distance he put between himself and his family. No matter how much time passed from that day.

This, he knew, *will send her flying.*

And still, he didn't know if he could make himself go back home.

In the Chilling Cold

In the chilling cold, Emilia and Ian walked to his car on the last day of school before winter break.

"Are you happy?" he asked.

"I guess . . . ," she said, and looked at him funny. He'd meant was she excited, now that they would have almost three weeks of no school. But it came out weird, and now he thought he sensed that strangeness between them again that seemed to creep up more frequently ever since the other day in her room.

"I mean, about vacation."

"Oh yeah," she answered, but it was all she said.

Maybe she hasn't completely forgiven me, he thought.

She said she had. And most times it felt like she had, but there were other times like this. *Are you sure we're okay?* he wanted to ask. But she'd repeatedly told him they were. And also to stop asking. He looked at her out of the corner of his eye and thought, *Maybe it really is just the weather, like she keeps saying.*

He thought back to last winter. Had she been like this then, too? He remembered her face, sullen, in the cold. She did sort of get quiet like this, more to herself. But this time felt different. He couldn't forget the way she'd started crying out of the blue that day outside the museum and again in her bedroom.

But you know why she cried that time, idiot.

"Are you?" she asked, suddenly bumping into him playfully, then smiling and pulling him from his thoughts. There she was again, seemingly okay. "Happy, I mean?"

He nodded and squeezed her hand. "With you? Always."

She took a deep breath, blew smoke signals in the cold. "So, will we get to hang out over vacation or are you working?"

"Working," he said, feeling a small bit of dread. "A lot, actually. I opened up my availability and now I have all these hours. I'll basically be stacking shelves all day every day."

"That sucks." Emilia frowned, seemingly genuinely disappointed. He was both saddened and touched by it.

"I know. But I owe my parents two months of car insurance. You know my mom will hound me until I pay her back every last cent. I have a day off here and there, though, so we'll still have some time together."

"Cool," she said. She watched other students drive out of the school parking lot and said, "God, I wish I had a car."

"Why? You want to drive far away from here or something?"

She shrugged. "Maybe."

He felt slightly betrayed but didn't let her see it. "You could always get a job and save up for one. Fill out an application at Pathmark. You'd get a job there easy. Then I'd see you all the time." He smiled, thinking of Emilia checking out groceries while he stocked shelves.

"Yeah, I should. I *want* to. But, you know . . . my mom." Emilia rolled her eyes.

Ian knew Emilia's mother didn't like the idea of Emilia working, or having to worry about how she'd get to and from work, or Emilia having to work nights. Emilia had told him that her mother basically wanted her home, safe, as much as possible. He was about to complain about the unfairness of it and suggest maybe Emilia talk to her mom again, but then he looked at her, saw she still looked happy, and decided against it.

"Hey, you know, I'll try to get out of another day or two of work, call in sick or something. Okay? I mean, screw it. It's winter break."

Emilia smiled and they got in the car. As they passed the elementary school, he noticed she was suddenly so quiet again.

"You okay?"

"Yeah," she said quickly. They drove in silence for a while. The air felt thick, so he talked about anything he could think of.

"Hey, know what I heard?" he said. "They're going to bulldoze the elementary school. My mom knows somebody on the school board or something, and I guess they decided to bulldoze it. Sell the land."

She turned and looked at him. "Really? When?"

Ian shrugged. "I don't know, just heard that's what's going to happen to it."

"Wow," she said.

She looked stunned and he regretted it immediately. He had

thought maybe she would be happy to hear it was going to be bulldozed. Or maybe she wouldn't feel anything at all. But he hadn't thought that she would look the way she did now.

"Hey," he said. "Sorry, I . . ."

"No . . . no, it's not a big deal. It's just . . ." She shrugged. "It's just . . . wow, you know?" She shook her head.

They arrived at Emilia's house. She was out the door before he could lean over and kiss her, and he watched as she hurried up the steps. When she reached the front door, he waited for her to turn and wave or blow him a kiss like she always did, but she just went inside.

He imagined she turned. He imagined a kiss landed on his lips.

And that's when he remembered that the day Emilia went missing all those years ago was the last day of school before winter break, too. It had been a cold, bleak day, just like today.

Ian shivered.

The Old Elementary School

The old elementary school was the first thing that came to Emilia's mind the next morning, that first day of winter break.

They're going to bulldoze it, she thought.

Emilia cracked open the window a few inches and put the peanuts in a row before lying back down. She listened to the soft whistle of the wind, the rustling of dead leaves as they fell to the ground and scraped along the pavement.

So what? What do I care?

In bed she closed her eyes. Her flock of birds appeared in her imagination, circling the sky above the school, perching in the trees outside of it.

You were trying to get my attention when you circled over me the other morning, weren't you? Emilia asked them.

The white puffy trails from that morning flashed in her mind, and her birds circling in the sky, before she and Ian headed to their first class.

What is it? What do you want to tell me?

"I'm leaving!" Emilia's mother called from the bottom of the stairs. "Emilia?"

Emilia opened her eyes and stared at the bare branches outside. The sky was beginning to stay that winter white all the time now. She wondered when the sun would come out again.

"Emilia?" Her mother was at the bedroom door now, and even in that brief moment before she saw Emilia on her bed, there was a recognizable hint of panic in Ma's voice.

Sometimes Emilia was sure her mother must think Jeremy Lance had escaped and climbed into her bedroom window in the middle of the night to finish her off.

Sometimes Emilia thought this herself. And now, with eight years of anger and oppression built up, it would be worse. What would he do to her? She shivered as she tried not to think of it.

"I'm right here," Emilia answered, turning in bed just in time to see her mother sigh with relief.

"Well, how about answering me at least? Is that so hard?"

Emilia noticed the extra edge in her mother's voice. She was agitated, more than usual, and even though she tried, Ma never hid it well.

It's the weather, Emilia wanted to tell her. *You're off, too, because of the cold. This is what happens to us, to you and me.*

The salt and pepper shakers flashed through Emilia's mind. She'd noticed more little items around the house lately, and she couldn't be sure if they'd always been around and she hadn't noticed, or if they were new.

Don't worry, Ma, I won't tell. I understand. It's just the cold.

"Sorry," Emilia said to her mother. And she meant it.

Ma shook her head, fussed with her purse. "Fine, fine. I just . . . listen, I'll be home late. Tomás is at work but I think he only works until four, so just a little after you get home from school. You guys have dinner without me. Here's some money. Maybe a pizza?" She set the money down on Emilia's dresser, gave her a puzzled look. "Why aren't you ready?"

"No school," Emilia said, and smiled.

"Oh . . ." Ma shook her head. "Crap, I completely forgot." A bird swooped onto the ledge and picked up a peanut in its mouth. It watched Emilia and Ma.

"I really wish you would stop feeding those damn birds," Ma said. "They carry diseases, you know."

Emilia looked at her mother. She had closed her eyes and was rubbing her head.

"Ma, relax, I'm home alone all the time."

"I know, I know. It's just that . . ."

"I'll probably just stay in my pajamas and watch TV," she said, hoping to ease her mother's worry. But Emilia saw the lines deepen on Ma's face.

"Why don't you come with me?" Ma said finally. "We'll be in the city together. We can go somewhere new for lunch? Come on, get ready. It'll be fun."

Emilia saw the hopeful look on her mother's face, but Ma had made her tag along before, and it was never actually fun. The appointments were always back-to-back and there was never time to do anything.

"Ma," Emilia groaned. "You know I just complain and you get stressed out and annoyed. Besides, I'm not a little kid. I'll be fine."

"I *do not* get annoyed. And I'm not treating you like a little kid."

"So then what's the big deal if I stay home? It's not like I'm going to go to work with you every day of vacation."

Her mother looked at her watch. "I don't understand why you can't just come with me," she said. "If you get ready in five minutes, we can still make the train."

"I don't *want* to go."

Her mother stood there like Emilia was being extra difficult.

"I don't understand. Why is this even an issue?" Emilia said.

Her mom was silent, then looked away and shook her head.

"Fine, Emilia."

But she said it in a way that really meant it wasn't fine. She pulled her keys out of her purse and sighed.

"And I don't want you watching television all day, got it?" she said, giving Emilia a funny look. "You can't just sit around watching that . . . crap."

Emilia stared at her mother.

"Understand?" her mother demanded.

Emilia nodded. "Fine, Ma . . ."

Moments later, Emilia heard the opening and slamming of the front door. She got up and looked out the window as Ma drove away. Then sat back down on her bed.

What the hell was that all about? she thought.

Why did Ma think she was so incapable of taking care of herself?

You know why.

But I'm older now, stronger.

Hadn't she survived the worst already? Emilia listened to the silence in her house now that everyone was gone.

Nothing's going to happen to me.

She tried to believe this.

But after arguing with her mother, the house felt so quiet. Almost eerie. And for a second, Emilia wished she'd gone with Ma.

Don't be such a fucking baby!

Only now she didn't know what to do with herself. It seemed like everyone had something to do. Everyone always had something to do, except her. And now she sat up here in her room like some girl in a tower, waiting to be saved. Waiting to throw down her hair and be rescued.

I'm not that girl, Emilia thought.

She looked in the direction of Ian's house and saw his car in the driveway. She wondered what time he started his shift at work.

See, there you go. This is why Ma wanted to take you with her, she thought. *I mean, you could actually do something by yourself, Emilia. Stop being so helpless.*

Why did she feel like this when she was alone? Why couldn't she be just a little more at ease by herself?

She knew why but didn't want to think about it, so she thought instead about what she could do today. Go to the library. Or pick up a sandwich at Carro's, maybe.

She reached in her drawer for more peanuts and waited for

more birds to show up. Finally, another one swooped in and landed on the ledge.

"You think I'm exciting, don't you?" She smiled at the crow, knowing it wouldn't be long before more came. "Go on, tell them it's breakfast time," she said. She watched him fly away, a nut in his beak.

Geez, Emilia, you're so exciting, she thought. *Feeding birds. Is this what you're going to do all winter break?*

No, she would do *something*. She didn't know what just yet, but she knew she had to do *something*. Anything.

Emilia shut the window and rolled out of bed. She got ready, and when she stepped outside an hour later, even the drop in temperature from yesterday did not stop her. She shivered, but closed the door behind her and trudged into the cold day.

Emilia Searched

Emilia searched the sidewalk for the little gifts her birds often left for her, trying not to think of how strange her mother had just acted. She came across the little gifts all the time—curiously tiny pencils, forgotten fallen beads, red-and-white twine from bakery boxes, so many extra smooth or unique pebbles, lovely leaves still intact, and so many lost mates of earrings. How many of these she'd collected in her room over the years. It was how her birds said they were thinking of her. They hadn't forgotten that day when they watched from the treetops and saw what happened to her in the woods near the playground.

Maybe the search would lead her to *something*. A strange thrill filled her as she walked and played this game. *Something, something, something.* She was looking for *something*. The word filled her mind. She wanted to do *something*. *Something* was going to happen.

Up ahead she saw the flag flying over the old elementary school.

They're going to bulldoze it.

And suddenly she knew.

Ma doesn't think you're strong. Nobody thinks you're strong. Here's your chance to prove them wrong.

Emilia looked up and noticed a single black bird flying in the direction of the school. She looked at the flag again.

She'd assured her mother that morning that she'd be fine. And she would be. She knew exactly what she was doing.

You can't go around scared just because it's cold, Emilia.

She told herself this as she walked toward the school. Her pace slowed the closer she got, but she kept telling herself, *Just go.*

As she approached the building with its peaked roof and red brick, her heart beat faster and seemed to slide upward into her throat. But she made herself walk up to the doors anyway.

Don't be afraid. You can do this.

But Emilia couldn't help it. Her eyes wandered over to the house on the corner, the spot where she'd picked up that bracelet so long ago. She still remembered so clearly when she'd looked up to see Jeremy Lance looking right back at her, trying to get her attention.

That day, Emilia had turned her head away, looked at the aide on the bus, hoping the woman would notice Jeremy Lance banging on the window like that. But she was helping other kids buckle up. So the banging got louder, and he hit the window harder with his fist.

Bam! Look. Bam! At. Bam! Me.

Bam! Look. Bam! At. Bam! Me.

That's what Emilia heard in those thumps. But she wouldn't look at him.

Bam! Look. Bam! At. Bam! Me.

Harder.

And harder.

Emilia should have walked away, or run to her classroom, but she felt stuck to the sidewalk. She kept her eyes on the aide, who was still buckling in children. How could it take her so long? And then she couldn't resist. The thumping grew even louder. Slowly, she looked back at Jeremy.

He *was* trying to get her attention. Emilia was sure of it.

He had looked desperate, out of control. His distorted face yelling in anger as he kept hitting the window so hard and wouldn't stop. And then—*crack!*—his hand came crashing through the sharp plastic. The broken window slashed into his arm and suddenly there was so much blood. The plastic was smeared with blood and his screams filled the air. The bus driver and the aide ran to him, but it looked like not even they knew what to do.

On and on Jeremy screamed.

And on he bled. Looking at Emilia as her brother came running back to her, how she stood there, crying.

Don't be afraid, Tomás said, hugging her hard as she covered her ears and shut her eyes tight. But still she saw Jeremy's face and heard his screams.

Don't be afraid, Emilia told herself now, and let out a breath as she turned back to the two large school doors in front of her. She wrapped her hands around the ice-cold metal handles and pulled hard.

Locked. Neither door budged.

She stood there, relieved. She couldn't get in. That was it.

You tried, she told herself.

She stepped back and looked up at the school.

Why do you even want to go inside, anyway?

Because.

Because everyone has always treated you like you couldn't.

But look, here you are. And you can't, Emilia thought.

This sent a ripple of anger through her body. Anger she hadn't known existed, that had come from some deep part of herself she'd forgotten and now filled her eyes with tears. She looked at the school again.

Why should she have to stand out here in the cold when she wanted to go in, take a look around, return to the place so many people thought she was too weak to return to?

I don't need to be protected from this place. Or anything. I lived through the worst, didn't I?

She stared at the doors that refused to let her in. That shut her out. Soon this place would be gone, bulldozed, as if it never existed. And she would lose her chance.

Why did Ma take me out of school, anyway? she wondered as she pulled at the doors again. She would get in; she would find a way to get in that school now. Emilia's determination made her forget how the past really happened, how she didn't talk for so long afterward, how it took her so long to recover. Right now all she could think was how her sudden withdrawal had only drawn more attention to everything. And how when she was out with Ma sometimes, she'd suddenly feel someone looking at her. And each time she looked up, it was a kid her age staring at her like she was a yeti. She knew that the next day, the kids at school would be whispering about her.

Guess who I saw? Emilia DeJesus.

I thought she was dead.

No, no, she's alive. But I heard she hardly ever comes out of her room, much less her house.

Oh, I heard they had to put her in one of those institutions.

In two years, Emilia's absence made the kids come up with their own stories of what had happened to her. How she became a bird, a crazy bird, kept in a cage. And when Ma couldn't homeschool her anymore because Dad left and she had to work full-time, Emilia had to go to middle school, where everyone stared and stared at her for that whole first year.

She should have just come back to this stupid school right after it happened. She pictured herself walking into her old classroom that next day.

Look, I lived! she would have told them.

Emilia kicked the door in frustration.

What did you expect? That they would keep it open for you to come and face your demons?

She turned and looked at the day, the unremarkable day, but

one she'd sort of decided was her day of liberation. The day on which not even locked doors could keep her out.

Emilia slowly walked the perimeter of the school, looking for a way to get in without being obvious to anyone who might be watching. She noticed a broken window near some bushes along the side of the school. She looked up and down the street—when she was sure no one was around, she walked over to the window and reached in to release the latch. In moments, it was open and she slipped inside.

The window led to the lower level of the school, where the art and chorus and orchestra rooms were located. She dropped carefully to the floor and landed in the chorus room. It smelled just as it always had. There was a fluttering in her gut as she took in the musty scent of chalk and pencil shavings. There were a few chairs left behind, strewn about and forgotten. In the corner, a crumpled paper. Emilia walked over to it and smoothed it out. She read the title on the sheet of music.

"Ghost of John."

The melody instantly came back into her mind. She remembered. This was the song they always sang around Halloween! She'd forgotten it until this very moment. Emilia began humming it as she folded the paper and put it in her back pocket. How many other songs had she forgotten or never learned? A chill ran up her spine, but she ignored it. Ma's words echoed in her mind.

Don't ever ignore your instincts, Emilia. If something feels wrong, it is. You know that.

Ma's voice and warnings were always with her now, always invading her thoughts.

Nobody is here, though, she reasoned as she walked to the door. Her hands were shaking; she was scared, but determined. She turned the knob, looked up and down the hall, and then stood there listening for any noise or signal that someone else might be there, too.

Nothing.

She stepped into the dark hallway and carefully walked down toward the art room.

Jesus Christ, Emilia, what the hell are you doing? she thought. Every one of her senses was on alert, her heart was beating fast, and her body felt weak.

Be brave! Be brave! You can do this! This is the day of your liberation!

Emilia stifled a nervous laugh that swelled out of nowhere. She imagined what her mother might say if she knew where Emilia was at this very moment, but Emilia continued because underneath the fear, she also felt a strange sense of freedom. Of power. She ran her hand against the smooth paint on the hallway walls just as she did when she was younger.

Remember this?

Her stomach fluttered.

The door to the art room was open and she went inside. There was no furniture, but *there*, *still*, was the large metal cabinet where her teacher had kept the art supplies. She opened the door and found several bottles of red, blue, and yellow paint.

And the glittery paint!

She unscrewed the cap and dipped her finger into the bottle, smeared the paint on the cabinet. How many projects had she missed out on while she was at the dining room table with Ma, the textbooks spread out before them, her mother growing upset and frustrated with her?

There was a new wave of excitement in Emilia's stomach as she thought of the school filled with so many classrooms. There was the room just at the end of this hallway, she remembered, the one where they stored all the instruments parents would rent for their kids throughout the year. So many instruments that didn't fit in the orchestra room. Emilia had started violin that year. Ma had rented it for her and she loved walking with that violin case, to and from school, feeling so important. But then, one day, it was gone from her room and she knew Ma must have brought it back here.

Emilia took a deep breath, pushed that aside for a moment, and focused again on all the places she could freely explore now. There was the front office, which must still hold some office supplies, paper clips, and sticky notes. And the gymnasium with sports equipment. And the library, perhaps a book or two left behind.

All these things, left just for her.

All of them, waiting to be found.

Emilia grabbed the rest of the paint bottles, unscrewed the caps tight with dried paint, and saw they were still fresh. She thought of all the gifts her crows had ever left her. She thought of how the cold this year was making her particularly uneasy, and she thought of her old third-grade classroom.

Eagerly, she ran upstairs to it. And there, she stood looking around, imagining that room filling up.

And she suddenly knew.

This is it! she thought.

The Next Night

The next night, Emilia smiled at Ian in a way that made his heart and stomach flip. She was the happiest he'd seen her in a while.

"Hey," he said, smiling at her.

"Hey," she said, getting up and rushing to hug him from where she'd been sitting on her front steps.

He laughed. "What's that for? What are you doing out here?"

She shrugged. "I dunno. I haven't seen you in a couple days. I've just missed you."

"I know. I'm sorry. I've missed you, too," he said, burying his face a little in her hair. He took a deep breath, inhaled the scent of her shampoo. He wished Anthony weren't back in town for Christmas. He wished that instead of letting Anthony talk him into going over to his aunt's house after work to hang out and spend the night, he'd hung out with Emilia instead.

She pulled away and grabbed his hand as they walked toward her house. She told him she'd rented a movie. And with each passing minute, every moment he noticed Emilia seemed more herself, a sense of dread filled him. He'd made a huge mistake last night. The memory of it made him uneasy.

When he got to Anthony's, his aunt and uncle had already left for a benefit dinner and wouldn't be home until very late. Ian had thought it would just be him and Anthony, but Jane was there, too.

They'd gotten bored and started making mixed drinks with whatever booze they found in the liquor cabinet. Ian had just wanted to keep up with Anthony, who could easily outdrink him now. And maybe, though he didn't want to admit it, a part of him didn't want to seem like a wuss in front of Jane.

Eventually Anthony drifted off to sleep on the couch while they watched TV, and Jane said she was going for a smoke.

Want one? she asked, holding up a cigarette.

Sure. Ian followed her outside.

He wasn't much of a smoker and he sort of hated the taste, but he liked being around Jane. She was actually nice, and he could tell she really cared about Anthony. As they smoked, they started talking about relationships and all kinds of things. Jane told him about the guy she'd dated before Anthony.

He was one of those types who thought he could bully me, you know what I mean? Like he could talk to me like I'm trash because of what I do. I could outsmart that guy any day of the week. She looked over at Ian. *Bet you didn't know I had a full ride to college if I'd wanted it.*

Ian was surprised, but he didn't say anything and tried not to show it.

Who knows, maybe I'll still go. Anyway, I wasn't having any of that guy's shit. See, that's why I love Anthony. Even before he knew where I lived and that my parents have money, he treated me as an equal. You know what I mean? She looked into the house through the glass door at Anthony sleeping on the couch. *He's genuine.*

Ian nodded as Jane took in a long drag and let out little smoke rings.

Ian's tongue felt fuzzy and his head heavy, and he found those smoke rings so mesmerizing, rising in the cold night. He looked at Jane as she took another drag and dispersed another series of *perfect O's from her perfect lips.*

Ian shook the thought away and closed his eyes.

So, you and Emilia, Jane said. *You guys have been together awhile, huh?*

Yeah, since middle school. Actually, really before then in a way. More like elementary school.

Really? Elementary school?

Yeah . . . He could feel the stupid grin on his face, even though his cheeks felt numb.

You guys are really serious, then?

Yeah. He closed his eyes for a moment and thought about Emilia. He was committed to their relationship. And he was sure Emilia felt the same way. Even if lately, she'd seemed off.

He could almost hear Emilia's voice in his ear. *It's just the weather,* she'd said.

But was that really it? Or was there more?

Of course there's more—you fucked up the other day, he thought.

Maybe she was just done with him? Maybe she didn't know how to tell him.

Ian felt the world tilting a little, and when he opened his eyes again, Jane was closer to him and he realized he'd said some or all of this aloud.

She looked at him sympathetically. And he was moved by the way she looked at him with genuine concern. He wanted to reach over and kiss her.

You okay? she asked.

Yeah, he said, as he felt a small burn on his hand. He looked down at the unsmoked cigarette that had burned down to the filter, and he dropped it to the ground. *I just . . . I mean, I think we're serious. Like, I know we are, but . . .*

It was so easy to talk to Jane. No second-guessing. She was so open with her feelings and experiences that it seemed easy and harmless to be honest, too. And he'd been feeling so confused around Emilia. And lonely, so lonely.

So here was this girl, *your cousin's girl,* who seemed to care. *Maybe it'd be good to talk to a girl, get her opinion,* he reasoned, ignoring how much he liked having someone listen to him. So he told Jane all about his and Emilia's relationship, about the way she'd been acting lately. And how he worried she was going to break up with him, or maybe she really was acting this way because winter brought back terrible memories for her. Because it was so entwined with her attack, an attack so terrible that Emilia had only spoken to him about it once. She'd seemed like she was in a trance when she told him.

Jane had listened. She'd told him Emilia was lucky to have

him. And that everything would be okay, because she could tell Emilia really loved him, too. She put her arm around him and pulled him in close. He shut his eyes and filled his mind with Emilia. The girl he loved.

It wasn't until Anthony woke up and took Jane home, when Ian was left on the couch by himself with his thoughts and the conversation echoed in his head, that he felt he'd said too much. And that he had betrayed Emilia as surely as if he'd kissed Jane.

Emilia, who had waited for him outside in the cold today and was acting like her old self. He fought back the urge to say sorry to her because then he'd have to explain what he was sorry for. So they popped popcorn, and watched the movie, and laughed, and when he had to go home, she walked outside with him. She threw her arms around his neck and kissed him over and over on the stoop. He held on to her waist and pulled her close to him and told himself, *Don't worry about it. You didn't do anything wrong.*

Even though he knew he had.

What If

What if the crows hadn't saved me? Emilia thought as she walked to the school again the next morning. She hadn't told Ma or Tomás or even Ian about the classroom. It was her secret, her purpose, her *something*, and she didn't want to share it with anyone.

Yesterday she'd lost track of time and stayed there too long. Her mother had gotten angry and suspicious, and Emilia told herself she'd stay home today. But as soon as Ma left for work this morning, Emilia couldn't help it. She felt pulled back to the classroom. And today she was going to stop at the consignment shop to see if she could find anything there to bring.

She'd already taken from her father's office a book he had of El Salvador, his homeland. And so many books of poetry. She'd been late yesterday because she'd sat in the classroom picking out her favorite poems to write on the walls and then spent too much time looking for one in particular. Something about the cold and winter and Sundays. She remembered how he'd read it to her once and told her it was his favorite.

Why, Dad?

Because it is sad, and it is beautiful. Like people, Emilia. Like life. It is all sad and beautiful.

She'd found it, finally, and felt like it meant something that she did.

After finding the poem, she picked out the perfect spot for it and told herself to bring a thick marker from home to write it on the wall.

Emilia felt for the marker in her pocket now. And adjusted her backpack, where she carried a folded-up, deflated air mattress from one time long ago when she and her family went camping.

She'd had so much fun exploring the school the last few days. And she'd found more art supplies in classroom cupboards and closets—chalk, staplers, papers—and hauled it all back to the classroom. The room was becoming a shrine to forgotten things; what others had discarded or forgotten, Emilia would bring here and make beautiful again. She could picture it all so perfectly. And then she'd left late. And her mother had completely over-reacted when Emilia came home.

Could she tell I was lying about being at the library? Emilia wondered. *Was she mad enough to follow me today, to see where I went?*

The classroom floated into her mind again, but a cold, biting wind whisked the image away. Instead, her mind crowded with the questions that came the colder the weather got.

What if the police hadn't checked the woods just beyond the school play-ground? What if Jeremy Lance had dragged me off somewhere else?

Emilia thought of Jeremy Lance. She could still hear his

breathing in her ears. She could still feel his hands around her ankles, the same hands that pounded and broke through that school bus window. Her ankles had felt bruised even weeks later from Jeremy Lance's tight grip.

Where would he have taken me if my birds hadn't come? What if I'd kept flying?

Emilia was shivering when she finally arrived at the consignment shop. She didn't know if from the cold, or the memory of Jeremy Lance.

The store smelled just as she remembered: of sweat and musk, unfamiliar people and sweet tobacco and houses not her own. But now she thought she also smelled death through the damp musk, and a faint sterile scent that tried to mask unwashed flesh and bandages, urine and blood, tears and mucus. It had surrounded Emilia those days she was in the hospital, traveling the hallways and wafting into her room. It clung to the nurses' clothes and brushed against Emilia when they checked on her.

The smell turned her stomach.

Emilia used to come here often with her mother when she was younger, while Tomás was off at school. Whenever Ma got frustrated with homeschool lessons, with Emilia wanting to make origami crows instead of following along, she would tell Emilia they needed a field trip and off they went, just the two of them, to fancy department stores on the other side of town. Ma never bought anything, but afterward they would stop by here, and Ma would have something to sell at the consignment store.

Eventually, Emilia understood Ma's secret. But back then, it was just a field trip. And they'd get ice cream afterward, their special sundaes.

All without Tomás.

Emilia felt a sudden pang of sadness for her brother.

"Looking for anything in particular?" Up at the counter, the salesgirl who had been flipping through a book was now staring in her direction.

"Just looking," Emilia answered as she cut through the thick scents to look at an old coat. She wondered who it had belonged to.

The girl went back to her book and Emilia looked at some shoes and wondered who had worn them. One pair in particular reminded her of the shoes her grandmother used to wear all the time.

Emilia was seven when her grandmother on her mother's side came from Mexico and lived with them for a year. Emilia's room became her grandmother's room, and Ma set an extra mattress in Tomás's room for Emilia.

Eres un pajarito, her grandmother would say to her all the time—*You are a little bird,* because she was always fluttering about. Emilia could hear her grandmother's voice as she closed her eyes and thought back to a day they were in the yard together. Her grandmother stared at the sky and got tears in her eyes as she spoke.

Cuando me valla. Al cielo, mija.

Emilia didn't understand, so her grandmother pointed to the

sky. This was how she and Emilia communicated. With gestures, plus some words her grandmother had taught her in Spanish and some Emilia had taught her in English. At first, Emilia was confused, but she eventually understood her grandmother meant that when she died, when she went to the sky, Emilia could still talk to her.

Emilia reached out for the shoes and tried them on.

Did I call out for you that day, Abuela? Emilia wondered. *Maybe you're the reason the birds showed up.*

Emilia clasped the straps around her ankles. The shoes were scuffed, but she thought they were lovely and decided to get them.

Her grandmother had died within a month of returning to Mexico. Emilia's eyes filled with tears as she thought of that long-ago grief. And then she remembered her eighth birthday, how they'd celebrated right before her grandmother had left. She'd given Emilia a beautiful pastel checkered dress that Emilia immediately put on and wore the rest of the day.

Emilia continued walking around the store, lost in her memories. She wondered who had that pastel checkered dress now. She hadn't seen it in years. Had her mother given it away?

Emilia remembered, too, about that time, how she would sometimes climb into bed with Tomás and tell him jokes and they would laugh until their mother came upstairs and threatened to make one of them sleep downstairs in the living room if they didn't go right to bed. They would pretend to be asleep, and when their mother was gone, they would go back to whispering and laughing into their pillows.

Except that one night, Emilia thought. On the night of her eighth birthday, actually, when Tomás had suddenly started crying softly in the dark. And when she asked him why, he kept repeating, *I'm just scared.*

Of what? she asked. He ignored her at first, but she kept asking. Finally he said, *Of the dark, that's all.* But she knew it wasn't true. He'd never been afraid of the dark before. Emilia held his hand, but he turned away and pretended he was sleeping even though Emilia could hear him quietly crying.

That was one of the last nights she slept in her brother's room. Then her grandmother was gone. And Emilia's room became her own again. And then that day in the woods happened. That terrible day. And for over a year afterward, she slept at her mother's side each night, tucked safely in her arms.

Emilia stared at some old scarves and thought of her brother, crying in his room. The sadness she'd felt for him earlier deepened as she turned her attention to a shelf lined with books. *Why wouldn't you tell me what was wrong?* she wondered.

Emilia opened an art history book with a bright yellow USED sticker on the spine and looked through it.

Angels and saints, demons and sinners filled page after page.

She flipped through it quickly, but one painting caught her eye and she went back.

It was dark and light and interesting. The first thing she noticed was the backside of a horse, then the man on the ground with arms raised, his body in danger of being trampled. He'd fallen, but there was a peaceful look on his face and he was completely oblivious to any danger as an older man looked on. *The Conversion of Paul*, read the caption under the picture.

She closed the book and carried it with her as she continued through the store.

Next she saw a stuffed squirrel. A starburst-shaped neon sign above it read, *I'm real!* Emilia looked over at the girl at the counter and pointed to the sign.

"What do you mean, 'real'?"

The girl barely glanced up. "Oh, it's like an *actual* squirrel," she said. "Just living life, minding its own squirrelly business, and then—*bam!* Somebody killed the little sucker, took out his insides, and stuffed him with who knows what to preserve him forever."

Emilia inched her face closer to the squirrel mounted to look as if it were scurrying across the wall. She looked at its dark, glassy little eyes. And even though she knew it was dead, she swore something in it was alive and aching to be rescued.

"Believe it or not, people are into that kind of stuff," the girl continued. "Pose them in little scenes from movies, even. I once saw one of Thelma and Louise. You know that scene, where they drive off the cliff? Yep, there was little squirrel Thelma and little squirrel Louise in a tiny little Thunderbird." The girl shrugged. "Kind of cute, but still super weird. I just don't know what kind of person does that. Anyway, some guy said he was going to come back for this one tomorrow, but if you want it, I'll sell it to you today."

Emilia shook her head and walked to another part of the store. "No, thanks. It's kind of terrible."

The girl nodded. "I know. Not a good job. I've seen some good jobs but this little guy looks kinda haunted, if you ask me. We get these critters more than you'd think. And this one's definitely not one of the best."

Emilia had meant it was terrible to take its insides out, to preserve it forever, instead of letting it be part of a food chain or whatever happened to dead squirrels. But she didn't correct the girl.

Instead, Emilia thought about the animals her father must be killing out in Alaska to stay alive. She wondered if he was lonely. Maybe even scared.

Suddenly, she saw him delicately skinning animals, with the care and precision of a surgeon, removing each organ and carefully placing it on the table. And then stuffing each limb, the head, the chest cavity with . . . *what? Cotton? Old clothes that have turned to rags?* And she suddenly saw his cabin fill up with animals—a squirrel like this one on the wall, a raccoon in the corner, a rabbit peeking out from behind a chair.

She couldn't erase the thought from her head and she hoped she wouldn't always picture her father this way, in a cabin surrounded by dead animals to stave off the loneliness.

But the more she tried to empty the cabin, the more she saw it filling up. Suddenly there was a bear, a deer, a crow on the mantel.

And her father sitting at the table, drinking hot coffee to keep warm, surrounded by all those creatures. Talking to them, calling them by name.

Maybe he called them *Nina, Tomás, Emilia.*

Emilia walked back over to the squirrel and stared at it.

Maybe you're Sam, she thought.

"I'll take it," she told the girl.

Emilia Couldn't Wait

Emilia couldn't wait to see her new items in the classroom.

Once there, she displayed the shoes on a small table she'd found in a storage room in the cafeteria. She put them near the window, brushed them with some of the glitter paint. They transformed into art and made her smile just looking at them.

Then Emilia turned her attention to the art history book. She cut out pictures and tried to decide which ones she'd put together and where they would go.

Finally, on an old hook, she hung Sam the Squirrel.

"What do you think?" she asked him as she looked around. The room still felt a bit cold and the lighting was dim. But she could bring candles next time! And more items from home. Books that she could stack and use like tables. And maybe that blanket her grandmother had brought from Mexico. She imagined the room glowing with so many candles. She imagined wrapping herself in the colorful striped blanket.

That would be perfect! Emilia smiled just thinking of her project.

Again, she didn't want to leave. But she didn't want to risk Ma asking more questions of where she'd been, so she left way before Ma ever got home from work.

My room is beautiful, Emilia thought as she walked in the cold. Her stomach flipped with excitement and she was lost in the idea of that classroom when she turned the corner and spotted Ma's car in the driveway.

Emilia started running. She'd made sure not to stay at the school too long today, and yet, there was her car. Ma was home.

Emilia ran faster, her mind racing with excuses. She hurried up the three stoop stairs and pushed open the heavy front door. The smell of cigarettes hit her right away. With a strange kind of sudden certainty, Emilia knew something was wrong.

She stood in the entryway for a moment, waiting for her mother to rush out and yell at her, because she felt something barreling toward her.

What's my biggest fear? she thought. And suddenly Emilia just knew.

Her father was dead.

She could feel the cold, the freezing cold, seeping into her skin, stopping the flow of blood.

She knew a person could freeze to death, how it took over the entire body. First your mind got fuzzy. You couldn't think or remember. She wondered if their names had briefly gone through her father's mind before he'd forgotten them, before the fuzzy black set in around him and he lost consciousness. She saw him buried in mounds of snow.

Or was it freezing water?

Emilia felt it as if it were happening to her, the loud cracking of ice in her ear as it gave way underneath. She felt the shock of freezing water, the black and blue rushing in around her, as she caught one last glimpse of the world, the clouds and sky, at the end of a faraway tunnel.

She fell to her knees as the cold found its way to her heart and stopped it. She clutched her chest and cried.

"Emilia!" Her mother was crouched down next to her. "Emilia, what is it? What's wrong? Tell me!" Her mother's voice was frantic, tinged with anger, the way it always was when she was worried.

"Dad?" Emilia choked. "Is it Dad?"

Her mother held her. "How'd you know?" she said.

Emilia cried harder.

But then she heard his voice. She heard him calling her name, telling her to open her eyes.

Emilia did. And he was there. Her father, right in front of her, looking at her, holding her shoulders.

It was a blurry image of him through her tears, but it was him.

Alive! Here!

"Dad!" she yelled, hugging him. She felt like she had come up for air, as if she had reached the surface of the cold black water and pulled herself out.

Moments ago she'd felt like she couldn't stand or walk, but she was on her feet now, hugging him, unable to believe he was really here. He led her to the couch, where they sat. And she stared at him.

Her father. It hardly made sense. The beard made him look older than she remembered. His hair was not neatly combed as it used to be. But his clothes were the same—khakis and a tucked-in button-down shirt.

"Dad," she said, shaking her head. "Dad."

★　★　★

Sam DeJesus looked at his daughter's face and saw, somewhere, the child he left six years ago. But she was different now. He didn't know why he was shocked that she hadn't stayed ten. He didn't know why all the times he pictured them here, without him, he never let them grow.

"Emilia," he said. Yes, this was her.

"When did you get here? How . . . ?"

The questions. He was surprised by them even though the anticipation of those questions were what had kept him away day after day, any time he thought of returning.

When he'd left, he didn't know he wouldn't return. He'd gone to interview for the job in Seattle thinking he would move them all there if he got it. But then came that day when he sat on the hotel bed staring at the return ticket in his hand. The time came when he might still catch his flight if he rushed into action. He pictured the plane on the runway while he sat on the stiff hotel bed, staring at the return destination. And then the clock hit 7:45 PM and he knew the plane was taking off. He imagined it in the sky, his seat, 16B, empty.

He called Nina, told her he'd have to reschedule his flight because the dean just called to offer him the job and wanted him to start right away.

I'll get everything settled here, then come home and we'll figure out the move, he told her.

Each day he came up with new excuses. Until she knew. Until *he* knew. He was not coming back.

Each week he thought, *I'll go this week.* At first, the pressure to go back was unbearable, but so was the idea of actually going back. To that life, to that reality, to his failure. Each month that passed filled him with dread and took him closer and closer to the point of no return. How could he explain himself after being gone for two months? How could he explain when two months turned into four, six . . . then *a year.* Two. And now, *now six.* He swallowed his shame.

Sam looked to his wife, but Nina stood at the window with her back to them.

"I got in this morning . . . ," he told Emilia.

She was smiling at him.

My god, how can she smile at me this way? How can she bear to look at me?

"God, Dad!" she said suddenly, laughing and wiping away her tears. "You're here!" Her laughter made him want to cry. "I can't believe it!"

How can she still love me?

He swallowed the sobs, the joy, the fear he felt in his chest, and smiled back at her.

"How long did it take you? Did you have to take one of those super tiny planes first?"

He looked at her. "What?"

"Is it always cold? That's how I imagine it, but doesn't it warm up sometimes? Do you feel . . . better now?" She looked at him meaningfully.

"Emilia," her father said.

"Forget it. Tell me what you did."

"What do you mean?"

She smiled at him again. "Did you eat raw fish? What was it like?"

"What . . . what are you talking about?"

Emilia looked at her mother, but her mother would not turn around. She looked back at her father.

"You know . . . ," Emilia said. "Alaska. Where you've been all this time."

"Alaska?" Sam asked. He looked to Nina for help or an explanation, and while she glanced back briefly with a strange look on her face, she offered neither.

"Emilia . . ." Her father reached for her hand, but then couldn't bear the thought of her pulling it away from him as he was sure she would do in a moment. So he folded his hands, *his too-soft hands*, which he had come to hate so much because they were fine and gentle and did not know how to fight, or punch. That did not dare to kill, not even his daughter's attacker, though his mind had fantasized about it so many times. No, his hands only knew how to turn the pages of so many useless books and hold on to each other like they did now.

"Why do you think I've been in Alaska, Emilia?"

The room filled with silence. He closed his eyes. Waited.

"What do you mean?" she said, confused by his question.

"I haven't been in Alaska," he told her slowly. "I've been living in Seattle. That's where I work. I . . . I've never been to Alaska."

"What?"

"I haven't been in Alaska, Emilia. Not at all." He tightened his grip on his hands, hands that still couldn't protect Emilia when she needed him most. Hands that even now refused to unclasp and reach for her because he was sure she would shrink away from him.

Emilia stood up, walked to the front door, and went outside.

Nina watched her from the window. "Go after her, Sam," she said.

He looked at his hands.

Emilia's mother grabbed her jacket, tugging at it hard from where Sam was half sitting on it, and walked out the door to follow her daughter.

* * *

An invisible umbilical cord seemed to connect Emilia and her mother. She could feel her mother walking behind her, not losing sight of her no matter which way she turned. Until finally, Emilia walked to the small diner on the main road and went inside.

An older, bearded man sitting by himself in a booth looked up as she came in, and she could feel the way his eyes fell on her body as she walked by. It made her angry and embarrassed, and she wanted to sink deeper into herself and disappear as she quickly slid into a booth near the back. Her mother came in and spotted her in the corner. She walked over and sat across from Emilia.

Emilia looked out the window. They sat like that for a long time until Ma placed her cold hands over Emilia's. Emilia looked at her mother, her skin paler than Emilia's, and remembered the time her mother translated the story her grandmother told about their family. About the Irish ancestor who fought for Mexico, then fell in love with and married a Mexican woman, and ever since, a fairer-skinned, auburn-haired baby was born into their family every few generations. Ma was one of those babies, and she often reminded Emilia, *Mexican blood and Irish blood produce the strongest, most stubborn human beings in existence. Never forget you are part of that strong line, Emilia. That blood that runs in your veins.*

Something in Ma's eyes told Emilia she had to be strong now, even if Ma didn't think Emilia was strong.

"So, he left us?" Emilia said.

Ma rubbed her forehead. "I didn't know you still *really* believed he was in Alaska. I . . . I knew you wanted to believe it, wanted us to believe it. But I guess I thought somehow, deep down, you really knew the truth." Ma shook her head, closed her eyes. When she opened them again, she looked deep into Emilia's. "Didn't you *know*? Somewhere in the back of your mind? Didn't you know the truth?"

Emilia looked back out the window. Maybe. She couldn't tell anymore if this story she told herself all these years was one she really believed or had come to believe over time. Obviously he'd left. She knew this. But she thought it was because her father couldn't function anymore. She thought he'd had to go deep into the woods, into the cold. She thought he couldn't be around anyone.

"I guess. I just thought . . ."

But all this time he'd been in civilization. All this time he was buying groceries, getting mail, working. All this time he'd been talking to people, laughing even . . . laughing *with them*. He wasn't isolated in some cabin. He was living a normal life. Somewhere else. Somewhere far away from them. Had she known the truth the whole time?

"Is he married? Does he have . . . other kids?"

She saw her mother wince. "No," she answered quickly. "I mean . . . I don't think so . . ."

Who is he? Emilia wondered. She didn't know her father anymore. Not the man he used to be. And not the man she'd made him out to be all these years. What had he really been doing when she imagined him walking through all that snow, when she imagined him chopping down trees, hanging hide, cooking small, sad, terrible portions of moose or rabbit?

"Does Tomás know? Has he seen him yet?"

If he hadn't been in Alaska, why, then, did he write poems, Emilia wondered, about being alone? In his journal that she'd found and kept for herself for the times she missed him most. Why did he write about the cold? Why did he say *that's where I'd go, that's where I'd go, if I wanted to feel nothing*?

Her mother shook her head. "He's still at work." She looked at her watch. "But he'll be home soon."

Emilia thought of her brother walking into their house and seeing their father. She didn't want Tomás walking into their living room unprepared.

"Let's go," she told her mother. She started to get out of the booth, but her mother wouldn't let go of her hand and instead held on to it tighter.

"Emilia . . . wait . . . ," her mother said. And in that moment, her heart filled with some inexplicable fear at the tone of her mother's voice, at the grip of her hand on Emilia's, at the sudden realization that something, *something* had brought her father back.

Why now? Why is Dad back now?

A coldness went through her body as she looked at her mother. At those green eyes that were warning Emilia to prepare herself, *be strong*.

Her mother took a deep breath. "There's a reason he's back."

"Why . . . ? What is it?"

She saw the struggle on her mother's face, the tightness in her body.

"Sit down," she told Emilia.

Emilia did and her mother held both of Emilia's hands in hers. It looked like they were praying.

"Emilia," her mother said. Her name came out funny and her mother cleared her throat, tried again. "Emilia."

This reminded her of something. Another time.

Ma held on tight to Emilia's hands then, tighter with each attempt Emilia made to pull away because something was telling her to run. To fly. Instinctively, Emilia looked out the window to the sky. Something was wrong. And her mother was going to tell her. But all she could think was, *No. Don't. I don't want to know, whatever it is.*

She heard her crows even though she couldn't see them; somewhere a thousand crows were cawing, warning her, screeching over her mother's voice. She willed them to cry louder.

Emilia felt like she was floating. The booth seat disappeared from under her and she could feel her body wanting to go up.

Her mother squeezed down harder on her hands.

"Look at me," she demanded. So Emilia looked at her mother's lips, tuned into her voice, and listened as Ma told her about Carl Smith.

The House Was Dark

The house was dark as Tomás approached. He walked up the three stoop stairs and opened the door. In the time it took him to reach for the light switch and click it on, he wondered where Emilia was. Why was the door unlocked? His mind suddenly registered that the car parked in front of their house was one he'd never seen before, and he assumed it belonged to someone visiting a neighbor.

"Hello?" he called, not expecting an answer, but trying to calm his nerves with his own voice.

"Tomás."

Tomás stood still, trying to understand what he was seeing. His father, in their living room. He'd been sitting in the dark. In their house.

"What are you doing here?" Tomás asked, still standing in the open doorway.

His father didn't answer. "My god, look at you," he said instead. "You're a man."

"What are you doing here?" Tomás repeated.

His father hesitated. "I just . . . I had to see all of you," he said finally.

Tomás stared at his father. He was lying. Tomás knew why he was here. He just hadn't thought he would come.

"We don't need you," Tomás whispered. His father looked down at his hands. They were shaking. He looked embarrassed and ashamed.

"Where are Ma and Emilia?"

"They left."

"Where?"

"I don't know. They just . . . left."

Tomás wondered if it was true. For a strange moment, he wondered if his father had done something to them. He didn't know the man sitting in their living room anymore. He didn't trust him.

Tomás looked around.

His father stood up, grabbed his jacket. "I'll leave," he told Tomás.

Tomás wanted to say something more to him. He wanted to make him answer questions, listen to his anger. He wanted to make him stay there and suffer discomfort and judgment. But Tomás could hardly stand to look at him.

When his father walked past him, out the front door, Tomás had the strangest urge to both push him out faster and hug him.

He watched him get in the car. And drive away.

His heart exploded in a million pieces.

But then he rushed through the house, looking for his mother and his sister. And when he didn't find them, he sat wondering where they would have gone. If their father was back, then maybe

Emilia knew. Maybe he and Ma had told her about Jeremy Lance's release, about the real attacker.

Tomás's heart beat faster as he thought back to the day he picked up the phone and listened in on a conversation between Ma and a man he eventually figured out was a detective who had worked Emilia's case.

He noticed how Ma had started acting so strangely after that call in the middle of the night, and then again when the phone rang the next morning, how she raced to answer the phone in her room whenever it rang. So he started picking up the line in the kitchen, holding his hand over the mouthpiece as he listened. Some of the calls were from bill collectors, a few from telemarketers. But then one day he heard a man tell Ma that Jeremy Lance had been released. It took Tomás a moment to realize what had happened, to piece it all together. But he did, and he wouldn't forget how strange his mother had sounded, how she choked back tears but spoke with such anger in her voice.

Tomás sat on the couch, trying to decide what to do, when the front door opened and Ma and Emilia walked in.

He took one look at Emilia's face, stunned and shocked and drained, and knew their mother had told her. Oh god, she knew. He knew it was best, that she needed to know. But the look on her face now, it was exactly why he hadn't told her himself. This look, what she was feeling now, was exactly what he'd wanted to protect her from, too.

The million pieces of his heart shattered into a million more.

Emilia immediately ran upstairs to her room and their mother stood at the bottom of the stairs, helpless, and watched her go. Ma's face looked a thousand years old.

"Does she know the truth about Jeremy Lance?" Tomás asked.

Ma stared at him, stunned.

"I . . . I picked up the line and heard you on the phone," he admitted. "When the detective called and told you about his release."

Ma closed her eyes. She shook her head and fresh tears slid down her face. "So you know about Carl Smith, too?" she asked.

Tomás nodded. "I heard his name. And enough to figure it out."

"Oh god," Ma said, shaking her head. "What if Emilia had found out like that?" He could see his mother shaking.

"Go, check on her. Please," Ma said, looking at him. "She won't . . . say anything to me. Make her say *something*, please."

Tomás stood outside Emilia's bedroom and knocked on the door, gently calling her name. She wouldn't answer. He tried to open it, but the door was locked.

"Emilia," he said. "Let me in, please."

He kept calling to her softly, waiting, and after what seemed like forever, he finally heard the gentle click of the door unlocking. He turned the knob slowly and carefully entered her room.

"Emilia?"

She was sitting on her bed, leaning against the wall with her legs drawn up, her arms around her knees, her head down. Tears filled his eyes. She looked so small, her hair hanging around her. Sitting just as she used to back then, *when she didn't want any of us to come near her.*

The memory of Emilia in this exact pose when she was little came upon Tomás so fast, so suddenly, that he felt disoriented. She'd had so many ways to shut out the world back then. How could he have forgotten?

Tomás took a deep breath and went to his sister. He wouldn't let her shut him out this time. Gently, he sat next to her. "God, Emilia. I'm so sorry," he said.

She wouldn't look up at him, but he heard her saying something over and over, and it took him a while to understand what she was saying. Finally, he made sense of the words.

"What have I done?"

"Emilia, you didn't do anything. Nothing."

"I ruined his life. All those years in jail." Her voice was choked. "Because of me."

"It's not your fault," he told her.

"People will find out. Think I'm horrible," she said through sobs. "They'll think . . . I'm a horrible person. A liar. Worse."

Tomás hadn't thought of what others would think. All he'd thought of since he found out was that someone out there hadn't paid for what he'd done to Emilia. That all this time, her attacker had still been out there.

"Don't worry about other people. You don't need to worry about other people. They have no idea what—"

"Exactly. They have no idea! All they'll know is *I* named him. That Jeremy Lance was arrested because of *me*. Everyone will know. And . . . the real attacker . . ." His sister clutched her arms tighter around her knees, made herself even smaller as she cried. "He's been out there this *whole* time. This whole time . . . What if . . . what if he's been *watching* me?"

"Emilia . . ."

"All this time." She cried harder. Her voice was muffled and her back shook with sobs, but she wouldn't look at him. "How can I . . . go out there . . . in the world with everyone knowing what I did?"

"*You* didn't do anything," Tomás said, louder than he'd meant.

He saw her jump, but she just kept saying, "I did. I did."

Tomás was almost afraid to touch her, but he put his hand gently on her arm and then pulled her close to him. "It'll be okay," he told her. "We'll handle it. I'll be with you."

Tomás held his sister and didn't let go. He held her like that, until her crying became less and less. Until she was exhausted and slowly fell asleep. Tomás covered her with a blanket. Then he lay next to her, on the floor, so she wouldn't be alone or scared if she woke up in the middle of the night.

I won't leave you alone, he thought as he listened to her breathing, an occasional soft sob bubbling up even in her sleep.

I won't, Tomás thought as he finally let himself drift off to sleep. *I won't.*

Neither of them heard when their mother came in, or how she cried when she saw them together that way. Neither of them knew she sat on the floor all night, too, watching over them, until they woke and saw her there the following morning.

PART THREE

Late December 1994

Several Miles from Emilia's House

Several miles from Emilia's house, Jeremy Lance rode his bike up and down the block. Katherine Lance watched him from the kitchen window.

He's home, she thought. *He's actually home.*

It had only been a couple of weeks since she'd watched her son exit Haven Bourne Correctional Center. She'd waited for him outside as he was escorted by two guards. It was cold, but the sun had managed to break through the gray sky for a little while that day and she watched as Jeremy blinked fast, just like he used to, and his eyes filled with tears. He'd always been so sensitive to sunlight.

The gate opened and the guards deposited him outside the doors that had kept him locked up, away from her, for so long.

Mom, he said, looking at her. He wiped his eyes, but the tears continued and he blinked and blinked.

She nodded and smiled. *Jeremy,* she said. Her voice was steady. *Ready to go home now?*

He looked back, confused by the two guards walking back inside now without him. *I don't think I'm allowed to leave,* he told her.

She kept her voice soft and smiled again so he wouldn't be scared. *Remember, I told you it would all be okay?* She stepped forward with a coat she'd just bought for him. *Everything is okay now. You can leave. You don't have to stay here anymore,* she said.

Jeremy looked back again at the door. *I do. I haven't been good,* he told her, looking down. She knew he hadn't been good. She knew he'd been uncooperative. As if anyone who is innocent should be cooperative. *They* should *scream and cry and pound the walls,* she thought. Which was just what Jeremy had done.

But this was real life, where that kind of outrage, even if justified, only made a person more of a threat. Where innocent people were not only jailed, but also killed. She should be grateful he wasn't put to death. She should be grateful she didn't have to sit in one of those horrible seats other mothers sat in as they watched their child be killed. She kept her eyes on her son's face and tried to remain calm.

They're letting you go, Katherine explained.

Why would they let me go now?

They know they made a mistake. Everyone knows the truth now.

Everyone? he asked, squinting as he looked back at the doors of Haven Bourne. He shivered in his short-sleeved shirt, but she resisted putting the coat on him and waited until he was ready.

She nodded. *They will soon.*

Jeremy took a step toward the car, waited. Then took another.

You wouldn't be tricking me, would you, Mom? Checking if I'll be good?

Her heart broke with his distrust in her. *I would never, ever trick you, Jeremy,* she told him. But she understood why he might think so. After all, hadn't she told Jeremy, who had been born afraid and distrusting of the world, that it was a beautiful place? Hadn't she enlisted the help of so many teachers, specialists, therapists at New Heights, the home for mentally and developmentally delayed children, and insisted that there was nothing to be afraid of? Little by little, he had believed them.

Until that day the police came for him.

Jeremy looked back at the prison and took another cautious step, then another. And he kept stepping until he was farther and farther away from it. When no alarms rang, when no dogs were unleashed and no guns were pointed at him, he laughed.

No joke, Mom? I can really go?

No joke, she told him, his laughter filling her with bittersweet joy.

He looked around, still blinking, and shook his head. He whispered something to himself but she couldn't hear him, and she wondered what he was saying.

What is he thinking? she thought. *How is he feeling?* She wanted to ask but not yet. *Give him a little time,* she reminded herself.

You ready? She held the coat open. Jeremy nodded and came forward; she scanned his arms and found fading bruises, blotches of yellow and green and blue, as she wrapped him in the coat.

He's out, she thought. *And here. And you're holding him.*

He felt so small and thin in her arms.

Jeremy shrank a little from her and she hurried to open the passenger door for him. Slowly, he got in the car.

The whole ride home, Katherine kept looking over at him. She couldn't believe this was real. She smiled, hoping her anxiety didn't show. *You okay?* she asked, noticing the way he held on to the door handle.

It just feels like . . . we're going so fast, he said. She looked over at him, noticed the way he blinked, turned away from the window even though the sun was gone now and a cold rain had started to fall. She reduced her speed significantly, let cars pass her, and ignored the impatient look of drivers as they glanced into her window and hollered.

Drive on, sonsofbitches, she whispered.

Jeremy laughed. *Drive on, sonsofbitches!* he repeated.

They laughed together, and she reached over and held his hand.

Don't worry, she said. *Everything will be okay now.*

He nodded, but she saw the way he was getting agitated as they continued driving.

Close your eyes, focus on your breathing until you feel better.

He nodded, closed his eyes, and did just that. She'd taught him the technique a long time ago, whenever he got worked up or scared. And he'd come so far before all of this. He'd made so much progress, especially that last year at New Heights. Every dime she'd ever made went to his tuition, to more therapy sessions. They'd said he could attend regular school, but she'd wanted him at New Heights, where he knew everyone and was safe. Where he eventually even started working, *working*, as a custodian. She'd seen so clearly in her mind's eye a normal life for Jeremy. She never ever pictured what ended up happening.

Katherine tried not to read too much into how afraid and anxious Jeremy looked just from the car ride, how he struggled to keep his eyes closed. She tried not to think how far back he'd slipped into his reclusive ways. How each time she'd been allowed to visit him at Haven Bourne—only twice a month, one hour each visit—there was less and less of him there.

Stay with me, she had thought each time she saw him, but his eyes grew colder and further away. And even though she brought his old schoolbooks with the idea of reviewing lessons, she no longer tried to coax him back after those first few months. Because she knew he was doing whatever he needed to survive in that horrible place.

But we worked so hard, she thought each time she left, and now, still, as she drove. *So damn hard! Just to have all this happen a month after his eighteenth birthday. Just in time to be tried as an adult after that bastard detective drilled him for hours, got Jeremy so damn agitated and confused, got a false confession from him.*

Katherine Lance clutched the steering wheel and looked over again at her now twenty-six-year-old son. He smiled at her nervously before looking away quickly. And it was only for a moment, a millisecond, but she was sure she saw in that smile a glimmer of her son as he used to be, when he'd been doing so well.

God, she thought, her heart racing. *Maybe we can start over. Maybe, maybe he'll still be okay.*

She wiped quickly at her tears.

Katherine Lance stared ahead again, her heart filling with possibilities and determination, as her mind tried not to think of the moment when the unfairness of all those days Jeremy spent imprisoned would hit him. When he tasted freedom again, Jeremy would feel the complete weight of the injustice done to him.

She *knew* he would.

And she felt a new fear blossom in her heart alongside her hope.

Will it finish breaking him? she wondered. *Will I lose him then for good? Will he blame me because I couldn't protect him?*

Katherine Lance smiled at her son.

We'll be okay, she told him. *Everything will be okay.*

And she kept driving.

The Day After Telling Emilia

The day after telling Emilia the truth about Jeremy Lance and Carl Smith, Ma didn't go to work. She spent all morning calling makeup artists she knew, asking if they would take over the few Sunday appointments she had as well as her appointments for the next several days.

I've had a family emergency, she explained over and over again.

I'm an emergency, Emilia thought each time. *A crisis.* Emilia could hardly stand it. It made her eyes sting with shame and the threat of more tears.

It's not true. That's not what I am, she told herself, even as part of her wondered, *Are you sure?*

Emilia sat on her bed, by her window, watching her crows come for the peanuts and looking out to see if her father would come back.

Where is he? she asked the crows.

Yesterday he was gone by the time she and Ma got home, and now she wondered if her dad had left again for good.

He wouldn't leave, just like that, would he? she asked her birds. *What do you think?*

She watched the crows and wished they would come inside, fill her room, and stay with her. She pictured them on her dresser, on her floor, perched on her shelves.

"Emilia?" her mother called. The crows startled.

"Upstairs," she answered as they flew away.

Ma came upstairs and before she could say anything, Emilia said, "I don't want to talk about it." Ma stood there for a moment.

"Okay, I understand."

But throughout the day, Ma kept calling for her.

"Emilia?" she called when Emilia was in the next room.

"Emilia?" she called when Emilia went downstairs to surround herself with books, though she'd already taken her favorites to the school.

"Emilia?" she called when Emilia went back upstairs.

Emilia finally went to the only place she thought her mother would leave her alone and not look at her the way she was looking at her. She filled the tub with hot water, as hot as she could stand it. She took off her clothes, shivered with each article she stripped off, and stepped into water so hot it made her prickle with pain before she finally went numb.

"Emilia?" Her mother knocked on the bathroom door.

"I'm just taking a bath, Ma."

Then, in a small voice, Ma said, "Not too hot, Emilia."

"I know."

She knew Ma was thinking about the times after the attack. When no matter how many sweaters Emilia wore, or how many blankets she covered herself with, the cold found its way into the very marrow of her bones. That's when Ma would run a hot bath for her. Emilia remembered how she would shake and shiver, how her teeth would chatter as she whispered to Ma to make it hotter.

It's already so hot, Emilia, Ma would say. But it never felt hot enough to Emilia. Not even when her skin itched and crawled from the heat. Instead, it felt like she was still lying in the woods.

She looked at the rising steam around her and sank into the hot water. She felt the cold ground beneath her.

Don't, she told herself, *don't.*

But she felt the sense of a cold breeze brushing over her legs. In her ears she heard the call of the crows, so many crows, and her mind conjured up the images of the branches above—thin, breakable, intertwined.

She was eight years old and looking to the sky like she did every day during recess.

No. Don't go back to that day, she told herself again. She closed her eyes and sank just below the surface of the water.

She held her breath for as long as she could stand. Then her mouth came to the surface, took a gulp of air, and went back down again. She looked at the silver blur of the world, of her bathroom ceiling, wishing she could stay underwater.

Hotter, she thought as her body shivered.

She reached for the hot water faucet. Turned it. Sank under the surface again.

★

That evening, as Emilia sat in her thickest sweatshirt and swirled uneaten spaghetti on her plate, Ma said quietly, "I know we talked about Jeremy Lance, how he's out of jail. But you need to prepare yourself, Emilia. In case we . . . see him."

Emilia's stomach filled with dread. She swirled the spaghetti some more, willing the stinging sensation in her nose and eyes to go away. Her vision blurred as she swirled and swirled. She could feel her mother staring at her.

"Okay."

"I think it'd be a good idea to call Dr. Lisa, check if she's still practicing here . . ."

Emilia's mind filled with Dr. Lisa's office. The dollhouse in the corner. The round table stocked with paper and art supplies. Emilia would color sometimes. She didn't want to go back there.

"Ma, please," Emilia said.

"It's important."

Emilia took a deep breath. Soon Ma would insist on home-schooling her. Soon she'd withdraw Emilia from school. She could feel their lives whirling back to the past. Going back to how things had been. Soon she would be shutting Emilia away in the house while the rest of the town, the school, the neighbors talked about her. She'd be her mother's shadow again.

Emilia looked over at Ma, saw in her eyes a confirmation of everything she'd just thought.

"Please, Ma," she said. "Can we just . . . slow down? Can't we just stay the same?" She didn't know how to explain to her mother what she meant. "Please."

"Nothing is the same," Ma said. The words made Emilia feel hollow, like a large hand had scooped out her insides. But she was careful not to let Ma see how she felt.

"I know, Ma. But just for a little while. Please."

Ma took a deep breath.

"I'm going to my room," Emilia said. She didn't want to sit there any longer. She half expected her mother to come after her, force her to talk about it, but she didn't, and Emilia was relieved when she was able to close her bedroom door behind her.

She locked it. And flopped onto her bed, letting the tears she'd been holding back come flowing out.

Jeremy Lance.

He was out of jail. She might run into him. She might actually have to face Jeremy Lance again.

The image of him covered in blood flashed in her mind, the image of him pulling her by her ankles on the playground, pulling off her clothes, came rushing back.

Emilia shook her head. It wasn't him. That's what Ma said.

But it was *him,* she thought. Emilia pulled the covers over herself, even though it didn't warm her or stop her shivering.

The House Felt Heavy

The house felt heavy, burdened with silence and memories in the days that followed.

Ma called the office where Dr. Lisa used to practice only to find out, no, she wasn't still in town. Emilia was relieved, but then heard Ma calling around to other therapists, heard her mother's soft murmur as she explained the situation over and over again *to who? The receptionist? Strangers?* And then she heard Ma's frustration, again and again, as she was told they were not taking new patients until after the holidays.

Emilia shrank into the couch, ashamed and embarrassed. She didn't want to go to a therapist.

I'm not going to talk about this, Emilia thought. *Not to anyone.*

She didn't want to admit what had happened, what she'd done. She could barely stand to think about it without feeling sick.

And Ma can't force you to go, she thought.

She wasn't little anymore. Ma couldn't just scoop her up and put her in the car like she used to.

But Emilia knew Ma would only push harder if she resisted. And she couldn't stand the way Ma was looking at her, following her around the house, watching her every move, just like she did before.

Tell her you'll go to therapy, Emilia thought, *but just to give you some time. Then just act as normal as possible. Tell Ma you're fine. And maybe she'll believe it and forget about making you go.*

So she told Ma, *Okay, I'll talk to someone, but please let me have my winter break. And please go to work. I know you have all those appointments anyway, with all the rich women getting their makeup done for their fancy holiday parties. So let's just be normal for a little while longer, okay? And I promise I'll go. In a few weeks. Once I have a little time. Okay? Please?*

She could see how anxious it made her mother to leave her alone again. Even when Emilia suggested she could call her father if she needed anything.

"He's still in town, right?" Emilia braced herself for the answer to the question she hadn't wanted to ask but couldn't keep in.

Her mother hesitated. "Yes, I just . . . I think we should ease into things is all."

Emilia wasn't sure she believed her mother, but she nodded. Maybe it was mentioning her father that finally made Ma agree, but eventually she did. And when the moment came just a week into winter break, when she watched Ma's car pull away slowly once again, Emilia breathed a little easier. Tomás was at work. Now Ma was, too. And her father was somewhere out there as well. Everything was back to how it had been. Even though nothing was the same.

*

Now she was alone. And it was Christmas Eve. Ma had a couple of appointments and Tomás, who was always looking for extra hours and pay, took the double shift nobody else wanted. Emilia should have been relieved to be alone, but she felt like she was being watched. She couldn't stop the thought that kept running through her mind.

He's out there.

Emilia hugged herself as she looked out her bedroom window, scanned her block.

Carl Smith might be outside, hiding in the bushes. Or down the street, parked in a car. Watching. Waiting.

No, she reminded herself. Ma had told her he was on his deathbed. That he couldn't get her. That the detective was going to try his best to have him prosecuted. But that, for now, he was on a breathing machine and hardly conscious.

But was he really dying? How could Ma know that for sure? Had she seen him? Had anyone?

Fear crept in and Emilia immediately rushed to check the doors. All locked. She clicked on the television, turning up the volume more than usual, and when the house felt too big, too loud, too empty and silent all at the same time, she went back upstairs to her room. But there, too, the thoughts she didn't want to think kept coming back to her anyway.

Emilia took a deep breath, let it out slowly.

Ma said he's dying. And he'll rot in that bed.

But what if he doesn't? What if he gets better? Emilia had asked Ma at the diner where she first told Emilia about Carl Smith.

He won't, Ma said, *but if he does, they'll lock him up forever for certain.*

Emilia thought about that for a moment. A sickly, faceless man dying slowly in prison, over years and years. Yes, that's what he deserved.

Stop, she told herself.

Emilia reached into her drawer, into the bag of peanuts she kept there, and realized there were none left.

A crow landed outside her window and looked at her quizzically.

"I know," she said. "I'm sorry."

She looked inside her drawer, hoping to find a few stray nuts, but found none. And then panic set in. That empty bag, for a moment, distressed her in a way she didn't expect. She'd have to get more. She'd have to leave the house. She'd have to go out, in the cold, and buy more.

It's no big deal. You can do this! You wanted Ma to leave you home alone and she did. You can do whatever you want. Prove you can do this.

Emilia looked outside at the empty street and cold day.

She'd overcome her fear when she'd made herself go to the elementary school. And those red doors, too, that refused to let her in but couldn't keep her out.

Emilia got dressed and grabbed the bottle of Mace Ma had

given her a while back but that Emilia never bothered carrying. She put on her coat and headed out the door before she could change her mind.

Outside, she kept her hand wrapped tight around that bottle and took deep cold breaths as she walked to the market across the street from Carro's. Each step made her feel stronger somehow, even though she was scared. Once at the market, she passed the Salvation Army Santa standing outside, ringing a bell, and headed directly to the peanuts. Emilia grabbed a bag and paid for it.

You see, perfectly safe, she told herself, letting out a deep breath and feeling accomplished as she left. She slipped a quarter into the bucket of the Salvation Army Santa she'd ignored on the way in. He winked at her.

Emilia quickly looked away. She clutched the peanuts in one hand and the bottle of Mace hidden in her coat pocket with the other. Suddenly she felt sad and ridiculous, terrified of Santa, certain he would harm her.

"You okay?" the Santa asked.

Emilia nodded without looking back at him.

You're so stupid, she thought as she stood there and felt tears threatening to rush forward. She hurried to the corner to cross the street. All she wanted was to get back home. But as she stood there, a bus passed by and Emilia's mind flickered with the memory of Jeremy Lance banging on the window, calling out to her as it went by. Emilia sucked in her breath with the sudden vivid image.

It wasn't him, she told herself.

But you saw his face. Maybe it was.

Or maybe you just can't accept that you ruined his life.

The thoughts came bubbling into Emilia's mind and, with them, an overwhelming sourness erupted in her stomach. She rushed to some nearby bushes and threw up. With each heave, her mind flashed with Jeremy Lance's face. Emilia shut her eyes and tried to think of something else.

The classroom.

Her *something.* Her project that she'd kept a secret. What if someone had discovered it? With her father's return and the news about Jeremy Lance and Carl Smith, she hadn't gone back.

Emilia wiped her mouth and tears with a trembling hand. When she looked up, she turned her gaze in the direction of the old elementary school. It was just a few blocks away.

Sam the Squirrel was there. And her dad's poetry books. She'd written that poem she'd finally found on the wall in thick black letters. She'd planned to make that room so beautiful.

You still can.

Emilia took a step toward the school, then another. All she had to do was keep walking in that direction.

But Carl Smith.

His name filled her mind.

Emilia thought of climbing in through the window and dropping into the dark chorus room, having to go up the flights of stairs alone in the dark, and she stopped.

What if he's waiting there for you? You wouldn't even know him if you saw him. He could be anyone. He could be watching you right now. This could all be some twisted trick he's playing on you.

Emilia looked around, kept her finger on the nozzle of the Mace bottle.

Just go home, Emilia, she thought.

But she wanted to see that room again. She remembered how brave and amazing she'd felt when she finally went back into that school. How she'd found so many little treasures and brought them to the classroom. She couldn't just forget about it. And she *had* left a flashlight near the window in the chorus room.

But Carl Smith.

He's dying, Ma said.

Emilia looked down at her feet, and without looking up, she willed them to move, one in front of the other, until suddenly, she was in front of that school again.

And then she was climbing in through the window, her heart beating so loud in her ears. She was jittery and the flashlight fell from her hand, thumped loudly on the floor, and rolled all over the place, making the room flicker eerily. She rushed to get it.

Just relax! she told herself. *You've been here before. Just like this. And you were okay. Just go upstairs. Get to that classroom.*

Emilia hurried down the eerie hall. The sound of her footsteps echoed off the concrete walls, and in those echoes, she thought she heard his name, *Carl Smith.*

The name repeated over and over in her mind.

Carl Smith. Carl Smith. Carl Smith. Carl Smith.

Emilia tried to shut out the echoes.

He can't get you, Ma's words whispered in her ears.

Emilia's heart thumped faster and she raced up the stairs to the classroom.

If you get to the classroom, you'll be okay. Everything will be okay.

Emilia told herself this each step of the way. Finally, she made it to the classroom and ran in, slamming the door behind her.

She leaned against it and caught her breath. She waited until her heart calmed down and her limbs regained their strength. And then she looked around, taking in the room. Everything was just as she'd left it. Nobody had been here. Nobody knew about this place.

Carl Smith.

No! Emilia shook her head and closed her eyes.

She wouldn't let herself think of him or Jeremy Lance here. Or of anything else that was happening *out there*. This place, this room was separate from all that and only for beautiful things.

And you made it here! You did it.

Emilia smiled. Yes, it meant something that she'd been able to make herself come here. It meant that she was strong. Brave. That she could handle everything that was happening. That Carl Smith couldn't get her. That she never ruined Jeremy Lance's life. That even the attack, somehow, could be left far away in the past, out there.

Emilia reached for the boxes and boxes of paper clips she'd

found in a cabinet last week. She mindlessly started linking them together, focusing on how shiny and new and silver they were. When she was finished, Emilia tacked up the long chain with pushpins in a large, swirly pattern on one of the walls.

She stepped back and looked at it. Strange, *but beautiful*.

Emilia started another chain. Then another, and another.

With each linked clip, she felt a small bit of relief.

Emilia Jumped

Emilia jumped, looked over, and saw Ian's car had pulled up next to her. How had she not heard it?

"Come on," he said, and smiled at her. "I just got off work."

Emilia slid into the passenger seat, feeling disoriented. Ian leaned in to kiss her, and the warm kiss felt both familiar and unreal on her lips.

"Where are you coming from, anyway?" he asked, looking at the bag in her hands.

Emilia's mind was filled with strange images of shiny gold pinwheels. Of every beautiful thing she'd left behind in that classroom. She looked down at her hands, suddenly remembering the peanuts.

"Getting peanuts," she said, holding up the bag. Ian laughed and kept driving. It seemed so strange and normal to be riding in the car with him, the way he was glancing over at her, the same as it used to be.

They got the wrong person, Ian. I accused the wrong person. The wrong person went to jail. The real guy is still out there somewhere.

The car screeched and the thoughts that had invaded her mind were silenced.

"So Anthony and Jane were wondering if you wanted to hang out again," he said. "Jane keeps asking about you."

Emilia turned to Ian, tried hard to keep her tone light, their conversation normal. "Why would she ask about me?"

"I guess she just really liked you. Says you two could be great friends."

"Really?"

Ian laughed. "Yeah, really. She's all right, you know."

"I guess you've gotten to know her a little better?" Emilia asked, trying not to let the idea bother her.

"A little."

Another date with Ian, Anthony, and Jane. She didn't really want to go. Just the thought of it made her stomach churn again. She could almost picture them—laughing and having fun. Oblivious and normal. Except her.

But maybe it'll make everything seem okay again, Emilia thought. *Maybe it'll make you feel okay.*

Ma's face loomed in her mind as Emilia remembered the doubt and uncertainty she'd seen when she'd tried to convince Ma she could be left home alone.

Will she always look at me that way?

Emilia wanted Ma to see that she could be okay, that she could be normal. And she wanted to feel that way, too.

"What do you think? You up for it?" Ian asked.

"Sure, sounds fun. When?"

"I have tomorrow off, but we'll be at my aunt's because she's throwing her annual family Christmas party," Ian said. "But sometime after that?"

"Sure," Emilia said again as they pulled up to her house. He leaned in, kissed her, and smiled.

Yes. Maybe she could get lost in her boyfriend's smile. Maybe she could tuck herself into him, into his car, into his bed, and she'd never have to tell him. Maybe she'd never have to say the words, to anyone, not ever. Maybe she could forget about all of this, and everyone else would, too.

"Call you later?" he said.

She nodded, got out of the car, like she'd done so many times before. This was how life had been. *This* was normal.

The sound of cawing crows up in the trees caught her attention. Emilia clutched the bag of peanuts and slowly walked up to her house.

Who Is It

"Who is it?" Tomás called out, biding some time as he gathered what he'd been working on in his bedroom and quickly shoved it all into his junk drawer.

"Me," Emilia answered. Tomás scanned his room one last time before he opened the door.

"Hey," he said. "What's up?"

"Nothing," she said, sitting at the foot of his bed near him.

"You okay?" he asked. She nodded.

He wanted to hold her. But he knew she would hate that, so he said, "It's going to be okay."

She nodded again, but didn't say anything. His stomach flip-flopped as he remembered his sister, back in those early days. How silent she became. How her mouth had seemed to become hollow. When he was younger, the phrase *Cat got your tongue?* haunted him. It went through his head repeatedly whenever he looked at his sister. Like some horrible thing came and snatched her tongue away and rendered her mute forever.

"I'm reading this book," he said to her, and began telling her about it. She lay down. "Want me to read you some pages?"

She nodded. Tomás read. He used to do this when they were little. The way they seemed to slip right back into the past startled him and he was relieved when, after a while, she finally spoke. A part of him was afraid she wouldn't.

"Is he really still in town? Or is Ma just . . . trying to protect me from the truth?" she said.

She meant their father. Tomás wanted to tell her to forget about him, they didn't need him, but he shook his head.

"He's here. He's just being himself. I think he's afraid of us, you know." Tomás looked over at Emilia and saw the confused, hurt look on her face. He'd let too much of his own thoughts slip out. "I mean, Ma. I think he's afraid of her. I heard her on the phone with him. Told him it would be best if he . . . gave us a little room. Time to adjust. She was pretty direct." Now he sounded so clinical. He wished he'd said it better.

"Oh," Emilia said, but he could tell she was still hurt. By her mother keeping him away or by her father listening or by the way he had explained things, Tomás wasn't sure.

"Don't worry. He's still in town."

She nodded. A minute later she said, "I haven't told Ian about any of this."

"It's okay, take your time."

"We have a date. With Anthony and his girlfriend again. He's back in town."

Tomás looked at Emilia. She stared at the ceiling.

"You don't have to go."

"No, I mean I want to. I have to act normal and I think it would be good for me . . . I just, I should tell Ian about it. Right? It's just so . . ." Emilia closed her eyes.

"Do you want me to tell him?" Tomás asked.

She took a deep breath. "No . . . I'll do it. Just not yet." Emilia got up and headed toward his door.

"Wait," Tomás said. She turned.

"You don't have to, Emilia. You don't have to do anything you don't want to. And you . . . you don't have to pretend like everything's okay."

"I'm not pretending," she said. "Really, I'll be okay." Emilia smiled sadly then and looked at her brother. "You're such a good person, Tomás. Always there for me."

His heart broke. And a sense of guilt and unworthiness hit him. He was relieved she didn't notice.

"You want to . . . talk? More?" he asked carefully. But she shook her head and he didn't push. She left his room, and moments later, he heard the click of her door.

Tomás got up and stared at her door for a moment. Then closed his own and locked it, feeling unsettled. He returned to what he had been doing before Emilia knocked—gluing together the bones of a bird that had been dead for seven years. He'd gathered them from the shed the morning after his father suddenly showed up and his sister cried herself to sleep, when Tomás had stood staring out their kitchen window, trying to make sense of them, their family, their past. That's when he found himself staring at the rusting white shed in the corner of their backyard. And he remembered.

When Emilia was nine and he was twelve, Tomás found his sister in their backyard, in the black coat and hat she'd asked Ma for. Ma didn't know it, but Tomás knew it was so she would look more like her black birds. That was when Ma got Emilia anything she wanted, as long as she asked.

As long as you use your words, Emilia.

But that day Emilia wasn't flapping around like usual. She was staring at an almost dead bird, crying. Her head was bent in grief and her long black hair fell around her face like a mourning veil.

Tomás crouched down. It was terrible. The bird's little head twisted at an odd angle, its legs limp against the ground. A small streak of white was coming from beneath it. The small bird quivered and shook, and with each quiver, Emilia cried harder.

It was alive, but so damaged. So irreversibly damaged, and in its final throes.

Tomás had been jealous of all the things Emilia got from Ma. Of the attention she received, and the way she absorbed their mother's energy. It all went to Emilia, only Emilia. He'd once not spoken for a day to see if Ma would notice, if she would turn her attention to him, but she didn't. And their father made himself so scarce that even when he was home, he might as well not be.

So he was left without Ma or Dad, and Emilia, too, had left

him. Gone somewhere after the attack and never fully come back, even when he tried to reach her. He'd try to make her laugh. He remembered sitting next to her, watching *Tom and Jerry*, and how he'd put his arms up like they were paws, and meow. But Emilia would only sort of smile, reach for his paw, and hold it.

He'd laugh at the funny parts, but she wouldn't, and then he felt so guilty. How could he laugh, exist even, when his sister felt this way? And what would she think of him if she knew what he had been doing as she lay near the playground dying?

Each day he grew more ashamed. He kept more to himself, so as to not bother anyone. He found ways to not need anyone or anything.

But that day, it broke him to see his sister crying over the small bird that wouldn't stop quivering. How Tomás wished it would stop quivering like that.

You're upsetting her, he wanted to tell it. But of course, he could hardly expect the bird to understand.

I want to keep it, Emilia cried. *I have to keep it. Find a box, Tomás, please, please find a box.*

You can't keep him, he told her. *It will rot and smell. Come on, we'll bury him. We'll have a bird funeral for him. Is that okay?*

Emilia nodded. *A bird funeral,* she repeated. *For* her.

What? Tomás asked.

She's a girl bird.

Okay.

So Tomás went inside, found a box of Ma's tea, and emptied

it. He ran back outside, picked up the bird, which, finally, in his hands, stopped quivering. Tomás swallowed the lump in his throat as he placed her in the box. How sad it looked, *she* looked, with her little eyes closed.

Tomás found a garden trowel in their dad's shed and dug a small hole. He and Emilia buried that bird by the shed and he said some words he remembered from church when they would sometimes go. Together they stared at the ground in silence for what seemed like an eternity. Emilia didn't want to leave the gravesite, and Tomás didn't want to leave her, but he worried their mother would come out soon. He put the trowel back on the high shelf as his stomach growled.

Come on, Emilia, he said.

Okay, she said. But she didn't move, and Tomás finally went inside.

Their mother was in the living room. *Emilia okay?* she asked when he came inside.

Fine, Tomás said. *Me too,* he thought.

He went to the bathroom to wash his hands. He looked at himself in the mirror of their medicine cabinet as he lathered, startled like he always was now at who he saw there.

Don't, he said to the person just below the surface. *Please, don't.*

He tried to look past the image, pictured instead the bottles of ibuprofen and cough syrup lined up just behind the mirror.

When he went back to the kitchen, his mother called out to him from the couch, where she was nursing a headache. *Tomás? Check and see if Emilia's okay.*

I was just out there. He grabbed the ham and cheese from the refrigerator, the bread from on top of the toaster.

Please, Tomás, his mother called. He could hear the weariness in her voice.

Fine, he said. But Tomás started making himself a sandwich instead. He was hungry and he'd just stood out there with Emilia forever.

Tomás? his mother called. *Is she okay?*

Yes, I see her. She's just playing, he insisted, even though he hadn't looked out yet. He took a bite of his sandwich, then another. And only when he was done did he bother to look outside.

That's when he saw Emilia standing by the shed, that little box in her dirty hands.

She'd dug it up. She'd clawed it out with her bare hands.

Tomás ran outside, grabbed the box from Emilia, and hid it in the shed. *Emilia, why'd you do that? You shouldn't have done that.*

But she just kept crying.

Why? she asked him. *Why?*

He told her to be quiet, to stop crying so Ma wouldn't worry. *Come on, I'll help you wash your hands and make you a sandwich. Okay? And . . . I'll figure out a way for you to keep the bird, I promise, just stop crying, please.*

He'd just told Ma she was fine and now she was filthy and crying and Ma had a headache, and oh, she would be upset at *him*. Not Emilia.

His sister nodded and they went inside. Tomás breezily told

his mother, *I'm going to help Emilia wash her hands.* And he quickly wiped her face and scrubbed at her hands with so much soap. The dirt was almost all off when Ma knocked and then came in. She stood behind them both, looked at their reflections in the mirror.

You're a good brother, Ma told him after a while, kissing his head. He returned his mother's gaze in the mirror and instantly felt bad about not checking on Emilia sooner.

I'll make her a sandwich for lunch, he told Ma. She smiled and went back to the living room.

Tomás dried Emilia's hands, took off her coat and hat, and whispered to her not to tell Ma about the bird.

You can keep it, he said. *Just don't tell Ma about it. She won't understand. And don't go looking for it again. I'll . . . I'll give it to you when it's ready.*

Her, she said.

Tomás nodded and Emilia hugged him so hard. When she smiled, he could almost see the Emilia of before, the one he missed so much. He just about cried right there and then.

Go, he told her.

He hung up Emilia's coat, tucked her hat into its pocket. Made her a sandwich and went upstairs. He had to think of how he could keep his promise to Emilia. He had to think of what he could do to make her happy again, like she used to be. Because he owed it to his sister. And because he couldn't shake off the phantom sensation of that small bird quivering and then becoming so still right in the palm of his hand.

Tomás stared at his ceiling a long time before it finally occurred to him. He'd keep the bones. And put them back together again. Like they do in museums.

His stomach turned a little as he realized he'd have to let it decompose as much as possible first, then clean the bones carefully.

But he'd do it, for Emilia. He'd put that little bird back together and give Emilia a tiny bird skeleton she could keep forever.

And maybe, in some small way, it would heal his sister and bring her back, too.

Tonight, in his room, Tomás opened his drawer and looked at the bird bones and the various photocopies of bird skeletons he'd made from a book at the library. And when he reached in to retrieve them, he caught a glimpse of pastel checkered material—the dress his grandmother had given Emilia for her eighth birthday. The dress he'd loved so much it hurt, so he took it from her closet. The dress that never would have possibly fit him, but that he took one day and didn't return anyway. Instead he'd crumpled it into a tiny ball and shoved it back there in a drawer his mother never bothered to look in.

He thought of the nights he would wait until everyone was asleep, lock the door, and hold the dress up to his body while he looked at himself in the mirror. How he'd lie in bed afterward, confused and angry and scared. Then later, after Emilia's attack, he thought about the word *suicide*. He'd go to sleep thinking of all the horrible ways people did it, how some hanged themselves, others slit their wrists. He learned people shot themselves and gassed themselves by running a car engine in an enclosed space.

All the images so horrific he couldn't imagine himself ever going through with it. But he used to think about it, too much, on those nights he was alone and Emilia was downstairs, sleeping in their mother's arms, protected like a baby bird.

Tomás returned his focus to the bird bones in front of him.

Emilia.

Life had been unfair to her, cruel. He wanted to do something. But those bird bones looked so frail and gave him second thoughts about what he was planning. How would this possibly help? Emilia probably didn't even remember that day. And if she did, would she understand why he was giving this to her? Did *he*?

He was sure he would get it all wrong anyway; he didn't even know what kind of bird this was.

But Tomás stared at the pastel checkered material and the bird bones and he remembered his little sister. Lately, all he saw every time he looked at Emilia was that girl, the one who had cried her eyes out that day in the yard and clawed at the earth to scoop out this small dead bird. The girl he'd taken this dress from.

Tomás wiped away the tears in his eyes.

He had to give both back to her.

Emilia Closed the Door

Emilia closed the door to her room and lay in bed, willing the heaviness and pain in her head to soften. She knew she could deal with this; she knew she had to prove she was strong, but it all made her feel like someone had whacked her hard on the head.

Her head thumped and an old song from a game she played with her friends came into her mind.

Concentration. That was the game.

She and her friends would pretend to crack eggs on one another's heads. They would give one another a big whack on the head and then laugh like it was the funniest thing.

How stupid, Emilia thought now, her head thumping as if one of those little friends from her childhood had just whacked her.

She felt herself drifting to the memory of yolks dripping down her back, of little fingers fluttering through her hair and down her shoulders.

Concentrate!

Concentrate!

It wasn't Jeremy Lance!

But she'd *seen* him. She remembered his face.

She thought of all the things she'd noticed lately, all the signs. The sky and the clouds and the white puffy trails. The birds, they'd been trying to tell her something was coming, but she hadn't understood. And her father was back. And her mother had revealed something so horrible.

Concentrate, concentrate.

Listen to the words I'm saying,

People are dying, babies are crying.

Concentrate, concentrate.

Why had they sung such a horrible song as kids? And laughed. Maybe because, back then, they didn't really know the world was horrible. They didn't know strangers watched from trees. Waited. Did horrible things.

But Emilia did. She knew.

Concentrate!

But she didn't have to concentrate. What she'd tried so hard to hold back now came rushing forward. And she remembered all of it.

Emilia had been in the woods behind her school.

   She was eight years old and looking to the sky like she did every day during recess. All she noticed were crows circling and circling around as she searched for a spaceship and waited to be abducted by aliens. After she saw the movie E.T. with her father, she became obsessed with the idea of life-forms on other planets far away. Though she didn't kid herself about all aliens being nice and cute.

They must be watching us, me, all the time, *she thought.*

Some of them, she imagined, were scary—terrible even, like the ones she read in the comics she'd started buying for a dollar at Connie's Arcade down the street. She'd sit and chew bubble gum in the aisles until Connie's son would say, "All right, Emilia. You gonna buy it or what? You're gonna get the pages all crumby." *Then she'd set down her dollar and read about the takeover of planet Earth by a giant squid-looking thing as she walked all the way home, always making it to her house just before it got dark.*

Emilia knew they would soon be coming for her. She knew too much about them. They could read her mind. The idea both scared her to death and thrilled her.

How would her parents find out? Would she be one of those kids on the milk carton, MISSING, *because she was on another planet? Would she become some kind of empress on that planet, and be allowed to return to her parents in the future and show them how important she was to the aliens?*

She stood in the far corner of the playground, the part where it became the woods, and listened to the crows cawing. She wondered how her classmates would react when the spaceship appeared, when a magnetic beam of glowing light pulled her into a whirring, humming disk and took her away!

Emilia smiled, thinking how surprised they would all be. She was sure it would happen any day now.

What are you smiling about? *Jasmine asked.*

Nothing, *Emilia answered, and resumed walking carefully so as to not disturb any of the tree twigs the aliens used to send her messages.*

Sometimes they were in the form of a Y. *That was their code for* Yes! We are out here. We are sending you messages.

Sometimes there was an X. *That meant* Stop, don't tell anyone. We are only entrusting you with these messages.

/\ There's a point to all this.

Emilia. Of course we know your name.

†

Someday our paths will cross.

Trust us, you can trust us.

Emilia knew she was the only one who could decode the messages. She kept walking around, searching the ground.

You're doing it again, *Jasmine shouted.* Looking for your stupid clues, aren't you? I told you already, aliens don't exist.

Emilia tried to ignore Jasmine. She didn't really like Jasmine, with her wrists full of jelly bracelets that somehow made her the leader of all of them.

Helloooooo, Earth to Emilia! *Jasmine sang.* Stop being so stupid.

Jasmine walked past Emilia, purposely stomping on as many twigs as she could. The other girls followed, past the swings and metal spiderweb, where kids hung upside down by their knees. Emilia half expected the metal web itself to start creeping behind Jasmine, too. For all the kids on it to be shaken violently before they fell on their heads. For the lunch aides to run in that ridiculous way adults run—toward the chaos while calling for help for all the children. But to Emilia's disappointment, it stayed in place.

Emilia didn't care. She liked her game more. And she was glad she was the only one chosen to look for and decode the messages. Yes, *she thought,* I am the chosen one.

Emilia looked to the sky, imagining the aliens watching her, but only a bunch of crows sat in the trees. She waved at the sky, trying to get in the aliens' good graces, in case they wanted to use her as a medical experiment or a human pet instead of turning her into an empress.

She kept walking.

———————————————>

Look!

Look at the leaves. See how they blow, Emilia? That is us, too. We are in everything. We see everything. And we are watching you, Emilia, waiting for you.

They were getting closer. Emilia knew it. Their messages were getting stronger. She knew she didn't have long.

When the recess bell rang, they went back inside to their classroom. Mrs. McNary passed around holiday coloring sheets and set out art supplies to keep them busy for the rest of the day. Emilia chose a Christmas tree to color as Mrs. McNary started the projector. Frosty the Snowman *played on the screen that pulled down in front of the chalkboard while Emilia's classmates laughed and sang along, colored and added glitter to their sheets.*

But Emilia looked out the window, thinking of the messages out there. She remembered a movie she'd seen a few weeks ago, about a man driving through the desert when his car radio suddenly went berserk, his car lights flashed on and off, his engine died, and his car came to a stop as a bright light suddenly appeared in the sky.

Emilia wondered if he'd received the messages, too. She wished she could talk to that man.

She wondered if they would come for her at home, at night. Would they come while she slept? Would they do something to Ma and Dad and Tomás? She thought about her family waking to prodding green fingers and large black eyes. Should she warn them? Maybe they would leave her family alone and just beam up Emilia. Which meant she'd have to leave her parents and brother behind and possibly, likely, never see them again. Emilia's eyes filled with tears and she felt a little scared.

She also felt someone's gaze on her. Emilia looked over and saw Jasmine staring back. She quickly wiped her eyes and reminded herself, Don't be stupid, Emilia! It's just a game! A game you made up! Nobody is really coming for you.

Those of you in Girl Scouts, just a reminder that Brownies is canceled today, *Mrs. McNary shouted over everyone hurrying to get their books and lunch boxes and backpacks together. Emilia looked at the clock, at the rolling credits of* Frosty the Snowman, *and was surprised it was time to go already.*

She quickly gathered her things and wondered if she'd heard her teacher correctly. And though she dreaded it, she turned to Jasmine and asked, No Brownies today?

Duh! It's winter break, *was Jasmine's answer.*

Emilia tried to ask Mrs. McNary if she could go to Tomás's classroom so he wouldn't leave without her, but then immediately remembered Ma telling him that morning of his dentist appointment in the afternoon. She would pick him up at noon, Ma had said.

You too, Emilia. If you want.

But she hadn't wanted to miss the holiday party or Brownies.

Emilia felt a small wave of panic as Mrs. McNary quickly rushed her back into line before leading them out of the classroom. She scanned the hallway for Tomás, just in case, but no luck.

Call home, *said a little voice inside her head. Emilia giggled despite her panic as an image of E.T. came to mind. She quickly snuck out of line near the pay phone outside the gym and retrieved the one quarter she always kept in the small side zipper of her purple sneakers. She slipped it into the pay phone and dialed her home number.*

After the third ring, Emilia knew nobody was home, but she let it ring four more times before finally hanging up.

Maybe they're still at the dentist, *Emilia thought.* Ma will pick me up later. I can just hang out on the playground, decode more messages, and then go out in front of the school, where Ma will be waiting like always.

Because it was the last day before winter break, the school emptied quickly. And by the time Emilia headed out across the field and to the playground, she didn't see anyone else around.

She puffed little smoke clouds out of her mouth and watched them disappear. By the time she got to the trees, she was out of breath and a little dizzy. She stopped, felt a strange stillness, and the cold found its way under her coat and her Cheerios sweatshirt, right to her spine.

A disturbance.

Emilia looked up, saw the crows watching her. "Have the aliens been here?" she asked them.

She got to work and searched for new messages but found none.

I know they were here! I can feel it!

Emilia looked all around but saw nothing. She walked and reexamined the same sticks, positioned just as they'd been during recess. Maybe the messengers had moved on. Perhaps she was not worthy of their time. Or maybe she'd misread their messages. Maybe they were just testing her patience.

Emilia sat down, waiting, wondering.

The day looked just like a winter day should, the sky so gauzy and white, filled with the long, thin, nearly bare arms of tree branches except for all the black birds. As she sat there, it started getting colder, so Emilia stood up, zipped her heavy jacket, and spun in circles to keep warm. She let out more puffs of smoke.

Can you decode my puffs of smoke? she asked the aliens.

After a while, she figured it must be close to time to go. She was sure she'd been walking and sitting around long enough and her mother would *soon be parked in front of the school waiting for her. She started walking, but suddenly a strong wind blew, sending leaves and a ton of twigs falling to the ground. Emilia raced to them.*

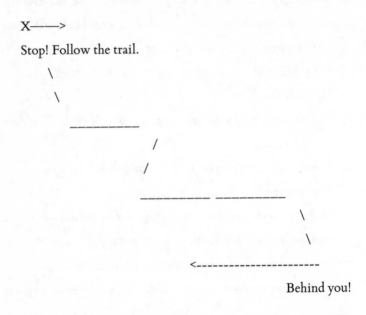

X——>

Stop! Follow the trail.

Behind you!

Emilia turned, but too late. A firework exploded in her ear, filled her world with streaks and spinning lights, and sent her falling to the ground.

The messengers! They were here! They were finally here!

Just like in the movie.

Emilia tried to remember if they had knocked the man unconscious before taking him into their spaceship. Oh god, they've come! They've come to take me away! She couldn't believe it was actually happening. She tried to open her eyes for a moment, to look up at the sky, past the tree branches in search of the blinding light of a hovering mother ship, but all she saw were the branches crisscrossing above her.

The aliens trampled her. Attacked her and throttled her. They hit her on the head, again and again, filling it with black and then aching, flashing color. And it was nothing like Emilia thought it would be. They were terrible. Horrible. They were going to kill her.

The realization sent her into a panic and she called out, screamed, but they drummed their fists on her body, grunted like wild pigs, and made terrible, terrible sounds. She felt herself being dragged over exposed roots and hard ground. She turned and saw the dirty white sneakers the messenger wore. One messenger.

She occasionally caught a glimpse of the world as her eyes fluttered. Her head hit the ground again. She tasted blood. She felt it seeping out of the sides of her mouth.

She saw flashing dots. And she thought, It's here. The ship is here.

Emilia wondered if what she thought was the spaceship was really the space shuttle Mrs. McNary had told them about all month. The space shuttle carrying the first teacher into space. It was scheduled to go off next month, but what if it was taking off right now and that's what she was seeing? What if Mrs. McNary had lied?

Maybe she'd lied about the Brownie meeting, too. Maybe it wasn't canceled. Maybe all of them were inside and she was out here.

Emilia felt herself being dragged hard by her ankles. This wasn't what she'd imagined. This was something else, something frightening and inhumane, but not aliens.

Oh god! Someone help! Please! she thought as she looked at the *sky. She saw the birds in the trees.* Help! *she tried to scream, but felt the blood bubbling in her throat; she heard herself gurgle.*

Her vision was darkening, but then she saw a huge black bird coming toward her. And then more. And more. And more! The sky darkened, was almost blackened completely, with so many birds. Or maybe she was passing out. She couldn't concentrate anymore. Help me! *she told them.* Please!

You can talk to me, you know, when I'm gone.

Emilia thought she heard her grandmother's voice.

Help me, *Emilia thought.* Help me!

She heard more shrieking, cawing in the distance, then the sound of hundreds of wings. And a man's voice, scared, getting higher.

Emilia focused on the trees, blurry and getting farther and farther away. She had a strange sense of falling, of going under. How much time passed before she realized she was alone? Before all she heard was silence and her own breathing.

She imagined floating up to the treetops, so high no one could ever get her. The wind blew again and Emilia realized she had no clothes on. She was cold, but somehow numb, and her body felt heavy. She felt herself falling, sinking deeper, into herself.

Am I dying? *she wondered.*

She went further inside herself, until she couldn't hear anything anymore. She slipped into the red of her veins, and traveled in the river of her blood, and arrived in the soft glow of her belly and lodged herself there. Her ears were stuffed with silence. Her blood, and body tissue, and insides muffled all the noise outside. She slipped into darkness and peace. And she didn't know how long she stayed there before she heard the crows crying.

Emilia! Emilia!

She heard the wind howling and felt it blowing against her bare skin.

The wind lifted her and carried her upward, past the tree branches, all the way to the top. And then they closed up beneath her, hiding the ground below. Hiding whatever, or whomever, she left behind.

It was dark.

And now she was a black bird, perched on the highest branch. And her mind felt soft and oozing. And she was trying to understand how she could be both up here and down there at once.

It wasn't aliens, Emilia, *she told herself.* It was someone. Someone scary.

Her mind filled with the blurry image of that someone. Someone horrible and violent and dangerous.

Emilia Was Crying

Emilia was crying softly in her sleep; her head was buzzing, and from somewhere far away, someone called her name.

"Emilia?"

She wondered if her tongue was intact or split. She tried to move, but her body hurt. She knew it was covered in bruises.

"Emilia?" It was her brother's voice, in her ear.

But how had Tomás gotten in the hospital room? They wouldn't let him in. Ma wouldn't let him see her.

"Wake up, Emilia. It's a bad dream, that's all," he said. His voice was gentle but urgent in her ear. She heard a soft whimpering and suddenly realized it was her own. "Just a bad dream. Don't cry."

Emilia opened her eyes and saw Tomás's worried face. Hot tears came out of the corners of her eyes and a sob was stuck in her throat.

"Are you okay?" he asked.

She nodded, unable to speak, and took a deep breath before letting it out slowly. She stared at the ceiling as she tried to come back to reality. Her brother held her hand.

"It just . . . it felt so real," she finally managed.

It was, but this *was just a dream,* she told herself. *You're home. In your bed. It was so long ago.*

She wiped her face. Took a few more breaths.

Tomás had started coming into her room in the middle of the night and sleeping on her floor ever since the night Ma told her about Carl Smith.

In case you have a bad dream, he whispered one night when she woke to find him there and asked him why. She was secretly grateful.

"I'm okay," she told him before he could ask again. And they stayed like that for a long moment before a knock at the door startled them both.

Ma peeked her head in. "Merry Christmas," she whispered.

Downstairs, they sat around the tree, opening gifts. Each item made Emilia think of back when things were normal. Ma usually finished her Christmas shopping months before the holidays. These gifts came from that time, those moments, when things were as Emilia had always thought they were.

"Do you like it?" Ma asked about a sweater Emilia had just unwrapped.

"I love it."

Tomás opened a new pair of sneakers. Then a new book. Emilia wrapped a new scarf around her neck.

"Now your turn," Emilia said, handing Ma a small box. Ma

looked at it, her eyes glistening before she even opened it. The box was shiny and pretty, wrapped carefully with a bow.

Emilia had bought Ma earrings. They were the kind of dangly earrings Emilia vaguely remembered Ma wearing. She didn't know what made her buy them for her mother. Maybe because she knew Ma would like them, but would never get them for herself. She usually bought her mother two or three small gifts, but these had taken her whole budget. Still, she wanted Ma to have them. She wanted Ma to look like she was going to a fancy party instead of just prettying up the women who went to them.

"Emilia," Ma whispered, lifting one of them from the small box.

"I know they're a little flashy, but, I don't know. I thought they'd look so pretty on you. Do you like them?" she asked.

Ma's eyes filled with tears. "I *love* them," she said, putting them on immediately. They glimmered as they caught the lights from the Christmas tree, and Emilia thought they looked beautiful. The sight made her think of the classroom, of making that room sparkle somehow.

She wished she could go there again. Right now.

Then the doorbell rang, and Emilia and Tomás looked at each other as Ma opened the door. There stood their father, holding three presents and a white bakery box wrapped with red-and-white twine. He'd shaved his beard and looked so much like he used to that it took all of them a moment to recover.

"Come in," Ma said finally.

They all watched as he cleaned his feet on the welcome mat

and came inside. Emilia looked at Tomás and saw how he stared at their father with so many mixed emotions on his face. She wondered if her face carried the same look. Their mother looked at the floor as he came in.

Their father just inside now, not knowing what to do next, clutched those boxes. Emilia knew what the bakery box must hold inside. The favorite treats he would occasionally surprise them with so long ago. An éclair for Emilia. Pignoli cookies for Ma. And crispy chocolate cookies for Tomás.

"Merry Christmas," he said, standing there.

It was like having a stranger in their house, which, Emilia supposed, was exactly what this was.

But it wasn't.

Sam DeJesus cleared his throat, took in the wrapping paper on the floor. "I guess I'm a little late," he said. His words seemed to take on so many meanings, and they all shifted uncomfortably as each one realized it.

"I'll put these here," he said, putting the gifts under the tree. Emilia glanced at them. She took in her father's handwriting on the labels. What had he been thinking as he wrote their names on those gifts?

"Would you like some coffee?" Ma asked him. He cleared his throat again, nodded.

"Yes, thank you."

"Merry Christmas, Dad," Emilia said when she realized that neither she nor Tomás had said a word to him.

His eyes filled with tears, and when he was finally able to speak again, he said, "Merry Christmas, Emilia. Merry Christmas, Tomás."

Ma came back with the cup of coffee. Emilia noticed how his hands shook as he took it. She'd forgotten about his shaky hands, and she wondered how many other things she'd forgotten about her father, as he sat there clutching the cup.

As the hours wore on and they watched different parades and old holiday movies on television, some of the strangeness wore off. Ma cooked and their father sat in the living room, awkwardly. But he stayed. And when they ate, he joined them. It was mid-dinner when Emilia thought, *He must not have another family. Because he's here. With us.*

She looked over at him. He met her gaze, and she offered him a smile.

"Are you hanging out with Ian today?" Ma asked her. This attempt at normalcy felt bizarre and out of place.

"He's at his aunt's," Emilia said, just as Dad asked, "Who's Ian?"

Emilia moved the food around on her plate. "My boyfriend," she said quietly.

"Oh," Dad said.

The silence that kept finding them surrounded them again. Ma tried to fill it up. Tomás said nothing. Their father looked lost.

The bakery box contained exactly what Emilia had suspected. Emilia forced a bite of the éclair. Ma said thank you. Tomás went upstairs.

"Well, I . . . better go," Dad said finally. Nobody argued with him. But Emilia watched as he put his coat on and opened the front door. She saw how he quickly glanced at the unopened gifts under the tree.

"Bye, Dad," she said.

He locked eyes with her for a moment. "Bye, Emilia." Then he looked at the ground as he turned and headed out into the cold.

Tomás Was Jolted Awake

Tomás was jolted awake that night, and he immediately sat up and looked over at Emilia's empty bed partially lit from the moonlight coming in through her window.

It was snowing.

Tomás stared at the flurries, and for a bizarre moment, perhaps because he had been dreaming of her when she was little, he half expected to see his sister out there, perched on the tree outside her window with the birds she was always feeding.

"Emilia?" he whispered as he got up and checked the bathroom. She wasn't there. Tomás hurried downstairs.

"What are you doing?" he asked when he saw her standing in the kitchen, staring out the open back door, the snow coming down harder.

She didn't answer.

"Emilia?"

It was cold, and any minute the draft would find its way under his mother's bedroom door and she would come out and ask them what they were doing.

"Close the door," he whispered to Emilia. The cold traveled

up the leg of his pajama pants and sent a shiver running through his body. But Emilia didn't respond and instead continued looking out into their backyard.

The way she leaned her head against the frame and crossed her arms in front of her body made him sad. She seemed so lonely. As if she were locking away some part of herself, just like she used to right after the attack. In some ways, Tomás felt like he really did lose Emilia that day. His sister had never been quite the same again. Once in a while bits and pieces of who she used to be would come out in an unguarded laugh or sudden rush of excitement or happiness. That's when he saw his little sister, the one he used to call Mia because he couldn't pronounce her name when they were little. That was who had always, *always*, been at his side, laughing. Until she wasn't.

When had he stopped calling her Mia? After the attack? When she seemed so far away always?

"You remember the dog, Tomás?" Emilia suddenly said to him, still looking into their backyard through the open door.

"The dog?"

"The one that chased me." She turned and looked at him, but he couldn't make out her face in the darkness. "Don't you remember, in first grade? I went outside to get the paper for Dad and that dog chased me."

Tomás remembered. He remembered Emilia's face, and the way fear took over and contorted it as she ran toward him, her eyes pleading, *pleading for what? Her life?*

She'd thought she was going to die. She was waiting for that dog to tear into her, for its teeth to pierce her skin.

"I remember," he said.

She turned back to look out the door. "I've been thinking . . . maybe it was a warning," she told him.

He didn't know what to say.

"No," he answered, because he didn't know how else to respond. "It was just something that happened."

"Do you know I used to think aliens were going to get me?" She laughed. "I didn't know it was going to be some guy in the woods."

Something about the way she spoke, the way she stared outside at the snow, coming down harder still, scared Tomás.

He didn't want to think of how she'd looked that day when the dog almost ate her. That's what he had thought, that the dog was actually going to eat her. And yet he'd stood there motionless in the kitchen, near the refrigerator, as she came running. It just happened so fast. He didn't have time to think of what he should do. And the strange whines coming from her scared him. Not even screams, just strangled whines, and the look on her face, just before she reached the door, just before she swung it open and threw herself in. The screen door slammed behind her and that dog, foaming at the mouth, saliva dripping, baring its ugly teeth, rushed at her and slammed its snout against the screen.

But right before the door closed, in a split second, Tomás could see the dog's jaws opening wide. Wider and wider, and swallowing

Emilia whole into the dark abyss of its mouth. That's what Tomás saw and still, he hadn't done anything about it.

I didn't do anything, Tomás realized. He swallowed the bitter taste that rose into his mouth. *Why didn't I run to her? Why did I just stand there?*

Their mother had come running, shouting at the dog until it retreated, but it didn't run away. Not until Ma filled a pot with cold water and threw it on the dog did it cry and whimper and leave.

Don't worry, Ma had told a trembling Emilia, who was crouched on the floor. Tomás could still see them here, on this very floor, together. Ma holding and soothing Emilia. *I won't let anything get you,* she said.

The memory and the thoughts that rushed into Tomás's head took his breath away.

What must she have looked like that other *day?*

It hit him in that moment in a way that it never had before, the gravity of what Emilia had gone through. He didn't know why he never really let himself realize it before, but right now, in this darkness, his sister looking so . . . fragile, he understood.

And he felt sick.

He looked at Emilia, the back of her head, her long black hair as she stared out the door at the falling snow. He was afraid of her turning around. He was afraid he might see on her face the terror she felt that day.

"It's beautiful," she said.

"What is?"

"The snow. The cold. I guess it can be beautiful."

"You think so?" he asked.

She must have been so scared.

She turned and looked at him over her shoulder, not with that scared look he imagined, just as Emilia. His sister. "I do. I really do," she said before turning back to the door.

He looked out then, too, and he saw what she saw. It did seem an especially beautiful, odd snow; it glowed.

"I caught Ma watching the video of us today, that time she and Dad woke us in the middle of the night to play in the snow. Do you remember? They bundled us up and we ran outside. We were so little, Tomás. It was so . . . long ago."

A lump rose in his throat and he thought any minute now he would start crying, for her, for all of them, for who they used to be and what they had become.

What if things had been different? Would we be different, too?

He felt a tingling in his nose, but he wouldn't cry. Not now, not in front of Emilia, who had suffered so much more than him. Even though he felt as if he had just buried his family. Even though his knees felt weak.

"Oh god, Tomás! You know what would be so lovely?" she said suddenly, in a rush, flashing a smile full of genuine excitement.

"What?" he asked.

I'm so sorry, Mia.

"If cherry blossoms bloomed in winter! Can you imagine

that? All those beautiful flowers, against so much white! Can you see us back there, running around in the snow, with all those cherry blossoms around us?" She gestured with her hands, in a way to mimic the falling of snow, and Tomás saw the silhouette of her thin fingers. "It would be so beautiful, to have a little bit of spring."

He looked at her face. "Wait here," he said, and ran to the entry-way closet near the front door. He gathered their winter gear in a rush and returned to the kitchen moments later.

"Here, here. Put these on. Come on! There aren't any flowers, but it can still be beautiful, Mia," he whispered. "We can still be beautiful."

Emilia turned quickly at his words and stared at him. "Life is beautiful, Tomás," she said.

He threw a coat and a pair of boots in her direction, a spare pair of gloves and a hat. She hurried to put on her gear, quietly laughing in a way that forced Tomás to blink back tears. Neither of them zipped up their jackets, just like when they were kids, and they rushed out the door into that biting cold snow, and started running.

The world was so silent, wonderfully silent, and it felt like only they filled it up. Emilia's soft laughter, the crunch of their boots, the sound of their own breathing, Tomás's voice as he urged on Emilia, telling her to run as he formed a snowball and threw it at her, the loose snow exploding in a soft spray of white, like a gentle, powdery firework.

She laughed and they ran. She stopped and he continued showering her with snow until she fell and made a snow angel. And Tomás quietly tucked this night into his memory, every moment, every detail, so he could recall it one day when he was scared or sad.

★　★　★

Nina watched Emilia and Tomás from the kitchen window.

It was two o'clock in the morning.

As she watched them run, she wished there was a way to wrap them back into her womb, protect them forever.

But Emilia wasn't even supposed to be born.

The thought she tried so hard to keep away drifted into her mind like a cold draft.

You were selfish, she told herself.

It was because of Nina's insistence that Emilia was even brought into this world. It was because she wanted *more than one child, Sam. I always imagined at least two. We have our little boy; maybe we'll have a little girl!*

She'd wanted a sibling for Tomás. She'd wanted to feel a life inside her body again.

But her body refused. Her body told her she was only meant for one child.

Be happy, her body told her. But she insisted. *No!*

And they wiped out their bank account on tests and in vitro fertilization, and finally a surrogate.

Only later did Nina think about it. Maybe Emilia hadn't wanted to be born. Maybe, like those calcified babies she'd read about, the ones who embedded themselves in their mother's body forever until they became little mummified stones, Emilia had sensed how cold and cruel the world could be and didn't want to be born into it. But her mother, her unstoppable mother, *insisted*, *insisted* she be born.

So Emilia came from the body of another woman, and every now and then, Nina caught a glimpse of something in her daughter's face that made her think Emilia was not for this world. That made her worry even before the attack, that she had asked for too much, that she had taken something that wasn't hers, and that the universe would take Emilia back. Nina worried; even before anything bad happened, she worried.

That was why her body shook the day they couldn't find Emilia, why the life drained from her. Because she knew.

Didn't you always know?

Nina pushed her thoughts away and watched her children.

When they started heading back to the house, she toyed with the idea of making them hot chocolate. But she couldn't even bring herself to turn on the light. She was afraid the switch, the fluorescent white, or the beep of the microwave, would completely break the spell that was already wearing thin. And so she quickly made her way back to her bedroom, left the door slightly ajar as they crept back in, muffling their laughter and trying to be quiet.

She heard their boots plop onto the floor and she knew there would be puddles to clean in the morning. She listened to the stairs creak under the weight of their bodies as they tiptoed back upstairs to their rooms, the opening and closing of their drawers and the creaks of the floorboards above her own room as they settled back into their beds.

And then silence.

She opened the door and looked down the hall, into the kitchen, feeling like she'd just seen and heard them for the last time. Like they were ghosts.

Nina stepped into the kitchen, resisted going upstairs to look at them safe in their beds. She looked at the melted snow from their boots that had gathered in a puddle on the kitchen floor, just as she knew it would. She left it there and looked at the snow falling harder, covering the ground outside.

She kept telling herself to go back to bed, but she couldn't. She stayed looking at the backyard, picturing Emilia and Tomás running around out there still. In that thick silence, she heard the echoes of their laughter and laughed softly with them, even as the snow kept falling and hid all evidence of their play from just moments ago.

And then, so suddenly, Nina saw a blanket of now fresh, undisturbed snow.

And she began to cry.

★ ★ ★

Upstairs in his room, Tomás breathed normally again after the running and cold. Emilia had told him, in the kindest way she could, that he didn't need to sleep on her bedroom floor.

"I'm sure I won't have bad dreams tonight," she told him, a smile on her face and her cheeks still flushed from running around outside. She looked happy. "And I can be okay, Tomás," she said.

"I know you can," he said. Still, he waited a moment longer in case she changed her mind. But finally, he simply said good night because he didn't want to ruin the moment. The idea of her having another nightmare made him anxious. He should be right there, to wake her from whatever horrible images crowded her head at night. But he didn't want her to think he didn't believe her.

He wanted to believe her.

So he went to his room, listened for any possible noise coming from Emilia's, before he finally closed his eyes and drifted into an uneasy sleep that intertwined tonight with that overwhelming worry he'd been carrying lately.

In Tomás's mind, he saw the two of them in all that brilliant snow. He saw them lying down, making snow angels, and he saw, suddenly, cherry blossoms fall on them in all that velvety white. And he was laughing. He looked at Emilia and saw her laughing, too, opening her mouth. The blossoms fell from the sky like snow and landed in her mouth, turning it pink, then red.

She reached out to the sky and Tomás saw her fingers again. He worried because they seemed so breakable and fragile and delicate. And he wondered how breakable his sister was.

Tomás looked over and saw Emilia eating the flowers. Her lips turned purple. Then blue. And Tomás panicked as he realized she was choking—she couldn't breathe.

But he didn't do anything. He just watched, even though something inside him screamed, *Help her, help her!*

He just watched, until she was buried and only a mound of flowers. When he finally felt he could move, he scrambled to her, reached to dig her out. But she was no longer there.

The Morning After Christmas

The morning after Christmas, when Ma and Tomás were both at work, Emilia sat in the classroom with her father's journal. She read the poem she'd read so many times after he left.

Al Frio

Me desperté con frio,
preocupado que la muerte había llegado por mi
y me chupo la vida,
lambió mis huesos,
devoró mis intestinos,
dejando nada.
Esto es lo que puede hacer el frio.
Y pensé,
al frio me iria,
al frio me iria,
si nunca quisiera sentir otra vez.

She had translated it into English using a Spanish-English

dictionary she'd found in her father's office, so she could understand it a bit better.

To the Cold

I woke up cold,
worried death had come for me
and sucked my life,
licked my bones,
devoured my intestines,
leaving nothing.
This is what the cold can do.
And I thought,
to the cold I would go,
to the cold I would go,
if I never wanted to feel again.

When she was younger, Emilia thought Alaska was the coldest place in the world. It was always Alaska she thought of when she pictured her father going to the cold. And she was fascinated by the books in the library about Alaska, with pictures of so much snow and, sometimes, a person among all that white bundled in so many layers. She tried to look past the goggles, the fur-lined hats and bulky coats, wondering if that was him, her father, in those pictures. So close she could touch him.

Emilia sighed. It had never been him.

She got up and wrote the poem on one of the walls. She wasn't too much of an artist, but it didn't matter. Not here. Everything could look beautiful in this room somehow. So she drew a man on the wall, his back to the viewer, and snowcapped mountains in the distance. In the mountains, she wrote her father's words.

Around the room, Emilia used chalk, paint, and markers to add more images, anything that came to mind. Clouds and birds. Cherry trees full of blossoms. She wrote more lines of poetry, from her father's journal and his poetry books. She loved how full the walls were getting, but they still seemed to be missing something. She looked at the glittery paint.

I'll paint them, and make them sparkle somehow!

Emilia didn't realize how much she loved this room, what she was turning it into, until she wasn't able to get away from her house yesterday. Now she sat among all the cut-up books and paper, feeling better and energized.

She rushed to her backpack and took out some pictures of her family and Ian. She'd gone through old school pictures and found one of her third-grade class. She cut herself and Ian out and laughed at how little they were. She would figure out the perfect thing to do with this.

Then she took out the Christmas gift her father had given her. She had unwrapped it alone last night and now she stared at the silver ribbon she'd put back on so carefully. She slipped it off the plain white gift box and opened the lid. Inside was a turquoise music box, adorned with delicate gold leaves around a border framing a picture of a tree. In gold lettering, it read, LIFE IS BEAUTIFUL. Emilia opened the box, and a sweet but melancholy tune played.

Her eyes filled with tears.

Last night, before Tomás had caught her watching the snow falling from the back door, Emilia had snuck downstairs to the living room to open this gift. And she'd sat by herself, next to the Christmas tree, and cried quietly as it filled her with bittersweetness. How much time had her father spent looking for this? Had he picked it up thoughtlessly because it was pretty, or gone on the recommendation of a salesperson? Or maybe—what she liked to think—he saw it and immediately knew she would love it.

Emilia stared at herself in the small oval mirror inside the music box. Was it possible her father still knew her, somehow, even after all this time? Even if she felt more and more like she didn't know herself?

Emilia took a deep breath and slowly closed the lid.

When she left the school a little while later, her head was filled with that music and that room. But the farther she walked, the more reality set in and thoughts of Carl Smith slipped into her mind. By the time she got home, it was all she could think about. Her mind flashed with the image of a body wasting away in its deathbed, too decrepit to be hauled off to prison. But what Emilia wanted was to see *his face*, to see that he wasn't Jeremy Lance.

Emilia sat on her bed, alone in her house, and looked at her crows pecking at the peanuts on her window ledge. She closed her eyes, trying to think of that classroom, but instead her mind clouded with the image of a gray-and-white sky, of tree branches. She felt the cold on her skin. Emilia felt herself drifting back to the past, swayed with the sense of falling.

Look at his face.

But her eyes snapped open and her body jerked as she came reeling back to reality. It was the same at night when she tried to fall asleep. She didn't want to go back to that day and relive it. She didn't want to fall. But she wanted to see his face.

Not now, she told herself. *Just not now.*

Emilia took a breath and looked around her bedroom; she was here, not the cold playground. She was sixteen, not eight. And she had to decide what she'd wear tonight on her date with Ian and Anthony and Jane.

She went to her closet, and a sense of déjà vu overcame her. She brought out a shirt and held it against her body, studied herself in the mirror.

Emilia looked at herself, that girl in the mirror who all this was happening to. That girl who had been attacked years ago. She looked tired.

Who are you? she wondered. *I don't know you.*

The girl she saw looked sad, desperate. Emilia didn't like the look in her eyes.

I don't want to be you, Emilia told her. But her image stayed the same.

Emilia reached into the top drawer of her dresser.

I can be someone new. Someone different. Not you.

Emilia retrieved a pair of dull scissors she kept in the junk drawer of her desk. She returned to the mirror, held them to a long strand of her hair, and began cutting. She watched that girl she'd been staring at fall away with each grating, thick snip until someone new appeared. Emilia smiled at who she saw.

There, Emilia thought as she finished. *There I am.*

She studied herself, but the longer she stared, the more she noticed the girl, her old self, reemerging. Only now she looked sadder. With hair that looked torn, and shredded.

Emilia stared in horror.

It had felt like time was standing still, and now it was rushing toward her, thrusting her back into the present and reality. What had she done? Ma would flip out.

Everyone will think—no, they will know—*something is wrong with you!*

Emilia threw the scissors in the drawer, like they were burning her skin.

What did you do? What did you do?

Fix it! Fix it! an urgent voice inside her cried. But she didn't have money to go get it fixed. She ran to Tomás's room, to the top drawer, where she knew he kept the money from each paycheck he cashed.

Go, before Ma gets home. Emilia grabbed her hat. *Hurry, Emilia. Hurry.*

Emilia ran out of her house and down to the local hairdresser. The chain beauty salon was somewhere Emilia had never gone since Ma had friends who were professional hairstylists and cut her and Emilia's hair for cheap. They were far more experienced than the stylists at the salon.

All those stylists are recent beauty school graduates, Emilia. And your hair is too beautiful to let them get their hands on it.

Ma's words echoed in Emilia's ears as she opened the door and the smell of styling products and burnt hair hit her.

A man stood next to the receptionist, laughing at something she'd said. They both looked up when Emilia came inside.

"Hello," said the girl. "What can we do for you?"

Emilia stood there for a moment, both of them staring at her, before she finally got the words out. "A haircut."

"That would be with me," the man said. He gestured for Emilia to follow him to his station, where she sat down and he pumped up the chair. "Let's see what we have here," he said as he went to take off her hat.

Emilia reached up, held on tight to the hat. The hairstylist stared at her in the mirror. Emilia, to her surprise and horror, began to cry.

"Oh dear," he said, his tone softening. "It's okay."

Emilia shook her head. It wasn't okay. It was terrible.

"I'll fix it, I promise," he said. "Let's take a look, okay?"

Emilia took a deep breath, watched in the mirror as he gently, slowly took off her hat.

He studied her hair, ran his fingers through it. "Oh, it's not that bad," he said. "I see this a lot. You're not the only one who's tried to cut her own hair," he told her image in the mirror. "Let me get some books, some pictures of what we can do, okay?"

Emilia nodded and watched him walk away. She hoped he wasn't telling the receptionist, rolling his eyes at Emilia's stupidity. She shifted in her seat and he returned in a few moments with several hairstyle books. Emilia studied his face to see if he'd been laughing, but his kind look erased her suspicions.

"We could do this," he said, pointing to a cute, short cut. "It really would look amazing with your bone structure."

Bone structure.

Emilia looked at her face, imagined all the tiny bones underneath her skin. She nodded. She didn't care what he did, as long as she didn't look the way she did now. So tragic.

"It's a little short, but I think it would look really cool." He smiled and she took a deep breath.

"Yes," she said finally.

He gave a quick nod, draped a black cape around her shoulders, and got to work. She closed her eyes, each snip of the scissors echoing in her ears as she thought of herself in her room. What had she been thinking? Her hair was still on the floor.

"You know what else might be fun?" the stylist said. "A few streaks of color. Would you like that? I'm bored as hell. We were swamped with everyone who needed their hair done before the holidays, but now not so much. Besides, looks like you could use a little cheering up." He smiled and winked. "No charge."

Her chest swelled with emotion. She nodded.

"What color? I could do something really punkish. Something that says, *look at me!*"

Emilia didn't want anything that said *look at me*, but she did want something. She thought for a moment. "Blue?"

He continued to cut. "Blue . . . yeah, that would work. It won't be super obvious with your dark hair, but when light catches those strands, at just the right angle, it'll look perfect."

His excitement was contagious as he worked. He started applying the bleaching agent and Emilia concentrated on how he separated portions of her short hair and foiled them. When he put her under the hot dryer, she closed her eyes and relaxed under the warmth of it.

The hot air blew around her, and with the soothing hum of it in her ears, Emilia felt she could never be cold here. But too soon, the hairstylist was back to wash out the bleach and add the blue hair color. Emilia smiled when that was finished and she went back under the dryer.

Twenty minutes later, back at his station, he styled. Emilia kept her eyes closed for as long as she could while he applied various products, tugging and twisting pieces so they lay perfectly imperfect.

When he was finally done and told her to open her eyes, she

did. And how changed she looked. Her eyes seemed larger, wider. Her face more delicate. But fiercer somehow, too. Emilia touched the soft, sleek, glossy strands and stared at herself. She turned her head and saw the shimmering iridescent blue as it caught the light. Her hair looked like feathers.

"What do you think?" the stylist said, meeting her gaze in the mirror.

She loved it. She loved him, this stranger who had fixed it.

"It's perfect!" she told him.

"Emilia?" Her mother's voice reached out to meet her even before Emilia stepped inside the house. Then she saw her daughter.

Ma covered her mouth as if quieting a scream that might come out at any moment, and Tomás, who sat just behind where Ma stood, stared at Emilia also. They both looked frozen, eyes wide with strange looks on their faces.

"What have you done?" Ma whispered from behind her hand.

Emilia immediately reached up for the short strands. She'd been so happy about it moments ago, had felt so fierce and amazing and giddy the whole walk home. But now she suddenly felt self-conscious under their gazes, and she pulled at the short strands as if it would make her hair grow. "I . . . I cut it," she said.

"I can see that," her mother said, but her green eyes shone as they filled with tears.

"It's no big deal. I wanted to do something different for my date tonight with Ian and his cousin," Emilia said, tugging at the short strands. She looked at her brother for some kind of support.

Tell her it's no big deal. It's not. Right?

But Tomás just sat there, looking almost as shocked as her mother.

"It's just a haircut," Emilia mumbled into the silence. "God, Ma. You're acting like I just killed someone."

Her mother stood there. "How can you say that? Don't say that." She continued looking at Emilia as if a ghost had walked into the house. Then she cleared her throat. "Why did you cut it?"

Emilia shrugged. She'd felt perfect when she left the hair salon. Why did Ma have to ruin it with this question? What kind of question was it? Why does anyone do anything? It was impulse. It was wanting to see someone else when she looked at herself. It was wanting to *be* someone else and trying to rid herself of something or someone she didn't want to be.

And it's because you fucked up your hair, a small voice reminded her. But Emilia silenced that voice and decided it didn't matter. Everything was fine now.

"I told you." She looked from Ma to Tomás.

Her mother shook her head. "No," she said. "That's not it. Tell me the truth, Emilia. Why?"

Emilia could hear the no-nonsense therapist tone Ma used after the attack when she was trying to get Emilia to talk again; it had crept back into her mother's voice.

"I told you. I wanted to try something new for tonight."

Tomás cleared his throat. "I think it looks good," he said finally. "I've seen a lot of girls with this kind of cut."

A lot of girls. Yes! She was just like a lot of girls.

No different, Ma.

Her mother looked at both of them, disbelieving. Tears slid down her face and Emilia knew what she must be thinking.

Can't you just be okay, Emilia? Can't you just be okay?

The words echoed in Emilia's head from the past, when her mother had had to pick her up from school once she finally went back. She hadn't been able to speak the words to make her mother understand then, either, what it was like to walk those halls, to go back to school after being home for years, surrounded by kids who'd made up their own truths about Emilia. They all thought they knew everything about her. She felt naked when she walked those halls, exposed for all to see. Sometimes, she even imagined that she had huge, gaping wounds, revealing her insides, her thumping heart, her pulsing veins. They looked at her as if that's what they saw. And when she heard someone laughing, she couldn't help but think they were laughing at her.

There's the freak who Jeremy Lance attacked. Do you think he raped her? Do you think he even can? Oh my gosh, I'd die . . .

And then she would remember the playground. The teachers would send Emilia to the nurse's office then, because suddenly, she would get lost in those memories, in the woods of the playground, and she couldn't find her way back.

Have you seen her pull the zombie act in class? She completely zones out. I've taken her to the nurse's office. She doesn't say a thing, just starts shivering like a weirdo.

Sometimes, even the nurse's voice couldn't reach her. Emilia would feel that woman gently pull her onto the paper-covered cot, the crinkling sound hardly making sense as she saw a sky full of birds.

We'll call your mother, okay? she'd hear from somewhere far away. Emilia would try to focus on the woman's face, one moment seeing the kindness there, the next minute seeing the outline of a beak, a glossy round head, small dark eyes.

We'll call your mother.

One by one, she'd watch more birds fly over her. Some of them coming down to perch next to her, their wings fluttering, shuffling in her ears, as they landed and took off again.

The nurse would lay a blanket on her because of the way she shivered. And Emilia would wonder at how it came floating down from the sky. How could she exist in two places at once? How could she be in the nurse's office and out in the woods by the playground at the same time? Maybe she was a time traveler, a ghost, who floated back and forth between worlds.

Mrs. DeJesus, Emilia is not feeling well again.

Over and over this happened. How many times had Emilia drifted back and forth, feeling the ground beneath her, the nurse's hand on her forehead, the sky above, the sound of her mother's voice, the crows crying.

And her mother would suddenly be there, slipping her hand into Emilia's and saying, *I'm here now. Let's go.*

But then there was that time when her mother got angry. When she pulled Emilia into the car a little harder. After speeding away from the school, Ma pulled over to the side of the road, brought the car to a jerking stop, and Emilia almost slid off the back seat, where she was lying down. Emilia could hear the slap of Ma's hand as she hit the steering wheel over and over again, as she cried and asked, in a whisper, *Why can't you just be okay? Can't you just be okay?*

She didn't say these things to Emilia. It was almost as if Ma had forgotten Emilia was even there as she said them to the wind blowing outside, carrying her words off to a world that wouldn't listen and didn't care.

But Emilia heard her. And she wondered why she wasn't okay and if she ever would be. Her mother sounded so tired. Emilia hated being the reason Ma was so tired. Emilia opened her eyes, saw her mother resting her head on the steering wheel, holding on to it, knuckles white.

Emilia ran her hand up the back of her hair, playing with the fuzziness of her short new cut. She forced a smile. "I'm okay, Ma," she said as she stood in the living room feeling like that small child, like a tiny plucked chicken. "Look, look, it's blue. Can you see? Doesn't it look cool? Tomás, look! I did it for fun. For tonight. I thought it would look cool. I just wanted something . . . different."

"I thought you wanted everything to stay the same," Ma said.

Ma searched Emilia's face for the truth, but Emilia disguised it as much as she could. Why couldn't Ma just trust her? Why couldn't she believe her instead of always looking for signs of weakness? Emilia felt the sting of oncoming tears but refused to look away.

"Don't make it into something it's not, Ma," Emilia said. "Please." She stared at her mother.

Prove you are stronger than she thinks, Emilia thought.

Finally, Ma nodded, wiped her eyes. "You have a date?" she asked. "Are you sure you're . . . you want to go out?"

Emilia nodded. "Yeah, Ma. I want to go out. What am I going to do? Sit around here all the time, not live my life?"

Ma took a deep breath. Emilia saw how her mother shook her head. "It's just that, I'm just worried about you. You have to . . ."

You have to talk! You have to say something, Emilia! Her mother's words from the past came to her now.

Emilia felt like she was in the back seat of the car, felt the steady hum of the drive when Ma finally pulled away again, the sound of the turn signal and the dizzying sway of turning this way and that as they headed home.

Emilia sensed the floor moving, rocking her ever so slightly off balance. But she smiled. "I'm okay, Ma. It'll be good for me to hang out with friends and just be normal."

Life is beautiful. I can be okay.

Oh, how she needed this to be true.

Her mother nodded, even though she looked doubtful.

"I'm going to change out of these clothes. I've got all these little pieces of hair pricking me." Emilia laughed a little. "Stop worrying about me," she called down as she went up the stairs.

When she got to her bedroom, she sucked in her breath and quickly picked up the strands of hair she'd left there only hours earlier. She shoved them into her top drawer and turned to look at herself in the mirror again.

Be okay, she told herself. She smiled at the new person she saw there. Just a normal girl, getting ready for a date.

★　★　★

Tomás sat in the living room and Ma turned to him as if for some kind of reassurance. He felt torn. He wanted to be on Emilia's side, he wanted to reassure his mother. But his sister, with her hair like that, *looked just like a bird, her eyes larger, her head small and glossy.*

And it scared him.

Ma stared at Tomás and he could almost read her mind.

Is she okay?

What's happening?

How much time do I give her? How much space?

Should I lock her up in this house, never let her out of my sight?

What do we do? What do we do?

"Don't worry, Ma," Tomás said with more conviction than he felt. He remembered those first few months, the way his mother pushed for Emilia to speak. The way Emilia looked out with vacant eyes and seemed to get farther away from them. And how he would whisper to her when their mother wasn't looking, *It's okay. You don't have to say anything until you feel like it.* And he'd squeeze her hand and she'd squeeze it back.

"If you push, you know she'll—"

His mother looked at him. "If I push, she'll come around."

Tomás stared at his mother. She shook her head. "Okay, okay," she said.

Maybe Emilia just wanted to see someone different when she looked in the mirror. If anyone could understand that, it was Tomás.

That's all, he thought. Because the only other explanation was that Emilia wanted to look like a bird. That she was transforming into one right before their very eyes. That at night, he might wake up to her cawing, crying out into the cold air.

Tomás looked out the window.

What do we do? What do we do?

I Can't Get over It

"I can't get over it! You look so different," Jane said as she looked at Emilia again. They were in the video store since Jane thought renting movies and getting pizza would be the perfect date night.

Emilia shrugged and played with her hair again as they continued looking at the rows of movies.

"Anthony will probably pick some wartime thing," Jane whispered into Emilia's ear as they walked the aisles. "He pretends it's the action part he really likes, but he's actually a sap. I think the part where the soldier comes home to his girl is always what gets him."

Emilia looked over at Anthony, and she knew Jane was right. Anthony had a surprisingly soft heart.

Jane held her finger to her lips. "Don't tell him I told you that."

"I won't," Emilia said, finding herself, somehow, enjoying this moment.

Like two girlfriends, she thought. *Just two ordinary girls out with their boyfriends.*

The most normal thing in the world. She smiled at Jane and

felt special somehow, knowing Jane wanted to be friends. She wondered if Jane was as lonely as Emilia was. For a moment, she pictured herself leaning over, whispering the truth into Jane's ear.

"So what about you, sweet Emilia?" Jane said, picking up another movie and reading the back summary. "What kinds of movies do you like?"

"I don't know. Not action, I guess."

Still, Emilia couldn't decide whether to like Jane or not. Just when Emilia found her laugh too loud and a little fake, Jane would say something sincere. And just when she thought Jane was cool, Jane said or did something to make Emilia wonder again. Like the way she smiled at Ian. Did she even know she did that? Or got so close to Emilia when she talked.

Jane shook her head. "I hate action, too. Okay, let me guess. Do you like foreign films, with subtitles?"

Emilia shrugged. "I've never watched a foreign film."

"You haven't? They're pretty great. My mom used to take me to these film festivals back when I wasn't a *stripper* . . ." Jane silently mouthed the word *stripper* and rolled her eyes. "I've brought such shame to her. Anyway, it was fun, you know. Going to theaters, listening to strange languages. Well, actually, I knew some of it because my mom hired a French nanny who spoke to me in French when I was growing up. She thought Spanish was too common. Isn't that so obnoxious? I mean, I'd probably get more use out of Spanish, but"—Jane shrugged—"*c'est la vie. Vous ne recevez pas de choisir, ma douce Emilia.* Or something like that."

Jane laughed at herself and Emilia looked at her as Jane grabbed a movie. "Where'd you say you went to school?"

"Oh." Jane rolled her eyes. "Pendulum Prep." She said it like she couldn't stand the words in her mouth. "Entitled bunch of snobs."

"Wow," Emilia said.

"You've heard of it?"

Emilia nodded. Of course she'd heard of it.

"Oh, this one," Jane said. "You have to watch this one. We'll get another one, too. What about a comedy? Do you like comedies?"

"Sure," Emilia answered.

"Romance?"

"Yeah, romance, too."

Jane nodded. "I know. I just love sweet stories. I mean, see, that's what my mom doesn't understand. Why does everything have to be so . . . highbrow. I like cheesy romance movies. I like renting movies and doing ordinary things. I like my guy in the service, waiting to come home to me."

Emilia looked at Jane and wondered at the way Jane saw the world. The way she saw Emilia.

"Don't tell anyone, but . . ." Jane came closer to Emilia's ear and whispered, "I think he's the one." Jane looked over at Anthony. "We've actually talked about it. Did you know a lot of guys get married young in the army? And their wives get to go along with them wherever they're stationed and it's like a little wives' club. They all live near one another and have little parties and game

242

nights. Don't you just think that's so cute?" Jane smiles. "I think it's absolutely perfect."

Emilia couldn't imagine anyone she knew actually getting married, even Jane and Anthony, who were slightly older. Anthony was nineteen and Jane, Emilia assumed, was about the same age. But Jane looked . . . hopeful. And Emilia didn't want to crush her hopes, so she nodded.

"Sure, I can see you doing that," Emilia said. And a part of her, for a moment, actually saw Jane and Anthony like that; she wished the best for them.

"Yeah," Jane said, "I mean, I know it seems fast and all. But we haven't exactly taken it slow. I slept with him the very first night I met him." Jane looked at Emilia. "You probably think I'm déclassé, right? Low-class."

"I don't think that," Emilia answered, resenting both Jane's vocabulary lesson and the idea that Emilia was some naive little kid who would judge someone on their decisions about sex.

Jane studied Emilia's face and nodded, seemingly satisfied with whatever she saw there, and continued. "It's not like I go around doing that or anything," she said. "I just . . . knew. I knew he was different."

Emilia nodded. "You guys are sweet."

"Really? You think so?"

"Really."

Jane nodded in the direction of Ian and Anthony. "Good guys must run in the family, then, right?"

"Yeah," Emilia said. "Must."

Ian and Anthony were laughing over something. Ian saw Emilia looking his way and their eyes locked; in that moment it felt like they were by themselves. She held his gaze as long as possible, and let herself think for a moment of the two of them, *married*.

"You guys have something real, too," Jane said.

Emilia nodded and picked a movie off the shelf. She tried to imagine Ian at the end of a church aisle, waiting for her. The two of them in a little apartment. Late night with friends they'd just made. Emilia smiled. Was it possible? It would actually be sweet. But somehow, it seemed so unrealistic to her.

Emilia looked over at Jane, who had pulled a lollipop out of her coat pocket and unwrapped it, and was now twirling and sucking on it. For her, whatever she wanted was already a reality. It was only a matter of time.

She wondered about the differences between her and Jane. Jane, who'd had the chance to go to fancy schools and spoke French, who had probably been abroad for a year like most Pendulum Prep students. Who had . . . so much. But chose to dance in some strip bar on the other side of town. Jane, who, if she put on the right clothes, which Emilia had no doubt hung in the far corner of her closet, could easily pal around with her former friends, who were probably at prestigious colleges. But instead she was here. With Emilia. Telling her all about where she was really from, but how she chose to be here instead.

Jane picked up a movie and read the description. "Anyway,

enough about me," she said as she lowered her voice and inched closer to Emilia. "Tell me about you and Ian . . . Have you two, you know . . . ?" Jane smiled slyly and sucked on her lollipop.

Emilia knew what she meant.

"Ummmm, well . . . no . . ." She'd never talked to anybody about her and Ian. The few girlfriends she'd had in elementary school scattered after that day in third grade. And when she came back to middle school, they'd only ever felt like acquaintances. They were okay, but they never felt like friends ever again and she knew she didn't really belong with them.

But now Jane was asking. And she was open and direct and experienced. And she seemed like she really did want to be Emilia's friend. So, maybe, *maybe she isn't that bad. And maybe it wouldn't be such a bad idea to talk to her about it.*

"Are you scared?" Jane asked, her face full of understanding as they kept walking down the aisle.

Emilia shrugged. "No, not exactly . . ."

Did she really want to explain this to Jane?

Maybe she could talk to Jane, but she couldn't tell her about anything without explaining the past. And she didn't want to talk about that.

"Don't be scared," Jane said gently. "How far have you two gone?"

Emilia shrugged and looked away without answering.

"Okay, I'm guessing you haven't done much. But obviously he loves you and you love him, and there's nothing wrong with showing that. And sure, sex is a little scary the first time, but you can do other things if you're not ready." Jane looked at her lollipop. "Like this," she said, laughing and her eyes widening.

Emilia laughed, too. Soon, they were cracking up, even though Emilia still didn't know what to make of Jane. Could they ever be friends? A few other people looked over at them, and Emilia looked down. But Jane didn't care. It was as if she could pretend everyone else wasn't there. As if she were above them somehow. She didn't care if anyone looked over at her, because they would never say anything to her. It was as if they recognized in her something, or someone who could do whatever she pleased. Something they prized. Nobody would ever harm *her*.

That was unfair. Emilia knew it was. But she couldn't help feeling this way. Because somewhere, deep in her gut, she knew it was true.

"What are you girls laughing at?" Anthony said, coming up behind them.

"Oh, nothing, I was just telling Emilia how delightful lollipops can be," Jane said. She met Ian's eyes and laughed. Emilia noticed how he looked away.

"Let's go, then," Anthony said.

They stopped by the supermarket, picked up junk food, and drove back to Anthony's.

Jane immediately put one of the frozen pizzas in the oven and made microwave popcorn while they argued about which of the three movies they should watch first.

"A fucking foreign film?" Anthony said when it was the first one Jane wanted to watch.

"I got it for Emilia," she said, and started the movie anyway. Jane curled up on the couch next to Emilia, the popcorn between them.

Anthony announced he was going outside for a smoke, and Ian followed.

From the window, Emilia could see Anthony and Ian talking. She watched as Anthony offered Ian one and was surprised to see Ian accept it and smoke it easily. It wasn't a big deal, but it made her wonder who Ian was when she wasn't around. Right now, from here, he seemed different somehow, and yet, the same. The Ian she'd always known, but not. He and Anthony looked like army buddies, laughing and talking, smoke coming out of their mouths from the cigarettes and the cold.

"Hey, come here," Jane said suddenly, clutching Emilia's hand and leading her to the kitchen. She unzipped her purse. "Lemme see something." She retrieved a tube of lipstick and applied it to Emilia's lips. It felt strange to have someone so close to her, and Emilia resisted the urge to keep pulling away. When she was done, Jane admired her work.

"You're a fucking stunner, you know that?" she told Emilia. "Look." She took out a compact and opened it.

Emilia looked at herself, at the same purple color on her lips that Jane wore, and couldn't decide if she loved it or felt stupid.

"It's cool. But . . . ," she told Jane.

Jane shook her head. "Yes, that's it. It's cool. Period. Jesus, Emilia. Don't be one of those girls who don't know that the guys fall all over themselves because you're beautiful and you don't even realize how amazing you are. Don't be afraid."

Jane was wrong. Emilia could tell when a guy looked at her, when he stared at her body. She could feel it a mile away.

"You shouldn't be shy about your beauty or your body, Emilia. There's nothing to be afraid of. The trick is to be in control. It's *your* fucking body. Nobody owns you. Nobody should have that kind of power over you. Unless you let them."

Emilia understood what Jane was saying. But it bothered her that Jane thought everyone had the luxury of thinking that way. *I* should *be allowed to be carefree,* Emilia thought. *I* should *be allowed to make out with my boyfriend without thinking of the past.*

I should be allowed to be like you, Jane. But I'm not. And I can't. So fuck you, Jane.

All Emilia said was, "You're right," without going into it as she looked out at Ian. He threw his cigarette on the ground.

Jane stood next to her and looked out, too. "You really love him, don't you?"

"A lot," Emilia said, without a moment's hesitation, but wondering why it even mattered to Jane.

"Then don't make the poor guy explode. He loves you."

The door opened and the guys came in, the cold and smell of cigarettes surrounding them like a cloud. Anthony pulled Jane to the couch and told Ian to put on the second movie instead. After

Ian did so, he settled next to Emilia on the small love seat, where she leaned up against him. He put his arm around her.

As the movie went on, Emilia could see the way Anthony's hand explored and caressed Jane under the blanket that covered them, like a mouse running up and down the length of her body. Emilia tried to pay attention to the movie, but couldn't help keeping track of the mouse's movements.

After a while, Jane whispered something to Anthony and went upstairs. Minutes later, Anthony followed.

The movie was slow, but Ian and Emilia kept watching it, even though her mind was wandering to what Jane and Anthony were doing up there.

Like this.

An image of Jane twirling that red lollipop flashed through Emilia's mind.

She swept the image aside as Ian began kissing her neck. She kissed him back, trying to push away the sick feeling in her stomach from the smell of cigarettes on his breath.

You really love him, don't you? Jane's question echoed in Emilia's ears.

She wished he hadn't had that cigarette. She thought she heard a bump coming from upstairs, but she tried to ignore it and bring herself back to the moment with Ian.

Don't make the poor guy explode.

Jane's voice whispered in her mind. Images of a space shuttle exploding in the sky filled it, jolting Emilia out of the moment. Her body reacted, and Ian immediately stopped.

"What's the matter?"

Why had Jane used those words, those *exact* words? Something in her mind clicked. She stared at Ian.

Explode.

"Have you been talking to Jane about us?"

"What?" Ian looked at Emilia, confused, but then she noticed the stalling as the inner workings of his mind tried to come up with some lie. "I don't know what you're talking about."

Emilia pulled herself up, forcing him back. She felt sick. Would he do that? Was he so desperate that he would put Jane up to this?

"What don't you understand? I'm just asking if you've talked to her about us."

She searched for the truth in his eyes, the one she already knew in her heart.

"Oh god . . . *you did.* You talked to her about us. You told her about me?"

"No, no . . . I didn't." He struggled for a moment, but then she *saw* the resignation. His shoulders slumped; his whole body gave up the lie. He let out a deep breath.

He could still not admit it, she thought. *In this moment, it's still not true.*

She almost wished for the lie. She waited for the next word out of his mouth, and then it came, the crushing "Yes" she already knew was coming.

"I'm sorry."

Emilia closed her eyes. The smell of the cigarette on Ian's breath that she could still taste, the smell of the house, perfume and leather and popcorn—it all made her sick.

"Oh god . . . ," Emilia said, realizing what tonight was. "Is that why we're here? So she could convince me to sleep with you? What the hell, Ian? Even after the other day?"

"No!"

"How much, Ian?"

"What?" he said.

"How much did you tell her? What exactly did you say?"

He shook his head. "I . . . I didn't . . . ," he tried. But then he got up and started pacing. "I . . . I don't even know how we ended up talking about it. We were just talking." Emilia turned away, unable to even look at him. She imagined him and Jane together, having that conversation. Talking about her and her hang-ups with sex? How she cried the last time? Planning how to fix her *after . . . after Jeremy Lance . . . no—someone else!—pulled off all her clothes, beat her, tried to . . .*

"It's just you've been so far away lately," Ian continued. "And I know, Emilia. I understand why you get this way in winter. But something else is up. I just don't know what it is. Or how to fix it. Or how to help you!" His voice cracked and she thought he sounded like he was going to cry. Any other time, it would have broken her heart to hear Ian like this. But all she could think about now was how he had talked to *Jane*. Of all people, Jane. And how he must have told her *everything*.

"I don't know what to do," he said. "I feel like I should *do* something, but I don't know what. I was just looking for advice, and we started talking . . . and . . . *please*, Emilia. I'm sorry. You have to believe me." He looked at her helplessly.

She closed her eyes, tried not to feel so sick as he repeated, "I'm sorry, I'm so sorry," over and over, and tried to hold her hand. But she couldn't stand his touch or his smell or his pity.

"Don't touch me!"

"Emilia . . ."

"Leave me alone," she said.

"I didn't mean to, you *have* to believe me. I just, before I knew it, we were talking about relationships and I had too much to drink and . . . I was just answering her questions and I knew I should just keep my mouth shut, but she has this way . . ."

"Shut up!" Emilia didn't want to hear it. "Don't say one more goddamn thing!"

She didn't want to imagine him drunk, talking to Jane.

Where had Anthony been? What else had happened?

She didn't want to imagine the way Jane must have looked at Ian, or the way he might have been mesmerized by her closeness, her lipstick, her smell, or how something about Jane had made him spill his heart out to her. But Emilia imagined it all anyway. And she imagined their bodies close to each other, Jane kissing Ian, promising him something Emilia wouldn't give him. No, not stupid, tragic, *sweet* Emilia.

"Please, listen to me . . ."

Emilia put her hands over her ears. She didn't want to hear his voice.

Don't let the poor boy explode!

"Take me home," she said.

"Please, Emilia . . ."

"Take me home," she repeated.

"Listen to me."

"Take me fucking home!" she yelled. She wanted to drown out his voice. She wanted him to shut up. She closed her eyes and refused to even turn his way.

Ian got up slowly, and then she heard him mumble something about not being able to find the keys. "Anthony's got them, from when he got his cigarettes from my car."

"Go get them."

"Emilia, please . . ." She could hear the desperate plea in his voice, and it pissed her off even more. She got up and ran upstairs, yelling for Anthony and pounding on the only closed door she could find.

The door swung open and Anthony stood there in his boxers. In the background, Emilia could see Jane in bed, the sheets pulled up to cover her body.

"What the hell is wrong?" he said.

"I need the keys. I need the keys . . . now."

"I don't have . . ."

"You do! You have them. Check your clothes."

"Okay, okay, relax," he said, his hands up like Emilia might shoot him.

How stupid, she thought. *Who do they think I am?*

Anthony backed up and went over to his clothes heaped on the floor, and to Emilia's relief, she heard the jingle of keys.

She felt Ian standing behind her, but she wouldn't turn around. She couldn't bear the sight of him. She couldn't imagine being in the car with him right now.

"Will you take me home?" she asked Anthony when he held the keys out to her.

Anthony looked past her at Ian. "What's going on?"

"Anthony," Emilia said again. "Take me home."

"Yeah . . . okay," he said. Quickly he dressed, shoved on his shoes. And the whole time, Jane stayed in bed, watching.

Emilia hoped Ian crawled into it with her. She hoped Jane comforted him. She hoped they fucked.

Emilia shoved past Ian and went outside to wait by the car.

Anthony came out, and soon they were on their way back to her house. After a long time, he finally asked, "What happened?"

She wanted to tell him, but she didn't know how to explain it. And she could hardly expect him to understand when the two people she hated most right now were people he loved.

"He's a jerk."

Anthony waited for more. Emilia stared out the window.

"He talked about shit I didn't want him to talk about. He told Jane things he shouldn't have. Like, poor him . . ." *And about that day.* She was certain of it.

Emilia had only told Ian about it when they were thirteen. Only him. Only once. She'd told him everything she could remember because it came to her so quickly. They'd been sitting at the park, she was on the swings, the weather was just starting to get cold, and she saw a little girl running around, laughing. And a part of Emilia remembered being that way. She said this to Ian without thinking, and how after the attack, she wasn't like that anymore. She hadn't spoken about it in years. But that day, the whole thing, the smallest details she could remember, started coming out. She felt like she'd been hypnotized, like she was out of her body and was watching herself recount the whole thing. It was the only time she had talked about it outside Dr. Lisa's office, the only time she'd told the whole awful story from beginning to end like that. And now Ian had told Jane. *He must have.* All those things Emilia never wanted to speak about, never wanted anyone to know.

"Oh," Anthony said in a tone that turned Emilia's stomach.

"You knew."

"Sorry," he said. After a few minutes, he added, "For what it's worth, he doesn't go around talking about it."

"Right."

"I'm serious. He's never brought it up. It was Jane who told me you guys hadn't . . ."

Emilia looked back out the window. "Of course."

"I'm sorry," Anthony said. "She's sort of like that. But she's harmless."

Emilia shook her head. "You shouldn't get in the habit of apologizing for her."

He didn't say anything and they drove the rest of the way in silence as she tried not to think of Ian, back at Anthony's. She tried not to think of Jane.

Jane.

Fucking Jane, who could be so free. Who could do whatever she wanted, dance naked under glittering lights and laugh about it, walk around with some naive assurance that nothing bad would ever happen to her. No, not her.

Anthony pulled up in front of Emilia's house, and as she got out of the car, he said, "He really loves you, you know. Don't break his heart."

Emilia shook her head. "Bye, Anthony. Thanks for the ride," she told him. She never wanted to see any of them again.

You're Home

"You're home," Ma said, standing up from the couch. She looked stricken at the sight of Emilia. She quickly reached for but fumbled with the remote control, and it clattered to the floor. Emilia looked at the television, at the woman on-screen saying that she would never forgive what had been done to her son. That everyone involved should be ashamed.

The name below the angry face on the screen read KATHERINE LANCE, and everything registered in Emilia's mind just as Ma turned off the television.

"Emilia . . . ," Ma said.

"Oh my god."

Ma rushed to her side. "Don't worry," she said, wrapping her arms around Emilia.

"How can you say that? How . . ." Emilia's chest felt crushed. She could hardly breathe as she pulled away from her mother and paced around the living room. Winter break would be over soon. She'd have to go back to school. People would be talking. They'd stare at her like they used to. Like she was some sort of freak, some kind of monster.

It would be on every news channel. And everyone would know exactly what she'd done.

Ma came over to her again, held her tighter and closer. "Emilia, stop, please. Listen to me. Are you listening? It's only a small segment, at the end of the news. It's not a huge story. Probably no one else has even picked it up."

"Yet," Emilia said.

Her mother just stared at her.

"People will blame me."

"*Nobody* is going to blame you. Not as long as I'm around. We'll get through this. Together."

Emilia tried to pull away, but Ma wouldn't let go. Emilia took a breath and closed her eyes, afraid of everything that might happen. Of how things seemed to get worse when she thought they couldn't possibly. Of how tight Ma was holding on to her, like she was never going to let go.

"You think they'll come looking for me? Reporters?"

"I had our name, number, and address unlisted years ago," Ma whispered into Emilia's hair. "And if anyone comes near here, near you, I'll kill them."

Emilia heard the strange tone of her mother's voice, and it only scared her more.

That night, all kinds of scenes played in Emilia's mind. Katherine Lance on the television. Jane and Ian talking. She and Jane talking.

Jane licking a lollipop. Jane and reporters watching from somewhere on the playground as Jeremy Lance threw Emilia around, hit her, dragged her like some kind of . . .

No! Not him! Carl Smith. Who is dying. And might still be thrown in jail for what he did.

So many scenes were getting jumbled up in her mind. She felt like she couldn't keep anything straight. Her head hurt from trying to make sense of it all, and it reminded her of those days after the attack. Of being in this house, with Ma, closed off from the rest of the world. Of lying in bed, day after day, everything hurting. Not knowing if it was day or night. Not knowing if she was at home, or in the hospital, or still on the playground, whenever she woke up.

It had been such a terrible time.

And now here she was again. Cooped up in the house. Afraid and confused. Ma and Dad whispering in other rooms, checking on her every few minutes, peeking out the windows for news vans. The phone ringing and Ma running to answer it when it was only Ian calling to apologize over and over. And Emilia couldn't even talk to him, because Ma and Dad would hear it all. So she quietly had to tell him to just leave her alone.

Ma was finally allowing her dad to come over, but only because he was now in charge of babysitting Emilia as they waited. And waited.

For something.

Something.

Emilia's mind flickered with the memory.

The classroom.

Was it real?

Yes, she knew it was.

I already have my something, Emilia thought as the days passed. *I have a place to go and be safe. I don't need to be here, like this.*

She hated her father hanging around the house all day, her mother calling every hour but only her father answering in case it was a reporter. And how all day long, she couldn't even figure out how to talk to her dad. She hated having him around and it confused her. She wanted him here, but she didn't. Or maybe she liked the version of her father she'd come up with, and he wasn't that person. A part of her understood that all this time, *this* man, who kept watch over her now, had preferred to be somewhere else.

"You guys can't do this," Emilia said the third afternoon her father was leaving and her mother was coming home.

"Emilia," her father said. Her mother shot him a look.

"I mean it. It's fucking ridiculous. I'm not staying locked up like this, in the house all the time."

"Just until . . . ," Ma started, but Emilia shook her head.

"No!" She didn't feel anywhere near as strong as she sounded. But she didn't want them to know how broken everything felt, how broken she was, how she cried at night when she was sure everyone was asleep, over Ian, over the past, over everything that was happening. How it felt, how it *was*, too much. How she couldn't handle it.

No! You can. You're okay. You have to be okay. Or things will go back to just how they used to be, everyone feeling sorry for you or thinking you're weird. You will never be normal again.

And to prove her point, Emilia grabbed her coat and left, ignoring how her parents called after her, even as fear and loneliness and guilt closed in around her as soon as she rushed out into that freezing cold.

You have to survive this! she thought, and then she hurried toward the only place no one would find her, the only place that made any of it bearable.

Make it even more spectacular, Emilia told herself as she got closer to the school. With each step she took, she felt like she was leaving everything behind.

Leave it all in the past.

She wouldn't let herself think of how her parents had looked at her when she left the house. Or how Ian had looked at her the last time she saw him. Or how Carl Smith, or Jeremy Lance, or his mother, or reporters might be trying at this very moment to find her.

Leave it all in the past.

Emilia dropped down through the window, ran up the stairs to the classroom, filling her mind instead with what she could do. What she *did* have control over. *That room.* And when she finally got there, she felt everything else slip away.

Make it amazing!

Emilia looked around.

Her mother's words echoed in her head.

You can have anything you want, Emilia.

Emilia sat in the corner of the room, her knees pulled up to her chest, held tight, and looked at her surroundings.

Yes, she could have anything she wanted. And she wanted this room. She wouldn't stay home, no matter what. She would make this room more amazing than she ever imagined.

Emilia Came Home

Emilia came home that night, her mind full of ideas and plans and possibilities. She stared into the darkness of her room as she lay in bed, but saw only that classroom. And when she fell asleep, there was no room for nightmares.

In the morning, she headed to Tomás's job. Carefully, she snuck up to the counter and shouted, "Boo!" so loudly, Tomás nearly dropped the case of display candy he was filling.

"What the hell?" he yelled as he fumbled with the box. Emilia laughed.

"Relax, I just came by for a visit. I miss you," she said. It was true. She missed him and wished she could explain why she'd been brushing him off lately even though she wanted him close. She was sure he had noticed. But it was just that she didn't want to talk about any of this, and maybe Tomás wanted her to, at least to him. How could she explain she just *couldn't*? It felt impossible.

"Me too," he said. He stared at his sister and smiled. "I don't have a break for another couple of hours, but . . ."

"No, don't worry. That's okay. I just . . . I couldn't stay home anymore."

Tomás gave her a gentle look. "I think Ma and Dad got the message last night. I noticed he didn't come over this morning, and she still went to work."

She knew Tomás was trying to make it feel like a victory, but Emilia's mood shifted as she thought of her mother on the phone that morning before she left. Ma had set up an appointment for Emilia to see a therapist in a few weeks. And she hadn't even told Emilia. So it didn't feel like a victory. It felt like the walls were closing in around her, like Ma was taking over, and Emilia was running out of time.

"Anyway, I was planning to go for a walk or something. But I thought I'd come see you first."

He smiled. "Thanks."

"Also . . . ," she said, taking a deep breath. "I have to tell you something. I . . . borrowed some money. Actually, I kind of took it when I did this." Emilia reached for her hair.

"From my drawer?"

She nodded. "I'm sorry I didn't ask. I just, I got it in my head that I really wanted to look different and—"

"Don't worry about it."

"I'm sorry. It's been bothering me this whole time."

"Forget about it." He looked at her so kindly, Emilia had to look away. A customer came up to the register then, and Emilia moved aside and wandered down the aisle.

Her brother was probably the kindest, most beautiful person she knew. She was relieved she told him about the money. She knew he knew anyway. And would never have brought it up unless she did.

It made her feel bad for what she did next: grabbed cans of spray paint in the utility aisle of the pharmacy and shoved them in the backpack she'd brought, along with a bag of votive candles. She walked to the art supply aisle next and grabbed as many little containers of glitter as she could.

When she went back toward the register, Tomás was ringing up a customer. Emilia lingered by the makeup and looked at a small palette of green eye shadow.

"Pretty," she said when he was finished, and she came over to him. She placed the eye shadow on the counter. He didn't meet her eyes, or notice the soft way she looked at him.

He shrugged.

"If I had your eyes, I'd wear this color," she told him. "You have such beautiful eyes, Tomás. I'm jealous." She smiled, but he still couldn't look at her.

"Where are you going, anyway?" he asked. He sounded flustered, but Emilia didn't pay it any mind. "I mean . . ."

She looked outside and pretended not to hear the question. "Anyway, I better go," she said, trying once more to catch his gaze. When he finally looked at her, she smiled so big. She placed her hands on the counter and lifted herself to his height, leaning in to give him a small kiss on the cheek. It was impulsive and so much like how she used to be.

"See you," she said.

He nodded. "See you." His look was tender and his voice barely a whisper.

Outside, Emilia glanced back and saw Tomás staring after her as the doors swooshed closed behind her. She walked away, the green eye shadow now in her coat pocket.

Emilia carried the supplies on her back, the slight guilt and nerves she'd felt at the store quickly giving way to a growing sense of excitement. And in that moment, she thought she understood Ma better than she ever had.

In through the chorus room, and then up all the stairs to her old classroom, where she unpacked her new items.

Emilia walked around the classroom, touching the items she'd brought here already. She looked at Sam.

Finally, she popped open one of the many cans of paint she'd found in the janitor's closet along with the ladder and got to work. With an efficiency that felt good, that made her concentrate and think only about what she was actually physically doing, Emilia opened the other containers, swirled and mixed, and then started painting the wall with the stiff paintbrush she'd found here, too. After every few strokes, she carefully blew small handfuls of glitter onto the wet surface and watched it stick and sparkle. With each area she covered, Emilia was mesmerized.

Yes, she thought. *Yes!*

She liked the way her arms started to ache. She liked the way her back cramped up. She liked not thinking of anything but this paint, this glorious paint, as the walls became dusted with more and more glitter.

For a moment, Emilia felt euphoric. She worried that maybe it was the paint fumes, but then she didn't care. She wondered if she could die by paint fumes, but she decided she didn't care about that, either. All she cared about were those sparkling walls, those walls she would picture tonight when she closed her eyes.

Emilia Tried Not to Look

Emilia tried not to look over at Ian's house that night, New Year's Eve, when she opened her window to set down a row of peanuts for her crows. But she did.

His window was bright. She could see his shadow. He flicked the light off and on. She didn't return it.

Finally, his window went dark.

A moment later, Emilia saw a car stop in front of his house. A BMW that she was almost certain was the one Anthony had shown up in once or twice before, in the past. His mother's car.

Emilia watched as Ian came out his front door. He looked up to her window and met her gaze before getting in the car. And in the passenger seat, Emilia saw Jane.

There she was, with her white-blond hair. Somehow innocent and culpable. Ian got in the car, and a moment later, Emilia saw Jane look toward her window with a sad expression on her face.

Emilia stood there, waited for them to drive away. But instead she saw the passenger-side window open. Jane stuck her head out slightly, then the paleness of her hand flashed against the slate blue of early evening as she gestured for Emilia to *come, come with us*.

Emilia's heart beat faster.

She hated them.

But she could go with them. *She could*. And maybe everything would be okay. Maybe everything *could* be okay. A betrayal, yes. Apologies. Forgiveness. Could it really be that simple? All she had to do was walk out there.

But walking out there felt like being naked.

Come with us.

The car waited. And waited. Emilia stepped away from the window so they couldn't see her.

But she could see them. And she saw, too, the red taillights as they drove away in that car, without her.

"Emilia?" Tomás knocked on her door.

"Come in," she said, and he came in carrying a wrapped shoe box, held it out to her.

"What's this?"

"It's for you. It was supposed to be for Christmas, but it wasn't ready in time."

Emilia took the box from him.

"Don't shake it," he said. "Be really careful with it."

Emilia carefully tore off the paper. She lifted the lid and looked inside.

"You don't have to keep it if you don't want to, if it creeps you out or you think it's gross."

She lifted the small figure out of the box carefully, studied it. "A bird skeleton?"

"Don't you remember?"

Emilia stared at the skeleton.

Flashes of that day, her brother standing over her, came into Emilia's mind. "Oh my god . . . I dug it up," she whispered, seeing in her mind her small hands as they scratched at the dirt where Tomás had buried it. As they retrieved the dead bird.

Tomás nodded. "I was going to do this for you when we were little, but I couldn't figure out how then. So I left it in the shed, in the box. And then I thought maybe it was just better if I didn't. Anyway, I've been thinking of that day, Emilia. A lot. And you . . . and . . ." He looked at the skeleton. "I don't know."

Emilia picked it up, so gently, and looked at the delicate bird bones. "I was so sad."

Tomás's brown eyes were full of concern for her. "I know it's years late, and strange. I guess I was a strange kid, to think of this." He looked at the bones and laughed. Emilia wondered how long it had taken him to clean them up, to figure out how to put them back together.

"It's not the best job. I think I got some of it wrong. But it looks . . . okay, doesn't it?"

Emilia's eyes filled with tears. "It's perfect."

Tomás wiped quickly at his own eyes. "Don't make me cry."

Emilia put the bird skeleton down on her desk and hugged him so hard. "Thank you."

"There's more," he said, nodding toward the box. Emilia noticed something covered with tissue paper. She lifted the paper and gently took out the dress for a young girl.

She looked at Tomás, confused, then back at the dress, which looked like it had been carefully ironed.

She knew this dress.

"It used to be yours," Tomás whispered.

"Oh," she said, suddenly remembering opening this very dress on her eighth birthday. "I thought . . . I lost it. Or Ma had given it away."

"I took it."

Emilia looked at her brother. Was he trying to tell her what she'd wondered a few times over the years? "It's okay," she said.

He wouldn't look at her.

"Tomás," she said. Her heart ached as her brother sat next to her.

"You looked so pretty in it. I was so . . . I'm so sorry," he said, his voice choking up.

She suddenly felt so undeserving of her brother. He was the one always putting himself and his feelings last, always watching out for her, but what had she done for him? She should have asked him if he was ever scared, up here by himself, all those nights she spent with her mother. Why didn't she ever ask him? Now she was afraid to ask, afraid he'd say, *Yes, I really was scared.* And she was afraid to ask about all the things he'd had to keep to himself all these years, that she didn't ask him about because she didn't know if she should, or if he wanted to tell her. She'd ignored the way her clothes were sometimes hung just a little differently, or how her makeup disappeared from the bathroom they shared only to reappear there later. She always knocked on his closed door, never turned the knob in case he'd forgotten to lock it.

She didn't want her brother to ever scramble or feel ashamed. She didn't want him to feel found out.

And she didn't want to tell him all the things she felt lately. How strange she felt. How scared she was at times, and numb other times. How time felt unreal and she sometimes felt like she was stuck somewhere between the past and the present. How she couldn't even find the words to say any of this. Or how sorry she was for never thinking of him.

"I love you," she said, her voice cracking. She could hardly get the words out, but she had to. "I . . . I'm here for you. And whatever you think is wrong, it's not. It doesn't matter at all. I'm so glad you took the dress, you understand? You deserved it, and so much more."

She couldn't stand the thought of him here by himself, crying himself to sleep, in the dark, alone, misunderstood each night, for how long? Years? Why hadn't she been certain sooner?

"I'm sorry," she managed. "I'm sorry."

Tomás shook his head, crying. "Stop," he said. But he pulled her in and cried harder as she hugged him back.

She wanted to say more. She wanted him to say more. But he just held on to her and said, "No more apologies, okay?" before she could utter another word.

She nodded, swallowed the rest of her tears, and held on to him, hoping he understood in her hug the things he did not want her to say aloud.

He pulled away, wiped the tears from his face. And she got up and carefully placed the dress next to the bird skeleton on her desk. They were beautiful. Like her brother. She knew exactly where each belonged.

Emilia and Tomás sat on her bed for a long while, staring at those items in a silence filled with their memories and an understanding of the unspoken words between them.

The First Day Back

The first day back at school after winter vacation, Emilia said a quick goodbye to Ma and Tomás before either of them realized they hadn't heard the beep of Ian's car. She rushed out of the house into the January cold and began walking to school.

She'd dreamed of the attack again last night. She kept seeing Jeremy Lance's face. So, so clearly. And then she'd see him in jail, pounding on the concrete walls. Screaming.

Emilia felt weak as she walked, and the images kept running through her mind.

"Emilia." She jumped and turned toward the street quickly. It was Ian, calling out to her from his car. "Emilia, please talk to me," he said again as he continued driving next to her slowly. "Look, it's freezing. Come on," he said. "Okay, okay. We don't have to talk. Just, please, let me give you a ride at least."

She looked over at him. Ian. Why couldn't things be okay between them so she could tell him what was going on? Her face felt frozen and her legs unsteady, and she was struck with that strange sense of déjà vu she'd felt so much these days.

"I promise, just a ride to school," he said, his face kind and gentle, and, oh, how she missed him.

Emilia got into the warm car without a word. She wanted to ask him where he went the other night, with Anthony and Jane. If he'd had fun without her. If he'd talked more about her. What did they say? What did they think? She wondered if someone like Jane was easier to deal with than someone like Emilia.

She wanted to reach over and kiss him. And hit him.

Emilia blinked away her tears.

Don't think about it, she told herself.

They drove through the same streets, the same way to school as always. For a moment, if it weren't for the miserable pain in her heart and the dread in the pit of her stomach, she could pretend she was popping a piece of gum into his mouth and wondering about Bazooka Joe.

She wondered if that pack of gum was still in the glove compartment.

What would he say if she started talking about the *Challenger* explosion, if she reached over and unwrapped a piece of gum? If she asked him about Bazooka Joe's eye? Would he play along with her? Would he pretend these last few weeks had never, ever happened?

Don't be stupid, Emilia.

They passed the elementary school. Jeremy Lance's face loomed in her mind again.

Emilia closed her eyes, and memories of being dragged, by her feet, flashed into her mind. She saw his sneakers. His legs.

It wasn't him.

And yet, her mind kept flashing Jeremy's face each time she looked at the guy in her memory.

She shook her head, trying to shake the image of him away. She looked outside and focused on the sky, and a part of her stirred. She remembered being up there.

I used to fly.

It rushed back so quickly, the feeling of the wind under her, the sound of flapping in her ears. The view from up there, dizzying, twirling, going higher and higher. Her mouth felt strange to her. She touched her lips, half expecting to actually find a beak.

She remembered being a bird.

I was a bird, she thought. *I really was one. I remember.*

She was wings and feathers and beak. She could fly away from here and from conversations she didn't want to have. Her hollow mouth wouldn't need to form human words. She could make it cease to function, and her ears go deaf, and she would be in her own cotton-lined world. She could sink into the soft silence so easily and refuse the outside world. There were ways to refuse it. She remembered now, how to be in it but not be a part of it.

"Emilia," Ian said from somewhere far away.

"What?"

"Did you hear anything I said? Are you . . . are you okay?"

She looked at Ian, and she wasn't sure she felt real.

Are you okay? Are you okay? She had to get used to that again, over and over.

Are you okay?

Am I? Yes. I can function the way I'm supposed to. Tell him, Emilia.

"Emilia?"

"Did I tell you my dad's back?" she blurted out suddenly. She laughed softly.

"What?"

The car was warm. "He's back," she repeated. Her words sounded strange to her own ears. "And he thinks he can just come back into the house like nothing has happened. Like he doesn't owe us some kind of explanation."

"What? When?" Ian kept looking from her to the street ahead.

"And did I tell you Jeremy's not the guy who attacked me?" she said, letting the words she'd been holding back just flow from her mouth. She looked at the sky. "Yeah, it was someone else. Some guy named Carl Smith."

"Emilia . . . what the hell are you talking about? What's going on?"

"He's dying. So they might not even prosecute him. I don't know."

"Jesus Christ, Emilia. What are you talking about?"

Emilia focused on the lock of the glove compartment. The little silver circle. The bubble gum she hoped was still inside. "He's been in Seattle all this time."

"Who? Carl Smith? How'd they find him . . . ? How'd they figure it out? Emilia . . ."

"No, my dad, he wasn't in Alaska. He was in Seattle. This whole time." She didn't even feel like she knew what she was saying, or how to make sense of it all. She looked at Ian. Was she dreaming?

"Is he at your house? Where is he?"

She tried to process Ian's question. She imagined some faceless man in her house. Carl Smith. Where? In her room? In her bed? Waiting for her.

Maybe he comes by every night. Maybe he's watching me, sleeping out there, in the yard? In the shed? In the cold?

Her dad's face flashed into her mind then. No, *Dad* was the one out in the cold. *He* was the one hunting for food in the snow, hacking squirrels with the machete he used to keep in the shed. In Alaska. Seattle?

"Emilia?"

She looked at Ian. Everything was jumbled up in her head. She felt tears prickling her eyes as she tried to make sense of all her mixed-up thoughts, but she didn't want to cry.

Ian grabbed her hand and pulled it toward his chest, but all she wanted was to get out of the car that was now too, too hot. She felt trapped.

"I'm taking you back home." He looked like he was the one who had to deal with it, like he was the one who had to figure it out.

"No!" she yelled, louder than she'd meant to. "I mean, *I* can deal with it." She pulled her hand away, but he held it tighter.

"No, we'll deal with it together."

"Pull over," she said as they came closer to Carro's deli.

"What? No . . ."

"I said pull over."

"Emilia . . ."

"I mean it, Ian. Pull over. If you want to help, just listen to me."
She felt like she was hyperventilating.

Ian pulled over, right in front of the deli.

She had to get out of the car. Emilia opened the door. He held
on tighter to her hand. "Let go," she said.

"But . . . where are you going?"

"Please let go."

He let go of her hand, but got out of the car as she did. He came
around to her side.

"Please, just leave me alone."

He shook his head but stood there, like he was afraid to move.

Was this the effect she had on people? Her presence scared them.
They didn't know what to do about her.

Just like before. Just like that.

"I'm okay. I just . . . I need some space," she said. "I need time to
think. I just need to be alone." The cold was making her nose run,
and two guys sat drinking coffee on the ledge of the deli's big store-
front window, watching them. She couldn't stand it. She wanted to
tell them to go away, too. That it was none of their business. She
wanted everyone to go away. To not notice her. To leave her alone.

"I'm not gonna leave you alone right now, Emilia," Ian said.

"I mean it. I . . . I really want to be alone. I don't need you to
feel sorry for me. Or try to fix everything. You can't fix this—
don't you get that? I mean, what are you going to do?"

She looked at him and she felt more than a little out of control.

Don't make a scene! she thought. But she was making a scene. She couldn't control the words coming out of her mouth.

He looked at her and she kept going. "I mean, *what can you do? What can you do about all this?*" she asked.

"I'll . . ." But he stuttered, looked around like the answers might appear somewhere, on the sides of the cars passing by, in the sky.

"Go. Just go," she said finally.

Ian stood still.

"Please." She shoved her freezing hands in her coat pockets. "I mean it. Please do that for me."

He shook his head.

"Go away!" she yelled. "Go! Leave me alone!"

Slowly, Ian took a few steps back toward the car, turned to look at her, tried one more time. But she turned away from him.

He started up the car, slowly pulled away. Emilia watched him go and closed her eyes, trying to keep back fresh tears.

Why are you crying? You sent him off. You don't want him here. You don't want his help.

And yet, when she could no longer see his car, when he was gone, she regretted it.

"Sorry, sweetheart." A voice invaded her thoughts. One of the men on the ledge. He looked at her over the brim of his steaming cup with a bored but sympathetic look as he took a gulp of his coffee.

"Love sucks," the other guy said, smoking a cigarette. He smiled at her. His eyes were small and gleamed the way they do when someone is amused. "Trust me, baby," he said, inhaling deeply. "Not worth it." He exhaled and stared at her through the thin veil of smoke, cocked his head to the side. His eyes took her in slowly, from head to toe. "Or maybe you just need someone who's not such a little boy, huh?"

"Leave the girl alone," the other man said.

But the man with the cigarette continued. "Maybe you need someone, I don't know, more like me, huh? I'm nice." He sat there, somehow taking up so much space, as if he were the only person who mattered.

Emilia looked at the first guy, but he shrugged and smiled and continued drinking his coffee.

"What do you say?" said the gross other guy.

The cold started on the back of her neck, and traveled up Emilia's scalp. She hated this guy. Both of them. She wanted to take the steaming coffee out of their hands and pour it into their laps. She wanted to pluck their hair out, strand by strand. She wanted to punch this one in his small eyes and filthy mouth.

She wanted *him* to choke on *his* own blood.

"Fuck you," she said. She looked into those eyes, watched them flash with delight.

"Oh, nice . . . ," he said, laughing.

Emilia started walking away, but she could still feel his gaze on her, following her, staring at her from behind, so she started running. Fast. As fast as she could.

Before he could reach for her.

Before he could drag her back.

Before he could hold her down.

She wouldn't let him.

"Hey, don't be like that, honey!" the guy called after her, laughing, *laughing!*

She ran faster. She'd run so fast she'd fly. She wouldn't let him catch and overpower her.

Because that's the worst, the very worst fucking feeling in the world. To kick! And scream! To push and fight, against someone so much bigger. Stronger.

God, so much stronger than you, so small. So weak.

Get away! Fucking get away from here, Emilia.

Emilia ran *faster, faster, run faster!* Tears blurring the world.

She ran down block after block, the cars a blur, the streets rushing by. She ran across the street without looking, with the sound of cars screeching, someone yelling, another cursing.

Don't look back! Keep going! Leave it all behind. It's all in the past.

Her lungs were cold. They were frozen. They didn't work. They wouldn't contract and expand. Her breath just howled in those frozen caverns in her chest. She could hear the howling coming from inside her. She was splitting, breaking from the cold.

Still she kept running. Until she saw it.

The old elementary school was just up ahead.

Faster now.

Then in through the window of the chorus room, down the

hall of the basement level, up the stairs, down another hall, until there, there was the classroom.

She ran inside, closed the door, locked it.

She slid down against the door, and that howling from so long ago erupted from deep inside her and filled the classroom. It swirled with the cold and wind she'd brought in from outside, the cold that followed her everywhere. She felt the force of it rush under her arms, lifting her *high, higher, higher.* Until she was floating.

Until she was flying.

Emilia Flew

Emilia flew into a white sky, her flock around her, flapping their wings with hers against the cold.

We heard you, they said. *We are here, Emilia.*

It'd been so long since she'd reached these heights or heard their fluttering wings so close to her. She felt light and fast and powerful. She felt free.

They dipped in unison, and then up again. They swirled to the left and in a wide fluid arc, then right, riding the gusts of wind. Emilia flapped her wings faster.

Higher! she said to them. And they listened.

Faster! she said.

They flew in and through gauzy clouds, traveling great distances.

Just like we used to, away from everything down there. Gone, gone, gone.

Emilia looked at the blurring landscape beneath her. The white of snow on the treetops and woods of an Alaska she'd pictured in her mind for so long. She saw a smokeless chimney in the distance, and then the cabin she'd always pictured her father in came into view.

The flock slowed, swooped down, and landed in nearby trees, on the roof. Emilia landed at the doorway; the door was open and she peeked her head inside.

It was empty.

No pots or pans, no small black stove, no bed. No books. No table to lay dead animals on, no tools to open and stuff them. Nothing.

Where did you go?

She flew to the nearest tree and perched on a branch, waiting.

Where did we all go?

Emilia waited in that cold as her birds landed and took off around her, flitting. *Let's go,* they said. *There is nothing here.* And she knew they were right.

They flew back, back to the city, where, on a busy street, she spotted her mother's auburn hair and saw her rushing to her next appointment. The look on her face was the same as she always wore, one of worry.

And then back to their neighborhood, past the pharmacy, where Tomás stood staring out the front window.

Do you see me, Tomás? Do you know I'm here?

His gaze followed Emilia as she flew toward the school. Back through the window in the classroom. Back, somehow, finally, to herself. To the body she'd left and the reality she'd learned to escape so long ago.

When Emilia opened her eyes, she was weary and stunned to find herself in the classroom. She looked to the window, where her black birds were gathered outside, in the trees.

It had been so long since she had taken flight with them like that. But they came for her. They'd heard her cry and there they were.

The sun was so strangely bright, and if it weren't so cold in there, she could almost pretend it was summer. How long had she been in that room? How long did she fly?

Emilia looked around the classroom, then moved toward the window. She squinted at the daylight outside, which was not the same as this morning. She looked at the sky for some clue as to what time it was, but she couldn't tell. Then she looked to the ground. The streets were mostly bare, as if everyone was already where they needed to be.

I'll stay here until I see the high school kids walking home from school, she thought.

In the meantime, she looked at the origami paper she'd brought the other day that she'd found at the back of her closet and hadn't used in years. Her head still felt fuzzy—from *flying? Sleeping?* She didn't know. It felt so real. She'd never been able to explain to her mother or Dr. Lisa how real it felt when she flew.

Emilia reached for a piece of the origami paper and started folding, her fingers moving as if on their own.

Muscle memory? Emilia wondered.

Where had she heard that term? She watched as her fingers worked so quickly, how they seemed separate from her, how they remembered the order and precise folds she made so long ago, this way and that way until suddenly, a perfect little black crow emerged.

"I'll call you Henry," she told it. She called so many of them Henry, and so many of them Lulu because when she was little, she'd run out of names. She tossed it in the box, the one full of tiny little crows her small hands had made over and over and over all those years ago, and had recently brought here. The ones her mother hated but let her keep. Hundreds of little black birds. For hours Emilia would sit making them, until her hands ached. Then less and less over the years. Emilia couldn't remember the last time she'd made one.

But her fingers remembered. And they worked quickly. One sheet after another, over and over, until the hours passed and there was no more paper and Emilia's hands ached once more.

PART FOUR

Early January 1995

Some Days

Some days Emilia walked all the way to the high school and stayed there for half the day. Other days she walked straight to the elementary school. But each day she worked on that classroom. And when the automated call about her absence would come in the early evenings, Emilia was usually the only one home to answer it. Or she'd be the first to the phone. She wasn't as worried about getting caught as she should be, and she didn't understand why. Maybe because she knew she could explain to Ma that she just didn't feel like being around anyone and Ma would understand.

But she'll hurry the visit to the psychologist, Emilia thought. Still, it was a chance worth taking.

And maybe going to a psychologist wouldn't be the end of the world?

No, be okay, Emilia told herself.

All she wanted was to stay in that classroom. Safe. Where she painted each of the origami crows using the glitter paint and a small brush from a watercolor paint set she'd found in a kindergarten classroom. And she sat in the little patch of sun that came in from the window, and one after another, she painted those birds, until they were shining. She tilted them this way and that, watched the way the light reflected off them. She took in their small brilliance, getting lost in it, so she could forget the cold outside and the ugliness of the world.

Emilia searched Ma's closet for thread. She knew there was some in an old sewing box stuffed under the extra winter blankets. Emilia remembered when they'd gotten the string and crochet needles. She saw how Ma walked into the store and carried them around with her for a bit before casually dropping them into her purse as they walked, pretending to search for something. That was how Ma tried to pick up crocheting.

It's supposed to help, she would say, but Emilia never understood. Especially when Ma only became frustrated and threw the string and the needles across the room.

But now here they were, the spools of string, from all those years ago. Most of them were brand-new. And underneath them, an old photo album Emilia hadn't seen in years. She opened it, getting lost for a moment in so many aching memories of her family. There they were on that trip to Jones Beach. And here was a picture of Emilia in front of their house on her first day of kindergarten.

Emilia closed the album and shoved it, along with the string, into her backpack and carried them to the elementary school.

In the school janitor's closet in the basement, she found a chair that could be used as a table to display more of her items. She carried it past the chorus room, past the art room, up the stairs to the ground level, singing "Ghost of John" to herself. This was where the kindergarten through second-grade classrooms were.

Little Emilia, what did you know, what did you know? she thought as she walked down the hall to the other set of stairs, which led up to the third- through fifth-grade classrooms. Emilia hurried, not just because the chair was heavy and slipping from her grip, but because she thought she felt the ghost of herself. And she was afraid to turn around and see little Emilia. To see her, knowing the future she didn't know yet.

Don't follow me, she told her.

The chair banged against her shins. She'd have bruises. She bruised easily.

Maybe I'm not strong. Maybe I'll never be, Emilia thought.

But once she got into the classroom, she started working. There, she snipped piece after piece of thread in varying lengths.

She punched tiny holes in her birds with a rusty hole punch she'd found in another classroom. Then looped the thread through those holes and tied a slightly bent paper clip to one end. She climbed the ladder and tacked the metal edge of the paper clip into the soft cork ceiling.

And she filled that room with hundreds of her glittering birds.

Later that week, Emilia went through the photographs, wondering what she could do with them. And she brought more items she found around her house—the salt and pepper shakers she was sure her mother wouldn't miss. And her father's battery-run boom box and cassette collection, old romantic songs in Spanish that she used to think were funny but made him melancholy, like poetry. They filled her with sorrow now, too. She also brought chipped teacups and cracked bowls Ma kept in the back of a cabinet because she said it made her sad to throw them out. Emilia had never understood before, but now she thought she did. She brought anything else she could find. Anything else that felt right. Emilia filled that room. And she worked.

She used the cans of paint that had been waiting. And she set out the candles. And blew up the air mattress with the bike pump they'd always had to borrow from their neighbor when they were little, but that she took without asking this time when she saw his garage door was open.

You can have anything you want, Emilia.

This.

She wanted *this*. A sanctuary, a beautiful place to escape the cold and all the terrible feelings swirling around inside her, filling her more and more. A place where she could be safe from Ian's confused and pitying looks, Ma and Tomás's worry, the rest of the world, which up to now had spared her the publicity but might still, at any moment, combust. They'd hate her, ask her *why* and *how*. Questions she'd asked herself a thousand times since finding out about Carl Smith but still couldn't answer. Emilia took a deep breath and closed her eyes; being here helped stop the relentless thoughts of Jeremy Lance and what she'd done to him. *How I ruined his life. And his mother's life. And why do I see, keep seeing, his face in my memory?*

She snapped open her eyes and a glimmering crow caught her attention. Emilia pushed away the thoughts that had crept in and instead looked around at what she'd built over the past few weeks. She stared at each item, beautiful in its own way. And the wall that had taken up most of her time. She sat on the air mattress, taking it all in, over and over again. It was done. There was nothing more she could do.

She opened the window just enough for some wind to sway her paper birds. She lay down, watched them shiver and shimmer above her.

What more can I do? she thought. Because she didn't feel like she was done. The room seemed complete and incomplete. There must be more she was supposed to do here. To feel complete. Normal. She wanted to feel complete and normal and whole.

Will I ever be?

The paper crows fluttered above her.

Detective Manzetti

Detective Manzetti looked at Emilia DeJesus, a small picture of her that he'd had in the back of his work desk drawer until recently. Now it lay on top of all the papers and reports on his desk. Her small brown face peeked out from behind her long dark hair, in front of the pink and blue beams they were using for backgrounds those days. He always thought she looked like she was hiding from the camera.

Do you have a picture where we can see her face more clearly? he'd asked Nina DeJesus back then.

She said something about this one being the most recent because she'd forgotten about picture day the year before, *so this is the best one. She still looks just like a baby . . . ,* she'd said, before her knees buckled and she grabbed on to his arm. *My god, my baby . . .*

Detective Manzetti sat at his desk and rubbed his arm where Nina DeJesus's fingers had dug into him eight years ago. He could almost still feel them.

Find her, she'd told him, gripping his arm harder. *You have to find her!*

We're already looking, he said. It was five-thirty and they'd been looking for half an hour. Emilia was eight; police were sent immediately. Not like teenagers, who could be runaways, so they had to wait a full twenty-four hours before they started an official search.

When did you realize she was missing?

She's a Girl Scout. The meeting today was canceled, but I didn't know. I was at the bank. I saw one of the girls from her troop standing in front of me with her mother. It didn't hit me at first . . . I remember looking at her and I said, "Missing Girl Scouts today?" and she looked up at me and said, "It was canceled." Just like that.

What time was that?

A little after four. Dismissal is at two-fifty and the meeting starts at three. I pick her up at four-thirty, at the front of the school. I was just going to the bank first and then to the school from there.

Have you ever talked about what to do if you're not home?

Nina shook her head. *I'm always home after school . . . I only work mornings. I never . . . except . . . except today.*

He saw the breath go out of her.

Anywhere you can think of where she might have gone after she found out the meeting was canceled?

Here. I thought she might be here. At the house. I was sure she must have walked home . . . Like I said, I was running errands. So I thought maybe I missed her. So I drove home.

Manzetti saw Nina going back in time, back to those moments. They all do it, when they're telling a story. When they're recounting the normal moments before the unimaginable.

It took so long to get home. I pulled into the driveway and ran inside, and I yelled her name. I ran upstairs, checked her room, ran through the whole house. Only Tomás, my son, was home—

Manzetti interrupted. *How old is your son?*

Nina gave the detective a look, anger and shame.

He's eleven. We've just started letting him stay home alone, but only if I'm going someplace nearby, for a short period of time. I only had to go to the bank and the school . . .

Detective Manzetti didn't react.

And your son, he said she didn't come home. Is that correct?

The doors were locked. He said he didn't hear the doorbell or anything. I scared him when I ran inside, yelling for Emilia. She shook her head. *But I didn't have time to explain. I . . . fell down the stairs.*

Nina gestured to the bleeding shin Manzetti had already noticed.

I was rushing. When I didn't find her here . . . I knew something had happened. Nina closed her eyes, leaning forward, holding her stomach. *As soon as that little girl, Jasmine—from Emilia's Brownie troop—said the meeting was canceled. I felt something, in my stomach, and . . . God, I just knew something was wrong.*

Her voice was strained and she started crying.

Does Emilia have a key to the house?

Nina shook her head, swallowed new sobs that came up.

Tell me what you did next, Mrs. DeJesus.

I kept yelling her name, hoping she was somewhere in the house. I . . . I wanted her to be here. Then I ran to my neighbors' house. I banged on their door asking if they'd seen her. Sometimes Mary bakes cookies and she lets Emilia help. But she wasn't there. I told her husband I was going to the school. I told him to call the police.

Nina shook her head. That's the part that always got parents. When the call to the police was made. Like ringing a bell that can't be unrung. Suddenly it became real.

So you went to the school. Did you drive there?

Nina closed her eyes, nodded.

Then what?

Nina DeJesus took a deep breath. *It was locked . . . Nobody was there. I banged on all the doors. I ran around banging on windows. Nobody was there. I . . . I didn't know what to do. I ran to the bike rack, the playground. Nobody. Anywhere.*

She was sobbing. *I should've known the meeting was canceled. I should've . . .*

Nina was starting the list of all the things she could have done differently. Manzetti had seen so many parents do this, too. He wanted to tell her there was nothing she could have done differently, but right now he needed to get the facts. Before she forgot them. This was no time to indulge in guilt.

So your neighbor who called the police, what is his name?

Nina told him and Manzetti made a note to make sure their stories matched.

The door opened and a man came in.

Sam! Nina yelled as he went over and hugged her. *Oh god, Sam . . . Sam . . .* Manzetti realized this must be the father.

He looked at the man, the struck look on his face. *Shock,* Manzetti thought. He'd had to drive up to a house with police cars in front, red and blue lights flashing; he'd had to explain to them to let him in, that he lived here; he'd had to walk up to this house, where the unimaginable was taking place.

Manzetti had seen spouses hold each other, yell at each other, blame each other, accuse each other, and then there were the ones who couldn't quite take it all in at once, and sat there, lost in another world.

Like Mr. DeJesus was doing now as Mrs. DeJesus tried to explain between choked sobs.

Now came the harder questions, about close relatives, close family friends, if they thought Emilia would go home with anyone she knew, anyone she didn't know.

Nina DeJesus answered them all, occasionally turning to her husband, who either nodded or shook his head or stuttered a few words.

And you, Mr. DeJesus? You were at work.

Yes.

And there are people there who can corroborate this?

Sam DeJesus nodded again. Eye contact, no anger. *Probably not him, but check out his story,* Manzetti thought.

Then Nina asked about the recent incidents with strangers, if they'd ever caught the person who flashed that little group of girls. She asked about a missing teen from last year who had received only a little publicity because it was first reported as a runaway.

Did they ever find that girl?

Manzetti paused, then shook his head.

Could this be the same guy? Could she have been kidnapped . . . ?

This was how it happened, one descending layer upon another.

Oh god, no.

Oh god, missing.

Oh god, a search.

Please no, god, not kidnapped.

Please, please no, god, not a body recovery.

Detective Manzetti cleared his throat and told Nina DeJesus, *Let's take this one step at a time. We don't know what has happened yet.*

He knew Nina DeJesus would be the kind of parent who jumped in full speed ahead, doing anything and everything. She was the kind of parent who would still be searching years, decades later. Manzetti knew parents like that. But sometimes, often, they chased the wrong leads.

But you're searching, right? There are officers out looking? I should—we should—be out there, Nina said. She moved closer to the edge of the couch, as if she would jump up at any moment.

Yes. We're searching. We got all our guys on it. Please, just—it'll be more helpful if you give me all the information I need.

She looked outside. *It's getting dark.* He knew darkness killed parents. When darkness fell, there was another level of fear.

The same things that happened in the dark happened in the day, *in plain sight*. Manzetti knew this after so many years on the force. But parents didn't. They had a false sense of security during the day and they looked into the fading light, the impending night just as small children did. With fear, scared of the impenetrable black, of the terrible unknown lurking there and what was happening to their child at that very moment.

The detective looked at how Nina swallowed gulps of air, *the beginnings of an anxiety attack.*

Then another officer informed Manzetti that some news stations had shown up while he was questioning Nina DeJesus. He had to get Emilia's face out there. He looked at the picture. A gruesome image flashed into his mind. He didn't want to think of her in a field, dead, a cord wrapped around her neck and flies buzzing around her naked body the way they'd found the fourteen-year-old girl from Hempstead whom Mrs. DeJesus had asked about moments ago. They'd reported her as a runaway, even though her mom, just like Mrs. DeJesus, knew something bad had happened to her.

Nobody listened to that mother. Nobody immediately searched for her daughter, Lucy Soto. The news didn't keep showing her face like they do for other faces. Lighter faces.

Girls in her situation often run away, Detective Manzetti had said.

He'd actually uttered those words to her mother, when he found out she had an older boyfriend. When he found out her mother learned they were having sex. When she told him reluctantly, yes, they'd had a fight that day about it. When she closed her eyes and told him, *I hit her.*

He didn't need more information after that, even though her mother kept trying.

The shame he'd learned to push away over the years came creeping back, along with the memory of how Lucy's mother had winced at the word *runaway*, like he'd reached out and slapped her.

No, not Lucy, she wouldn't run away, she told him.

And then weeks later, how she screamed.

No, no, not Lucy! Not Lucy!

He'd driven Mrs. Soto to the morgue to identify the body. And numb as she was when he drove her back home, her last words to him were, *She would be alive if you'd believed me. If you'd bothered to do your job and look. But what do you care, what does anyone care, about girls like my Lucy?*

He wouldn't do that again, to another mother, to another girl.

We'll find her, he told Mrs. DeJesus, following her gaze out the window. At the night flashing blue and red.

And then, he heard his radio. He'd turned it down just low enough to keep track of what was going on, but not loud enough for the DeJesuses to hear. And in buzzed the miracle nobody ever got.

Female matching subject found, ambulance en route.

He was sure he heard it correctly, but excused himself from the parents while he stepped into another room for more information.

Is she alive?

Critical.

Where?

St. Mary's.

En route with mother and father.

They found her, he told Nina and Sam DeJesus. *She's on the way to the hospital. I'll take you in my patrol car.*

The cry that came out of Nina DeJesus still haunted him. It was so much like that of Ms. Soto. Primal. The way she fumbled getting up, like her legs didn't work, as she grabbed on to him again, asking, *Is she . . .*

She's alive—it's what she meant to ask but couldn't—and he quickly added, *but hurt.* It was all he said, all he really knew, as they hurried out of the house. But he wanted to prepare her. He felt her body go slack again.

What he remembered wanting to tell Nina when she cornered him in the hospital that night, when she told him to find the person who did this, was, *Be glad she's alive. So many aren't.* His mind flashed with the horrible image of Lucy Soto, with the horrible things done to her, to all the bodies he'd seen over the years, to the bodies of women and girls especially.

He couldn't tell Mrs. DeJesus all the ways the odds were stacked against Emilia—a girl, a girl with a brown face, a girl with a name like DeJesus.

Do you know how lucky you are?

No. Of course, he couldn't say that.

She would have spat in his face. Emilia? *Lucky?* With her black-and-blue body, her tongue she bit through, her cut face and missing teeth? With the uncertainty of whether there would be brain damage after her head was hit against the ground so hard, so many times? And with the certain emotional trauma she would endure the rest of her life? *Lucky?*

But she was.

All these years later, Manzetti understood more than ever how *lucky* Emilia was, how close she came to being another Lucy.

But the word went through Manzetti's mind and made him sick. Was that all he thought? She was *lucky?* Is that why he did a sloppy job? Why he followed the only lead he had and was willing to lock up anybody who might fit the bill? To make it easier? For whom?

For you?

Yes. That's how he'd managed.

But then Carl Smith called him.

Manzetti stared at the old file now marked REOPENED. Jeremy Lance stared back at him.

You prosecuted him. Another kid. Someone a traumatized eight-year-old identified. Someone you got to confess. Just because he displayed violent behavior at school. Just because you didn't want to think about Lucy Soto. Because her face, her neck, that cord, was all you saw when you shut your eyes at night and you needed to close each case. Because you didn't want anything else haunting you. Bad guy caught. The end. Another case solved. Move on to the next. And the next.

Good going, Manzetti. Fucking good going.

He put the picture of Emilia in the file, closed his desk drawer, and went home.

In the fridge sat two bottles of beer and leftover takeout. Manzetti grabbed a beer and closed the fridge. As he opened the bottle and took a long swallow, he stared at an invitation to a New Year's Eve party last week that he hadn't gone to. He crumpled it up and threw it out, then turned on the television.

The call he received from Carl Smith a few weeks ago was a punch in the gut. He couldn't have imagined eight years ago having to make the call to Nina DeJesus about it.

Or did you know all along, he thought as he got in the shower. *And just hoped it wouldn't catch up to you?*

Nina's voice on the phone a few weeks ago echoed in his head.

But why? I don't understand. How? Who? I don't understand. I don't understand.

That's what Nina DeJesus kept saying when she was finally able to speak. After he brought the past back through the phone.

Maybe I should've gone in person, Detective Manzetti thought. But he hadn't wanted to scare Emilia. What if she was home and she saw him, remembered him from the hospital and the trial?

He's dying, he'd told Nina over the phone. *He wants to . . .* He took a deep breath, had trouble uttering the next few words. *He wants to relieve his conscience,* Manzetti explained.

She'd hung up on him then.

He didn't call back. He knew he'd have to eventually, *but let her process this first, Manzetti,* he'd told himself. *Before you have to explain what a piece-of-shit scumbag this guy is.*

Detective Manzetti looked at his bare feet as the shower water fell around him. Here, when he was alone and the emergencies of the day were over and there was so much quiet, things haunted him. Like Carl Smith's voice when he called Detective Manzetti. He could still hear it. And his labored breathing. And the clicking sound of some kind of machine in the background.

I have to tell you something, Detective . . .

And so he began, the caller, telling Manzetti strange stories of his childhood that Manzetti listened to because he quickly realized the kind of person he was dealing with. Someone who reveled in the fear he instilled in others. Someone who, despite what Manzetti had told Mrs. DeJesus, didn't have a conscience at all, but rather was proud of what he'd done and couldn't stand going to his grave without boasting about it. Someone who identified himself as Carl Smith.

And you didn't even have to figure it out, did you? Manzetti thought. *He told you just what he'd done.*

Manzetti stood under the scalding water for a while longer, then got out and wrapped a towel around his waist. He headed back to the kitchen and opened the remaining bottle of beer as the day's crimes and misfortunes were recounted on the six o'clock news.

The phone rang and he answered.

Moments later, Manzetti placed the phone back on the receiver. He clicked off the television, drank his beer in the darkening apartment, knowing what he had to do next.

Emilia Walked Home

Emilia walked home from the elementary school. As she got closer to her house, she heard the loud shouts of children at the park. She looked at the sky; it would be dark soon.

They should go home.

Another scream. This one so shrill. And Emilia couldn't help but wonder if whoever that scream belonged to was okay. She kept walking home, but a gnawing feeling in her stomach made her stop again.

I should check, she thought.

Why hadn't anyone checked on her? Had no one heard her—the girl who screamed?

Emilia turned and headed toward the park.

When she walked up, no adults were around. She heard the crack of a bat hitting a ball, followed by urgent cheering and yelling, and she watched a boy run and a girl go up to bat over on the baseball field. The girl swung and another resounding crack filled the air, followed by more hooting and hollering.

Look at them, Emilia thought. *They don't know what can happen to them.*

She suddenly imagined the scene through the eyes of a predator. How easy it would be to overtake one of these kids, any of them, wait them out.

Emilia turned her attention back to the merry-go-round that was spinning with two children half hanging off. That shrill scream again, and Emilia spotted the girl it came from. She filled the air with her scream over and over again, all the while laughing. A moment ago, it had sounded so sinister to Emilia, a warning. But now, looking at the girl, she saw it was all just fun. Nothing to be afraid of.

Except it had sounded terrible. Emilia looked around, but no one came running to check on the children in the park. Nobody came at all.

Did anyone hear me? Emilia wondered. *Did they think I was just a kid, far away, having fun?*

Emilia sat on a bench under the tree and watched the kids spin.

She remembered spinning like that on the same merry-go-round when she was little. One time, spinning so fast she fell off and crashed hard onto the concrete. At the time, it was the worst thing that had ever happened to her.

Emilia watched the merry-go-round. No kids fell off this time, and instead it came to a stop and the two kids dismounted and walked out of the park. The playground was now empty except for the players who remained on the baseball field, too far away to notice her.

Emilia looked at the dome structure with tunnels next to the merry-go-round. She once wrote her name in there. She smiled, wondering if it was still there. Emilia went over and crawled into one of the tunnels.

Jesus, had she really been able to stand up in here? She crawled to one of the farthest walls, the one filled with graffiti parents never knew about because they never bothered to crawl in this far. Here were the hearts and initials declaring love **4ever**. The scattered names of people Emilia never knew. A drawing of a penis. The assurance that somebody out there thinks **You're stupid!** and the promise that **for a good time call 1-800-Ur-Sister!**

Emilia looked toward the bottom. In small letters on the yellow gloss–painted wall, almost undetectable, she saw her name. **EMILIA**.

She'd brought the black Sharpie from home that day, knowing the whole time this was what she was going to do. And her heart had pounded with each step she took as she walked to the playground. She'd had to wait for the perfect moment, when the tunnel cleared, to write it.

But what a thrill it had been. To see her name, to know it would be here. She remembered.

She stared at it now and tried to remember the girl who'd put it there.

EMILIA.

She touched her name, too. She'd written it just before that terrible day. She'd been this girl, this Emilia, the one who wrote her name. Unafraid, younger, and weaker, but not broken.

Am I broken? she wondered.

She traced her name with her finger now. *Had* **EMILIA** *ever really existed?* Had that girl who wasn't always looking over her shoulder ever really existed?

Emilia heard the crack of the bat again and remembered the kids on the field.

She touched her name one last time and quickly crawled out. It was dark now. The streetlights had come on. Everyone was gone except for one boy, doing a couple of practice hits on his own.

The white light of the bakery just across the street glowed while the man inside wiped the glass cases and put up a HELP WANTED sign. Suddenly Emilia felt someone's gaze on her, so she looked around but saw no one.

She turned, scanned every part of the playground. Her heart beat faster, and she looked back over at the boy hitting balls.

Go home! she wanted to yell, but she didn't want to startle him.

Come on, she thought as he hit one, two, three balls and ran out to retrieve them.

Go home. Go home now!

Her skin prickled and itched. She could feel panic crawling on her. And she tried very hard not to scream, not to run or leave that boy behind. He pitched each ball up in the air and hit them again.

She'd give him one more minute, and then she'd run over there and tell him, *You have to go home now!*

The boy collected the balls but sat on the bench, staring at the field.

You should be home. Someone should be worried about you.

Emilia looked down the block leading up to the baseball field. Someone would come for him soon, wouldn't they?

She heard a rustle and jumped. But then noticed a crow on the branch above her, looking in the direction of the field.

Go home! Emilia urged the boy.

Go home! the crow repeated.

Emilia blinked back the tears that were beginning to fill her eyes.

Go home now!

She kept sending the message his way, and finally, the boy gathered the balls and put them in various pockets. He picked up the bat and rested it on his shoulder before looking out at the field again and finally, finally, starting to walk home.

Emilia felt relieved. She watched him walk off the field and down the block.

Be careful, she warned.

When she started losing sight of him, she got up and followed. She stayed half a block to a block behind, losing track of him only momentarily in the shadow of a tree or bush. Each time he reappeared, she was relieved.

If someone grabs him, I'll be ready. I'll help him.

After a few minutes, he turned and walked up to a well-lit house, opened the door. The voices of other children tumbled out, and then silence as the door closed behind him.

Emilia walked past the house; the smell of food was in the air. She took a deep breath, imagined for a moment the boy not coming home. When would the house have started to settle into uneasy quiet? When would it start to shiver with fear and cold? When would the walls and floor and ceiling have split with uncontainable worry and grief and the unimaginable become suddenly very real?

Emilia imagined her mother, her father, her brother in that house, waiting for her to come home, possibly staring out the window, waiting.

And she, lying in the woods.

The tears came so fast, unexpectedly, and the pain she always carried with her suddenly filled her like a balloon and took up her whole chest. She choked on her tears.

Emilia hurried down the street, wiping her face. The wetness of her tears left patches of cold on her cheeks.

Why?

Why?

Why?

Why me?

The question drummed into her thoughts. It was one that sometimes floated into her mind, suddenly there without notice, and accompanied by others.

Why me?

Why had he done it? Why did he choose me? Why was the Girl Scout meeting canceled? Why didn't I just walk home? Why did I have to go into the woods? Why? Why? Why?

Emilia walked, but sensed, in the darkness, the weight of

someone's stare again. Someone was watching her. She glanced behind her and walked faster.

Maybe it's Jeremy Lance. Maybe he's found me because he knows what I did to him. He'll be angry.

She felt dizzy, her steps unreal. She felt like she was on the merry-go-round.

Why?

Focus! she told herself, because she had to keep her legs working. Because she couldn't sprout feathers right now and fly away. She had to stay in her right mind and keep her legs moving, make sure she got home.

Run.

Faster!

Her backpack bounced hard against her with each step.

Go home, Emilia. Go home! Don't fly away. Just keep running. Get home.

Her feet felt like they couldn't move fast enough. She felt danger at her heels, like the dog that chased her years ago, frothing at the mouth. She felt it on her back, like a hand was just inches away from grabbing her and pulling her into the darkness. She felt it all around her.

Then she heard strange little yelps and realized they were coming from her. She put her hands over her mouth.

Emilia braced herself for the explosion of light that would burst in her head—*any moment now! Any moment!*—as someone hit her from behind, blinding her.

Any moment now! Any moment!

You will fall.

And the world will go black.

And you won't be able to fight him off.

Again.

NO!

There was her house, up ahead, *just up ahead*. She pumped her legs harder.

Within moments she was cutting across her front yard, running up the stoop stairs and swinging open the screen door. It banged against the guardrail as she opened it.

The whole house shook with relief as the door slammed shut behind her. Emilia tried to catch her breath as a swell of emotion rose in her chest.

"Emilia? What happened? What's wrong?" Emilia's mother rushed to her from the couch, where her father also sat. And in another chair, a man Emilia almost recognized, but not quite.

Emilia caught her breath, quickly pushed down the sobs threatening to escape her.

"Nothing. I'm fine. The wind caught the door and I accidentally slammed it."

Her mother stared at her.

"Why are you shaking?"

"I'm not. It's cold outside. I ran the whole way because I know you worry. Just lost track of time." Emilia looked at the man.

"Look at me," Ma said. "You look scared. What happened? Tell me."

Emilia could hear the panic, the subdued hysteria, in her mother's voice.

"Nothing," Emilia repeated, trying to keep those same emotions out of her own.

The man smiled at Emilia and something flickered in her mind. She knew him. From where?

"Hello," he said to Emilia.

Ma looked nervous as she put her arm around Emilia's shoulders. "Emilia," she said. "This is Detective Manzetti. He worked your case years ago."

It took a moment for it to sink in, but then Emilia remembered. She had seen this man in her hospital room. He had given her the cards. Yes. No.

Emilia nodded. "Hello," she said.

Why is he here? Emilia thought.

The detective glanced over at her mother and a look of resignation passed on Ma's face.

"He's updating us," Ma said. She guided Emilia to the couch, where she sat between her parents.

The detective smelled like cigarettes. Emilia noticed that his clothes, while nice, were wrinkled. He reached over and took a sip from the glass of water on the coffee table, where Emilia also saw some papers.

He put down the glass. Looked at her.

"Hello, Emilia," he said, offering her a kind smile. "I've been in touch with your mother, but I've gotten some definitive information I thought would be best to share in person." His eyes were a strange light brown. They looked like the color had been rubbed out of them. Tired. He looked at Ma and she nodded for him to go on.

"Your mother has told you about Carl Smith—is that right?"

Emilia held her breath. Had he died? Was this detective coming to tell them Carl Smith was dead? A part of her hoped he was dead and gone forever. But another part of her wanted him thrown in prison. Who cared if he was too sick? Let him die there. Why should he be shown any mercy? Or maybe he'd come to tell them what Emilia secretly suspected, that Carl Smith had tricked them all. He'd never really been dying and now they couldn't find him. Because all this time *he's been hiding in the trees, watching you. Waiting. Again.*

Emilia exhaled and looked at the detective. "Yes, I know about him."

Detective Manzetti nodded, looked down at the floor. "Well, I'm sorry." He took a breath and looked back up at her. "I tried, but . . . the prosecutor confirmed they cannot prosecute the case, not in the condition he's in."

Ma had told her it was a possibility. But Emilia hadn't believed it, not really. How could someone do this to her and go unpunished? How could someone who *didn't* do this be the one who got punished instead? It was irrational, unreal, but here was the detective, and Ma, and her father, telling her just that. The confirmation felt like a crushing blow and heightened the fear she'd been trying to push down.

So, he would *still be out there*. And nobody cared that he did this to her, not really.

"He's in hospice care. In and out of consciousness, very close to death. There's no way he can hurt you, I promise you. But there's also no way he'll be able to stand trial." The detective shook his head. "I'm sorry."

Her mother put her arm around Emilia's shoulders, pulled her in close.

"I know you have no reason to believe me, but we know it was him. He confessed, gave us details we never released and no one else would know."

Ma hugged Emilia closer to her body.

Her father held her hand. Emilia didn't remember him reaching for it to begin with. She looked over at him. Her father's face was filled with so many emotions.

Emilia looked at the table in front of her. She focused on that report as the detective continued apologizing.

A few moments later, he collected the papers. Emilia's mother and father walked him to the door.

Emilia rushed upstairs to her room.

Ian Didn't See Emilia

Ian didn't see Emilia in school anymore, not in the halls or at lunch, and she was gone by the time he raced from his last class to hers. Except for the one time he looked out the window of his Algebra class and thought he caught a glimpse of her walking off campus, but couldn't be sure.

Emilia was nowhere to be found.

When he called, only her mother or Tomás answered. He didn't want to keep leaving messages and he didn't want them to know he and Emilia had broken up if she hadn't told them, so he stopped calling.

Maybe we didn't, Ian thought. *Maybe we never really broke up.*

A little hope rose in his chest, even though whenever he walked by her house, he was too chicken to go up to the door.

At night Ian would look from his dark window to hers, to that square of yellow light, in hopes of seeing her there, her silhouette, looking in his direction like she used to. But she didn't. She was never there. He didn't even see the birds on the ledge anymore.

Ian was suddenly afraid something terrible had happened to Emilia. Her mother and brother would tell him, wouldn't they?

For a moment, Ian wondered if they had. Had he blocked it out? Had something terrible happened to Emilia, again, and the world was keeping it a secret from him?

Tonight, he looked to the window again, at the yellow glow.

No, she was in there. She had to be. As long as that square was yellow, Emilia was there, safe.

He lay in bed, retracing the last couple of months. So much had happened.

What happened?

You were stupid, he told himself. *And then that strange and terrible news about Jeremy Lance.* And now she was closing up again like she had all those years ago.

The day he saw her on her front lawn, and he cawed at her before running home, he'd felt *something.* He felt, somehow, that he was chosen. That if everyone from their class had lined up and Emilia had to caw at just one of them, she would still choose him. She would caw at him. Because he understood her. They were linked forever in that moment. That's what he thought. He was the only one who understood her. He'd been so sure back then.

So after that day, he kept going back to her house, whenever he saw her outside, even when his mother said, *Stay away from Emilia DeJesus.* Because all he could do was think of Emilia DeJesus and how lonely she must be. And how she didn't go to school anymore. And how she was stuck in her house all day. And how she no longer talked.

All he wanted was to be her friend.

He'd sneak over to her house and knock on their back door.

Are you allowed to be here? her mother asked once. He shrugged and waited. But her mother would call for Emilia, and she'd come running to the screen door and he'd ask her to play.

She always nodded.

She wouldn't talk to him at first. Only cawed. And gestured. Pointed to where she wanted to go, or turned her face in the direction of what she wanted to do. She'd grab a rock if she thought they should play hopscotch. She'd point to the grass, where they would take turns doing cartwheels. She'd point to the hammock her father had hung in their backyard, and they would swing on it together.

Ian remembered.

I did understand her.

She would push them off from the ground and keep them going higher. Sometimes, she was able to swing so fast, so high, that the hooks of the hammock creaked as though they might break, and he would actually feel his stomach flip. He'd look over at her those times, to see if her stomach flipped, too, but she never looked back. Her eyes were steady on the sky, looking at it so intensely as her black hair fluttered. It was as if she thought that if she pushed hard enough, she could reach it. Sometimes, Ian believed she could.

It was there that she first spoke to him. Not a caw, but real words.

She suddenly reached over and held his hand. *Close your eyes,* she said quietly. He looked at her in surprise, but she still wouldn't look back. So he closed his eyes.

They were mostly in the shade, but they were going so high, they swung in and out of reach of the sunrays. With his eyes closed, Ian felt like he was going through a flashing tunnel, the wind swishing in his ears and through the trees.

He said to her, laughing, *We're going to fly off this thing!* because he was trying to cover up his fear. He hadn't expected her to speak again.

But she did.

That's the point, she'd said. He opened his eyes and looked over at Emilia still staring at the sky as she pushed her feet off the ground harder and swung them higher in the hammock.

And then she looked over at him.

Him.

And she leaned in and kissed him on the cheek.

Ian stared at the glowing yellow window. It flickered, like someone had just walked past the light.

Emilia. She's there.

He wanted to climb out his window and go to her, climb the tree and inch over on the branch closest to her window and knock on it. To make sure she was really there. She might or might not talk to him like back then. She might or might not ignore him. She might or might not let him in.

He imagined her, lying on her bed, staring at the ceiling with her arms behind her head.

Emilia. Let me in, please.

But he was sure she wouldn't hear him. And he both wished and was afraid she would look in the direction of his window. She didn't want him anymore. And he didn't know how to be her chosen one again. He wished he still had the nerve he'd had when he was a kid.

"Caw," he whispered into the silence of his room. But he only felt stupid and sad.

That Night, Ma Came into Her Room

That night, Ma came into her room and stood over her while Emilia slept. But Emilia was awake; she was always awake now. Her eyes were open and had already adjusted to the darkness, so she saw her mother's hunched shoulders and her ghost face as she stood in the light of the moon. And she knew how long her mother stayed. Not just a few minutes like before. Sometimes, it felt like hours.

Emilia thought of an old story her grandmother told her once of a woman who lost her children and roamed the night, weeping in search of them.

"You can't keep doing this, Ma," Emilia whispered into the darkness.

"You're awake," Ma said, her voice thin. "I . . . just had to check on you."

Emilia sat up. Her mother didn't sound okay. And she didn't look okay. Emilia imagined the woman from the story, crying, searching for her children. She saw her mother.

Ma sat on the bed.

"Emilia," she whispered. "I thought . . . when you came

running in like that, you looked so scared—" Her mother's voice broke and it frightened Emilia how Ma seemed to know exactly how she'd felt. "I immediately thought you'd seen Jeremy Lance. I . . . know it's a small chance, but you're not ready for that."

"I didn't run into him," Emilia managed, though earlier she had felt like she might see him at any moment, following behind her. What if she ran into him one day? What if she found herself face-to-face with him and was completely unprepared?

She couldn't let that happen.

Ma took a deep breath. "Okay," she said. Then, "I'm sorry the detective was here. That you just walked in without knowing. I should've . . ."

"It's okay, Ma," Emilia whispered.

"I always hated that he made you answer all those questions immediately after." Emilia knew Ma was talking about the past now, how she was questioned right after the attack. "They never should've done that. I should've . . . You couldn't even talk, for Christ's sake. Your mouth was—" Ma shook her head.

Emilia's memory flickered again with a hazy image of the detective and a notepad. With YES and NO note cards in front of her.

Did you see his face? Emilia had closed her eyes and one face came floating into her mind, one she was afraid of, the boy who'd punched his hand through the bus window.

Emilia stared at the cards.

I think so. Maybe, she tried to say. Hot pain shot throughout her jaw and mouth, immediately reminding her not to speak. She made a strange noise and both Detective Manzetti and her mother quickly urged her to use the cards.

She saw his face in the woods now. He was there. In the trees. Slowly she reached over and nudged one of the cards the detective placed so close to her fingers.

YES.

Do you know him?

She closed her eyes again. She saw his face floating there, hovering in the trees.

Stay with me, Emilia. Did you see a face? Someone you know?

Words she couldn't say ran through her head. *Maybe I think it was him, but . . .* She wanted to explain, but more hot pain pulsed in her jaw, her ears, her head. Emilia felt dizzy.

Use your cards, Emilia.

Again, she nudged the card that read **YES**.

Do you know his name?

NO.

Later that day—*or days later?*—they came back with pictures—of teachers, custodians, her father, her brother, neighbors, strangers she vaguely recognized, and then, *there*. The one she was afraid of. The one that floated in her mind.

That boy.

And she pointed to it.

"How much do you remember, Emilia?" her mother whispered now, on her bed. The hospital room faded away and Emilia was back with Ma in her room.

The way they were sitting, side by side, in the dark, not looking at each other, reminded Emilia of the confessionals she used to have to go to when she attended Sunday school. The patterned screen between her and the priest that separated them and invited some kind of confidentiality, the idea that you could tell him anything, even the very worst. Especially the very worst.

But she couldn't tell her mother the truth. That she could remember the smallest detail, the strangest things. That she'd tied a red rubber band around her pinkie at lunch that day. That she'd worn that sweatshirt she'd sent away for with ten dollars and three proofs of purchase for the first time—the yellow Cheerios one that she never saw again—and that's why she used to throw each new box of that cereal across the room until her mother stopped buying them. She couldn't tell her that when she closed her eyes at night, she remembered exactly the way the tree branches looked above her, that she could see the finest lines etched in the bark.

She couldn't tell her mother this. Or explain why, no matter how hard she tried, whenever she imagined her attacker's face, it was *always* Jeremy Lance she saw, just as he'd looked that day through the window on the bus, right before he punched through the window. His mouth open in a scream.

Even now, when they told her she'd been wrong, why couldn't she change what she saw in her memory?

Why did I picture his face? Why?

Had she even caught one glimpse, one small glimpse of the

attacker? Or had she immediately thought she'd seen Jeremy Lance, because she was afraid?

Her breathing quickened and her stomach felt like she'd swallowed a bag of jagged ice.

Her mother reached for her hand.

"I'm sorry. You don't have to answer," Ma said. After a while, she spoke again. "Detective Manzetti says Carl Smith is pretty far gone . . . will likely be dead any day now. I know, I know it's not fair." Ma's voice took on an edge and she squeezed Emilia's hand harder. "But he can't get you. He's dying. There's no way he can do anything to you anymore. Don't be afraid. It'll be over soon, Emilia. And we can focus on you getting better."

The words *getting better* made Emilia feel terrible.

"But I'm fine," Emilia whispered, feeling small and stupid. And she *could be* fine. If everyone just gave her time and space. She *was* dealing with it, in her own way.

"Emilia . . . I made an appointment for you, to go see a—"

"Don't, Ma. I already know."

"It's for the best, and I—"

"Please, Ma." Emilia closed her eyes.

Ma got up. She let out a long breath. "Okay," she said. And then leaned down and kissed Emilia's forehead before she turned and headed toward the bedroom door. Emilia opened her eyes and watched her go.

Was it my fault, Ma? My fault? The question was somewhere inside her. But she couldn't ask.

Maybe it *was* her fault Jeremy Lance was imprisoned for eight years. And maybe she was the reason her family fell apart. And maybe it was even her fault the attack ever happened. Because she should never have gone out to that playground, into those woods, alone.

Emilia swallowed her guilt and her words. She never wanted to ask any questions. She never wanted to know the answers.

Ma stopped at the door. "You were just a child," she said, as if she'd heard Emilia's thoughts. And her mother stood there a moment longer before heading down the stairs.

Ma's Words from Last Night

Ma's words from last night echoed in Emilia's head as she rode her bike from Uniondale to Levittown. *You were just a child.* Did Ma mean it *wasn't* her fault? Or that it *was*, but that she couldn't really be blamed because she was just a child? Either way, Emilia had to face exactly what she'd done.

You've gone fucking crazy, Emilia, she told herself.

Maybe, she answered. *But anyway, I can't take the chance of running into him.*

If Ma knew what you were doing, if anyone knew what you were doing, they'd kill you. You'd be institutionalized.

Maybe. But when I see him, I want to be ready.

Emilia looked down at the paper in her hand, not that she needed to. If she closed her eyes, she could still see the address on the report the detective had brought over and laid on their coffee table. It was strange the way things happened. She didn't think she knew what she was doing when she stared at that paper, or what she would do later, but she ran upstairs and wrote it down as soon as she got to her room.

She knew she didn't want to forget the address. And she couldn't trust her memory anymore.

Emilia looked up and slowly rode past addresses displayed on mailboxes until she came to 346 Fort Road. She stared at the brick house with dead trees and bushes obstructing the windows.

She didn't have to do this. She shouldn't do this. She was sure her mother would grab her by the arm and pull her away from here as fast as possible if she knew.

But Emilia parked her bike and went up the walkway.

She rang the doorbell.

She waited.

Will she call the cops?

Will she push me as soon as she sees me, send me flying down the porch steps?

Flying.

Will he *answer?* She hadn't even considered it until that very moment, and now it was too late. The heavy door opened and a woman—Mrs. Lance—stood on the other side of the screen door between them.

"Hi," Emilia said. It came out funny. Like she'd been holding her breath. Katherine Lance stared out at her.

Emilia knew she should say something, but she didn't know what. Finally, she spoke.

"I'm . . ." Her words got stuck. "I'm . . . My name . . ."

"I know who you are," Mrs. Lance said. Her voice chilled Emilia and something told her to run, but she stayed.

Why are you doing this? You have no right to be here. She must hate you. You ruined their lives.

Emilia swallowed the panic.

"And you, you're Mrs. Lance?" Emilia felt the need to confirm. Her voice trembled in her throat.

"Yes," she answered. She let Emilia stand there awkwardly, uncomfortably, before speaking.

"And you're Emilia. Emilia DeJesus."

Emilia nodded, though she knew Mrs. Lance was not asking for confirmation. Here they were, face-to-face, staring at each other in silence.

"Why are you here?" she asked finally.

Emilia's mouth went dry. Why was she here? Because she was afraid of running into them somewhere. Because she didn't want to hide. Because she wanted to apologize even though it would mean nothing.

Because I'm so sorry. I thought I saw Jeremy that day, but I was wrong, so wrong.

"I asked why are you here?" Katherine Lance repeated sharply.

Emilia startled, but her mouth refused to utter a word, and now her body refused to run.

The woman shook her head. "So you ring my doorbell, and now you have nothing to say?"

"I'm . . . I'm sorry," Emilia said.

Katherine Lance stared at her. She didn't say anything.

Emilia looked at the ground. "I . . . I'm sorry. I don't know why . . ." Tears filled her eyes. Her heart beat faster. Her body felt like it was shaking.

Go home, she thought. She turned to leave.

"Wait."

Emilia looked back. Jeremy's mother looked disgusted with her, but she reached for the screen door and opened it.

"Come in," she said.

As soon as Emilia entered the kitchen, she noticed the sign on the far wall.

WELCOME HOME, JEREMY!

She swallowed the bitter taste in her mouth and tried to find somewhere else to look as she sat down at the kitchen table. She kept on her coat and scarf even though the house was warm, stuffy. Mrs. Lance stood by the kitchen sink.

Mrs. Lance must have made the sign, right here, at this very table. Emilia ran her hand over the surface, imagined a welcome-home cake, Mrs. Lance here with Jeremy, looking at him, *how? The way Ma looks at me? Like she can't quite believe I'm really there sometimes?*

"Tell me why you're here." Mrs. Lance's voice cut into her thoughts.

But Emilia couldn't tell her it was because she felt like she should show her face. That she should come here and tell Mrs. Lance, Jeremy, that she was sorry. How silly and simplistic and terrible and impossible it felt in this moment. Why did she ever think this would make a difference? Had she done this to feel better, for herself? Or for them? As if they cared about anything she would have to say.

And maybe, a small voice told her, *if I see him, I'll know once and for all. And I can be* sure *it wasn't him.*

All these thoughts raced through Emilia's mind. She glanced at Mrs. Lance, her pinched face, her narrow eyes. The woman hated her—Emilia knew she did. She had to.

How could she answer the question? Nothing seemed appropriate. She could feel Mrs. Lance staring at her.

"I don't know," Emilia finally said.

Suddenly a door to a room down the hall opened noisily and a young man emerged. He rushed through the kitchen, past Emilia, and headed to the side door that led outside. "Rec time," he yelled.

He was gone in an instant, the door slamming behind him, and Emilia caught her breath as it registered. It was him. She recognized him.

He was thin and pale. And the little bit she caught of his face looked hollow and gaunt.

His mother went to the door, yelled at him to be careful, and closed it slowly.

She turned and looked at Emilia. "That's Jeremy," she said, watching Emilia for her reaction.

Emilia nodded.

Mrs. Lance went to the window and looked outside. Emilia could see him from where she sat as he rode his bike. He rode in and out of their visibility.

Mrs. Lance took a deep breath. "Did you come here to tell me your side of the story? Is that it?"

Maybe. Maybe she was there to assure Mrs. Lance she never meant to name him. Maybe she was there to tell her *it wasn't my fault*. Or to be told it wasn't her fault.

I am so very sorry that I've ruined your life, your son's life. And now I want you to tell me I didn't. So I can go on with mine.

She looked at Mrs. Lance, who wouldn't even look her way now. "Let me tell you something. Let me give you our side of the story. Does that sound fair?"

She glanced at Emilia, her lips pressed together firmly as she waited for an answer.

"Yes," Emilia said.

Katherine Lance took a breath, and began. "Jeremy was a difficult kid. Didn't talk until he was eight years old." She looked back outside as she spoke. "I feel like he was somehow locked up, inside himself, ever since he was little. But *I* could see him in there, my boy, lost somewhere. And I had to pull him out. Do you understand me?"

Emilia didn't respond, just stared as Katherine Lance continued.

"No, of course you don't. But it doesn't matter. I *knew* I could get him out. I had to tell him, 'Come out to this world, be free. It's okay. I'll help you, I'll protect you.'"

Mrs. Lance wiped at her face quickly.

"He trusted me. I got him into that group home. Do you know how much he—we—had to work to get him to say his name?

But he did, and he trusted me. And he came out of himself. Sometimes, he'd have rough days." She looked out the window. "One time he punched his hand through a bus window because he'd lost a bracelet I told him gave him special powers." She shook her head. "It was stupid of me, but he refused to ever take it off because *he trusted me.* Because he thought it helped him. Because he was convinced it was the reason he made so much progress."

She turned to Emilia, who sat there, her blood running cold as she remembered picking up a bracelet that day. The way Jeremy was looking at her from the window.

"Then that day. And you said it was him. They arrested him . . . at the home." Emilia looked away; it was so hard to look at Mrs. Lance, the stone-cold face, and now with all this new information.

"I wasn't there when it happened," Mrs. Lance continued. "I was here when I got a phone call from one of his therapists." She closed her eyes. "I could hear him screaming in the background."

Emilia's eyes filled with tears.

"The group home is twenty minutes away. I drove to the police station where they were taking him. I got there before them, saw as they brought him in. Screaming. Yelling. He was . . ." She shook her head, as if trying to forget. "There was no calming him down." She took a deep breath. "And I saw it all unravel. All that work, since he was three. All kinds of therapies to get him to walk, to speak, to socialize, to interact with others. The things that come so easy for so many other kids, Jeremy had to *work* for, harder than I've seen anyone work before in my life. All that progress, just undone, right there."

Mrs. Lance looked at Emilia. Stared at her with that same impenetrable look. But then Emilia saw it crack, fall as Mrs. Lance was overcome with so many emotions. She brought her hands to her face, turned away.

Emilia closed her eyes, as if that would help shut out the sound of this woman's sobbing, profound sobs that had been pushed down deep, time and time again. It was too much.

What have I done? What have I done? Emilia wondered as tears spilled down her own face.

Finally, the sobbing subsided. Mrs. Lance took deep breaths, gained control of her voice, and asked, "So tell me, why did you name my boy?"

Emilia shook her head, wiped her eyes and running nose. "I don't know," she said.

"You don't know? That's not an answer."

"I don't know," Emilia repeated.

"That's not an answer. *You* came here. You came to *our* house. You showed your face here, so now give me an answer!" Her voice was firm and Emilia was scared.

"I . . . I was scared. I was scared of him!"

Mrs. Lance looked at Emilia, nodded. They stayed there in the silence of the kitchen a long time. Emilia wanted to leave, but she was afraid to move.

"Everyone's always afraid of him. At least you were honest."

Katherine Lance walked over and offered Emilia a few paper napkins. Emilia wiped her face, blew her nose. Her eyes fell on a schedule on the refrigerator with times for eating, showering, sleeping. Jeremy's mom followed Emilia's gaze.

"His daily schedule," Mrs. Lance explained. "Same one he kept in prison. It makes him feel safe. Keeps him calm. The first few days home were horrible. But then I remembered how he liked things just so as a little boy. And . . . if I keep to that schedule, just so, it helps. Except for the shower." A new edge came into her voice then. "He needs to keep to the schedule, and yet, as soon as he gets in the shower, he's yelling and screaming and . . ." Mrs. Lance turned and walked back to the window.

Emilia's heart filled with more horror and guilt.

What horrible things had happened to Jeremy?

A type of radio on the counter buzzed, and Mrs. Lance automatically reached out her hand and turned it up.

Something about an accident on a street Emilia somewhat recognized. She suddenly realized it was a police scanner and wondered why Katherine Lance owned one.

Mrs. Lance turned it back down.

"You'd be surprised what we're surrounded by every day, Emilia. There was a murder three weeks ago, barely made the news. A young woman was assaulted while jogging last year, found unconscious in the bushes by another jogger. She lived. That's nice, isn't it?"

Emilia stared at Mrs. Lance's face.

"Another was followed in her car for half an hour until suddenly, at a red light, some guy got out of his car and started banging on her window, threatening her, calling her names. There are so many, Emilia, I can't keep them straight. I used to study each case, any newspaper clipping I could find, took notes while watching the news, if they made the news, if I thought there was the slightest possibility it was *him*. The man who attacked you and got away with it. I looked for clues. I used to call the police, give them leads.

"At first they were . . . courteous, at least on the surface. But then they just thought I was a mental case. Too distraught, they said. Finally they told me I had to stop or they'd take legal action. And they said anything on my record would keep me from being able to visit Jeremy in prison." Katherine Lance stopped, shook her head, and took a deep breath. But Emilia could see the anger in her face at the thought of being forbidden from seeing her son.

"And what did they do when they found out about Carl Smith?" She looked at Emilia but went on, not waiting for an answer. "Sorry, they said. They are so sorry. As if that means anything."

Emilia got a sick feeling in her stomach.

A buzzer went off, making Emilia jump. Mrs. Lance looked at the kitchen clock. "I have to start his lunch," she said.

Emilia knew that meant it was time for her to go. She stood up and headed toward the kitchen door slowly.

She struggled to unglue her tongue from the roof of her mouth.

Tell her.

Now.

Emilia's hand was on the doorknob. She closed her eyes and forced out the only words she had. "I know it doesn't mean much. But I'm so sorry. I will always be sorry." Her voice was thin and weightless and she didn't know if Mrs. Lance heard her. Emilia was too ashamed to look back at her.

Emilia turned the knob and opened the door. A cold gust of wind rushed in.

She closed the door behind her.

Outside, Jeremy Lance approached Emilia on his bicycle as she picked up hers.

Even though she knew the truth—*he wasn't the attacker, Emilia!*—she couldn't help the fear that shot through her heart and the rest of her body. Emilia looked at the kitchen window, where Mrs. Lance stared out at her. She resisted jumping on her bike and pedaling away as fast as possible.

"Hi," he said.

Jeremy Lance pedaled past Emilia. He reached the corner, made a wide turn, and rode back at the same, even pace.

"Hi," he said as he approached again.

"Hi," Emilia managed. This time he stopped, just next to her and her bike. Emilia's heart beat faster.

The day was hardly bright, but he squinted his eyes as he looked at her, as if the light outside was too much, and Emilia realized, with a fresh pang of guilt, that maybe it was.

"You came out of my house. Were you talking to my mom?"

Emilia nodded, looked toward the kitchen window again, but now she couldn't tell if Mrs. Lance was still there.

"That's nice," he said. His lips were pale and his smile was too big, and Emilia tried not to be afraid of him, but she was shaking and even if she wanted to pedal away, her legs felt too weak now. She stared at the dark shadows under his eyes that made him look like he hadn't slept in days. "I love my mom," he said.

He looked at Emilia expectantly. "I love my mom, too," she said, swallowed the lump in her throat. "I should get going." She was afraid to turn her back on him, but she wanted to leave.

He nodded, put one foot up on his bike pedal like he was going to leave, too, but then set it back down on the ground.

"Hey," he said, cocking his head to the side before she could ride away. "Do I know you?"

Emilia's blood froze.

What will he do if he knows it's me?

Emilia couldn't help thinking this.

She shook her head. "No."

"Oh," he said. "I've been gone for a while." He looked down at his feet, at the untied laces of his sneakers. "I've been in prison," he said. "Shoot, I'm not supposed to tell anyone. You won't tell, will you?"

Emilia shook her head. He smiled. She wished he would stop smiling.

"Anyway, I thought maybe I met you a long time ago." He

kept his gaze on her. She saw drool puddling up in the corners of his mouth.

Emilia was scared—dizzy, and cold, and so scared.

She shouldn't have come here.

She wouldn't look him in the eye, but she felt his gaze on her. And she didn't want to make any sudden moves. He took out a pack of gum from his pocket, a red, white, and blue packet with one-eyed Bazooka Joe staring at Emilia. Jeremy held it out to her. "Want one?"

She was afraid to say no, so she reached for a piece. Her hand shook as he placed it in her palm.

"Chew it," he said, laughing.

Emilia could see his teeth and it made her feel queasy. She unwrapped the gum and reluctantly chewed it.

"Hey, you're cold," he said, noticing how she shivered. Her mind flashed with the memory of his face. On the playground. On that day.

She looked up at him, shook her head.

"Wait . . . I do know you," he said.

"No, no, anyway I gotta go . . ." Emilia turned away and got on her bike.

"Wait."

Emilia started pedaling, glanced back as he struggled with his bicycle, his shoelaces getting caught up in the pedals.

"Wait," he called. "I know you! Wait."

But her body prickled with fear and restraint.

"I said wait!" he yelled. He sounded angry. Maybe everyone was wrong. Maybe she *was* right. Maybe it *was* Jeremy Lance; maybe it had been him all along.

Emilia pedaled faster and tried not to look back. She didn't want to see his face, angry, coming for her.

But at the end of the block, she looked quickly—she couldn't help it—and saw him riding toward her on his bicycle so fast. His face twisted in confusion. And his mother was suddenly running behind him, chasing him, calling his name.

Emilia Replayed Everything

Emilia replayed everything in her mind—being in the kitchen with Jeremy's mother, listening to her, and then how he had pedaled toward her.

Jeremy Lance knew who she was, or he would figure it out soon. And his mother *knew* she was still afraid of him, hated her even more.

It made her angry and ashamed. But she made herself replay the day of the attack in her mind, over and over again instead of pushing it away. Each time was just as horrible.

Remember, Emilia. Remember!

She remembered, but . . . she always saw the same thing. The same sweatshirt she wore. And her blue coat. And the smoke-gray day. And the cold.

And then his face. Jeremy's face. Just as he'd looked on the bus. *Just* as he'd looked on the bus.

Emilia conjured up his face again, again, again.

It was always the same, not one change.

Jeremy, *exactly* as he'd looked on the bus. His hair disheveled *just* as it'd been on the bus. His shirt, the *same* shirt he'd been wearing that day. His expression, scary and horrified, *exactly* the same as his expression that day on the bus.

Emilia's blood ran cold.

Could I have cut his face from my memory, from that day, and put it on the real attacker, Carl Smith? Could a brain do that?

Emilia wondered this in the darkness of her room.

She shook her head. *No,* she told herself. *Impossible.*

But something told her it could.

PART FIVE

Mid-January 1995

I Need a Favor

"I need a favor," Emilia said into the phone as she looked out her bedroom window. The light went on in Ian's room.

"Emilia?" he said. She could hear the surprise in his voice, and she imagined him in his room, sitting up in bed.

"Will you take me to the train station?" she said quickly.

"Right now? What's wrong?"

"No, not now. Nothing's wrong. Tomorrow."

She heard him rustling around. "Why?"

She hesitated. "I'll tell you tomorrow, but will you? Please?"

There was a short pause. Then, quietly, he answered, "Yeah, of course. Of course I'll take you."

Emilia breathed a sigh of relief. She closed her eyes and pictured him. She pressed the phone to her ear, listened for his breathing.

"Thanks."

There was a long silence on the other end and she felt sheepish suddenly, for calling him, for asking him for this favor after she'd cut him out of her life. She heard his gentle breathing and thought of his mouth, of how it felt on hers. And she missed him.

"So, how are you?" he asked finally.

"I'm okay." She tried to sound convincing. "You?"

How are you? I miss you. What happened, Ian?

"I . . . ," he began, but then paused. She could tell he was being careful. "Good. I'm good," he answered. There was so much silence between them, and with each quiet moment, Emilia felt sadder and sadder. She closed her eyes and mouthed his name silently. She wanted to feel him on her lips even as she felt the two of them falling into some place they'd never get out of. She wished there were an easy way to tell him everything, but there wasn't. And it felt like there was too much to even try.

"Emilia?"

She opened her eyes, focused back on their conversation. "That's good," was all she could say. She could almost picture the look on his face, sitting on his bed, where they had lain and kissed when his mother wasn't home. It felt like so long ago.

"What time?" he said suddenly, and there was a distance in his voice that caught her off guard and pulled her out of the memories of who they used to be. "Tomorrow. What time?"

"Oh . . . like you're picking me up for school."

Another long silence before he asked, "Do you want me to come with you?"

Say yes, Emilia. Say yes!

"No," she heard herself say. She felt a pang of disappointment with herself and tried to explain. "The thing is . . ."

"Forget it, don't—"

"It's just that . . . I need to do this by myself, you know?"

"No, I don't know," he said quickly, then more softly, "What is it you're doing, anyway?"

She twisted the phone cord around her foot. "Can I just tell you tomorrow?"

"Why can't you tell me now?"

She wasn't being fair to him. If she were Ian, she would've hung up and had nothing to do with her ever again. But that wasn't his way. He'd always been there for her. When no one else was.

Even when she was a bird.

Just tell him, Emilia.

"Tell me tomorrow, then," he said. "Or, you know, don't tell me. Whatever."

She was about to reply, but she heard the sudden click of the phone.

See you tomorrow? she thought, and it was stupid because if he'd said it, she knew she would have resented him.

But he didn't say it. Of course not, Emilia. He doesn't owe you anything.

She looked over at his window, the yellow glow of his bedroom light. She reached impulsively for her lamp, to switch the light on and off, but then stopped when she saw his window suddenly go black.

Emilia hung up the phone.

The Next Morning

The next morning, Ian's car pulled up in front of her house, red and dull and screeching as he turned into the driveway. Tomás shot Emilia a funny look across the living room when he heard it.

"I'm going," she called to her mom as she slipped her backpack over her shoulder.

Her mother came out from the kitchen and stood in the doorway.

"Okay," she said, wiping her hands on a dish towel.

Emilia looked at her mother, dressed in a brown outfit she had worn weeks and weeks ago.

"Ma . . . ," Emilia said.

Her mother noticed the way Emilia took in her outfit, and she brushed her skirt. "I know. You hate this outfit."

"No," Emilia said, looking at her mother. Ma was pushing her auburn hair out of her face, revealing a beauty too often hidden by worry and concern, by a hardness that looked at the world with too much suspicion and worst-case expectations.

Ma turned her head, revealing the earrings Emilia had given her for Christmas, and smiled. "How do they look?" she asked.

"Beautiful," Emilia said. Her nose tingled with the oncoming tears.

Her mother looked at her. "You okay?"

Ian beeped the horn.

Emilia smiled and nodded. "You need to worry less, Ma. Gotta go."

Emilia rushed to leave, but her mother came over and gave her a hug. And Emilia suddenly felt such tenderness for her family, and sadness, too, that it threatened to come bubbling out.

Don't! she told herself as she pulled away from her mother. It would alarm Ma. She would move up Emilia's appointment, immediately take her to the psychologist, whom they'd be seeing soon enough anyway. Emilia had been able to avoid going by making excuses each time. She was bombarded with schoolwork; could they reschedule? She had an important test coming up; couldn't they wait just a little longer? Until Ma finally said no, they could not, and Emilia circled the day on her calendar, staring at it each day with dread.

I love you, she thought as she pulled away from Ma. If she said the words, Ma would know she wasn't feeling quite herself today.

"See you later," Emilia said quickly.

"Okay . . . have a good day."

"Yep." Emilia opened the door. She wanted to stay home. She wanted to climb into her mother's bed like she did when she was a child. She didn't want to go out into the cold. But she felt like she had to do this.

Go, she told herself, *before you don't go through with it, before Ma thinks something's wrong.* "Bye," she said before rushing out.

"Bye," her mother said.

Emilia stepped outside to a cold gray morning. She'd kept Ian waiting long enough, but she couldn't help looking back at her house.

She imagined her father walking up the steps later today.

He'd been coming by, at least for a little while, most days. But Emilia knew he was just waiting until he was convinced she was okay.

Then he'll leave again. That's why he hasn't gotten a job here. Or an apartment.

Emilia looked toward the living room window and her heart dropped. She spotted Tomás suddenly there, staring at her. She waved at him and saw the flurry of his hand as he waved back. It made her want to cry.

She quickly got in the car.

"So where are you going?" Ian asked as they came to a corner.

"The train station," Emilia answered, avoiding his look.

"No, I mean, where are you *going?*"

Emilia looked out the window, trying to figure out how to answer his question.

"Not far," she said, looking up at the sky.

"What's that mean?"

They came to a stop sign. But Emilia kept her gaze out the window and Ian continued driving. He didn't ask anything else, and only the screech of the car interrupted the cold silence between them as they drove past the street leading to the elementary school. Emilia looked down the block and then, suddenly, it was behind them.

She closed her eyes and pretended they were headed to the museum, that first time they went. That time they drove with the windows down and played the music so loud it drowned out the screeching of Ian's car. Emilia could almost feel the hot wind whipping her hair again like it had that day.

Where do you want to go? Ian had yelled over the whooshing gusts and loud music.

I don't know, she had yelled back, laughing, trying to keep her hair out of her face. She had said, *Let's go somewhere. Anywhere! Anywhere as long as I'm with you!* And that's what they'd done.

She could remember Ian looking back at her then, in a way he didn't seem to anymore.

He used to be able to see me. Not poor Emilia who was attacked. Just me. When did his look turn into so much pity and looming questions?

In that moment, on the way to the museum, Emilia's father was still in Alaska catching rabbits, and Jeremy was still guilty as charged instead of tragic, and Emilia didn't know his mother, who stayed up all night reading horrible articles and following strangers, and Carl Smith, whoever he was, didn't even exist.

And winter had still been so far away.

Why can't we hold on to summer? Emilia wondered.

The screeching sliced into her thoughts and memories and maybe sleep, and Emilia's eyes fluttered open as they turned into the parking lot of the train station.

"We're here," Ian said. He pulled into a parking space.

"Thank you," she said to him.

He nodded, glanced at her backpack. "Are you running away?" he asked.

"Of course not," she said as she pressed the tips of her fingers against the cold windowpane.

"Then why won't you tell me where you're going?"

Tell him, Emilia.

She turned and looked at Ian. Beautiful Ian. His eyes were pleading with her now. Ian, the boy next door. The boy who smiled at her when he handed back her graded test in third grade. The boy who grew wings for her. The boy she loved.

But he wouldn't understand what she had to do. He couldn't understand what she felt.

"Ian." She said his name and reached out to put her hand on his cheek. He closed his eyes and she leaned in, kissed his lips so softly.

Maybe he *would* understand if she tried. But she couldn't risk it. She would explain later.

"Don't worry," she told him. "It'll be okay." She exited the car and hoped he wouldn't follow her.

He didn't.

But he stayed there. And as Emilia headed to the platform, she turned to look at him one more time. Her heart ached for him.

"I'll call you later," she yelled. He stared at her for a moment. "I promise."

He nodded and smiled, his face lighting up a little. And she blew him a kiss.

Emilia looked up and saw crows flapping in unison, cawing to her as she bought a train ticket.

She knew what they were saying. She'd forgotten how clearly she used to be able to understand them.

Careful, careful, Emilia. You're getting too close.

They cawed their warning, and the whooshing of their wings filled the air, but Emilia got on the train anyway.

From the window, she saw they followed her.

Followed the train.

Waited for her to emerge again. She could feel their watchful black eyes on her.

Don't get too close, they cawed. *You must remember. You must stay away from those who hurt you. Stay away. Listen to us.*

But Emilia didn't listen.

The First Thing She Saw

The first thing she saw when she got off the train from Hempstead to Atlantic Terminal in Brooklyn were signs for a stoop sale. And when she turned the corner, she saw the sidewalk full of items. She walked on the opposite side of the street.

Emilia looked down at the other address she had copied and memorized from Detective Manzetti's report. That was the place there, right where a man in a red sweatshirt stood outside, selling old, used items.

Emilia shoved her hands into her coat pocket, along with the now crumpled piece of paper, and she quickly diverted her attention.

That's where he lived. That's where he ate. That's where he came home, after . . .

Emilia took a deep breath. She looked up just as the man in the red sweatshirt noticed her and they accidentally made eye contact. He smiled and waved.

It stopped her in her tracks.

Every nerve in her body told her to leave, to run. But Emilia kept telling herself, *Don't be afraid, don't be afraid,* because a part of her wanted to go over there.

But any bravery she'd felt earlier drained itself completely from her body, leaving her feeling hollow. She hurried to the end of the block, and into a small market she noticed on the corner.

She hadn't thought past just getting here. She supposed, somewhere in her mind, she'd imagined an alternate universe, some version of herself ringing the doorbell, stepping far away, and looking at his face.

Did you think he would just answer? He's dying. He's in a hospital, right? On his deathbed. Or maybe that was him, out there, in that red sweatshirt.

Emilia felt confused and disoriented, unsure of the truth and everything she thought or had been told.

Why would you do this? Do you really want to see his face? she asked herself. *Do you want it to haunt you? Do you want it to come floating into your mind at night, right before you fall asleep? Do you want it to jolt you awake?*

Yes!

She wanted to *see him.* She wanted to see *his face.* She wanted to know who Carl Smith was. She deserved to know exactly who had attacked her.

She looked outside, across the street, at the man standing in front of the address she'd scribbled on a piece of paper.

Is it you? Is it?

Oh god, Emilia. What are you doing?

Emilia stood by the market window and kept her eyes focused outside. She watched the man.

He was thin. He wore jeans, and his sweatshirt was tattered. He looked like he'd been working outside forever, his face leathery and weathered. A lady called out to him, raised a bowl in the air, and he made his way to her as quickly as he could, but he had a limp that slowed him down. His arms, unnaturally long and thin and bony, dangled at his sides. When he reached the customer, he looked at the bowl, crossed his arms in front of himself, and shrugged. The customer said something and the man disentangled his arms, swatted at the air in a way that said, *Take it, take it.*

That can't be him, she thought as she continued watching from the market window. *It can't be. Can it?*

No. Carl Smith is dying.

Her mind was spinning.

"Are you okay? Can I help you?" an older woman at the counter called.

Emilia spun around and saw the woman studying her curiously. "No, I'm fine."

She grabbed an apple and put it in a plastic produce bag, as if to prove she was perfectly normal. Perfectly fine. She looked at the house again, at that place where he lived. Where he breathed and ate *and what, remembered that horrible day?* Emilia imagined him in one of those dark rooms. She was almost positive he was in there, looking out the window. At her.

"I'm not scared of you," Emilia whispered.

Look at me. I'm here. And I'm not scared of you. I'm not scared of you!

Emilia kept in the words she wanted to shout. And she tried not to think of how she was hiding out at the grocery store.

He's dying. There's no way he can do anything to you anymore, Emilia. Don't be afraid.

That's what Ma had whispered in the darkness of her room that night.

Don't be afraid.

"Kind of weird to have a stoop sale now, isn't it? In the middle of winter?" she asked the woman, who was now looking at her suspiciously. The woman looked out the window.

"Oh, his brother's been trying to get rid of some stuff. The man who lives there is dying." Her face lost its suspicion for a moment as it took on that look people had when they discussed death.

"Oh," Emilia said, her body buzzing with nerves and fear.

"Yeah, poor Carl," the woman said.

Dizzying anger spread throughout Emilia's body.

The lady outside, who'd asked the man about the bowl, was raising more items to him. He answered with the same gesture. *Fine, take it, take it.* The lady began sifting through a large box, clothes and shoes and pillowcases. She held up a brown sweater, threw it back in, and dug deeper before pulling out a dingy yellow sweatshirt. She held it up.

"Are you getting that or what?" the woman at the counter said.

Emilia's memory flickered and she caught her breath. The sweatshirt. Its particular shade of yellow. Like a Cheerios box.

The lady held out the sleeves as if wondering whether it would fit someone.

Someone small.

No!

Emilia raced out the door.

"Hey, hey! You have to pay for that!" the woman yelled at Emilia as she came out from behind the counter, faster than Emilia imagined she could. Emilia looked down at the plastic bag in her hand with a single apple in it. She threw it in the woman's direction and ran as the woman complained and yelled some more from the doorway, something about being a thief.

But Emilia didn't care. She ran across the street, headed toward the house, faster and faster. Until she was there, rushing toward the box, dumping all of its items onto the concrete. Emilia dropped to the ground as the man in red came toward her, saying something Emilia didn't hear.

And there it was.

Cheerios yellow.

She didn't know how it was so clean. Where had the blood gone? What was this man saying to her?

It's mine! she thought, as she clutched the sweatshirt tight to her chest.

It's mine!

Emilia looked at all the items: a pen, a flashlight, sunglasses. She noticed a small change purse. And a terrifying thought entered her head.

All these things—were they souvenirs? Of what—other crimes? Of other girls, just like me?

The world felt muted and dizzying as she stood up, clutching that sweatshirt and looking up to the sky, seeing birds flying above her. The reflection of a window caught her eye as it mirrored the smoke-white sky and her birds.

Emilia stared at it.

He could be there. Just behind that window.

Her body filled with hate and anger and fear, but she stood there a moment longer, before she looked back down at all the items displayed before her. She tried not to cry, but tears and choked sobs rose in her chest as she began to wonder about, and collect, various ones.

The man who had come over to her asked her something she couldn't quite hear or understand. And when she looked at him, she took out all her money and held it out for him. But he shook his head and said more things Emilia couldn't hear.

Emilia felt herself floating. Flying. She hugged the sweatshirt to her chest and as she walked away, she didn't notice how the other items and her money slipped away and fell. But not the sweatshirt, not *her sweatshirt*. That she held tight.

Emilia walked in a daze, being pushed here and there as she finally entered the train station and into a throng of people rushing toward her as they exited. She made her way to the platform and stood there with closed eyes as the unmistakable screeching of an approaching train filled the air.

But all Emilia heard was the screeching of her crows.

A Guy in a Black Leather Jacket

A guy in a black leather jacket walked up to the register and threw a box of condoms on the counter. Tomás rang it up, avoiding eye contact. Without thinking, he mumbled, "Have a good night," as the man stuffed the change into his pocket.

He looked at Tomás and smiled. His hair was dark and stylish and he picked up the small plastic bag, but not in a hurry like most people would. And before leaving, he said, "You have a good night, too."

The man's face was kind and gentle and beautiful. And Tomás felt that if he looked at him too long, the man might be able to guess the secrets Tomás kept.

Tomás started wiping the counter and tried not to think about him after he'd left. But all he could do at this job was think. Ring up a customer, think. Ring up a customer, think.

The man was nice. And handsome. And Tomás felt funny noticing how handsome men could be. He worried they'd know he was admiring them. He wanted to be like this man. He wanted to walk like this man, and smile easily, and have the kind of subtle confidence and sleekness of this man.

But he also wanted to be like the women in the advertisements. He wanted to wear vibrant, glossy colors on his lips and jewelry on his earlobes. He wanted to wear eye shadow and look like he had just woken up from a luxurious dream. He was hypnotized by the beauty of women, how they surrounded themselves with, and draped and smothered themselves in, so many beautiful things. He wanted to be beautiful.

Tomás looked around, sprayed more cleaner on the counter, and wiped at it over and over, as if the motion might somehow help wipe away his thoughts. It felt dangerous to think this way. It felt strange and lonely and as if he would have to be full of secrets and strange desires forever.

Tomás tried not to think of himself. He willed his thoughts instead to Emilia.

Something this morning had bothered him and came prickling back now quietly. He'd caught a glimpse of her after he came down the stairs and looked out the living room window. She was walking to Ian's car.

Are they back together?

Why did he feel he knew so little about his sister since the attack?

Because she'd never seemed quite the same again.

She'd looked lonely somehow walking in the cold. She'd looked like he felt. As if she had some kind of secret. It had made him stop and watch her the whole way to the car.

"It's slow, Tomás. I'll keep an eye on the register. You start blocking, and I don't mean cosmetics. Looks pretty enough." His boss raised his eyebrows and Tomás felt a wave of shame. He was being careless lately.

"No problem," he yelled back to his boss, too loudly, and Tomás walked to the medicine aisle and started pulling up the different bottles of pills and making sure they looked neat and stacked and inviting.

Emilia's face that morning, as she looked back at him, came flashing through his mind.

Do you see me? he thought when she didn't notice him immediately. *Emilia, see me, please. Do you see me? Say goodbye to me.*

He almost ran outside because she wasn't looking toward the window.

But then she did, and she waved, got in the car, and they drove away. And Tomás was filled with relief, just before the same sadness he'd felt the night when he saw his sister's silhouette in the kitchen came over him.

Tomás pulled a box of ibuprofen to the lip of the shelf and remembered wanting to die. How he would open the medicine cabinet for a comb and look at those bottles of aspirin and ibuprofen and cough syrup and antacids. All of them there to help ease pain.

Sometimes he thought of taking them. Just taking lots and lots of them.

But he couldn't imagine, not really, ever *actually* taking them. No, not really. He knew he wouldn't because he loved life more than he hated his pain and he wanted to *live, really live,* one day.

He wondered how many other people thought these things he thought about. He worried the world could read his thoughts, especially when Ma looked at him one day after dinner and said in the most peculiar voice, *I don't know what I'd do if I didn't have you.* Her voice was steady, but her eyes looked full of sadness, and he'd wondered what made his mother suddenly think about this and say it out loud. *I love you,* she'd said to him.

He'd nodded, unable to speak.

Tomás pulled pill bottle after pill bottle to the front. He thought back to their snow-filled night, to his sister and how happy she'd looked. And delicate. And cold.

Tomás stopped. The same cold sadness from that morning washed over him again. He'd seen something in Emilia, something he recognized in himself. A kind of covering up *that slipped away for a moment? Is that what I saw? How sad she really is?*

All this time, she wanted them to think she was okay.

But she wasn't.

He hurried to the front of the store, to the phone next to the register, and called home as he quickly explained to his manager that he just needed to check up on his sister.

He looked outside at the early evening and pressed the phone to his ear.

It rang and rang and rang.

Emilia Was Cold

Emilia was cold. She didn't quite remember getting off the train, but at least she now recognized some stores and was relieved she'd somehow known enough to head in the right direction, toward her house.

There's Kmart, where Ma got me those boots, she thought as she also realized she was still a far walk from home and it would be dark soon. Her feet felt numb. And she was scared.

Maybe I should call home for Ma or Tomás. Or Ian—he'll come.

There was a pay phone up ahead. Emilia reached in her pocket for a quarter, but the money she thought she had, that she remembered bringing with her, wasn't there.

She had bought things at the stoop sale, hadn't she? Had she used all her money? She looked for the change purse she remembered grabbing. Maybe there was a quarter in it.

But she found no items, no money, nothing.

Emilia felt confused but kept walking.

She wondered if Carl Smith had been in his home. Was he at the hospital or was he right inside that house, dying? She should have asked the man outside. She imagined the conversation.

Do you know Carl Smith?

Yes, he's my brother.

I heard that he's not well.

No, he's not.

Is he inside? Can I see him?

What would the man have said? Emilia imagined the look he might give her, the same confused look he gave her when she didn't understand what he was saying to her.

Can I?

I suppose.

Emilia pictured the scene in her head.

Then what? Would I walk up those steps? Would I go into that house, that house that must smell like him? Where he lived, and breathed, and sat, doing what? Thinking of that day? Remembering?

She imagined herself going up the steps. Pushing open the front door. A television set would be on. The kitchen light, too. And stairs, leading to a bedroom she knew held Carl Smith. Dying.

Fear and anxiety fluttered wildly in Emilia's chest and she took a deep, heaving breath. Let it out slowly.

She kept walking and felt the world slipping away as she continued, as she became numb with cold.

In her mind she saw his bedroom door, open just a little bit. From it came those smells she remembered from the hospital. And she stood just outside. All she had to do was peek in, *and look at his face.*

371

The man who attacked you, Carl Smith, not Jeremy Lance, is just beyond that door.

She could smell his diseased body. It turned her stomach. She felt the cold wrap itself around her ankles, tightening, and then Emilia felt like she was falling.

Emilia felt herself being dragged away from the door—*Look at his face first!*—and the image became darker and farther away as she felt herself floundering, wanting to fly.

Emilia lunged forward, trying to reach the disappearing door. And suddenly the world whirled back into view.

A car horn blared and Emilia jumped back. The driver yelled at her as he drove by and pointed at the lit-up DON'T WALK sign. Emilia looked at it, and then at her surroundings, realizing she'd walked well past the turn to get to her house. Now she was just two blocks from the school.

She looked in its direction and thought of her glittering birds. Of that room. The sign ahead changed and flashed.

WALK.

FLY.

WALK.

FLY.

Emilia ran across the street and headed toward the school.

Sam DeJesus Sat in the Hotel Lobby

Sam DeJesus sat in the hotel lobby with an almost-empty cup of coffee on the table in front of him. He watched the coming and going of people outside, the lights of taxis flashing in the early night as they pulled up and away from the curb.

In another time, in another place, he would have been inspired by the strange elation and sadness of departures and arrivals. He would have gotten out his notebook and tried to capture the words that would precisely describe this feeling, the look in people's faces, the busyness and monotony of a moment, a day, a life.

But he didn't carry pens or small notebooks anymore.

Sam lit a cigarette and remembered the day the shuttle blew up. That was the day he'd stopped trying to capture all of this. He'd sat, trying to process his own feelings, through poetry. Fucking poetry.

Shame filled him as he remembered. What he should have been doing was trying to help his family. His daughter, his wife, his son. What he wanted was to take their pain away. But all he could think about was himself. How he felt. What a useless piece of shit he was.

He remembered distinctly sitting outside on the patio with his notebook in his lap. He knew he should go inside and help Nina. She was in bed with Emilia. He'd already started sensing Nina had finally discovered he was a coward. He could see how she was looking at him. How her eyes followed him when he would go outside or to the basement with his stupid journal at his side, unable to write a fucking word and unable to be around them, either.

He'd been sitting on the patio, near the bathroom window, when he heard Nina's weeping from inside.

Go inside, he told himself. *Go inside.*

He looked at his blank page and listened to his wife. He felt as if he'd split in two. Part of his mind and most of his heart disengaged themselves from his body. He closed his journal and vowed never to write again. He took another drag of his cigarette and looked at the sky, telling himself to go inside, but he couldn't.

Sam stared out at the hotel lobby and pulled another cigarette from his shirt pocket. He was just lighting it when he suddenly saw Nina rushing through the doors, frantic, running to the desk.

He felt his lungs collapse.

"She's gone," Nina said as soon as Sam went up to her.

"What happened? What happened?"

But she was already speaking over him.

"She hasn't come home, Sam. I don't know where she is. I

don't know where she could have gone. She was supposed to be home. And I just . . . I just have this feeling. Something is wrong, terribly wrong. I don't know where she is." She was on the verge of hysteria.

Sam felt all of his insides loosen.

Stay strong, he told himself. *For once, don't be a coward.*

"Okay, okay," he said, trying to wrap his mind around what Nina was saying, what he should say, what he should do. "Okay, come sit down. We'll call the police. We'll . . . She's okay, Nina. I know she's fine. We'll find her . . . ," he said. He said it with so much conviction that he almost believed it himself.

She must have gone somewhere with her boyfriend and lost track of time.

Or she's probably already home and we just don't know it yet.

Or she's sitting on the couch, worried, because she knows Nina must be worried.

Sam guided Nina to the couch he'd just been sitting on. He reached for the phone on the table next to it. "Call home and check. Maybe she just got there."

Nina nodded, reached for the phone as Sam dialed their home number. She waited, and slowly, as nobody answered, he saw her hand start shaking. She pressed the handset harder against her ear, closing her eyes and whispering, *Please, please.*

Sam saw tears slide out the corners of her eyes. He watched the way the sobs took over and came out in great gulps as he reached for the phone, which she was holding tighter and tighter with each unanswered ring, or maybe because she was afraid she might miss Emilia's voice on the other end.

He gently loosened the phone from Nina's hand as he fought back his own sobs.

"We'll call the detective," he whispered, bringing the phone up to his own ear, listening to the terrible endless ringing before hanging up with his finger.

Nina searched in her purse and pulled out an old business card frayed at the edges, the same one from so long ago, and handed it over to Sam.

He held her hand for a moment, just to stop the shaking, before he dialed Detective Manzetti.

The House Was Cold

The house was cold and dark and empty. It was nighttime by the time Tomás stood in the living room, listening to the silence, the echo of the phone still ringing in his ear. He hadn't unlocked the door in time.

Was it you, Emilia?

He had no way of knowing if it really was Emilia, but something told him it must have been her. Was she calling for help? Had he missed it again, like that day when he'd been so confused by that person he saw in the mirror he only *thought* there was a ringing phone? Only later, years later, did he learn Emilia had tried to call home that day.

Why, in all this time, had they never gotten an answering machine?

Tomás took in the empty living room. Where was his mother? Why did the house feel like a shell, so empty? Why did it feel like someone had just died?

Relax, he told himself. *Think.*

Still in his coat, Tomás ran over to Ian's house.

"Is Emilia with you?" he asked as soon as Ian answered the door.

The look on Ian's face let him know immediately that she was not.

"Do you know where she is?"

Ian looked at Tomás, silent.

"Ian, do you know where she is?" he asked, louder this time. "She's not home, and I need to know where she is."

"I . . . I don't know. But, Jesus Christ, are you sure she's not home? Or with your mom? Or something?"

Tomás caught the edge in Ian's voice.

"What's going on? Do you know something?"

"I . . . She asked me to take her to the train station this morning . . . She skipped school and she wouldn't tell me where she was going."

"What?"

"I tried, but she wouldn't. But I took her, because she wanted me to and—"

"Where did she go?" Tomás said.

"I'm telling you, I don't know! She wouldn't tell me."

"Think, Ian, where do you think she might have gone?"

"I don't know. She was acting funny and . . . I'm sorry. I really don't know."

"Fuck!" Tomás yelled, and he saw Ian sit down under the weight of what Tomás was and wasn't saying. His hands were on his knees and he was shaking his head.

"She wouldn't tell me . . . ," he repeated.

"Get your keys," Tomás said. "Let's go."

Ian jumped up, grabbed the keys from the counter. He yelled something upstairs to his parents, and just as they were pulling away, Tomás saw the door open as Ian's mother looked outside, confused.

"Where first?" Ian asked.

"I don't know, just . . . drive," Tomás said, his eyes already searching, already looking for Emilia's silhouette to emerge somehow, from somewhere.

Be okay, he told her, hoping his voice would reach her wherever she was right now.

Please just be okay.

The sound of Ian's car sliced through the silence of the night and echoed in the darkness.

The Crows Watched Emilia

The crows watched Emilia through the classroom window. She had lit candles and placed them all around the room so it glowed.

They'd watched her create this place, and for as much as they'd followed Emilia all these years, for as much as they saw, they cocked their heads to the side, as if perplexed. Something was happening, but they didn't know what it was. So they sat, vigilant, on the branches of the tree and watched as she put finishing touches on a mural she'd painted on the wall—a large black crow.

Because she was one of them. She'd been one of them for years.

But the rest of it, everything she'd dragged there, all these items. What did it mean? What did it mean that she'd spent so much time here by herself? Creating, memorializing?

Perhaps this was what made Emilia more human than not.

One of the crows cawed loudly, and she turned to look at them. Then looked around the room, as if taking everything in. She walked over to the different items, picked them up, touched them gently.

Emilia looked at the mural. And then at the art book she'd left open. And finally, she turned and looked out the window.

The crows flitted and stretched their wings and stood at alert as she came toward them. She unlocked one side of the window, then the other, struggling as she tried to pry it open. Finally, a loud screech broke the silent night as she dislodged the window and slid it up roughly. The cold swept in; it made Emilia catch her breath and tremble and turn away.

It's cold, Emilia.

What are you doing, Emilia?

Close the window, Emilia.

Emilia turned back toward the night, shivering like she was about to break but once again facing that biting cold. The crows waited for a look, or a word, or a few nuts. But she looked out past all of them, toward the playground, as if hypnotized, and stared for a long time.

The crows cawed louder but she didn't hear them; her eyes were faraway and set only on the playground.

Go home, they told her. *Go home.*

But Emilia closed her dark, dark eyes. "I'm coming," they heard her say. "I'm coming for you." The crows saw her lips turning blue from the cold. They watched as she lifted her arms, just as she did when she was a small girl, right before she would take flight.

The cold against Emilia's chest was like a thin sheet of ice as she swooped up, up, up toward the sky. She took flight and looked back at the school. All those windows, dark and smudged, except for the glowing candles in the classroom.

She and the other children had once looked out those windows when they were bored, when their minds had wandered from the story they were reading or the math problems that never ended. They stared out those windows, into the unremarkable world outside, and they waited. They waited for something remarkable to happen. She remembered being one of those kids—*yes, I was just like them once*—as she sat at her desk, staring out the window and across the playground. She would imagine herself over there, playing, running into the woods.

Emilia flapped her wings harder and looked over at the playground.

Where are you? Emilia whispered now as the wind blew and the night got darker. *I know you're there. I'm coming.*

The wind was cold, freezing even, but Emilia paid no mind to it. She sliced through the air, sailed through the dark sky, the endless dark sky, riding and dipping and catching the currents to get to the playground. The cold fluttered through her body. It swished under her giant wings.

And then Emilia thought she saw her. A little child emerging from somewhere on the other side of the playground, a smaller, younger version of herself, the one her brother used to call Mia. The sky around her lightened to gray, the same shade it'd been the day of her attack, and Emilia could suddenly see clearly.

Emilia focused on the girl. It *was* her. That was Mia.

Mia ran across the field, past the metal spiderweb and monkey bars, and then suddenly stopped right at the perimeter of the woods.

Emilia knew she was going in.

No, don't! Wait! Wait!

Mia faced the woods, looking at the ground.

Wait, Emilia called. *Wait for me. I'm coming for you.*

Emilia flew to the tree, perched in the branches, from where she could see any danger coming.

She saw the young girl look up at her for a moment.

Don't be afraid, she told that smaller version of herself. *I'm with you. We'll be okay.* It made Emilia want to cry, but she took a deep breath and watched Mia go into the woods, looking now at the sticks on the ground, following them.

Interpreting the messages from aliens, Emilia remembered. She looked away from the young girl and studied the woods.

Where did he come from? Where was he hiding? Where exactly was I when it happened?

Mia strayed farther and farther into the woods. Emilia tried to fly down to her, but she couldn't move.

Mia was almost to the fence that separated the school from the next property. And Emilia remembered, *Here, oh god, here. This is where I was.*

Emilia cawed, shrieked, but already felt a pain shooting through her head and jaw.

God, she remembered every blow, the fireworks she saw behind her eyelids, the confusion. She couldn't see anything. Nothing. Just flashes of light, flashes of the sky, crisscrossed branches, and dark dots.

Emilia spread her wings, tried to fly down, but she felt disoriented. She was in two places at once. *You'll be okay,* she tried to yell, but only more shrieking caws came out as she felt part of herself being dragged over cold ground and jagged rocks, *farther from the school, farther from her home, farther from her family.*

She could hear the gurgle of her younger self; she could taste the blood in her bird mouth; she knew her tongue was split and the blood was filling it up. She knew Mia was floating in and out of consciousness.

I'm here with you, she cawed to her younger self. *You're not alone. You live through this! You're not going to die! You'll be far from here soon. I promise.*

Her shoes were gone. Her pants were off. Emilia wrapped her wings tighter around herself. She watched the horrible scene from above. Then from the ground. Her mind flickered back and forth between the two views, back and forth.

Look at his face, she told herself. *Look at his face!*

The man was wearing a black knit hat. And a black coat. His pants were brown and his sneakers were white, but his face was turned away. Yes, she remembered now. She *had* seen him. What she'd forgotten, repressed, pushed its way through now. It flickered on, like a movie in her mind.

Show me your face!

Emilia saw Mia's eyes were now focused on the sky and she was looking far away. And Emilia remembered. This was when the crows, *my beautiful crows,* showed up.

Emilia lifted her head, opened her beak, and cried. Louder and louder.

Come! she told them. *Come now!*

She could see some in the trees high above, but much fewer than Emilia remembered. Why wasn't the sky darkening with so many crows like she remembered? Why were they just sitting on the branches, watching?

Panic filled her and Emilia screeched louder.

Please! she begged. *Help me! Someone help me!*

Only then did the crows respond, flying from the branches. She heard their wings fluttering. A few swooped down by the attacker casually.

And that's when he let go.

He saw just those few crows coming toward him. Flapping around him. And he let go.

Emilia watched him back away now in a frenzy as if they were the most terrible things he'd ever seen, yelling and holding his arms over his face, swatting at the crows, which only then became agitated.

Let me see your face.

He swatted at them harder. He was scared. Terrified.

Emilia saw him fall backward and trip over an exposed tree root. He tried to catch himself as he fell and brought down his arms.

And she saw him, his face.

She *saw* his ordinary face. His terribly ordinary face. Like that of any man she'd ever seen on the street, at the market, in a shopping center. Like that of *any* ordinary stranger.

That's him.

It rushed back to her now.

Brown hair around the edges of the knit cap, dark eyes. Thin lips. Sallow skin.

That was him. That was his face. His terrible face.

And it was not Jeremy Lance.

Emilia looked above for all the crows she remembered, for the darkening of the sky as more and more came.

But she felt dizzy with confusion and betrayal. There had been hundreds of crows that day, *hundreds*. They came to her rescue, surrounded and comforted her, kept her safe until she was found. But now only the same few remained, no more, no less, perched high in the trees once again.

Emilia heard the gurgle. She tasted more metal in her mouth and heard Mia's heavy breathing.

I'm coming. I'm coming for you. I'll save you.

Emilia swooped down.

Detective Manzetti Promised

Detective Manzetti promised Nina and Sam he would look for Emilia himself. He promised he would use all his resources to find her. He did not tell them his resources were limited, nor that now that Emilia was sixteen, the department would likely not start looking for her until she'd been missing a full twenty-four hours. He did not tell them the chances of someone taking Emilia were slim. He did not tell them he was worried for their daughter.

"We'll find her," he assured them, looking at Emilia's family. The same, only older. He looked at her boyfriend, the last person to see her, and asked him again about the conversation he and Emilia had at the train station. Ian told him they'd broken up and Detective Manzetti wished he hadn't. With her father's sudden return, the revelation of Carl Smith, and a breakup with her boyfriend, on the surface, Emilia was looking too much like a classic case of a teenage runaway.

But Detective Manzetti was sure she wasn't.

The night felt surreal to him, so similar to the night Emilia went missing eight years ago. He'd had that uneasy feeling then that he would have to tell another mother terrible news. It was like a stone in his stomach. He had the same feeling now.

When he returned to his car, he remembered the message that came through when they found Emilia. That night he'd been wrong.

He hoped he was wrong tonight.

Manzetti put his car in drive and turned on his lights.

Where are you, Emilia? he thought.

The night did not respond.

What Did I Miss?

"What did I miss?" Nina whispered to Sam. They were sitting at the kitchen table. They'd been instructed by Detective Manzetti to call any friends their daughter had, and Nina sat struck as she realized Emilia had none. "I missed something," she said.

"No, you didn't," Sam said as he looked at Tomás and Ian sitting near the window in the living room. Tomás sat with his arms crossed, chewing on the inside of his lip as he stared at the wall. They'd walked in just moments before, Sam's heart swelling with hope and Nina jumping up from the chair when the doorknob jiggled, and how crushing when it wasn't Emilia.

For a moment, when he saw Ian, Sam thought maybe they'd overreacted. For a moment, he thought Emilia would come in after them. They'd say they all just went out for pizza together. They'd wonder why their parents looked so worried, why Nina looked deathly pale.

But no, Tomás explained he had worried about her at work. He'd come home to look for her. He hadn't heard from her.

Tomás's worry compressed Nina's worry. Sam's also. Especially when Tomás said, *We looked everywhere I could think of, everywhere.* But still, no sign of Emilia.

"I can't sit here and just *wait.*" Nina's voice cracked.

"Detective Manzetti said it would be best."

Nina shook her head, went over to the window, and looked out.

"I missed her call," Tomás said suddenly. "The phone was ringing. It was her—I know it was. And I missed it."

Nina went to him, pulled Tomás close to her. "It was me. I called. I let it ring and ring and ring. I thought she might be home."

Tomás leaned into her, crying harder than Nina could ever remember her son crying. She felt his body go slack, as if relief was flooding through him, weakening his limbs. Nina held him tighter, and he allowed her to, at least for a few moments.

★   ★   ★

Tomás watched the clock tick away as they sat together, waiting for Emilia, waiting for the phone to ring. Waiting for news.

"I can't do this," Ma finally said again. "We *have* to keep looking for her."

His father nodded and quickly rose from his chair like he couldn't stand the waiting, either. "Let's go," he said. "Ian, you stay here in case she comes back."

Ian nodded and watched the three of them go.

They got in the car and his father drove, careful to go down each street slowly, so they wouldn't miss her, though Tomás really wanted him to speed through the whole town so they could get to Emilia immediately, wherever she was.

"Where would she go?" Ma said over and over again.

The library was now closed, the arcade, too. They stopped at fast-food places and went inside. Carro's. The small fruit market even. They stopped by the diner, where Ma rushed inside to check if Emilia was there. She came out moments later shaking her head. They headed to the park where Emilia used to play and where Tomás would cut through on his way home from work and see Emilia on the swings sometimes.

Aren't you getting too old for the playground? he teased her once when he saw her there. It had been just a few months ago. The first cool breeze of fall in the air. He could see her now, jumping off the swing while it was high in the sky, and running over to him to walk home together.

She had smiled and shrugged, and as they came up to their house, she said, *I try to remember how I used to be. When I'm on the swings, I almost can. Almost.*

She'd said it casually, moved on to something else. But there had been a pause in there, a few seconds of silence Tomás felt now he should have asked her what she'd meant. Emilia never talked about the attack. Any time he'd ever gotten too close to the subject, she'd change topics or say she had something to do.

Tomás sat in the back seat of his dad's rental car thinking of those few seconds. And he racked his brain trying to remember anywhere else she might have gone, anywhere she would go to remember how she used to be.

One of Emilia's favorite places when they were little was Playland. They'd gone at least once most summers when they were still a family. Emilia loved it. And she'd been happy there.

Tomás grabbed the headrests of the front seats and pulled himself forward. "Dad, remember how much she loved Playland? The boardwalk, the rides. The food. I think . . . if she took a train . . . maybe she might've gone there?"

His parents looked at each other. His father made a turn and pulled the car over. "Do you really think she'd go there? Why would she—"

"It's worth checking," Ma said. "We have to keep looking, Sam. I can go and you stay here and keep searching. Tomás, you come with me. We'll cover more ground together."

Tomás's father nodded. "I know, okay . . . ," he said, unsure at first but then with certainty. "Okay."

Tomás took a deep breath. He leaned his head against the window and looked up at the sky.

Is that where we'll find you, Mia?

He watched birds flitter about in a tree, so many of them, outside one of the windows of their old elementary school.

Your birds, Emilia, he thought. *Your birds. Come home, please.*

His father put the car in drive and continued down the street in tense silence.

Suddenly, Tomás noticed a soft glow in one of the windows of the school.

"Stop."

"What?"

"Stop the car!"

His father slowed, but Tomás got out of the car before it even came to a full stop and started running as fast as he could toward the old elementary school.

When They Saw

When they saw the glowing lights of the classroom, Ma was confused but relieved.

She must be here! Oh god, here. By herself. My Emilia.

They ran to the front of the school, pulling at the doors, pounding uselessly at windows, trying to find a way inside.

"Get a hammer, something!" Nina yelled at Sam, who ran back to the car and searched as Tomás continued looking for any opening. Emilia was in there, he knew she was; he just had to figure out how she'd gotten inside.

"Here!" he yelled suddenly as he came across the window that led to the chorus room. "I found a way in!"

Tomás made his way through the opening, his feet accidentally kicking over a ladder that had been placed there.

He dropped down into the room, which was darker than the moonlit night outside, darker than sidewalks illuminated by streetlights. He picked up the ladder and helped his mother climb in. They both stood there for a moment, disoriented, trying to adjust to the impossible darkness.

A moment later, Sam came through the window. Tomás

stumbled toward where he remembered the door being when he attended this school.

"This way," he told his parents as his mother reached out for his arm.

He led them through halls and staircases, as they made their way up to the room Tomás had seen from the street.

At the last stair, they turned the corner and saw the glow of the open classroom up ahead.

"Emilia!" Ma called as Tomás started running.

When they reached the doorway, they scanned the room for her, and were immediately struck by both her absence and the magnificence of the room.

"My god," Ma said. "Did she do this? All this?" Her mouth opened, as if she was on the verge of saying more, but then she was speechless with each new thing she took in. Never, never in all her life could she have imagined this. The glowing candles, bright and soft and holy. The walls, *sparkling*? And the room full of crows: shimmering rows of crows hanging from the ceiling, crows in flight painted on the walls, and on the largest wall, a mural of a single large black crow, its wings wide and outstretched.

But its face was Emilia's face, an old photograph of herself enlarged and cut out perfectly to fill the bird's face. Her dark eyes looked as if they were looking right at you.

And there *they* were, under one of her wings. Individual pictures of Sam, Ma, and Tomás under one, and under the other, a picture of Emilia when she was about eight years old. Next to her was a picture of Ian, just as young as Emilia. And between their little cut-out bodies, Emilia had drawn their arms reaching out toward each other and their hands clasped together. There was a heart around them.

Emilia had adorned their heads with little beads so they looked majestic, like they were wearing crowns. She'd put flowers in their hair, too, and around them, her father's poems written on the wall. Their portraits were connected with sparkling gold thread that reached from one to the other and back again, over and over, entwining all of them together in such a way so that they looked like they could never possibly come apart.

They looked so beautiful. And this room was beautiful. So many strange little objects assembled here.

"Emilia?" Ma called out in a shaky voice as she passed the air mattress, made up with a blanket from home. "My god, was she sleeping here? When?" Ma whispered as she brought a hand up to her trembling mouth. She noticed the striped salt and pepper shakers displayed on a stack of books, along with other small decorative trinkets she hadn't noticed missing from home.

The school was cold and frigid. It was a calm, windless night. The glittering walls and trinkets and paper crows, all of it was so stunning. That was why none of them immediately noticed.

It was Tomás who saw it first. The open window. It was he who suddenly felt the world fall away as his head started whirring.

He slowly walked toward it, telling himself, *No, no,* while another part urged him forward. He looked down just as his mother called his sister's name again.

"Emilia?"

He yelled without knowing the words were coming from his mouth.

"Emilia! Emilia! No, no!"

He looked down at his sister, her broken body illuminated by the light of the moon, as his mother ran into him, her whole weight against him as she screamed. His father grabbed her around her waist, pulled her away from Tomás and from that open window.

"Shut the window! Shut the window!" his father yelled. But Tomás couldn't move, and then his mother was running out of the room, and then somehow, Tomás heard her screams coming from down below.

Those screams, traveling up and into his ears as if she were right next to him still.

Those screams, shrill and inhuman, but full of his sister's name, coming from his mother as she held Emilia.

His father was outside now, too, and he ran to a house close by. Tomás ran down the stairs, pushing against each door he passed on the way, but all were locked and he frantically made his way back to the chorus room and out of the school, the world moving so slow and so fast.

"Oh god, she's so cold, she's so cold!" his mother screamed when Tomás reached them. She had taken off her jacket, wrapped it around Emilia, and was now rocking back and forth with Emilia in her arms.

Tomás kneeled down next to his mother, crying, and put his arm around her. He felt her shaking with cold and grief and sobs. He looked at his sister, at the blood that came out of her ears and mouth and blue lips.

Emilia.

Her shoes had come off.

One of her feet was twisted at a strange angle.

She was wearing striped socks.

Tomás heard his father's sobbing and then his father was holding him.

The sound of faraway sirens came closer and mixed with his mother asking God for help, his father's crying, Tomás's heaving breaths.

Red and Blue Lights

Red and blue lights flashed on the glossy feathers of the crows in the trees. From there, they watched the people below. Their faces were all drawn to the ground. Only Emilia's faced upward, at the sky, at them, before a zipper hid it from view and she was enclosed in a black bag.

They watched as she was rolled into an ambulance.

They watched as she was taken away.

They watched.

And they cried. *Caw. Caw.*

More crows arrived, filling the trees and the school roof as the people below them left. The night filled with silence as the world went to sleep. The crows stayed. All night and into dawn.

Until the sun rose, and the crows took flight.

★ ★ ★

Carl Smith lay in his bed earlier that day as a dozing hospice nurse sat in the corner of his room. He wished she would leave. He didn't care that she adjusted his pillows and held a straw to his lips so he could drink the water. He was disgusted by her, and if he'd been able to speak, he would have told her so.

But Carl Smith couldn't speak. And each breath he took, even with the machine pumping oxygen through his nostrils, was a struggle. He could barely move and only now and then opened his eyes and took in the world around him. His eyes flitted from the woman in the corner of the room to the window. His brother kept the shades open so Carl Smith would have a clear view outside whenever he managed to open his eyes.

For a brief moment, Carl Smith was able to do just that. And he looked out the dirty, smudged pane and saw his brother below, selling away his items. One by one.

A deep hatred for his brother stirred in him, not only because he had taken over his house, his life, even his death, but because his brother was good and gentle and kind. All the things Carl never was and never could be. He glared at the man his mother loved more. But the hate made him tired, and just when he was about to close his eyes, he caught a glimpse of a young girl running across the street.

Another time, he would have been thrilled to see a young girl like her. Like the ones he observed from his office at the university where he taught. Young female students walking through the parking lot, often late at night. Alone. He imagined the things he could do to them. How quickly he could drag them to his car. Sometimes he got carried away with these thoughts as they sat in his Classics class, never imagining what he was imagining. How close he let himself come to carrying out his fantasies, but didn't because he worried they could identify him. And because of the one time campus security had come asking him questions when a student complained she was being followed.

Too capable, the older ones.

It was what he was thinking the day he saw a young girl playing alone on the playground at the elementary school next to the university.

That day, every simmering slight he'd ever felt by those other girls, who'd thought themselves too good, who had even complained about him so he'd had to be careful—so, so careful—came to a boiling rage. But he'd shown them, all of them, that he was not someone to be dismissed. He wasn't intimidated by them. Any of them.

Except, this girl. The one he saw now outside his window as he lay helpless and dying. She scared him. With that black coat, and black hair, flitting around, gaping, squawking, she hardly looked human. Carl Smith blinked, strained his eyesight. The breathing apparatus calmly clicked as he struggled for a breath.

Yes, she looked more like a giant bird, the kind he'd been terrified of ever since he was a little boy, when children laughed at the sight of him cowering and trembling as they flapped their arms and ran circles around him.

He felt her dark black eyes looking straight at his window. She could smell his fear with her animal instinct. She knew exactly where he was. And what he was.

Carl Smith trembled in his bed. Closed his eyes, even as he was certain she was at that moment opening her beak and crying out, calling the rest of her flock to her.

Carl felt himself falling into an opaque darkness. He felt his lungs being squeezed as he tried so hard, so hard, to suck in more air. The clicking of a faraway machine echoed in his ears even as he sank deeper and deeper into a frightening darkness.

More air!

His heart raced as he realized he was dying. This was it. This was the moment. This was what dying was. Any moment he would see a bright white light. His mother would come and beckon to him, explain it was time to go with her. And he would go into the light.

Carl waited, but only more darkness and silence engulfed him as he slipped deeper and deeper into his death.

In that darkness, Carl was confused as he heard the inhuman shriek of a million birds. He tried to will himself back to living, he tried to will himself to see a bright light, but instead he heard more and more shrieks coming from the dark abyss that surrounded him, and the unmistakable sound of a million wings fluttering toward him. He tried to bring his arms up, but his body was useless.

Oh god, he could smell them. Millions of birds, their repulsive feathery smell. And the gush of wind as they descended upon him.

The birds had finally come for him, digging their sickening talons into his flesh. He felt them begin their pecking at his body and his heart drummed out of control, faster, as his lungs demanded more air.

More air!

But there was none, and Carl Smith felt himself being devoured by his sins and his fears in a place where there was no breath, no life, no salvation.

PART SIX

Spring 1995

The Cold Months

The cold months thawed.

Outside, trees that had been brittle and breaking were now full of leaves. The fluttering each time a breeze came through sounded like a collective sigh of relief at having survived another winter.

Ian sat in his car and watched from the corner as yellow bulldozers and cranes knocked down the elementary school. Walls were crushed; bricks crumbled and tumbled down. The crane nudged the room that was once his third-grade classroom—that place where he had handed back a graded paper to Emilia and she had smiled at him—and pushed it to the ground.

Stay away from Emilia DeJesus, his mother had warned him.

But I didn't. I loved you. And you loved me.

He had gotten to kiss Emilia DeJesus. And he knew her, *I did know you,* he thought. Even if he didn't. He knew how she was always thinking of something and what her back felt like under his hand. How she'd tuck her hair back, and how she'd relax a little when she thought no one was looking at her. The feel of her breath and her voice in his ear.

The rhythmic clanking of the machinery surrounded him and he watched. He'd been watching every day, but today was the day those metal teeth clamped into their old classroom. And he saw the large bird on the wall. For a few seconds, he saw it clearly, its enormous wings lifted to the sky, the sun shining on it before it, too, was cut away.

Emilia.

It was Tomás who'd taken him to the room days after the funeral. He'd told Ian he had to show him something. So they got in Ian's car, and Tomás told him to drive to the school.

I know Emilia would've wanted you to see it, Tomás told him as they drove. Their shoes scraped on each step as they walked upstairs, and then echoed in the hallway as they walked toward the room. He saw the way Tomás braced himself before he opened the door. Ian did the same, but even then he was unprepared.

The paper birds. The walls that looked iridescent. The mural with Emilia's face. Ian's eyes filled with tears and he took a deep breath before he walked to her.

He saw the picture of them as little kids and his heart crumbled in his chest.

He touched the heart she'd drawn around them and sobbed. He'd only loved one girl in his life. Emilia DeJesus. And now she was gone.

When did you do all this? he whispered.

She didn't answer, only that smile he'd never see again, that seemed now to hold back so many things.

He stood there a long time, searching for answers in that picture. A clue, some indication of why, but found none.

Finally, he walked away and looked around at all the items that decorated the room. The squirrel, broken bowls that had been glued together, striped salt and pepper shakers, a pair of kiddie boots, a bird skeleton Tomás held carefully in his hands.

Ian walked to the window.

He stepped closer and stared at the tree outside.

This is the last thing you saw.

He could feel Tomás's gaze on him. He reached out and touched the glass, and then he looked down.

He tried not to imagine her on the ground. But his mind conjured it up anyway.

He did not want to think of the force with which her body hit the concrete. The sharp, deafening sound of the crack of her skull. He did not want to think of the fluids that were excreted, the arms and legs at odd angles. He closed his eyes, but still, he saw her.

He was crying, saying her name, over and over, but didn't realize it until he felt Tomás's hand on his shoulder. Until he heard him crying, too.

She didn't mean to, I know she didn't, Tomás managed.

Ian nodded. He *knew* she didn't. He remembered the way she looked the last time he saw her alive. *I'll call you later,* she'd said to him.

I know, Ian said. She'd turned and looked at him at the platform. She had blown him a kiss. She never would have given him that hope if she intended to never see him again. She knew he would be waiting by the phone, waiting for her call that night. She wouldn't have him wait if she never meant to call. Would she?

Over the weeks it was he and Tomás who cleared the room. Took all the precious things Emilia had so carefully placed in there. Neither of them could stand for all those items she cared about so much to be crushed by a bulldozer. All of it fit in just a couple of boxes. Ian knew Tomás would someday take them out, look for clues in each item.

When they were done, only the mural remained. And the pictures of Emilia and her family. He and Tomás stood in front of the photos.

Let's go, Tomás said. He turned around and left the room.

Ian didn't feel like he had any right, but he knew Tomás would want them later. So he unpinned them from the wall, put them on top of the items in the box he was carrying, and followed Tomás down the stairs.

Ian watched the crane tear into the school. The only comfort he had was that Emilia's face was not being crushed in that rubble. If he hadn't taken the pictures down, he wouldn't trust himself not to rush and climb over the rubble now to find them.

Stay away from Emilia DeJesus.

The words felt so near and real, as if he were eight years old again, standing in the kitchen, and his mother had just uttered them.

He thought he couldn't cry anymore; he'd cried so much these last few months. So he was taken aback by how more sadness and pain swelled up inside him again, so quickly, so completely.

He wiped away fresh tears. He knew he'd feel this way for a long time, maybe the rest of his life.

But I didn't stay away from you, Emilia. And god, I'm so fucking mad at you. Why didn't you let us help you? Why didn't we figure out a way to help you? I'm so fucking mad at us. But I'm glad I didn't stay away.

He wiped away the hot tears that kept sliding down his face, and after a while, he took a deep breath and tried to collect himself.

He had somewhere to be.

Ian put his car in drive and made a U-turn, the screeching barely slicing through the sound of heavy machinery. He imagined Emilia next to him. What she'd say if she were here.

Looks so small, doesn't it?

It does.

I wonder what they'll do with it now.

Ian shook his head, drove to the other side of town, where Anthony was waiting. His cousin had come back for him.

A week leave, man. Let's get out of here awhile. A small road trip.

He was glad Anthony hadn't asked Jane to come along. He couldn't see a couple holding hands without thinking of Emilia. The thought of not being here—of not being home—felt like a relief, maybe, from picturing every moment they'd had together

411

each time he looked toward her bedroom window, or seeing her just ahead every time he turned down a block. He thought about highways and gas stations and miles and miles of road ahead.

What if it were you and me instead? he thought as Emilia's face filled his mind.

He wondered if he'd always wonder *what if*. And if every moment would feel like a strange version of what was because of what wasn't.

Ian rolled down the window, letting the warm air dry his tears as he drove faster, away from the school, Emilia's ghost now next to him.

I can't believe it's really gone. Her voice rang in his ears.

"Me neither," he answered. So much was gone.

He reached over, felt for her hand, and touched only air.

Sam DeJesus Was Flying

Sam DeJesus was flying. He left the place he'd returned to, had once called home, but which could never feel like home again. He had stayed and watched over Nina for three months. His mind filled up with those moments—sitting by her bed, begging her to eat. Those nights she sobbed herself to sleep and let him hold her.

He tried to be there for her, for Tomás, took on everything he could. All those things too horrible, or too mundane, or now too meaningless. And somewhere in the days that made up the months that followed Emilia's death, he thought maybe Nina forgave him a little for the time he wasn't there.

But then one day, the sun was too bright. And the chill in the air was less biting. And he could sense the slightest bit of spring.

It's getting warm, he told Nina one day as they sat outside, on the patio. The doctor said she needed to get out.

It is, she said. And then she looked at him the softest he could remember, and he knew she was releasing him. *It's time,* she said. And he was ashamed of how he almost collapsed with relief and gratitude.

So she knew. She would have to be strong again. He watched as she gathered herself, as she drew herself up, for Tomás.

Sam had never deserved Nina.

Or Tomás.

Or Emilia.

Just then the pilot announced they would be landing soon. Sam looked out the oval of the airplane window, at the vast snow covering the land below. He'd looked for the coldest city in Alaska where he could realistically survive. He wondered if it would be cold enough here. And he hoped the cold would help his heart pump the hot pain more slowly through his body.

I'll return, Sam thought. *I just need to stay cold a little longer.*

He'd told Nina the same, and she nodded, though he knew she didn't believe him. He didn't blame her; he wasn't sure he believed himself.

He stared out the window, at the snow that awaited him.

He welcomed the freezing cold; he prayed for the numbing of pain.

Nina Never Felt

Nina never felt her daughter inside her womb, never felt the kick of Emilia's small feet, or the turning and stretching of her small body inside Nina's own. But Nina felt her daughter's absence as if she'd carried Emilia inside her all these years, as if now she'd suddenly been ripped out of her. And along with her, all of Nina's insides, her heart, lungs, muscles, blood, and veins.

This is what empty means, Nina thought.

She was glad Sam was leaving. Not because she hated him. Hate seemed useless to her now. But because if he'd stayed, Nina knew she would continue letting him take care of everything. She knew she would stay in bed, in the darkness of her room, until she disappeared into that darkness. For a moment, she thought she understood Emilia.

But Sam said he was going. And she could hear Tomás's voice again. She heard in it how he needed her, though he didn't say it. She'd forgotten, in the grief of Emilia's death, that someone still did. So she got up, amazed at the heaviness of her own body. As if she'd been out in infinite space, and just been shot back to Earth; she'd never felt such heaviness in her life.

But she got up. And tried to live.

At first, she didn't think she could get through the days on her own. She found herself pushing a cart in a store and wanted to take everything, but couldn't take a single thing. Because none of it meant anything anymore, none of it could fill her, none of it made sense. She felt like Emilia was watching. And then she saw herself, from a great distance in the sky, through the roof of the store, pushing that empty cart. Nina left it and was almost out the door when she started to cry. She saw herself fall. Great, heaving sobs gushing from her as two people came to her side.

That wave of grief had almost crushed her, but she had to keep going.

The next day, she booked a few appointments, the first since Emilia's death, which had left her unable to function. Just local ones at first, then more. Her friends sent her old clients back her way, little by little. Until suddenly she was in her old routine again, standing on a train every morning and night, carrying her makeup supplies, not knowing how she got there.

One Saturday, she was driving and thinking of Emilia when she was little and wondering about time, how it passed and didn't. She looked at the address in her appointment book again. She turned into the neighborhood and recognized it.

No, she thought, *please no,* as she went down the street, knowing exactly where she was headed.

She drove through the gates, her heart already in her throat. When she knocked on the door, she could hardly contain her shaking, and she blinked back tears as she remembered being here only months earlier.

Only months earlier.

Her heart swelled with pain.

"Hello," the woman said.

"Hi," Nina whispered.

She set up in the same area as before. Only now it was brighter, even fuller with flowers than last time. Even as the past several months had been brightening, Nina's world had felt void of color. She didn't want the flowers to look so bright, but they did.

She felt the woman's eyes on her as Nina quickly set up, as she put the smock around her client's shoulders and quietly asked, "Evening or day event?"

"Evening," the woman replied.

Nina busied herself immediately. Worked quickly, meticulously, gently. She thought only of her work. Only of the blending, and smudging, and sweeping, and brushing.

She tapped the excess eye shadow off the brush and swept it across the woman's eyelids, *blue-black*, like Emilia's hair.

She handed the mirror to the woman, who nodded approvingly. "Thank you," she said.

Blue-black, her hair, and the cold, and the dark, and her body. Bruised. Cold. Blue-black.

Nina began shaking then. Her eyes filled with tears. She saw the woman's gaze in the reflection of the mirror as tears escaped and fell down her face.

She's gone, Nina thought. *She's gone.*

The thought wrecked her each time it forced its way in. It did so without permission, multiple times a day, demanding to be acknowledged, in the middle of everything and nothing at all. Sometimes she could withstand the pain that came with it; other times it knocked her down so completely.

Months compressed into nothing, into a second and a single breath. And it felt like no time had passed.

"I'm sorry," she said to the woman, through her sobs. "I've lost . . . my daughter . . . my daughter."

The woman got up, guided Nina into the chair. She told her not to apologize. Moments later, there was a tissue in Nina's hand. Moments later, she was alone, the woman having told her to *take your time, please, take your time.*

And so Nina did. And in that garden, she let herself cry until she was almost exhausted. She took deep breaths. And when she finally felt she had cried herself dry *at least for today,* she got up and began cleaning her brushes.

Pain comes in waves, she thought as she packed up her items. *In tsunamis of tears.* Nina reminded herself she couldn't allow the overwhelming grief to crush her. She had to continue. Even when thoughts of Emilia persisted. And somewhere, in the back of the garden, she heard the song of a bird. She walked in its direction.

She passed flowers and flowers, remembering the fern she imagined was back here. The one large enough to hold her and wrap her in its leaves.

She walked to the back, closer to a bird she could not see.

I wish you were here, with me. I want you back here. With me.

There were plants and flowers in every color. But no large fern. Nowhere to put her pain, tuck it away. No choice but to carry it with her.

When she returned, there was a cup of tea on the table. Nina slowly drank it, calmed herself as much as she could, before finally gathering her things and leaving the garden. The woman's kindness was so profoundly touching as she escorted Nina out, asked her to please come back, handed her a flowerpot with purple flowers to take home.

Nina refused it at first, but the woman said, "Pain is . . . so hard to carry alone." Her words echoed in that large house and her eyes flickered with some kind of recognition as she looked at Nina. "Please." And she pressed the flowerpot into Nina's hands.

Nina accepted it. "Thank you," she said.

She looked in the rearview mirror, saw the woman still at the door as Nina drove away, out the gates, until she could see her no more.

When she arrived home, Nina walked up the steps to her house. A breeze blew and she felt a cold left over from winter brush against her arms. She was sure no one else could feel it. But she did. She always would. And she suddenly pictured Emilia, shivering, even when it wasn't cold outside. Even when the water was hot. And she understood her daughter in that moment more than ever. The way the cold always found her.

Crows cried in the distance and Nina sat on the front stoop to listen to them for a moment, the flowerpot next to her.

Emilia.

Nina turned her head to the sky. She watched the crows dip and glide and circle above. She closed her eyes and her tears glistened in the sunlight.

The crows cried.

Emilia, she heard in each one.

Emilia.

Tomás Held On

Tomás held on to the little checkered dress and cried. It was folded so small, and tucked into the corner of his drawer. On top, he also saw the green eye shadow she'd shown him that day at the pharmacy and a small piece of paper folded in half. Tomás opened it. His hands trembled as he saw his sister's handwriting, read her words.

Don't be afraid to talk to me. I love you.

It, and all that it meant, took Tomás's breath away.

His chest filled to bursting with regret and sadness and the realization of being understood and understanding his sister. But too late. He cried tears he didn't know he had left. And thought of Emilia.

So she had known, and she had understood that day in her room.

It had scared him. How close she was to the truth. He'd been afraid to say any more that night.

If I had your eyes, I'd wear this color, she'd told him, so softly, so gently, at the pharmacy. He couldn't even look at her as his heart raced. All he could manage was to ask her where she was going.

He was planning to talk to her, tell her everything. He knew he could.

He held the dress tighter.

See you.

He remembered the gentle way she smiled just before the doors swooshed closed after her.

You did see me, Emilia.

But now she was gone.

Tomás cried harder, aching for his sister. For her smile and her words.

He stared at the boxes through his tears, the ones that had been haunting him for weeks now. Stacked neatly and undisturbed in the corner of his room. Each day he grew more afraid of them and pretended they didn't exist. Each day he was more afraid of coming face-to-face again with what was inside.

Because it was Emilia.

Emilia was inside those boxes. In bits and pieces, recognizable and unrecognizable. And opening those boxes was like pouring alcohol on raw wounds.

Tomás opened the first one and caught his breath when he saw Emilia's face staring back at him.

The pictures.

He had thought they were crushed and buried. He pulled out her picture and tacked it onto the wall. He stepped back, sat on his bed, searched Emilia's glossy eyes.

How? he asked her. How did it happen? How did she fall?

How did they let her?

She stared back at him, still and silent. She looked so lonely on the wall by herself. Tomás added the picture of his mother, of himself, and, finally, even the one of his father.

He sat back on his bed, wiped the tears that wouldn't stop coming, as he searched all of their faces, asking them unanswerable questions.

What did we know? What did we know?

He continued, unpacked the squirrel, and as he reached up to put it on one of his bookshelves, he saw Emilia had written *SAM* on the bottom of it. It made him laugh and cry. He unpacked one item after another, let himself get lost in thoughts of his sister. He heard her voice, felt her presence, as if she were with him. And maybe it was the unpacking—what he'd been so afraid of— or maybe it was seeing again all these things his sister had found beauty in, all those forgotten, strange items, that made him less afraid somehow.

We lost you, Emilia. But I'll look for you. Every day. And I'll find you somehow. I won't forget you, he promised her.

This is what he thought when he saw his mother on the patio later that week, pouring another bag of dirt into a large flowerpot.

Tomás watched as her hands dug into the dirt. How she would cry as she filled the pots. Her face became smudged with dirt as she wiped away tears with her hands—almost as though it were therapeutic—and still each day, more work. More bags of dirt and pots in every size, plants and flowers and seeds. Lattices and green support rods.

Today, though, he knew it was more than just the work of it all. The distraction. The ceremony. It was more than therapy.

She's looking for Emilia, Tomás realized.

His mother sat back and brushed her hair out of her face, exhaled. She looked up and saw Tomás watching from the window. She looked at him softly for a moment before waving him over. He opened the screen door and went to her. She looked up at him and he worried she noticed the slight hint of green on his eyelids.

She smiled, motioned for him to grab a bag of dirt. And together they filled more pots; they turned the earth, the smell of damp dirt and fertilizer filling their noses. Reminding them of life.

★ ★ ★

Through the rest of spring and summer, Nina and Tomás plant flowers and plants and watch as tears fall and penetrate the soil. They watch them bloom and thrive, the vivid colors so alive in the sun. They watch as crows begin showing up, perching on the edges of flowerpots. They think of Emilia.

They tend to the garden, knowing the cold will come and take it away.

And it does. Prickling and fast and so full of pain.

*

Ma and Tomás look out the window as winter approaches.

"I feel like I'll always be looking for her, waiting for her," Tomás tells Ma.

"Me too," she says.

Winter arrives, swirling and large and so, so cold. They watch as life is choked out of all the flowers and plants they so carefully tended, how they die bit by bit.

And then they wait.

For life to come back to them again.

Emilia's story was difficult to write for many reasons. Because I am a mother to daughters. Because Emilia, in many ways, became like a daughter to me. Because I am a believer in hope. And because, more than anything, I so badly wanted her to be okay.

I worried when I knew she wasn't going to be okay. I worried that I was writing a story without hope, that I was not providing the kind of story I feel we need most in today's environment, stories that are rallying cries of power, calls to action.

But I could not be untrue to Emilia, or to the depth of her pain and suffering. And I could not be untrue to you, the reader, or to the realities girls face in this world every day. I knew in this book I had to be honest about some ugly truths.

And the truth is, every day in this world, girls suffer. At every turn they are told they are not good enough. Society has made a habit of using and misusing, of discarding and preying on girls without thought or care. Of sexualizing them, perpetrating violence toward them, of turning a not-so-blind eye on it all, and refusing to acknowledge there is consequence to it. This is particularly true for young girls of color.

And *that*—that fills me with rage. It should fill us all with rage.

Because another truth is that it *doesn't* have to be this way. We can, and should, live in a society where girls are allowed to simply exist and are not at a constant risk. Where they are respected and valued and not objectified. I know at times it seems far off, this kind of society. But I am hopeful.

Change *is* coming.

I see girls and women coming together, marching and filling the streets with unwavering spirit, and calling for justice and change. There are girls and women in courtrooms refusing to let their attackers get away with the crimes done to them, lifting their voices, unwilling to be intimidated or ignored. And there are more and more people standing with them, joining the fight.

But this story is about a girl who doesn't get that chance.

I wrote it to acknowledge all the silenced voices. To acknowledge that there *is* consequence to this appalling treatment of girls and women. There are broken lives and long-lasting effects. There are Emilias, many Emilias in the world, whose stories go untold or are hidden away and who go without justice. I wrote *The Fall of Innocence* so we don't forget that. Because we can't. We shouldn't. And no girl's story should *ever* have to end like this.

I wrote it so we all fight like hell,

for change—

for ourselves,

for those around us,

and for those who have fallen.

Resources

Suicide Prevention

National Suicide Prevention Lifeline

1-800-273-8255

The Trevor Project

1-866-4-U-TREVOR (488-7386)

Sexual Assault

National Sexual Assault Hotline

1-800-656-HOPE (4673)

Rape, Abuse & Incest National Network

rainn.org

Girl Empowerment

WriteGirl

writegirl.org

Girls Inc.

girlsinc.org

Girls For A Change

girlsforachange.org

CARE: Women's Empowerment

care.org/work/womens-empowerment

Plan International USA: Because I am a Girl

planusa.org/because-i-am-a-girl

Acknowledgments

Many thanks to Kerry Sparks of the Levine Greenberg Rostan Agency for your tireless belief in my work. Thank you, Liza Kaplan, for your guidance, talent, and vision. I am so incredibly grateful this story ended up in your hands. Thank you also to Michael Green for your support, and to Talia Benamy and every member of the Philomel family who worked on this book.

A million thanks to my family: mis padres, Miriam y David Torres; my sister, Nancy; and my brother, David. To my beautiful little crew, Ava, Mateo, and Francesca Sanchez and David and Matthew Willibey. Each of you and all our days together, who we were and who we are and who we still have yet to become inspire me every single day of my life. And to Nando, with your incomparable heart and love, always believing in me. Thank you forever.